SCOOBY-DOO the BIG SQUEEZE!

Written by:
Chris Duffy
Joe Edkin
Terrance Griep, Jr.
Jesse Leon McCann
Paul S. Newman
John Rozum
Joe & Hilarie Staton

Colored by:
Paul Becton

Illustrated by:
Dave Cooper
Dan Davis
Mike DeCarlo
John Delaney
Manny Galan
Tim Harkins
Scott McRae
Andrew Pepoy
Joe Staton
Rurik Tyler

Lettered by:
John Costanza

...s-original series
...on
...cted edition

...Grosterman
...or Art Director

...aul Levitz
President & Publisher

Georg Brewer
VP-Design & Retail Product
Development

Richard Bruning
Senior VP-Creative Director

Patrick Caldon
Senior VP-Finance & Operations

Chris Caramalis
VP-Finance

Terri Cunningham
VP-Managing Editor

Alison Gill
VP-Manufacturing

Rich Johnson
VP-Book Trade Sales

Hank Kanalz
VP-General Manager, WildStorm

Lillian Laserson
Senior VP & General Counsel

Jim Lee
Editorial Director-WildStorm

David McKillips
VP-Advertising &
Custom Publishing

John Nee
VP-Business Development

Gregory Noveck
Senior VP-Creative Affairs

Cheryl Rubin
Senior VP-Brand Management

Bob Wayne
VP-Sales & Marketing

SCOOBY-DOO VOL. 4: THE BIG SQUEEZE!
Published by DC Comics. Cover and compilation copyright © 2005 Hanna-Barbera. All Rights
Reserved. Originally published in single magazine form as SCOOBY-DOO 16-20. Copyright © 1998,
1999 Hanna-Barbera. All Rights Reserved. SCOOBY-DOO and all related characters and elements
depicted herein are trademarks of Hanna-Barbera. The DC Bullet is a trademark of DC Comics.
The stories, characters and incidents featured in this publication are entirely fictional.
DC Comics does not read or accept unsolicited submissions of ideas, stories or artwork.

CARTOON NETWORK and its logo are trademarks of Cartoon Network.

DC Comics, 1700 Broadway, New York, NY 10019
A Warner Bros. Entertainment Company.
Printed in Canada. First Printing.
ISBN: 1-4012-0514-3
Cover illustration by Joe Staton.
Publication design by John J. Hill.

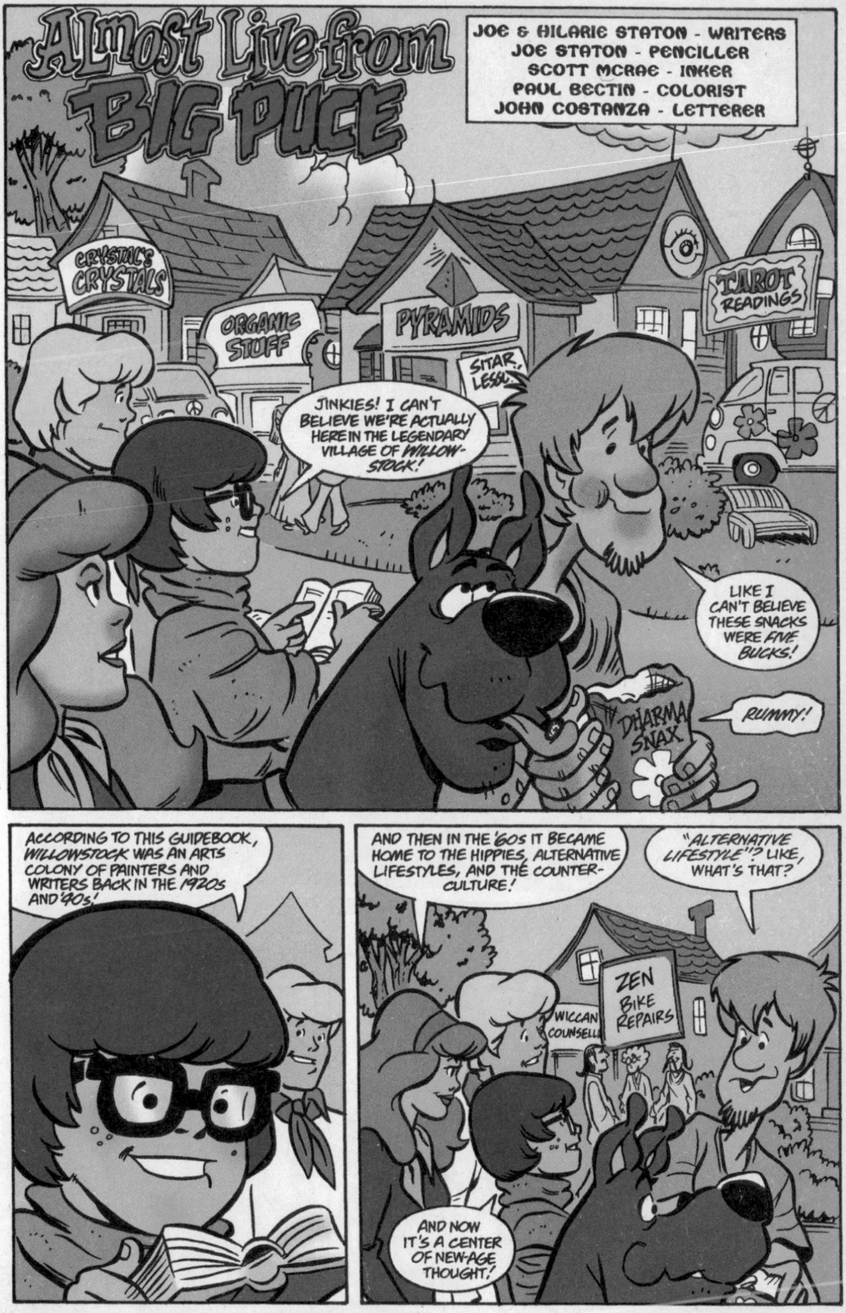
ALMOST LIVE FROM BIG PUCE
JOE & HILARIE STATON - WRITERS
JOE STATON - PENCILLER
SCOTT MCRAE - INKER
PAUL BECTIN - COLORIST
JOHN COSTANZA - LETTERER
CRYSTAL'S CRYSTALS
ORGANIC STUFF
PYRAMIDS
TAROT READINGS
JINKIES! I CAN'T BELIEVE WE'RE ACTUALLY HERE IN THE LEGENDARY VILLAGE OF WILLOW-STOCK!
LIKE I CAN'T BELIEVE THESE SNACKS WERE FIVE BUCKS!
DHARMA SNAX
RUMMY!
ACCORDING TO THIS GUIDEBOOK, WILLOWSTOCK WAS AN ARTS COLONY OF PAINTERS AND WRITERS BACK IN THE 1920s AND '40s!
AND THEN IN THE '60s IT BECAME HOME TO THE HIPPIES, ALTERNATIVE LIFESTYLES, AND THE COUNTER-CULTURE!
"ALTERNATIVE LIFESTYLE"? LIKE, WHAT'S THAT?
ZEN BIKE REPAIRS
AND NOW IT'S A CENTER OF NEW-AGE THOUGHT!

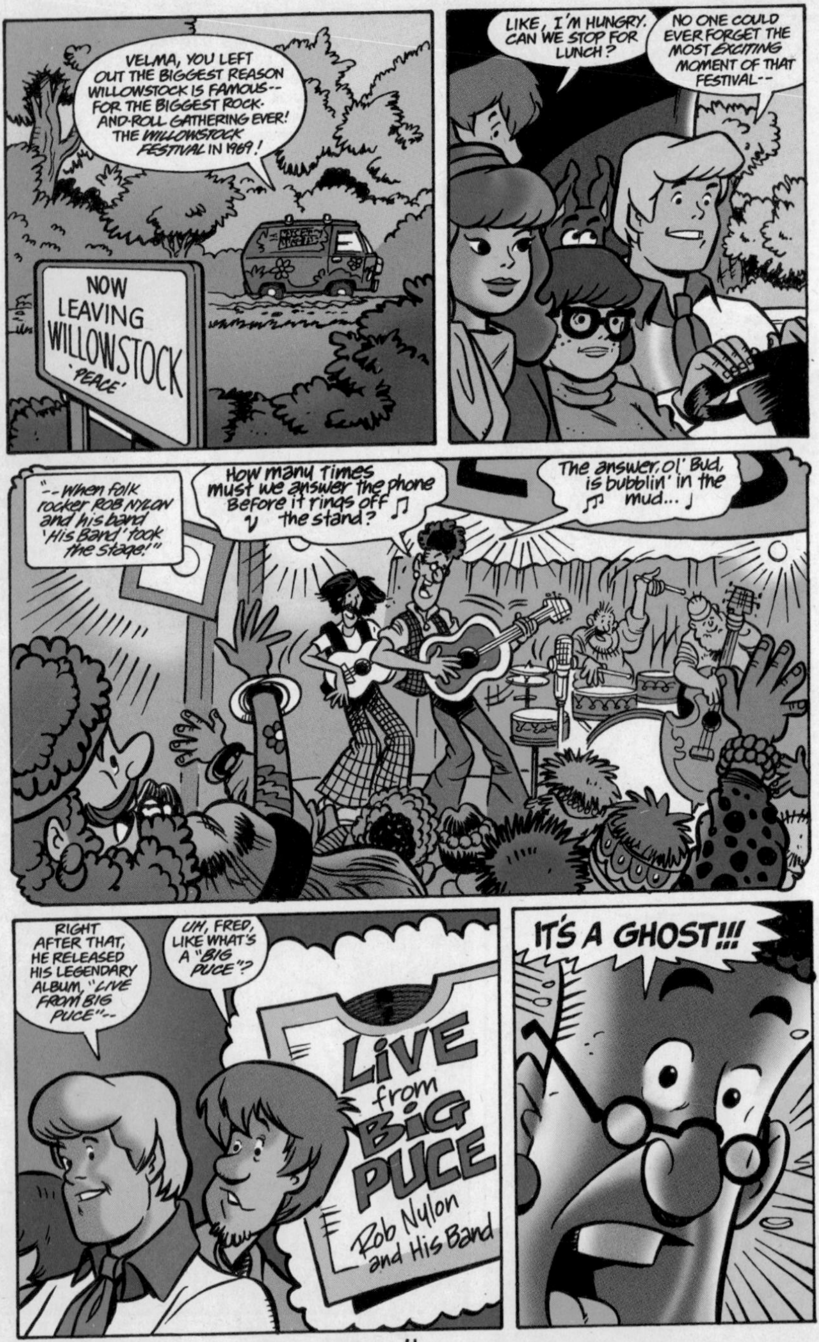
VELMA, YOU LEFT OUT THE BIGGEST REASON WILLOWSTOCK IS FAMOUS-- FOR THE BIGGEST ROCK-AND-ROLL GATHERING EVER! THE WILLOWSTOCK FESTIVAL IN 1969!
NOW LEAVING WILLOWSTOCK 'PEACE'
LIKE, I'M HUNGRY. CAN WE STOP FOR LUNCH?
NO ONE COULD EVER FORGET THE MOST EXCITING MOMENT OF THAT FESTIVAL--
"--when folk rocker ROB NYLON and his band 'His Band' took the stage!"
How many Times must we answer the phone Before it rings off the stand?
The answer, ol' Bud, is bubblin' in the mud...
RIGHT AFTER THAT, HE RELEASED HIS LEGENDARY ALBUM, "LIVE FROM BIG PUCE"--
UH, FRED, LIKE WHAT'S A "BIG PUCE"?
LiVE from BiG PUCE
Rob Nylon and His Band
IT'S A GHOST!!!

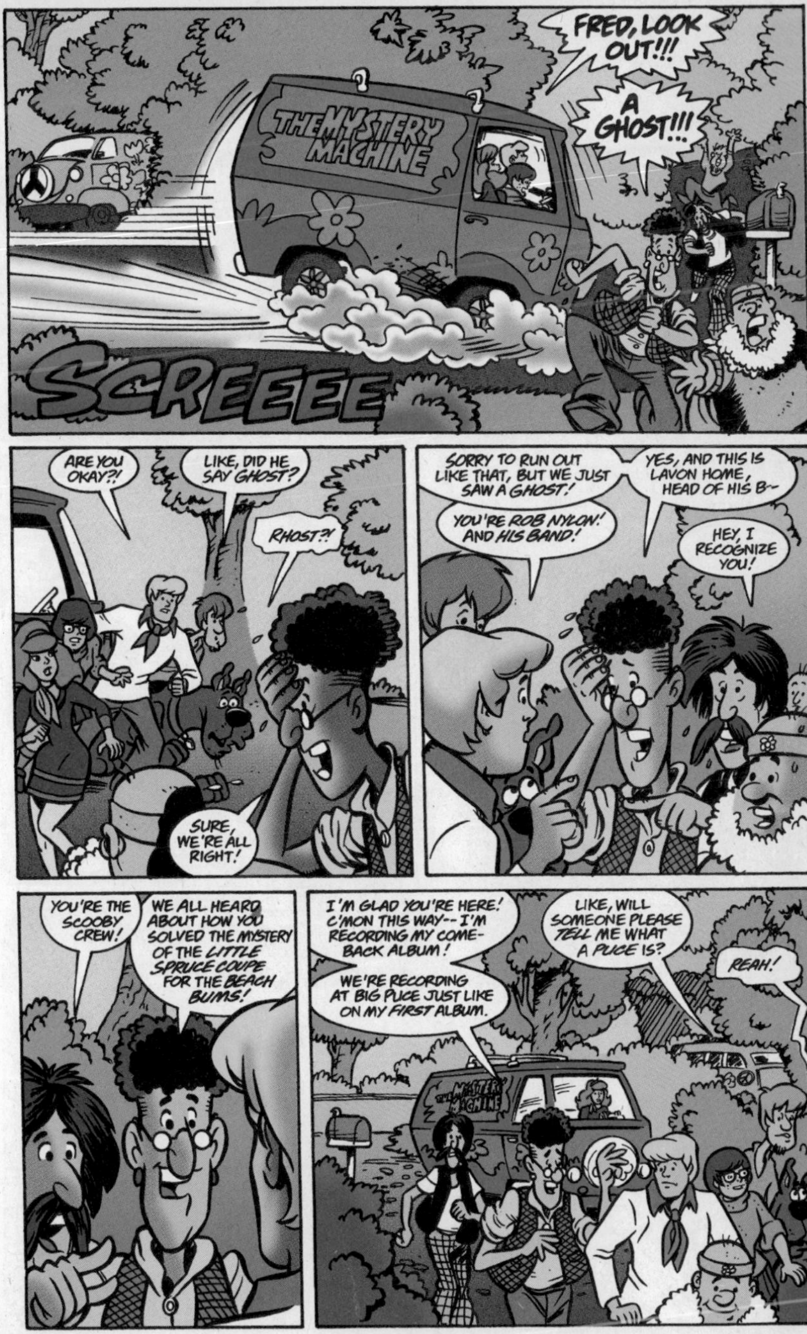
FRED, LOOK OUT!!!
A GHOST!!!
THE MYSTERY MACHINE
SCREEEE
ARE YOU OKAY?!
LIKE, DID HE SAY GHOST?
RHOST?!
SURE, WE'RE ALL RIGHT!
SORRY TO RUN OUT LIKE THAT, BUT WE JUST SAW A GHOST!
YES, AND THIS IS LAVON HOME, HEAD OF HIS B--
YOU'RE ROB NYLON! AND HIS BAND!
HEY, I RECOGNIZE YOU!
YOU'RE THE SCOOBY CREW!
WE ALL HEARD ABOUT HOW YOU SOLVED THE MYSTERY OF THE LITTLE SPRUCE COUPE FOR THE BEACH BUMS!
I'M GLAD YOU'RE HERE! C'MON THIS WAY-- I'M RECORDING MY COME-BACK ALBUM!
WE'RE RECORDING AT BIG PUCE JUST LIKE ON MY FIRST ALBUM.
LIKE, WILL SOMEONE PLEASE TELL ME WHAT A PUCE IS?
REAH!

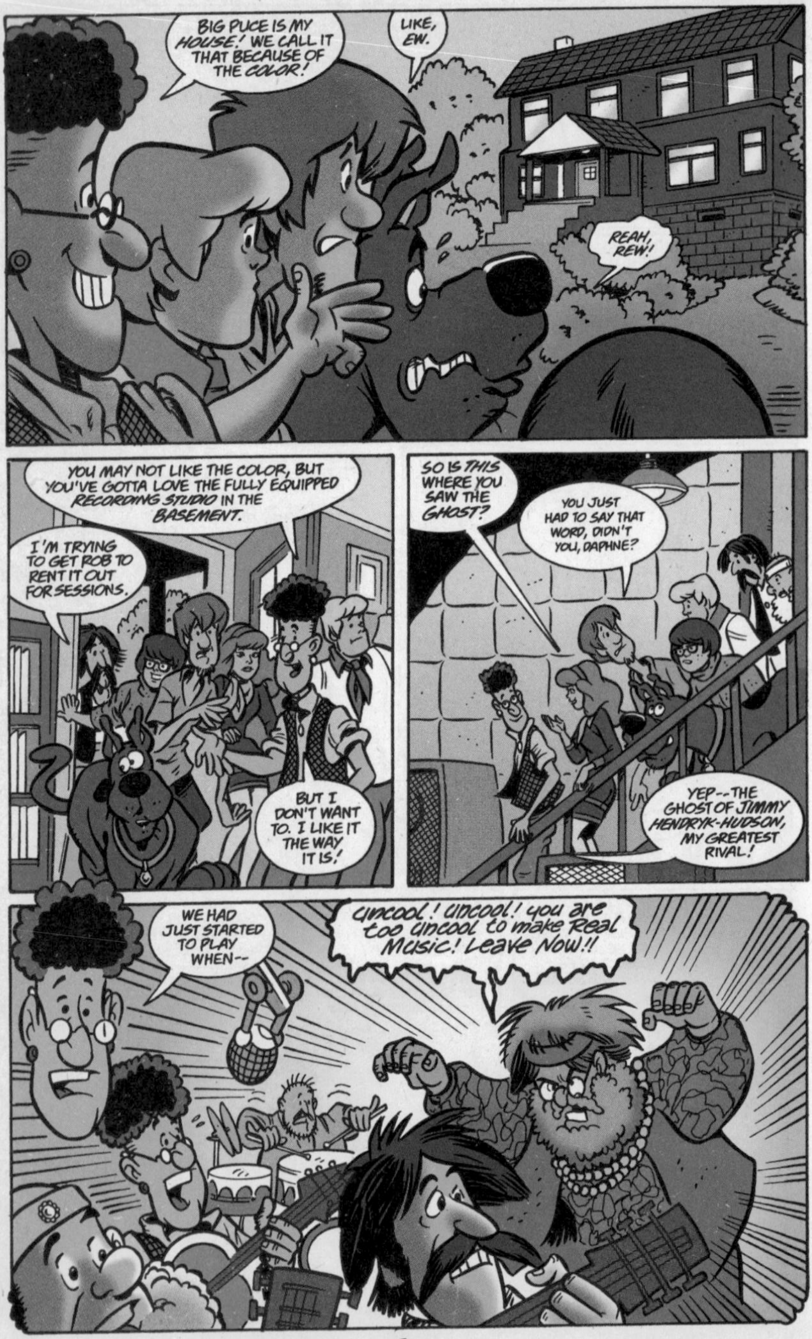

BIG PUCE IS MY HOUSE! WE CALL IT THAT BECAUSE OF THE COLOR!
LIKE, EW.
REAH, REW!
YOU MAY NOT LIKE THE COLOR, BUT YOU'VE GOTTA LOVE THE FULLY EQUIPPED RECORDING STUDIO IN THE BASEMENT.
I'M TRYING TO GET ROB TO RENT IT OUT FOR SESSIONS.
BUT I DON'T WANT TO. I LIKE IT THE WAY IT IS!
SO IS THIS WHERE YOU SAW THE GHOST?
YOU JUST HAD TO SAY THAT WORD, DIDN'T YOU, DAPHNE?
YEP--THE GHOST OF JIMMY HENDRYK-HUDSON, MY GREATEST RIVAL!
WE HAD JUST STARTED TO PLAY WHEN--
Uncool! Uncool! You are too Uncool to make Real Music! Leave Now!!

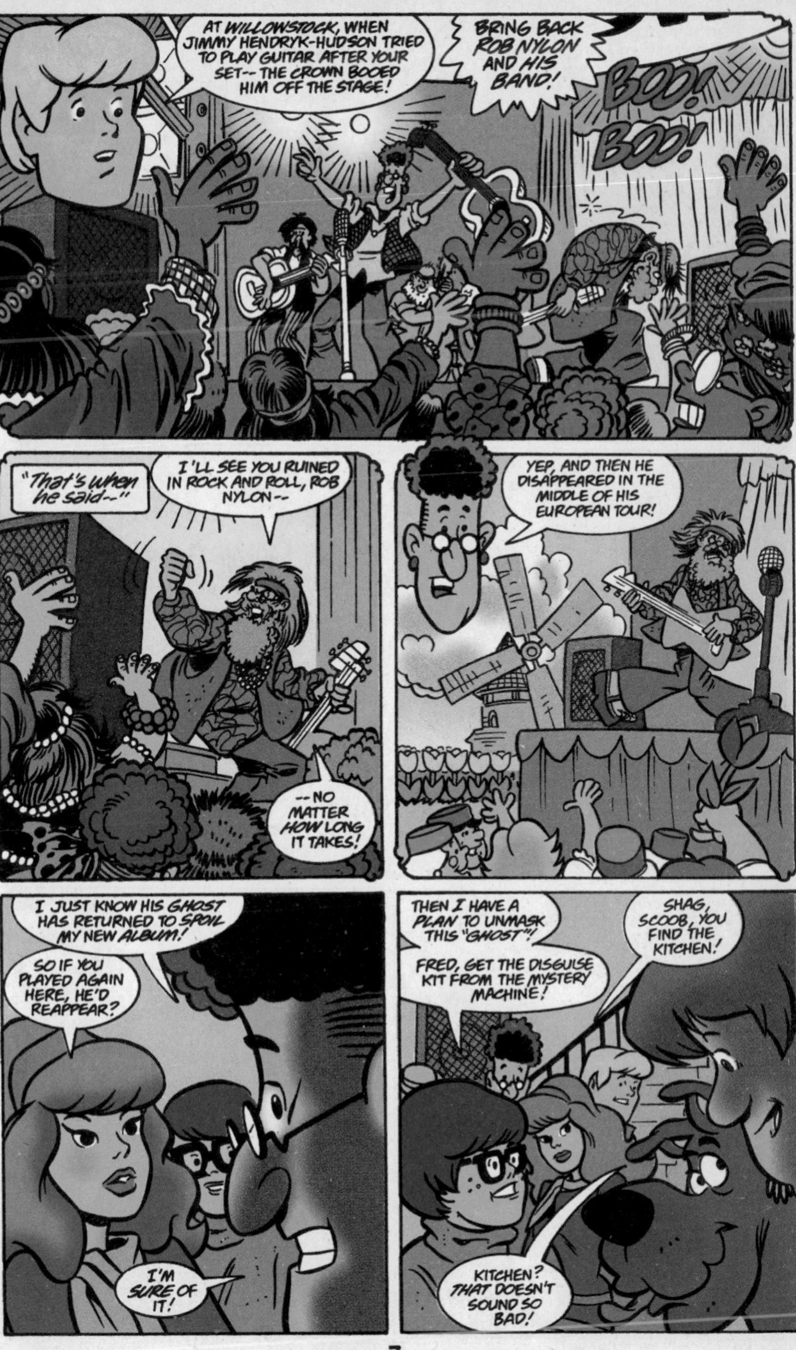
AT WILLOWSTOCK, WHEN JIMMY HENDRYK-HUDSON TRIED TO PLAY GUITAR AFTER YOUR SET-- THE CROWN BOOED HIM OFF THE STAGE!
BRING BACK ROB NYLON AND HIS BAND!
BOO!
BOO!
"That's when he said--"
I'LL SEE YOU RUINED IN ROCK AND ROLL, ROB NYLON--
--NO MATTER HOW LONG IT TAKES!
YEP, AND THEN HE DISAPPEARED IN THE MIDDLE OF HIS EUROPEAN TOUR!
I JUST KNOW HIS GHOST HAS RETURNED TO SPOIL MY NEW ALBUM!
SO IF YOU PLAYED AGAIN HERE, HE'D REAPPEAR?
I'M SURE OF IT!
THEN I HAVE A PLAN TO UNMASK THIS "GHOST"!
FRED, GET THE DISGUISE KIT FROM THE MYSTERY MACHINE!
SHAG, SCOOB, YOU FIND THE KITCHEN!
KITCHEN? THAT DOESN'T SOUND SO BAD!

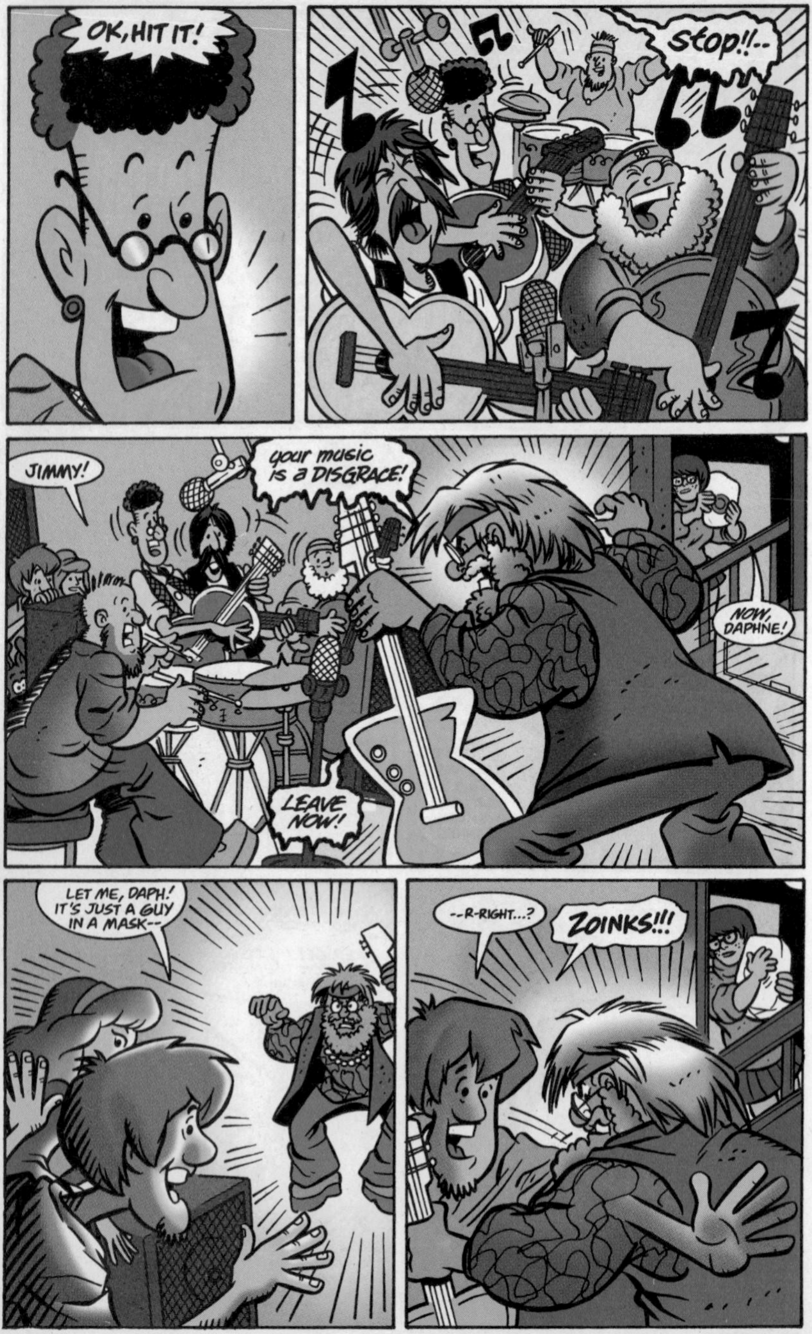
OK, HIT IT!
Stop!!--
JIMMY!
your music is a DISGRACE!
NOW, DAPHNE!
LEAVE NOW!
LET ME, DAPH! IT'S JUST A GUY IN A MASK--
--R-RIGHT...?
ZOINKS!!!

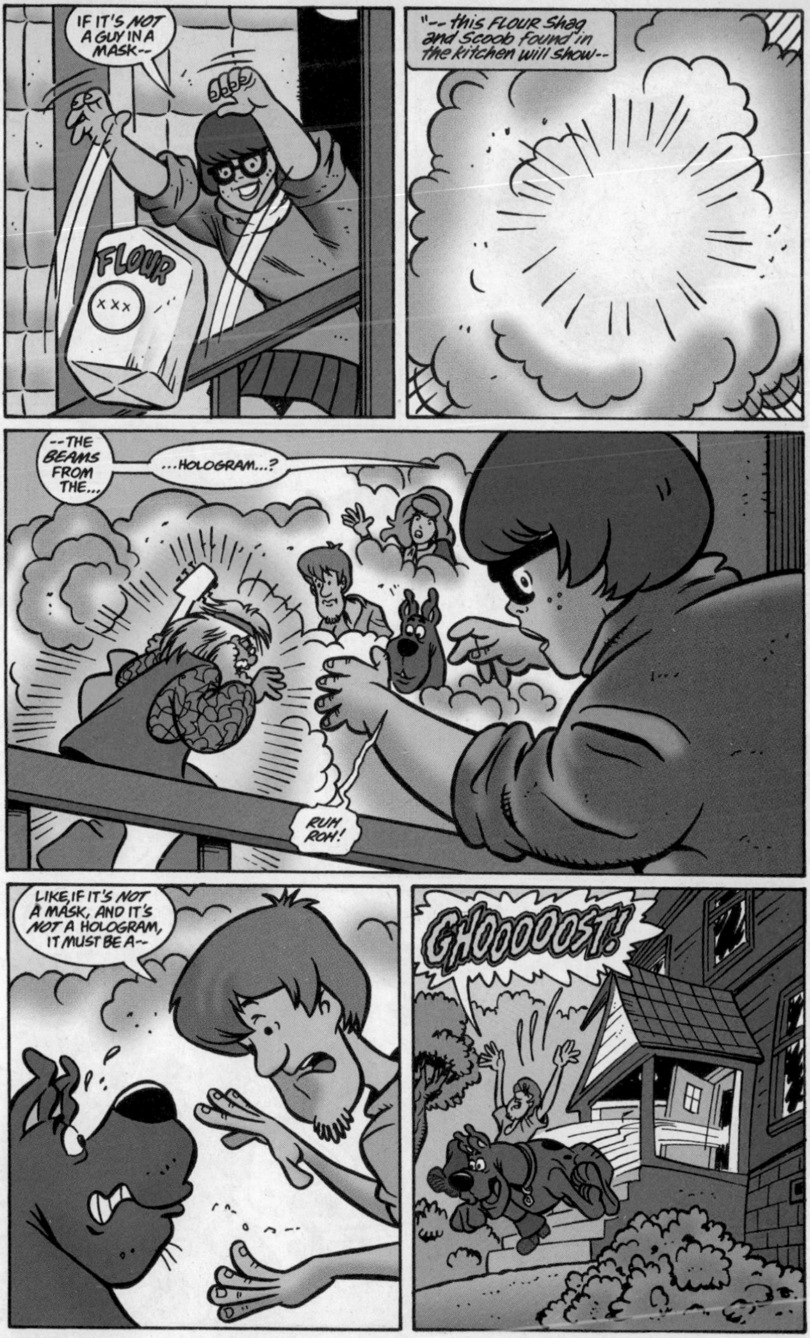
IF IT'S NOT A GUY IN A MASK--
"-- this FLOUR Shag and Scoob found in the kitchen will show--
FLOUR
--THE BEAMS FROM THE...
...HOLOGRAM...?
RUH ROH!
LIKE, IF IT'S NOT A MASK, AND IT'S NOT A HOLOGRAM, IT MUST BE A--
GHOOOOOST!

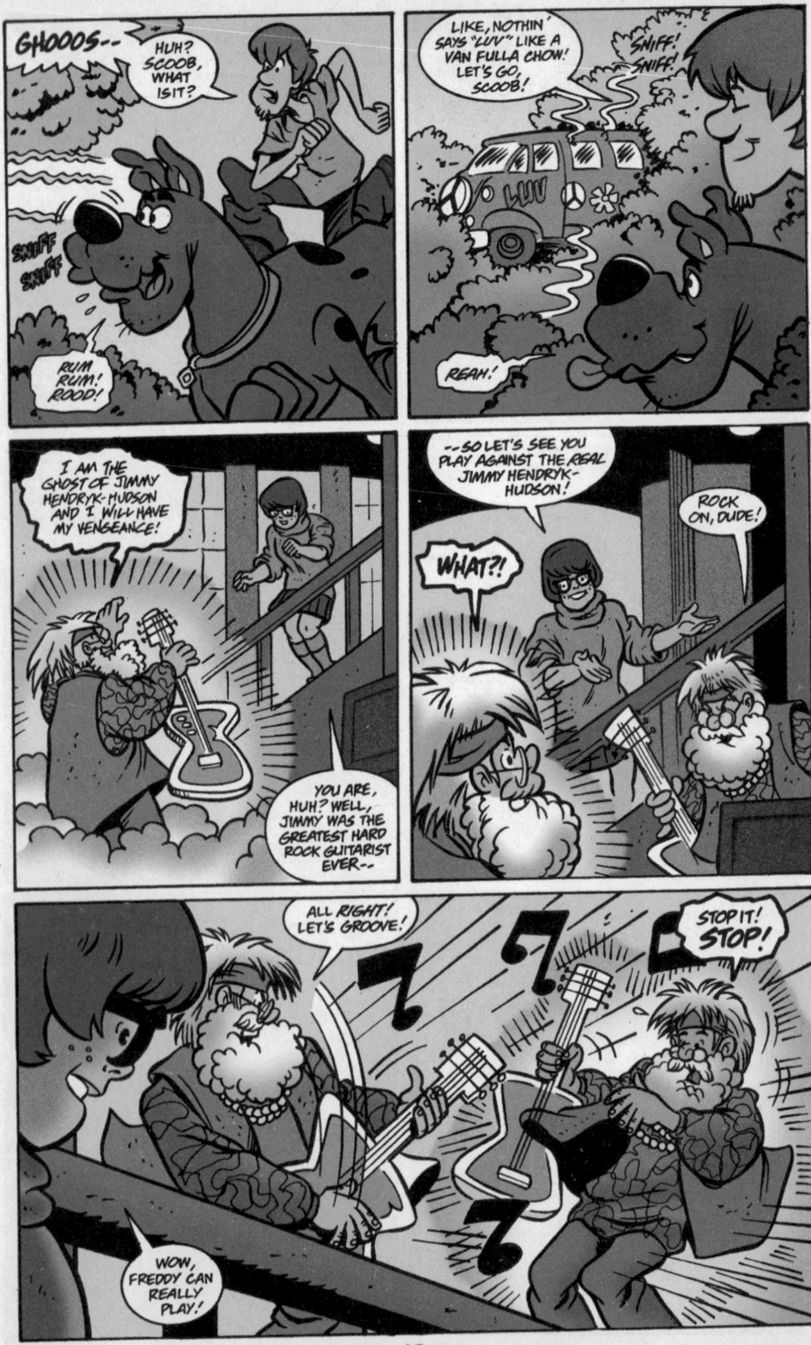
GHOOOS--
HUH? SCOOB, WHAT IS IT?
SNIFF SNIFF
RUM RUM! ROOD!
LIKE, NOTHIN' SAYS "LUV" LIKE A VAN FULLA CHOW! LET'S GO, SCOOB!
SNIFF! SNIFF!
LUV
REAH!
I AM THE GHOST OF JIMMY HENDRYK-HUDSON AND I WILL HAVE MY VENGEANCE!
YOU ARE, HUH? WELL, JIMMY WAS THE GREATEST HARD ROCK GUITARIST EVER--
--SO LET'S SEE YOU PLAY AGAINST THE REAL JIMMY HENDRYK-HUDSON!
ROCK ON, DUDE!
WHAT?!
ALL RIGHT! LET'S GROOVE!
STOP IT! STOP!
WOW, FREDDY CAN REALLY PLAY!

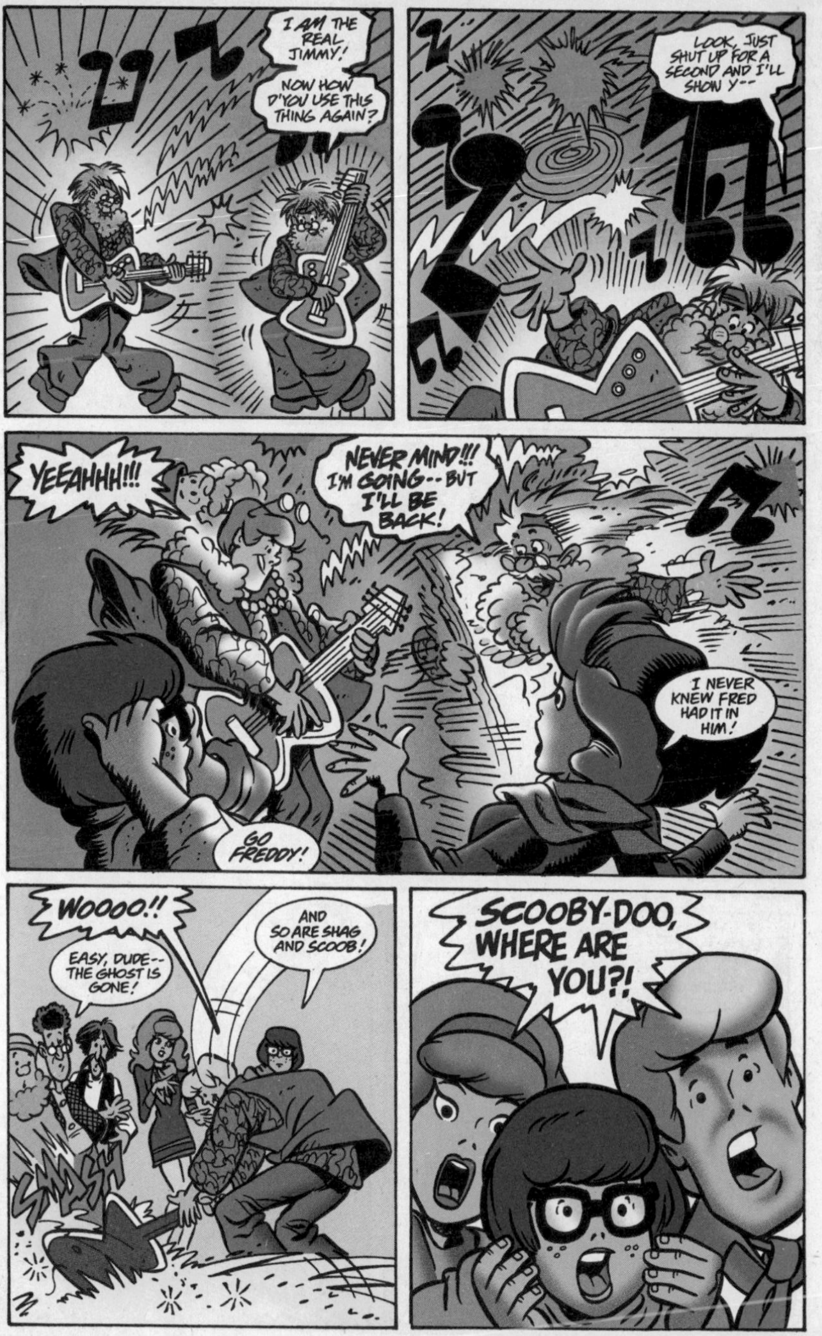
I AM THE REAL JIMMY!
NOW HOW D'YOU USE THIS THING AGAIN?
LOOK, JUST SHUT UP FOR A SECOND AND I'LL SHOW Y--
YEEAHHH!!!
NEVER MIND!!! I'M GOING--BUT I'LL BE BACK!
I NEVER KNEW FRED HAD IT IN HIM!
GO FREDDY!
WOOOO!!
EASY, DUDE-- THE GHOST IS GONE!
AND SO ARE SHAG AND SCOOB!
SMASH
SCOOBY-DOO, WHERE ARE YOU?!

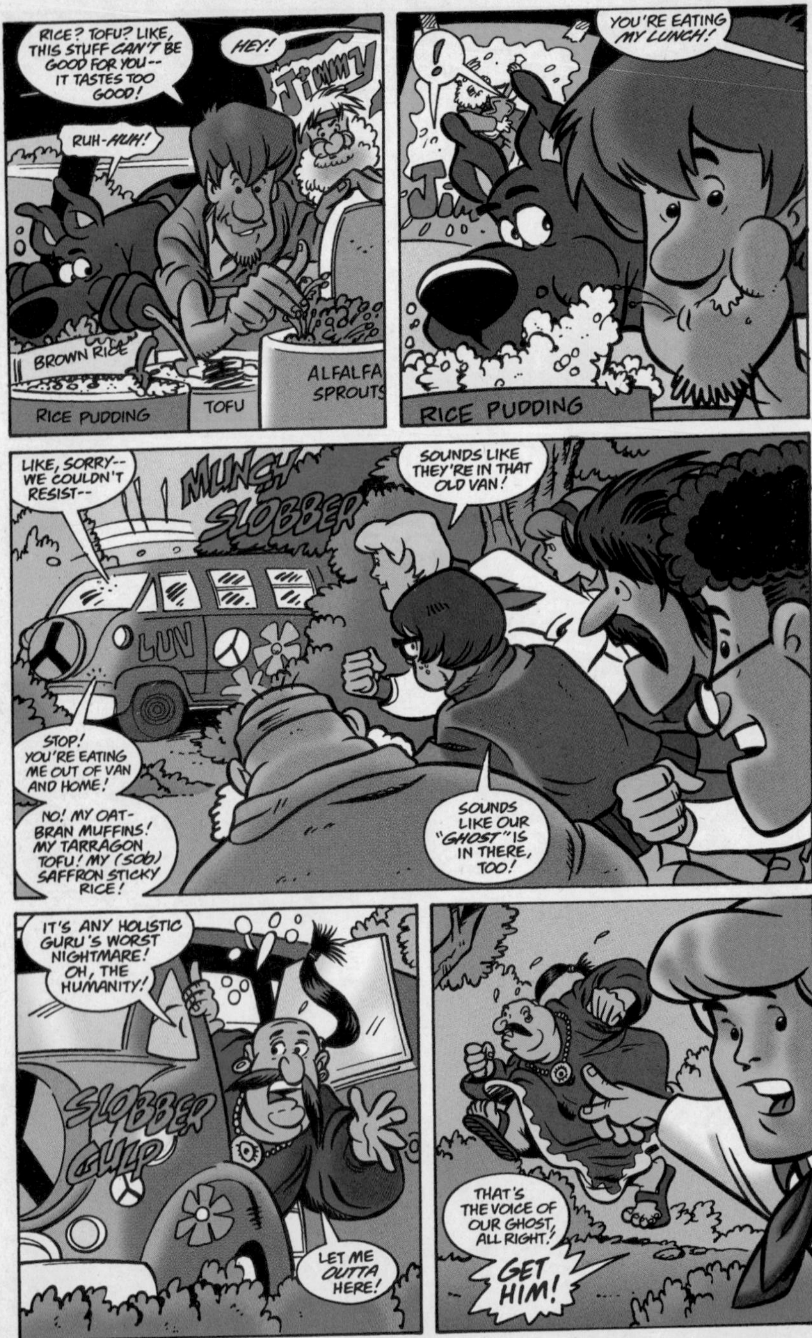

RICE? TOFU? LIKE, THIS STUFF CAN'T BE GOOD FOR YOU-- IT TASTES TOO GOOD!
HEY!
JIMMY
RUH-HUH!
BROWN RICE
RICE PUDDING
TOFU
ALFALFA SPROUTS
YOU'RE EATING MY LUNCH!
!
RICE PUDDING
LIKE, SORRY-- WE COULDN'T RESIST--
MUNCH
SLOBBER
SOUNDS LIKE THEY'RE IN THAT OLD VAN!
LUV
STOP! YOU'RE EATING ME OUT OF VAN AND HOME!
NO! MY OAT-BRAN MUFFINS! MY TARRAGON TOFU! MY (SOB) SAFFRON STICKY RICE!
SOUNDS LIKE OUR "GHOST" IS IN THERE, TOO!
IT'S ANY HOLISTIC GURU'S WORST NIGHTMARE! OH, THE HUMANITY!
SLOBBER
GULP
LET ME OUTTA HERE!
THAT'S THE VOICE OF OUR GHOST, ALL RIGHT!
GET HIM!

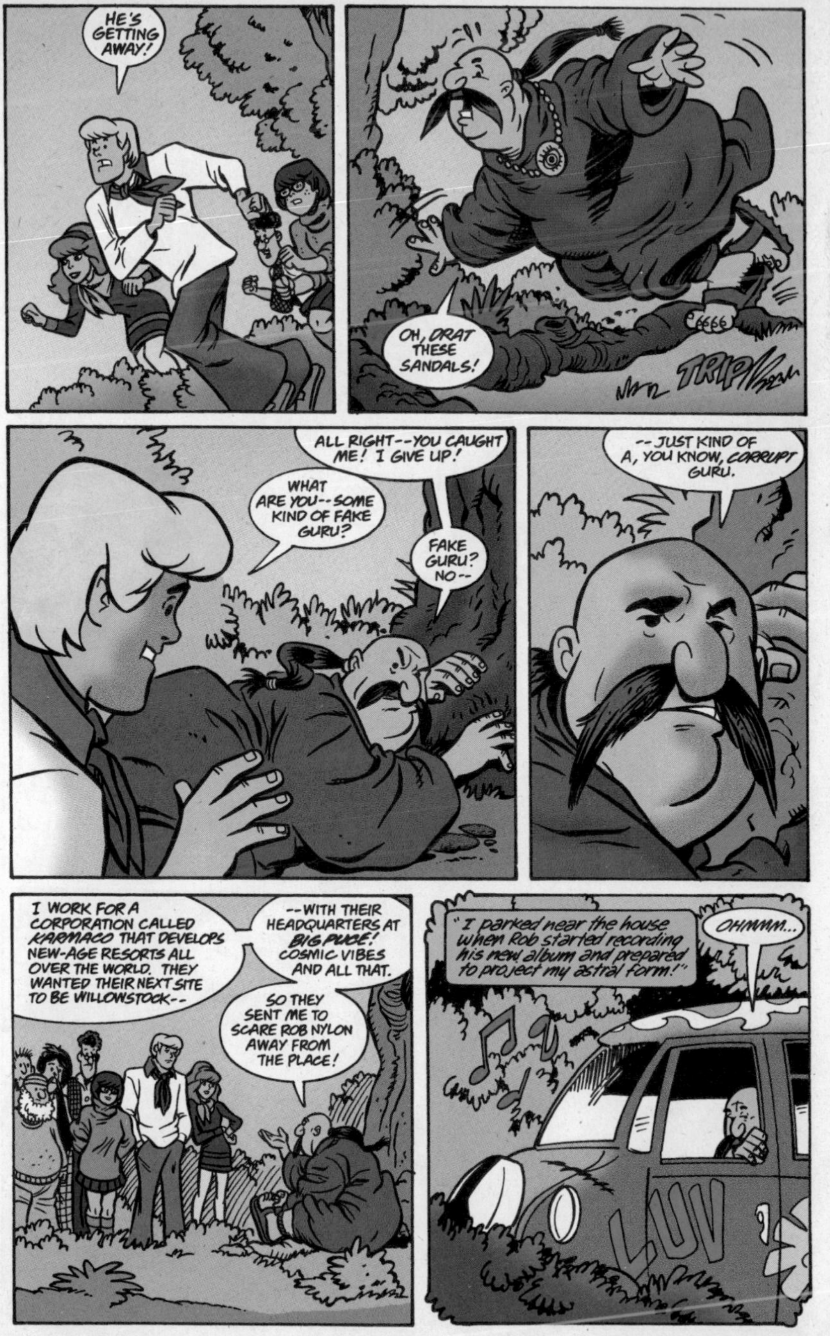

HE'S GETTING AWAY!
OH, DRAT THESE SANDALS!
TRIP
ALL RIGHT--YOU CAUGHT ME! I GIVE UP!
WHAT ARE YOU--SOME KIND OF FAKE GURU?
FAKE GURU? NO--
--JUST KIND OF A, YOU KNOW, CORRUPT GURU.
I WORK FOR A CORPORATION CALLED KARMACO THAT DEVELOPS NEW-AGE RESORTS ALL OVER THE WORLD. THEY WANTED THEIR NEXT SITE TO BE WILLOWSTOCK--
--WITH THEIR HEADQUARTERS AT BIG PUCE! COSMIC VIBES AND ALL THAT.
SO THEY SENT ME TO SCARE ROB NYLON AWAY FROM THE PLACE!
"I parked near the house when Rob started recording his new album and prepared to project my astral form!"
OHMMM...
LUV

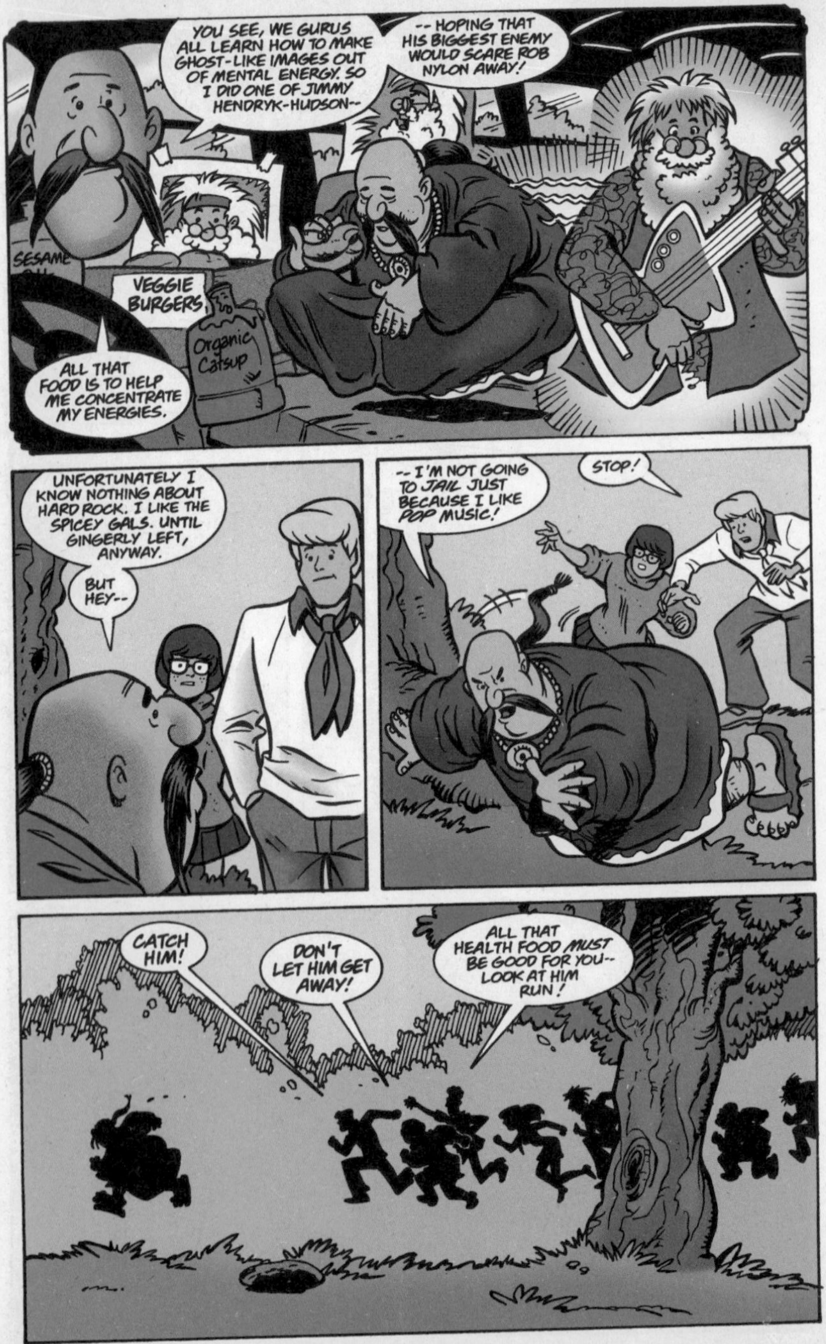
YOU SEE, WE GURUS ALL LEARN HOW TO MAKE GHOST-LIKE IMAGES OUT OF MENTAL ENERGY. SO I DID ONE OF JIMMY HENDRYK-HUDSON--
-- HOPING THAT HIS BIGGEST ENEMY WOULD SCARE ROB NYLON AWAY!
SESAME
VEGGIE BURGERS
Organic Catsup
ALL THAT FOOD IS TO HELP ME CONCENTRATE MY ENERGIES.
UNFORTUNATELY I KNOW NOTHING ABOUT HARD ROCK. I LIKE THE SPICEY GALS. UNTIL GINGERLY LEFT, ANYWAY.
BUT HEY--
-- I'M NOT GOING TO JAIL JUST BECAUSE I LIKE POP MUSIC!
STOP!
CATCH HIM!
DON'T LET HIM GET AWAY!
ALL THAT HEALTH FOOD MUST BE GOOD FOR YOU-- LOOK AT HIM RUN!

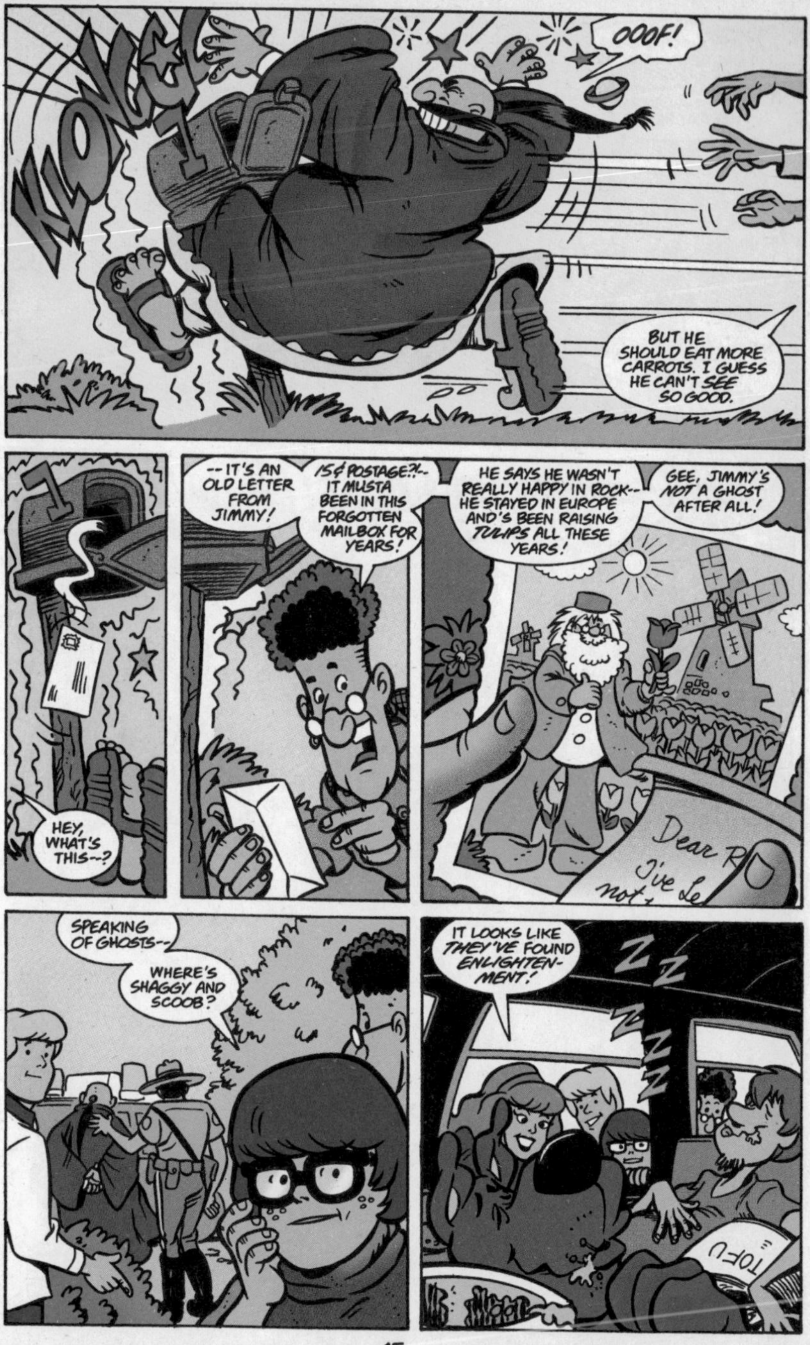
KLONG!
OOOF!
BUT HE SHOULD EAT MORE CARROTS. I GUESS HE CAN'T SEE SO GOOD.
HEY, WHAT'S THIS--?
--IT'S AN OLD LETTER FROM JIMMY!
15¢ POSTAGE?!-- IT MUSTA BEEN IN THIS FORGOTTEN MAILBOX FOR YEARS!
HE SAYS HE WASN'T REALLY HAPPY IN ROCK-- HE STAYED IN EUROPE AND'S BEEN RAISING TULIPS ALL THESE YEARS!
GEE, JIMMY'S NOT A GHOST AFTER ALL!
Dear R
I've le
not
SPEAKING OF GHOSTS--
WHERE'S SHAGGY AND SCOOB?
IT LOOKS LIKE THEY'VE FOUND ENLIGHTEN-MENT!
Z Z Z Z
"TOFU"

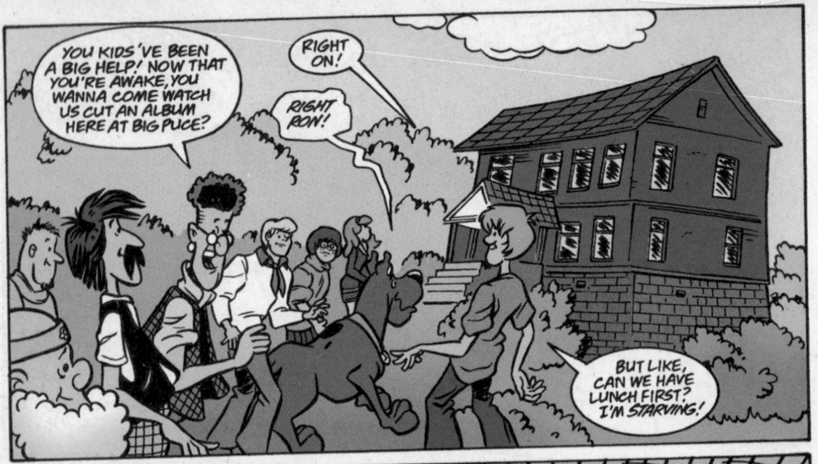
YOU KIDS'VE BEEN A BIG HELP! NOW THAT YOU'RE AWAKE, YOU WANNA COME WATCH US CUT AN ALBUM HERE AT BIG PUCE?
RIGHT ON!
RIGHT RON!
BUT LIKE, CAN WE HAVE LUNCH FIRST? I'M STARVING!

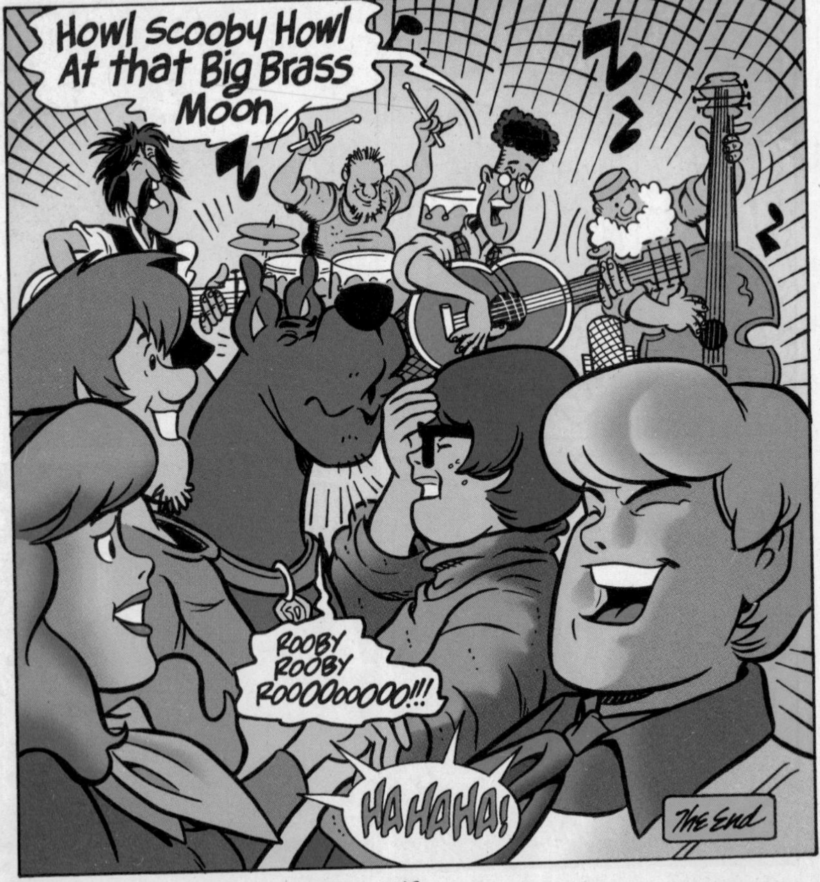
Howl Scooby Howl At that Big Brass Moon
ROOBY ROOBY ROOOOOOOOO!!!
HAHAHA!
The End

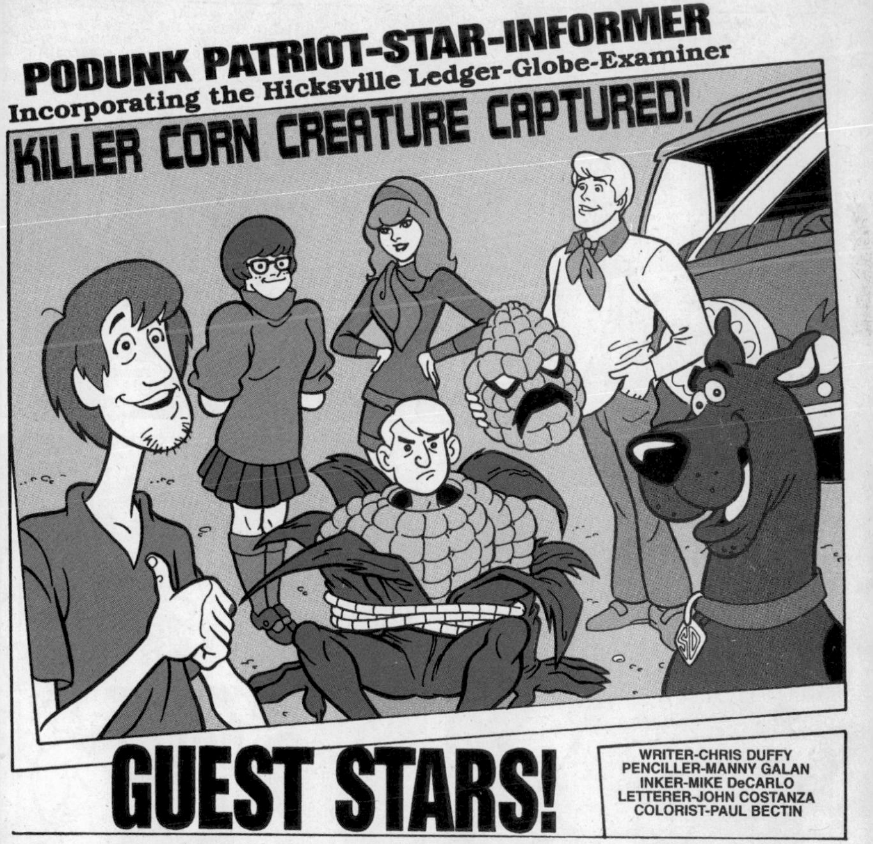
PODUNK PATRIOT-STAR-INFORMER
Incorporating the Hicksville Ledger-Globe-Examiner
KILLER CORN CREATURE CAPTURED!
SD

GUEST STARS!

WRITER-CHRIS DUFFY
PENCILLER-MANNY GALAN
INKER-MIKE DeCARLO
LETTERER-JOHN COSTANZA
COLORIST-PAUL BECTIN

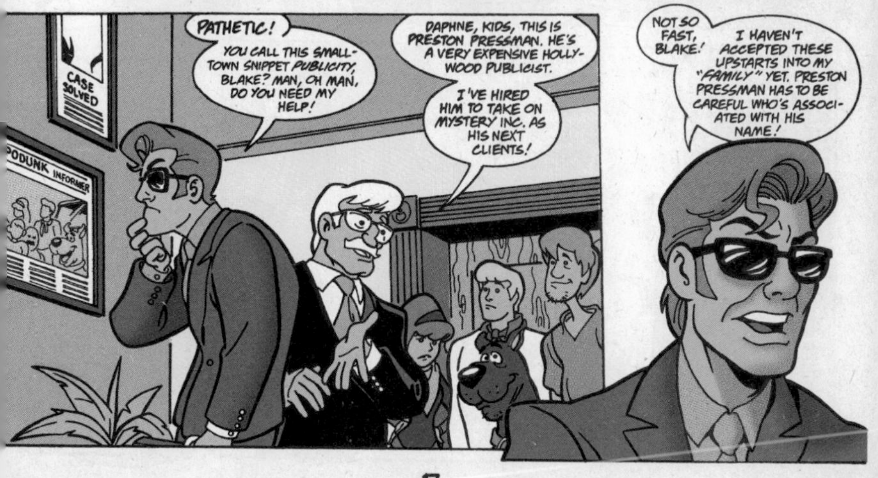
CASE SOLVED
PODUNK INFORMER
PATHETIC! YOU CALL THIS SMALL-TOWN SNIPPET PUBLICITY, BLAKE? MAN, OH MAN, DO YOU NEED MY HELP!
DAPHNE, KIDS, THIS IS PRESTON PRESSMAN. HE'S A VERY EXPENSIVE HOLLYWOOD PUBLICIST.
I'VE HIRED HIM TO TAKE ON MYSTERY INC. AS HIS NEXT CLIENTS!
NOT SO FAST, BLAKE!
I HAVEN'T ACCEPTED THESE UPSTARTS INTO MY "FAMILY" YET. PRESTON PRESSMAN HAS TO BE CAREFUL WHO'S ASSOCIATED WITH HIS NAME!

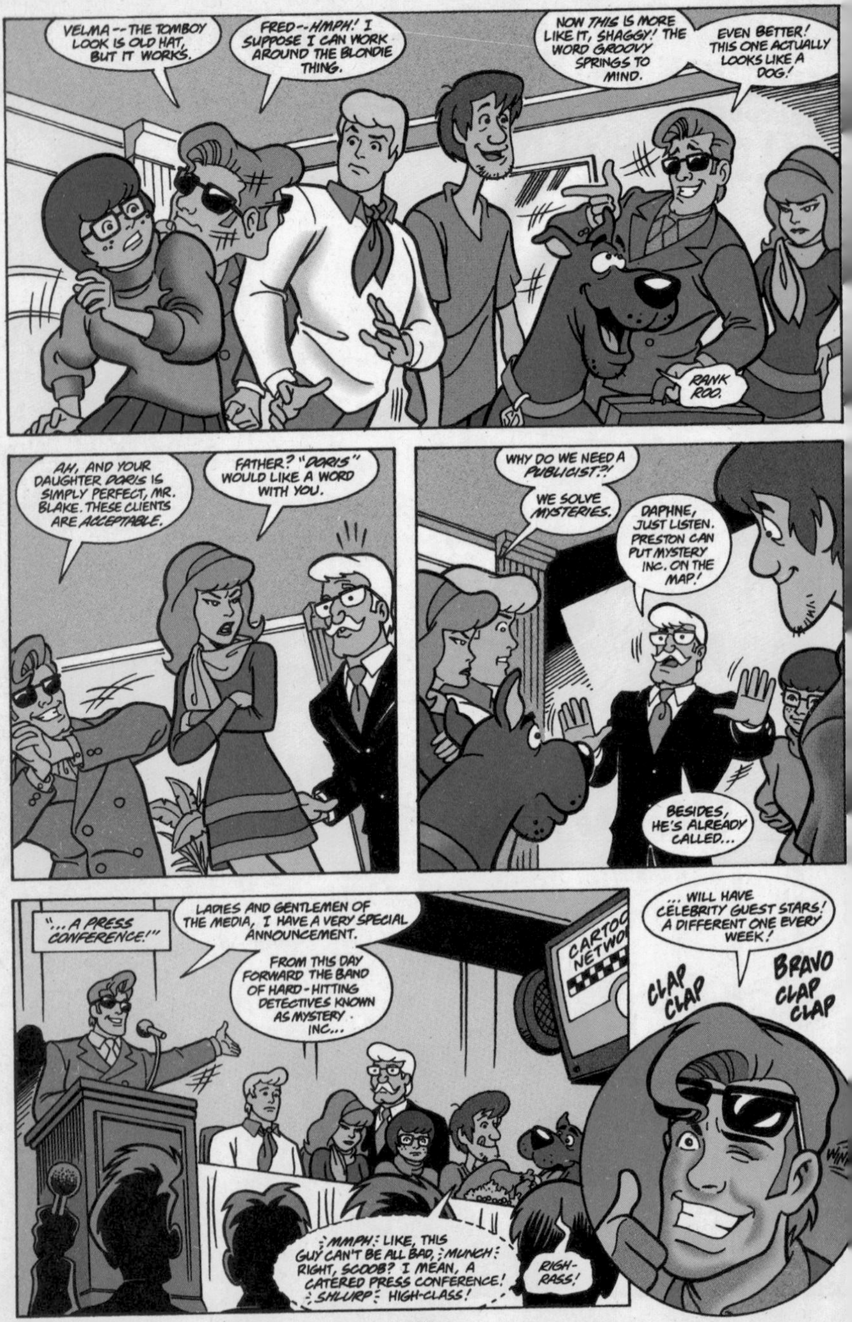
VELMA--THE TOMBOY LOOK IS OLD HAT, BUT IT WORKS.
FRED--HMPH! I SUPPOSE I CAN WORK AROUND THE BLONDIE THING.
NOW THIS IS MORE LIKE IT, SHAGGY! THE WORD GROOVY SPRINGS TO MIND.
EVEN BETTER! THIS ONE ACTUALLY LOOKS LIKE A DOG!
RANK ROO.
AH, AND YOUR DAUGHTER DORIS IS SIMPLY PERFECT, MR. BLAKE. THESE CLIENTS ARE ACCEPTABLE.
FATHER? "DORIS" WOULD LIKE A WORD WITH YOU.
WHY DO WE NEED A PUBLICIST?!
WE SOLVE MYSTERIES.
DAPHNE, JUST LISTEN. PRESTON CAN PUT MYSTERY INC. ON THE MAP!
BESIDES, HE'S ALREADY CALLED...
"...A PRESS CONFERENCE!"
LADIES AND GENTLEMEN OF THE MEDIA, I HAVE A VERY SPECIAL ANNOUNCEMENT.
FROM THIS DAY FORWARD THE BAND OF HARD-HITTING DETECTIVES KNOWN AS MYSTERY INC...
...WILL HAVE CELEBRITY GUEST STARS! A DIFFERENT ONE EVERY WEEK!
CLAP CLAP
BRAVO CLAP CLAP
MMPH LIKE, THIS GUY CAN'T BE ALL BAD, MUNCH RIGHT, SCOOB? I MEAN, A CATERED PRESS CONFERENCE! SHLURP HIGH-CLASS!
RIGH-RASS!

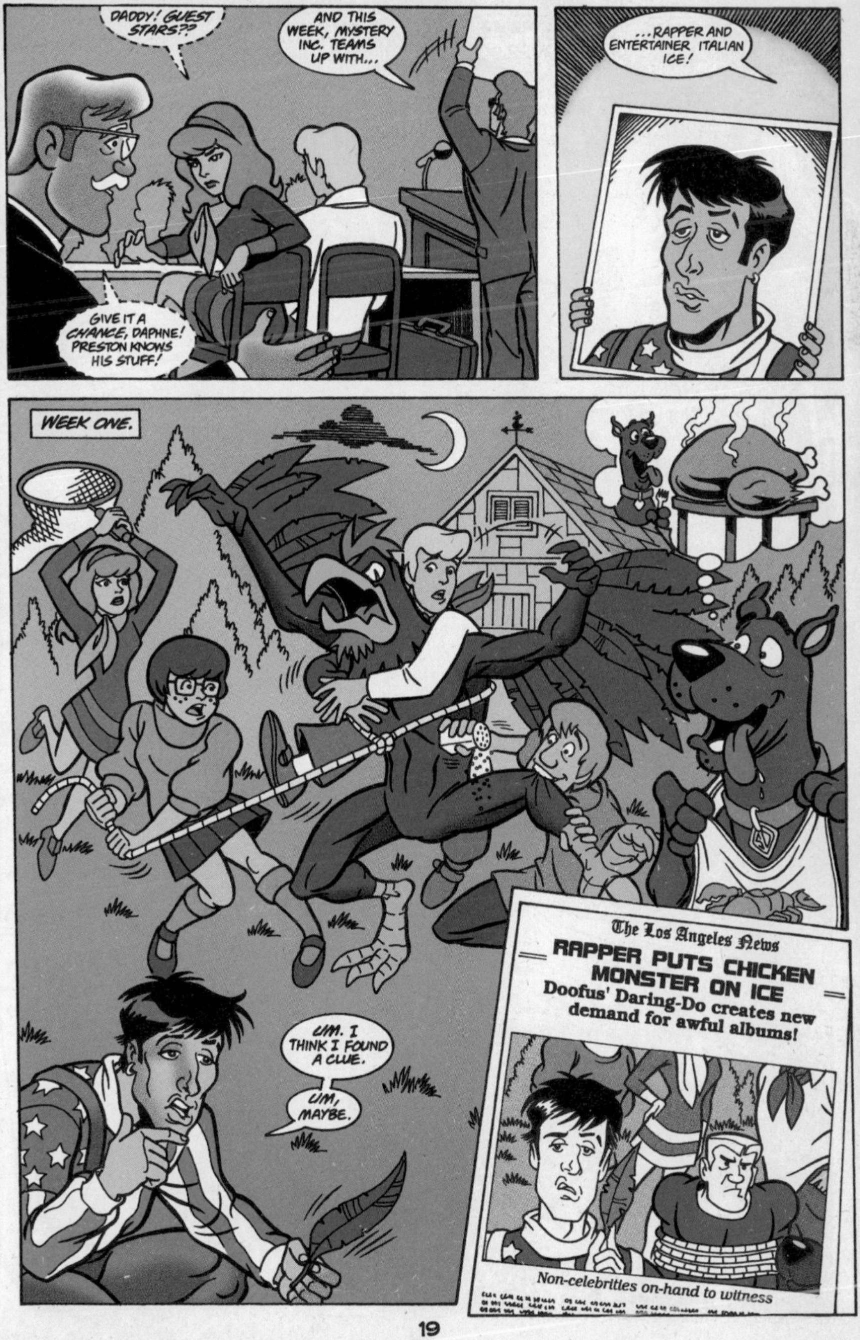
DADDY! GUEST STARS??
AND THIS WEEK, MYSTERY INC. TEAMS UP WITH...
GIVE IT A CHANCE, DAPHNE! PRESTON KNOWS HIS STUFF!
...RAPPER AND ENTERTAINER ITALIAN ICE!
WEEK ONE.
UM. I THINK I FOUND A CLUE.
UM, MAYBE.
The Los Angeles News
RAPPER PUTS CHICKEN MONSTER ON ICE
Doofus' Daring-Do creates new demand for awful albums!
Non-celebrities on-hand to witness

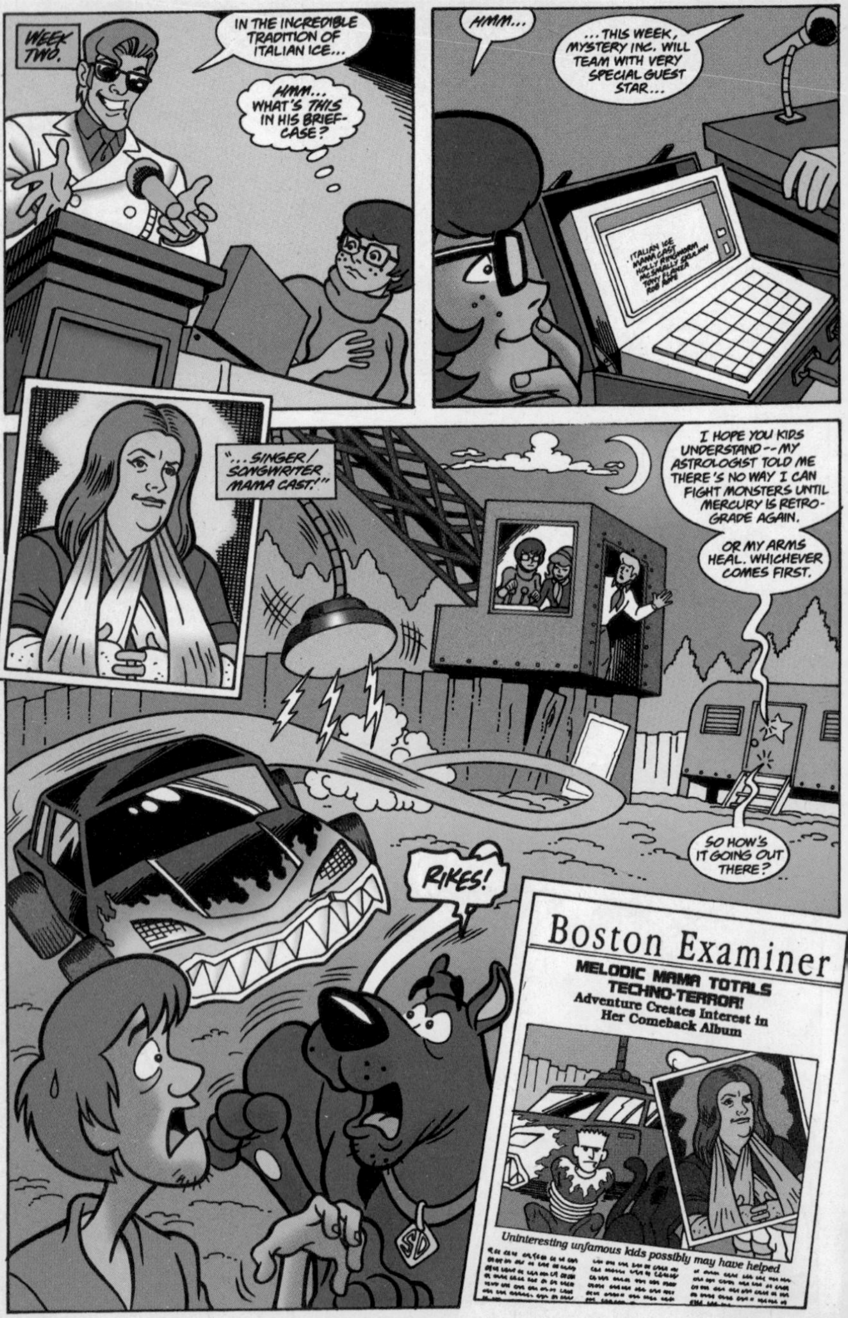
WEEK TWO.
IN THE INCREDIBLE TRADITION OF ITALIAN ICE...
HMM... WHAT'S THIS IN HIS BRIEF-CASE?
HMM...
...THIS WEEK, MYSTERY INC. WILL TEAM WITH VERY SPECIAL GUEST STAR...
"...SINGER/ SONGWRITER MAMA CAST!"
I HOPE YOU KIDS UNDERSTAND--MY ASTROLOGIST TOLD ME THERE'S NO WAY I CAN FIGHT MONSTERS UNTIL MERCURY IS RETRO-GRADE AGAIN.
OR MY ARMS HEAL. WHICHEVER COMES FIRST.
SO HOW'S IT GOING OUT THERE?
RIKES!
Boston Examiner
MELODIC MAMA TOTALS TECHNO-TERROR!
Adventure Creates Interest in Her Comeback Album
Uninteresting unfamous kids possibly may have helped

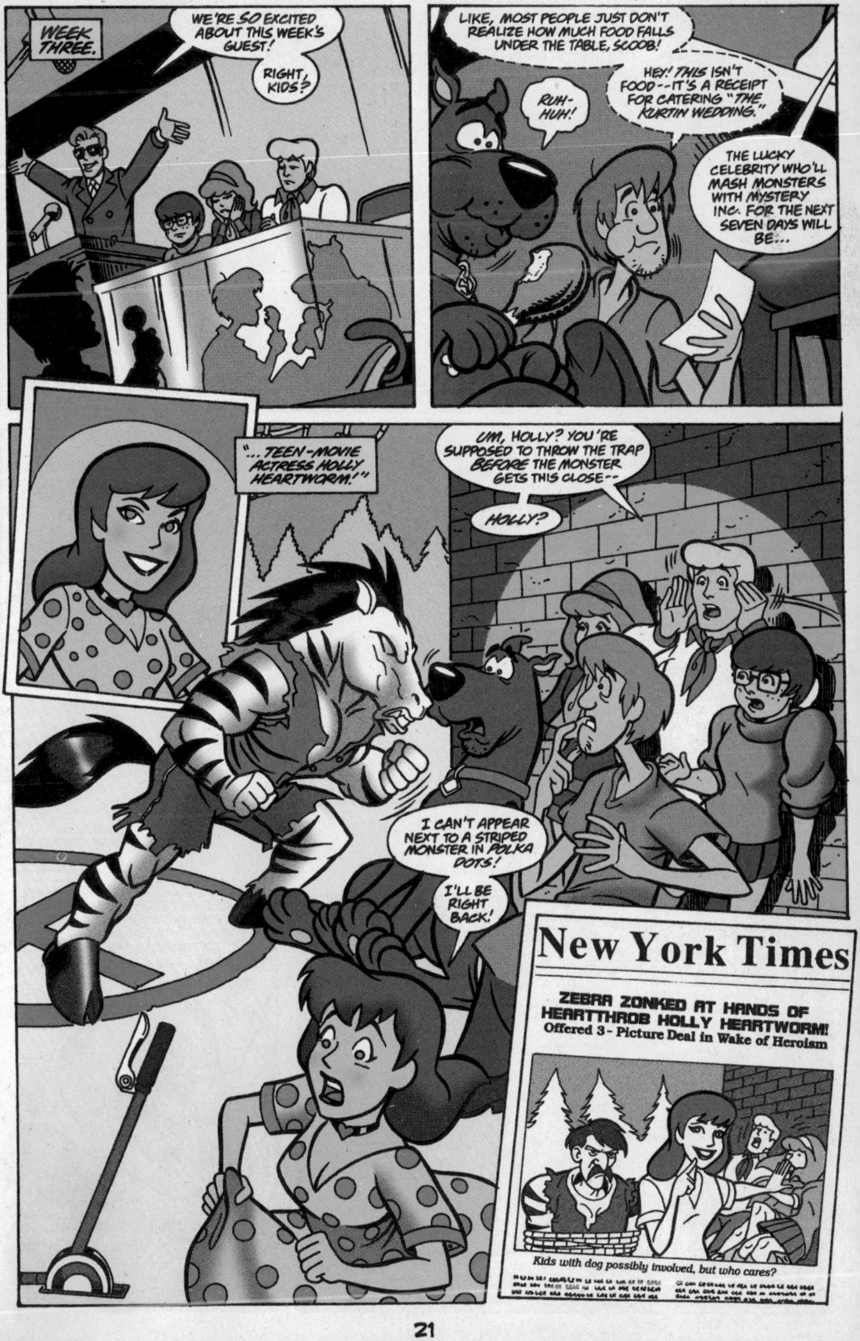
WEEK THREE.
WE'RE SO EXCITED ABOUT THIS WEEK'S GUEST!
RIGHT, KIDS?
LIKE, MOST PEOPLE JUST DON'T REALIZE HOW MUCH FOOD FALLS UNDER THE TABLE, SCOOB!
RUH-HUH!
HEY! THIS ISN'T FOOD--IT'S A RECEIPT FOR CATERING "THE KURTIN WEDDING."
THE LUCKY CELEBRITY WHO'LL MASH MONSTERS WITH MYSTERY INC. FOR THE NEXT SEVEN DAYS WILL BE...
"...TEEN-MOVIE ACTRESS HOLLY HEARTWORM!"
UM, HOLLY? YOU'RE SUPPOSED TO THROW THE TRAP BEFORE THE MONSTER GETS THIS CLOSE--
HOLLY?
I CAN'T APPEAR NEXT TO A STRIPED MONSTER IN POLKA DOTS!
I'LL BE RIGHT BACK!
New York Times
ZEBRA ZONKED AT HANDS OF HEARTTHROB HOLLY HEARTWORM!
Offered 3 - Picture Deal in Wake of Heroism
Kids with dog possibly involved, but who cares?

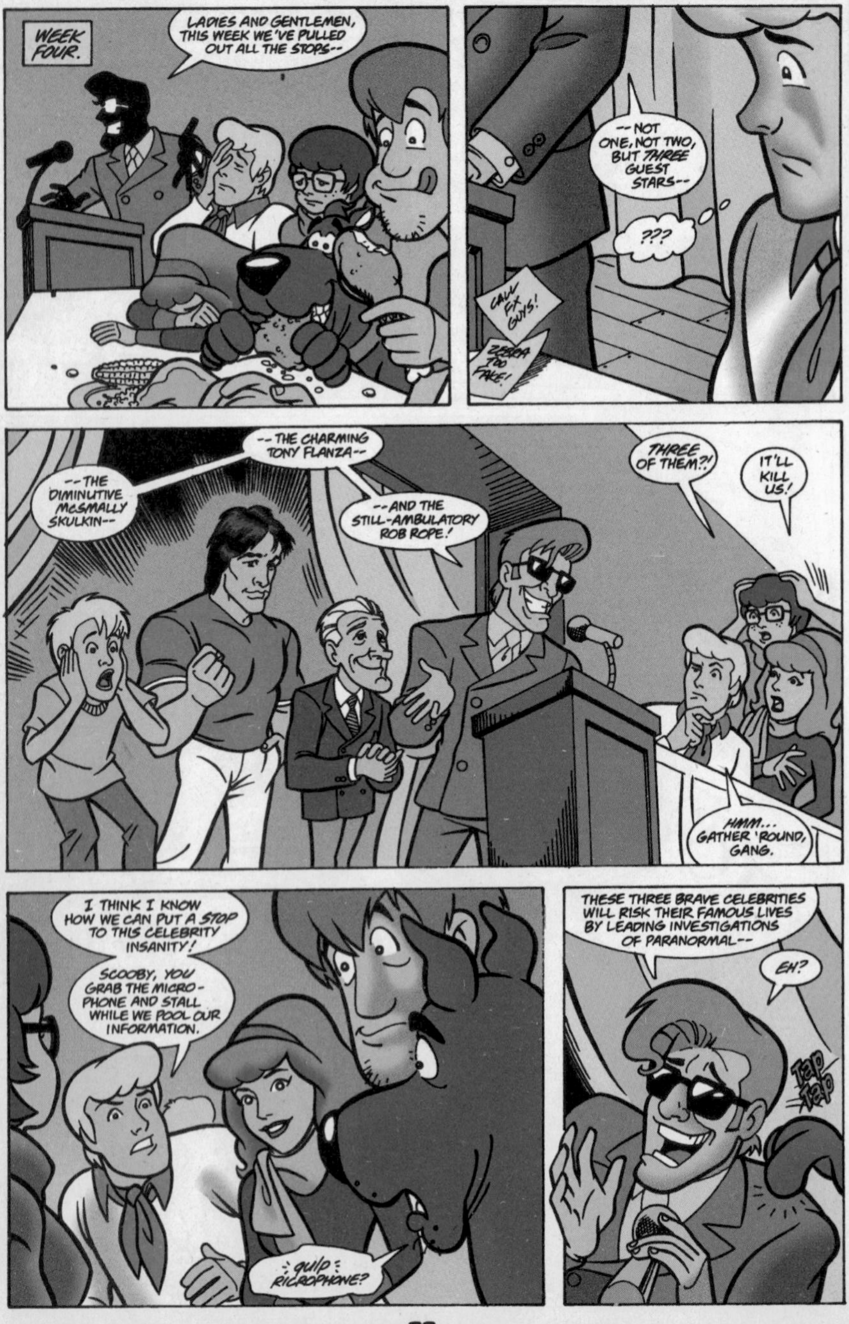
WEEK FOUR.
LADIES AND GENTLEMEN, THIS WEEK WE'VE PULLED OUT ALL THE STOPS--
--NOT ONE, NOT TWO, BUT THREE GUEST STARS--
???
CALL FX GUYS!
--THE DIMINUTIVE McSMALLY SKULKIN--
--THE CHARMING TONY FLANZA--
--AND THE STILL-AMBULATORY ROB ROPE!
THREE OF THEM?!
IT'LL KILL US!
HMM... GATHER 'ROUND, GANG.
I THINK I KNOW HOW WE CAN PUT A STOP TO THIS CELEBRITY INSANITY!
SCOOBY, YOU GRAB THE MICRO-PHONE AND STALL WHILE WE POOL OUR INFORMATION.
gulp RICROPHONE?
THESE THREE BRAVE CELEBRITIES WILL RISK THEIR FAMOUS LIVES BY LEADING INVESTIGATIONS OF PARANORMAL--
EH?
TAP TAP

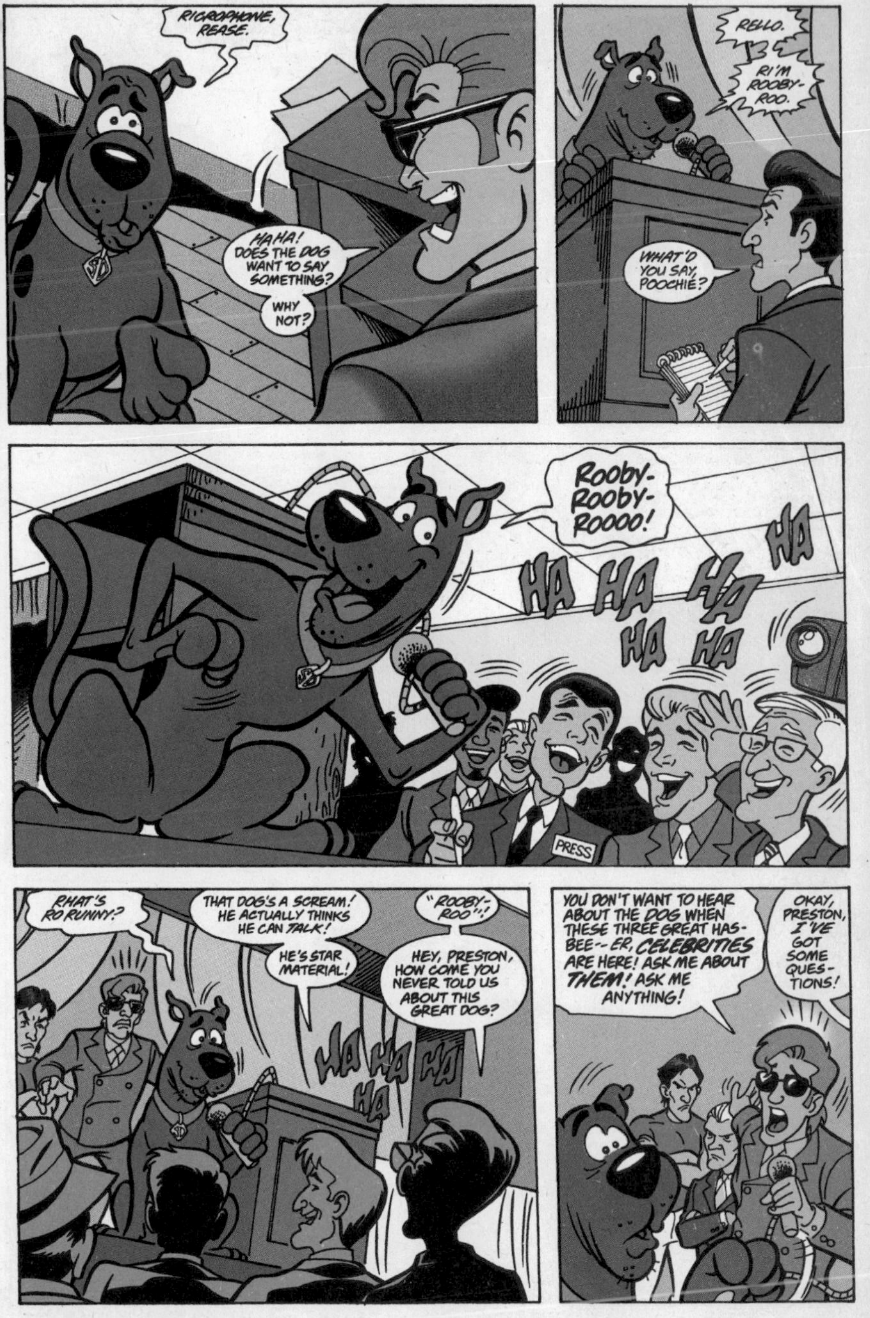
RIGROPHONE, REASE.
HA HA! DOES THE DOG WANT TO SAY SOMETHING?
WHY NOT?
RELLO.
RI'M ROOBY-ROO.
WHAT'D YOU SAY, POOCHIE?
Rooby-Rooby-Roooo!
HA HA HA HA HA HA HA
PRESS
RHAT'S RO RUNNY?
THAT DOG'S A SCREAM! HE ACTUALLY THINKS HE CAN TALK!
HE'S STAR MATERIAL!
"ROOBY-ROO"!
HEY, PRESTON, HOW COME YOU NEVER TOLD US ABOUT THIS GREAT DOG?
HA HA HA HA
YOU DON'T WANT TO HEAR ABOUT THE DOG WHEN THESE THREE GREAT HAS-BEE-- ER, CELEBRITIES ARE HERE! ASK ME ABOUT THEM! ASK ME ANYTHING!
OKAY, PRESTON, I'VE GOT SOME QUES-TIONS!

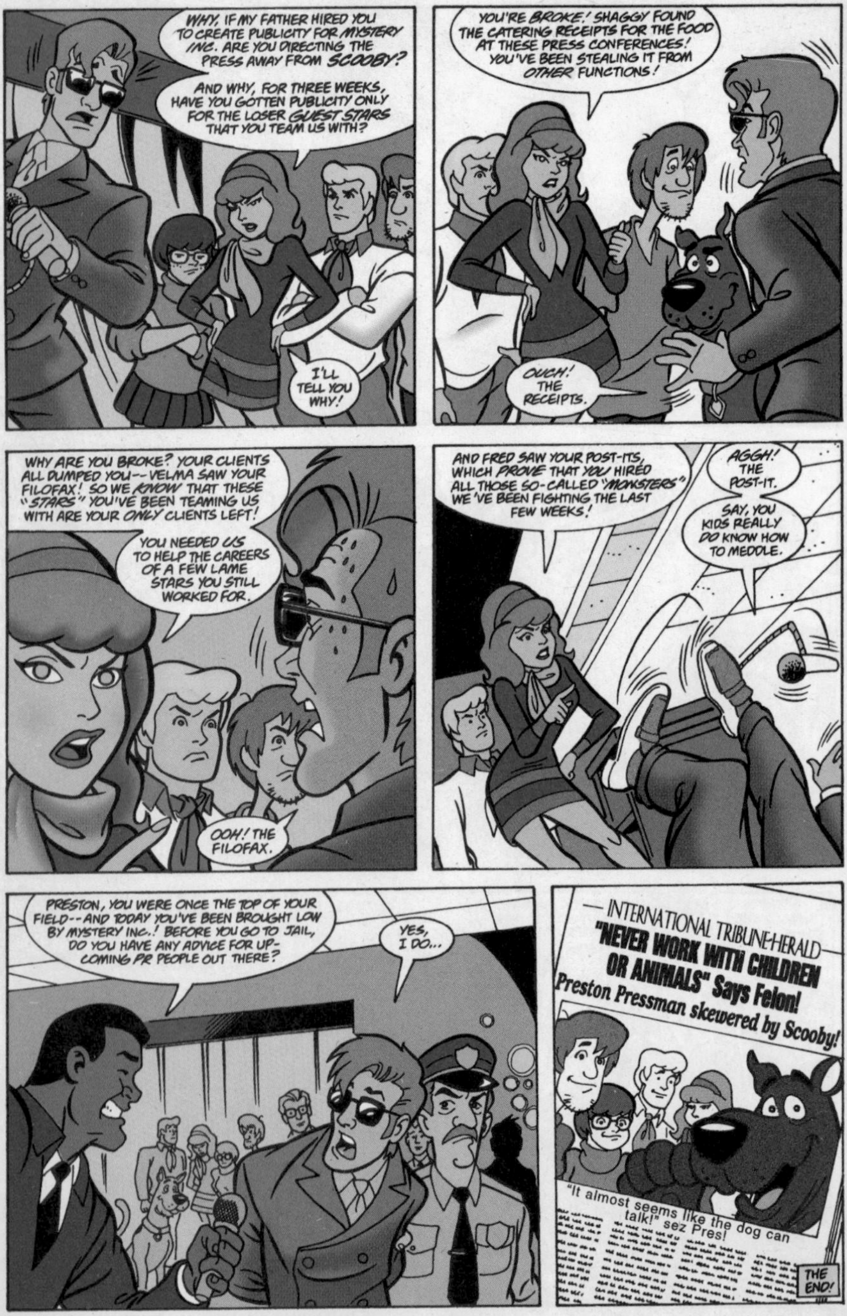
WHY, IF MY FATHER HIRED YOU TO CREATE PUBLICITY FOR MYSTERY INC. ARE YOU DIRECTING THE PRESS AWAY FROM SCOOBY?
AND WHY, FOR THREE WEEKS, HAVE YOU GOTTEN PUBLICITY ONLY FOR THE LOSER GUEST STARS THAT YOU TEAM US WITH?
I'LL TELL YOU WHY!
YOU'RE BROKE! SHAGGY FOUND THE CATERING RECEIPTS FOR THE FOOD AT THESE PRESS CONFERENCES! YOU'VE BEEN STEALING IT FROM OTHER FUNCTIONS!
OUCH! THE RECEIPTS.
WHY ARE YOU BROKE? YOUR CLIENTS ALL DUMPED YOU-- VELMA SAW YOUR FILOFAX! SO WE KNOW THAT THESE "STARS" YOU'VE BEEN TEAMING US WITH ARE YOUR ONLY CLIENTS LEFT!
YOU NEEDED US TO HELP THE CAREERS OF A FEW LAME STARS YOU STILL WORKED FOR.
OOH! THE FILOFAX.
AND FRED SAW YOUR POST-ITS, WHICH PROVE THAT YOU HIRED ALL THOSE SO-CALLED "MONSTERS" WE'VE BEEN FIGHTING THE LAST FEW WEEKS!
AGGH! THE POST-IT.
SAY, YOU KIDS REALLY DO KNOW HOW TO MEDDLE.
PRESTON, YOU WERE ONCE THE TOP OF YOUR FIELD-- AND TODAY YOU'VE BEEN BROUGHT LOW BY MYSTERY INC.! BEFORE YOU GO TO JAIL, DO YOU HAVE ANY ADVICE FOR UP-COMING PR PEOPLE OUT THERE?
YES, I DO...
INTERNATIONAL TRIBUNE-HERALD
"NEVER WORK WITH CHILDREN OR ANIMALS" Says Felon!
Preston Pressman skewered by Scooby!
"It almost seems like the dog can talk!" sez Pres!
THE END!

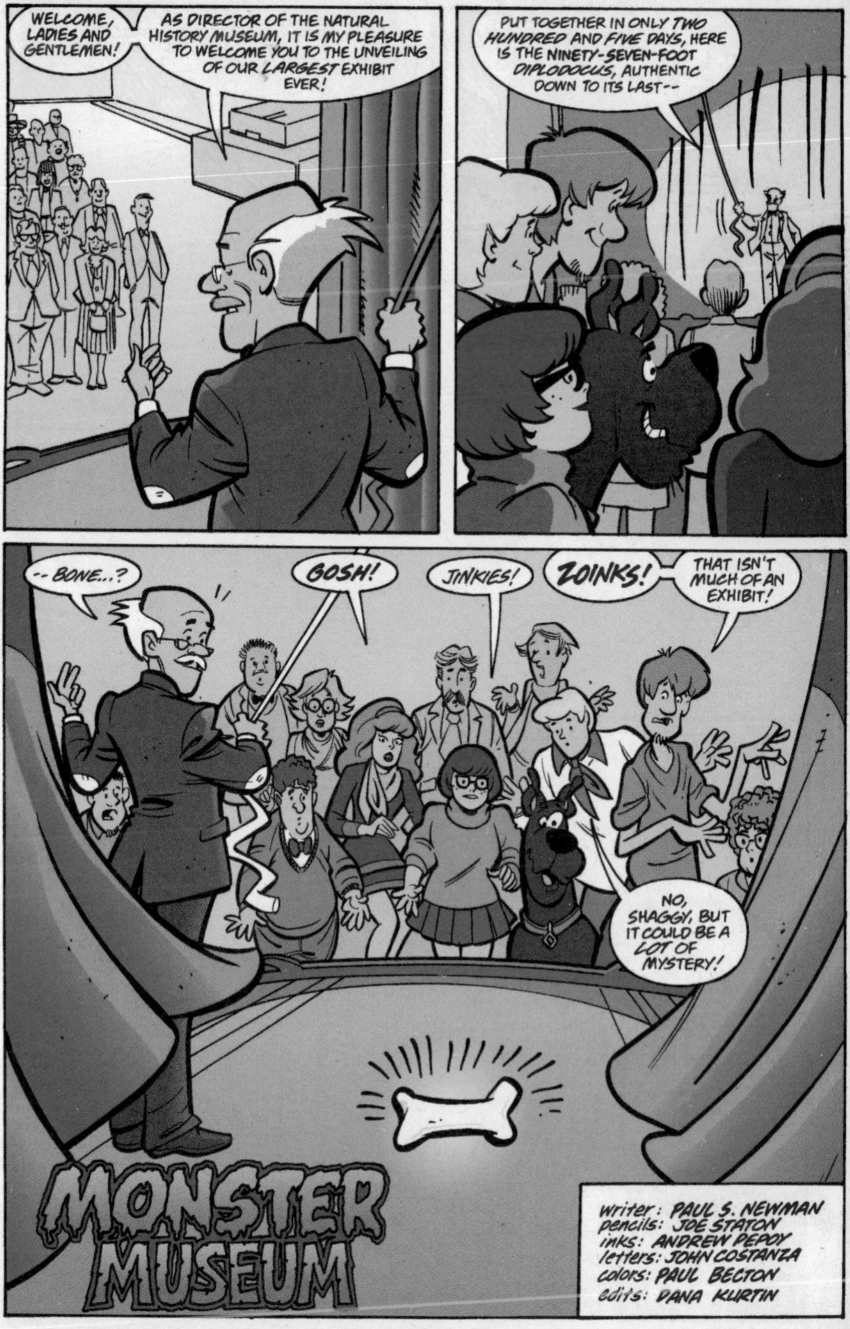
WELCOME, LADIES AND GENTLEMEN!
AS DIRECTOR OF THE NATURAL HISTORY MUSEUM, IT IS MY PLEASURE TO WELCOME YOU TO THE UNVEILING OF OUR LARGEST EXHIBIT EVER!
PUT TOGETHER IN ONLY TWO HUNDRED AND FIVE DAYS, HERE IS THE NINETY-SEVEN-FOOT DIPLODOCUS, AUTHENTIC DOWN TO ITS LAST--
--BONE...?
GOSH!
JINKIES!
ZOINKS!
THAT ISN'T MUCH OF AN EXHIBIT!
NO, SHAGGY, BUT IT COULD BE A LOT OF MYSTERY!
MONSTER MUSEUM
writer: PAUL S. NEWMAN
pencils: JOE STATON
inks: ANDREW PEPOY
letters: JOHN COSTANZA
colors: PAUL BECTON
edits: DANA KURTIN

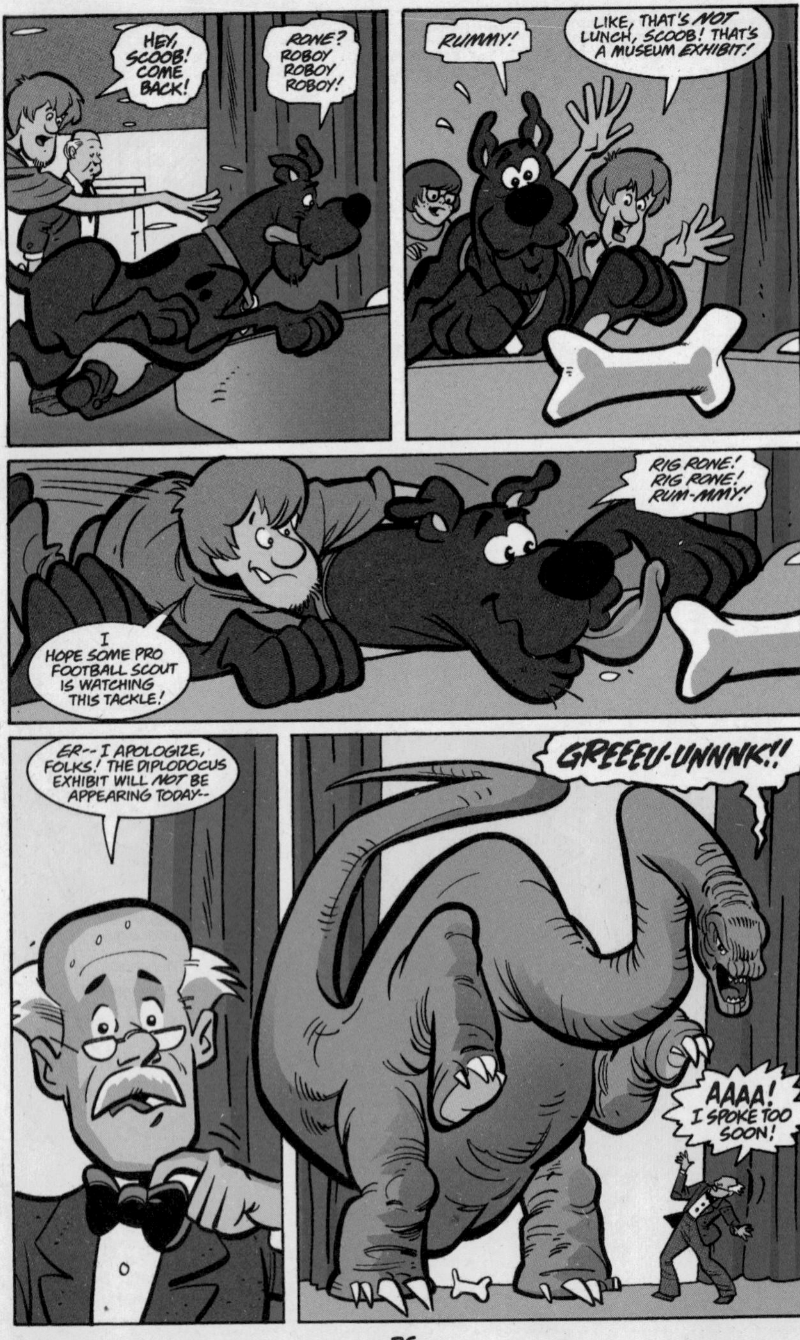
HEY, SCOOB! COME BACK!
RONE? ROBOY ROBOY ROBOY!
RUMMY!
LIKE, THAT'S NOT LUNCH, SCOOB! THAT'S A MUSEUM EXHIBIT!
RIG RONE! RIG RONE! RUM-MMY!
I HOPE SOME PRO FOOTBALL SCOUT IS WATCHING THIS TACKLE!
ER-- I APOLOGIZE, FOLKS! THE DIPLODOCUS EXHIBIT WILL NOT BE APPEARING TODAY--
GREEEU-UNNNK!!
AAAA! I SPOKE TOO SOON!

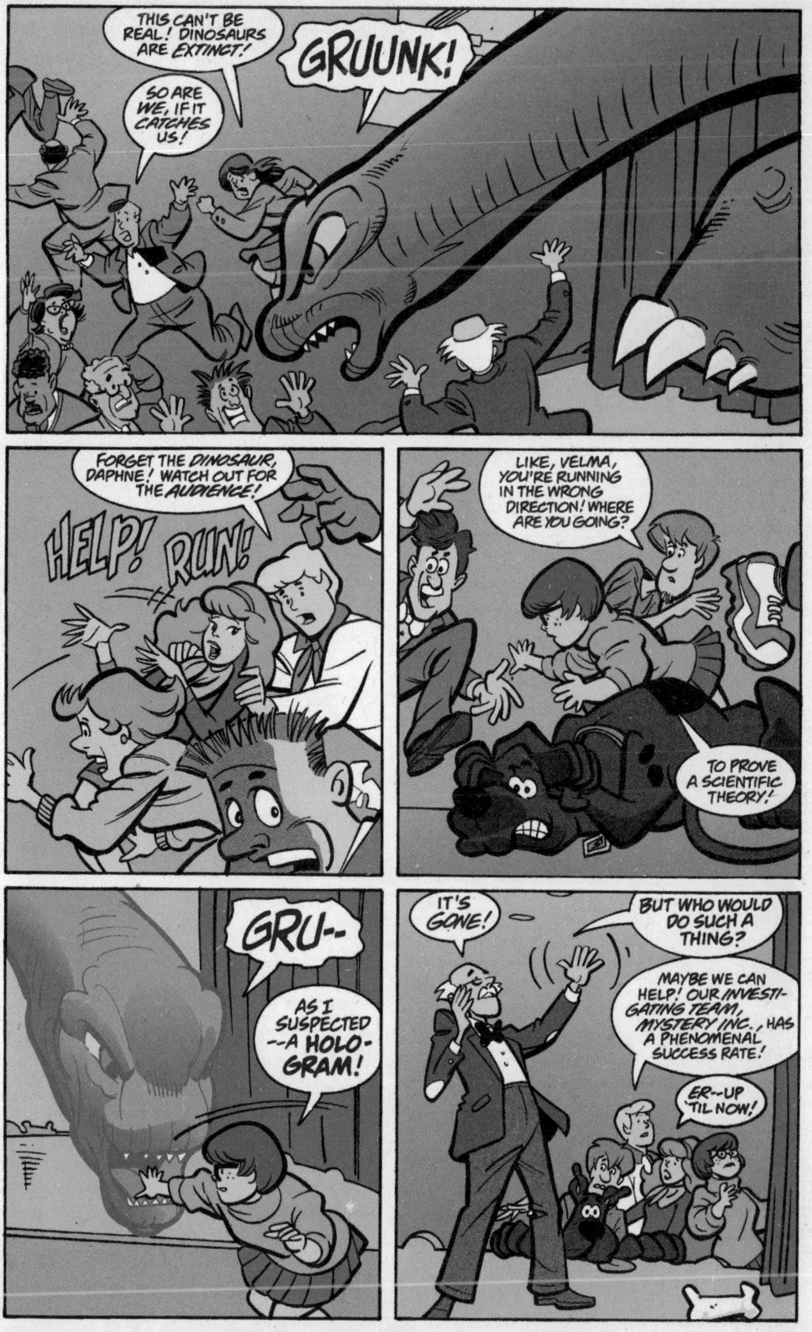
THIS CAN'T BE REAL! DINOSAURS ARE EXTINCT!
SO ARE WE, IF IT CATCHES US!
GRUUNK!
FORGET THE DINOSAUR, DAPHNE! WATCH OUT FOR THE AUDIENCE!
HELP! RUN!
LIKE, VELMA, YOU'RE RUNNING IN THE WRONG DIRECTION! WHERE ARE YOU GOING?
TO PROVE A SCIENTIFIC THEORY!
GRU--
AS I SUSPECTED --A HOLOGRAM!
IT'S GONE!
BUT WHO WOULD DO SUCH A THING?
MAYBE WE CAN HELP! OUR INVESTIGATING TEAM, MYSTERY INC., HAS A PHENOMENAL SUCCESS RATE!
ER--UP 'TIL NOW!

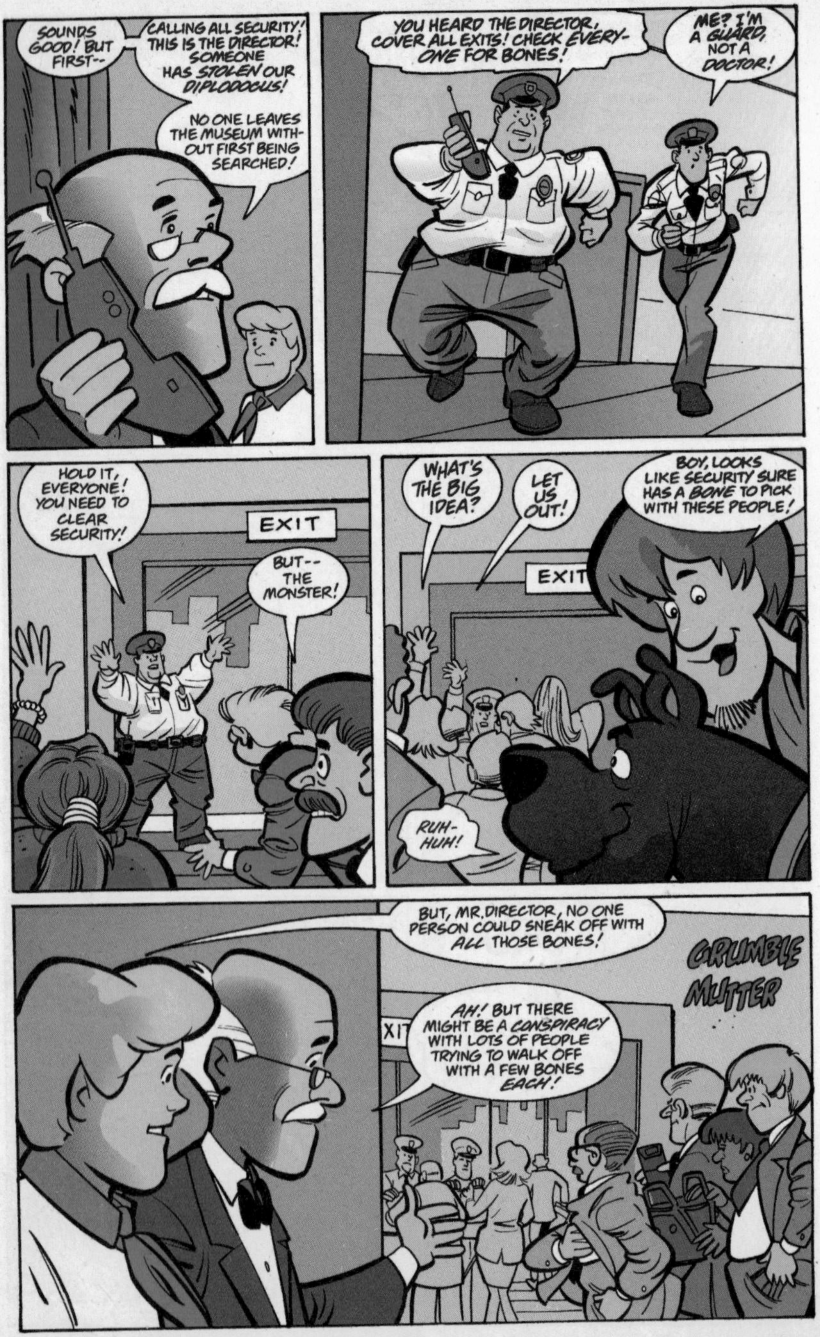
SOUNDS GOOD! BUT FIRST--
CALLING ALL SECURITY! THIS IS THE DIRECTOR! SOMEONE HAS STOLEN OUR DIPLODOCUS!
NO ONE LEAVES THE MUSEUM WITHOUT FIRST BEING SEARCHED!
YOU HEARD THE DIRECTOR, COVER ALL EXITS! CHECK EVERYONE FOR BONES!
ME? I'M A GUARD, NOT A DOCTOR!
HOLD IT, EVERYONE! YOU NEED TO CLEAR SECURITY!
EXIT
BUT-- THE MONSTER!
WHAT'S THE BIG IDEA?
LET US OUT!
BOY, LOOKS LIKE SECURITY SURE HAS A BONE TO PICK WITH THESE PEOPLE!
EXIT
RUH-HUH!
BUT, MR. DIRECTOR, NO ONE PERSON COULD SNEAK OFF WITH ALL THOSE BONES!
GRUMBLE
MUTTER
AH! BUT THERE MIGHT BE A CONSPIRACY WITH LOTS OF PEOPLE TRYING TO WALK OFF WITH A FEW BONES EACH!
XIT

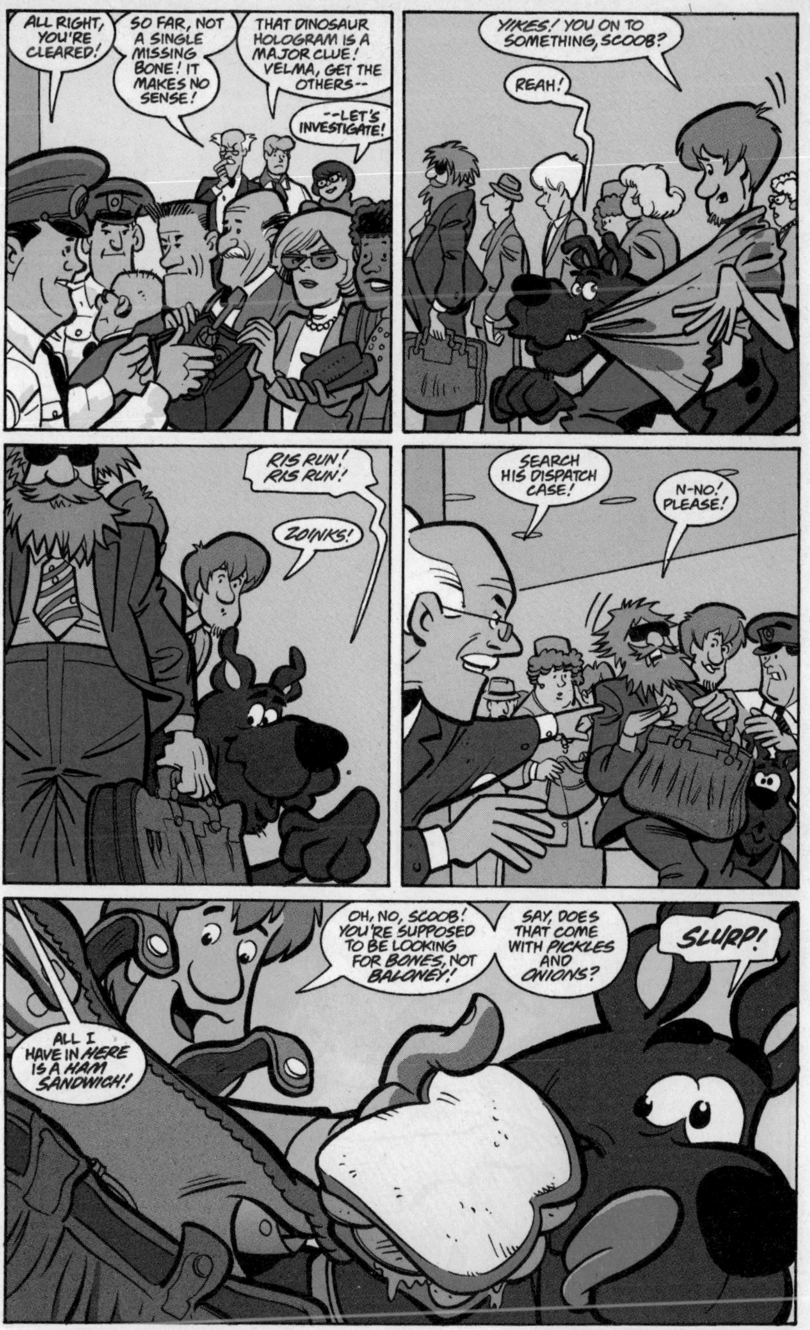
ALL RIGHT, YOU'RE CLEARED!
SO FAR, NOT A SINGLE MISSING BONE! IT MAKES NO SENSE!
THAT DINOSAUR HOLOGRAM IS A MAJOR CLUE! VELMA, GET THE OTHERS--
--LET'S INVESTIGATE!
YIKES! YOU ON TO SOMETHING, SCOOB?
REAH!
RIS RUN! RIS RUN!
ZOINKS!
SEARCH HIS DISPATCH CASE!
N-NO! PLEASE!
ALL I HAVE IN HERE IS A HAM SANDWICH!
OH, NO, SCOOB! YOU'RE SUPPOSED TO BE LOOKING FOR BONES, NOT BALONEY!
SAY, DOES THAT COME WITH PICKLES AND ONIONS?
SLURP!

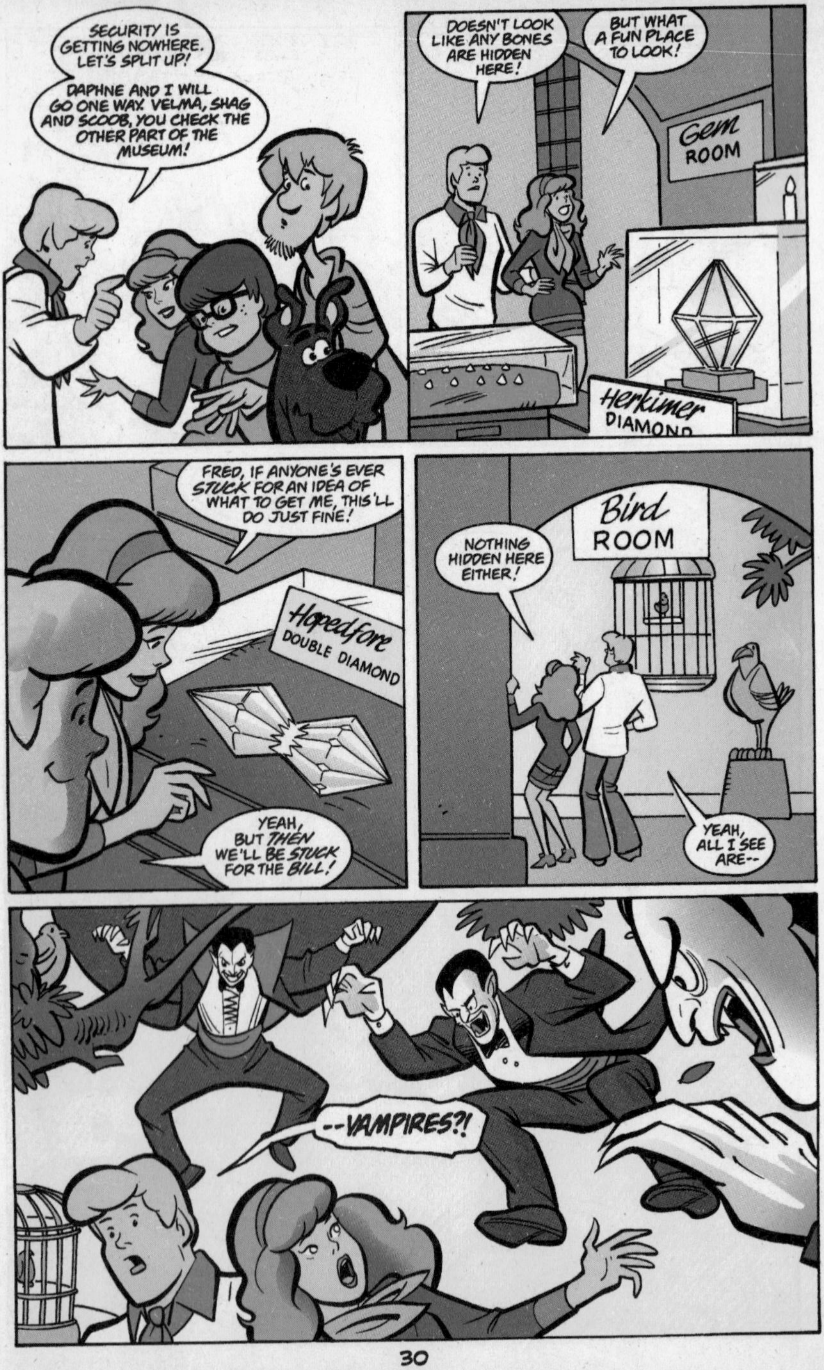
SECURITY IS GETTING NOWHERE. LET'S SPLIT UP!
DAPHNE AND I WILL GO ONE WAY. VELMA, SHAG AND SCOOB, YOU CHECK THE OTHER PART OF THE MUSEUM!
DOESN'T LOOK LIKE ANY BONES ARE HIDDEN HERE!
BUT WHAT A FUN PLACE TO LOOK!
Gem ROOM
Herkimer DIAMOND
FRED, IF ANYONE'S EVER STUCK FOR AN IDEA OF WHAT TO GET ME, THIS'LL DO JUST FINE!
Hopedfore DOUBLE DIAMOND
YEAH, BUT THEN WE'LL BE STUCK FOR THE BILL!
Bird ROOM
NOTHING HIDDEN HERE EITHER!
YEAH, ALL I SEE ARE--
--VAMPIRES?!

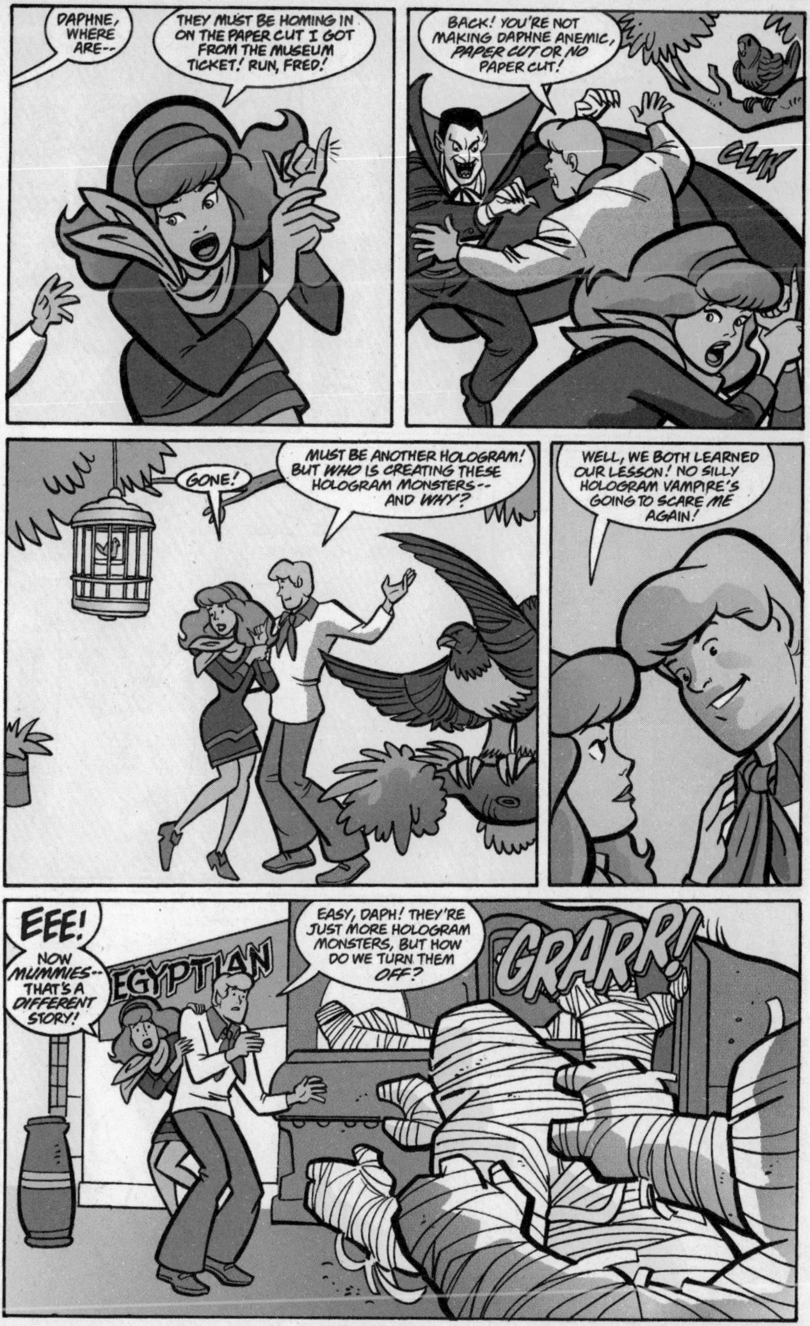
DAPHNE, WHERE ARE--
THEY MUST BE HOMING IN ON THE PAPER CUT I GOT FROM THE MUSEUM TICKET! RUN, FRED!
BACK! YOU'RE NOT MAKING DAPHNE ANEMIC, PAPER CUT OR NO PAPER CUT!
CLIK
GONE!
MUST BE ANOTHER HOLOGRAM! BUT WHO IS CREATING THESE HOLOGRAM MONSTERS-- AND WHY?
WELL, WE BOTH LEARNED OUR LESSON! NO SILLY HOLOGRAM VAMPIRE'S GOING TO SCARE ME AGAIN!
EEE!
NOW MUMMIES-- THAT'S A DIFFERENT STORY!
EGYPTIAN
EASY, DAPH! THEY'RE JUST MORE HOLOGRAM MONSTERS, BUT HOW DO WE TURN THEM OFF?
GRARR!

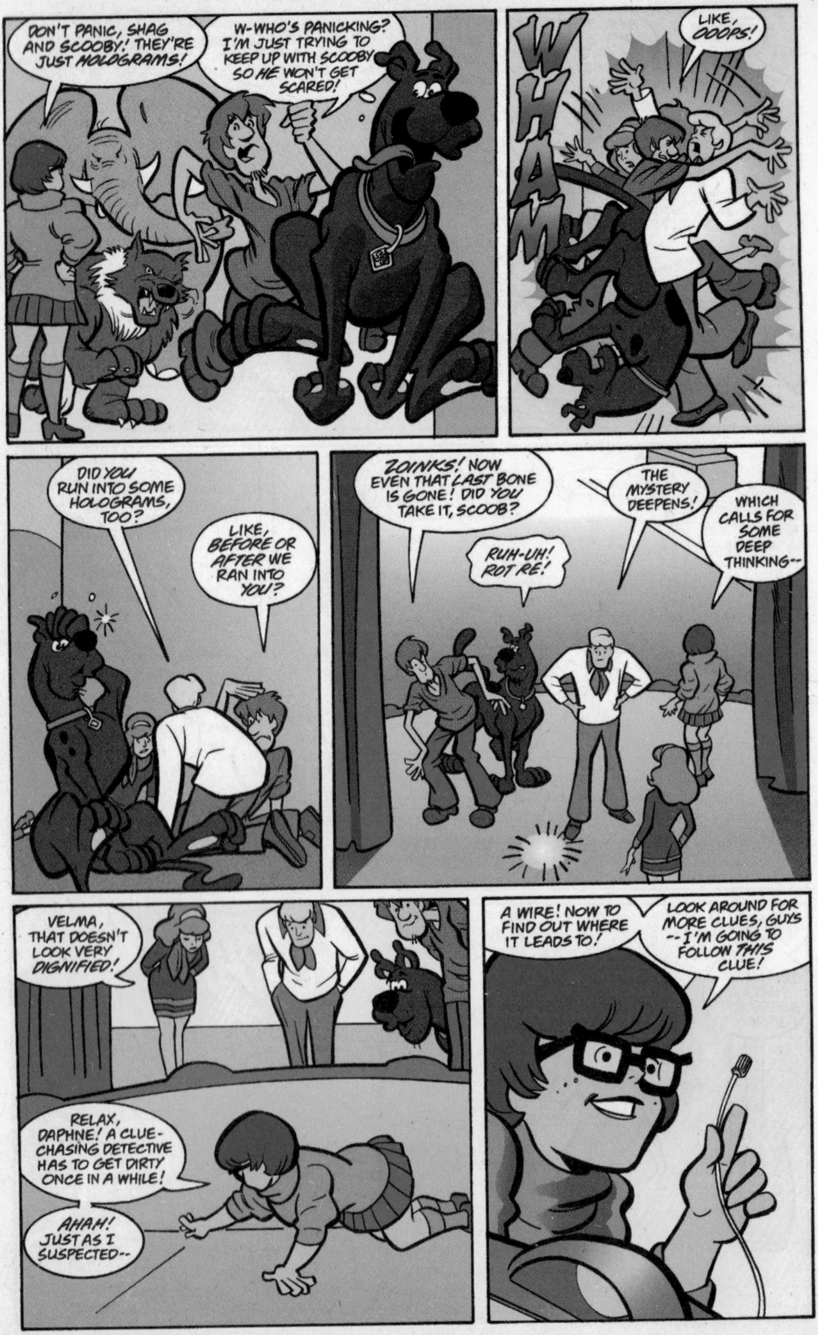

DON'T PANIC, SHAG AND SCOOBY! THEY'RE JUST HOLOGRAMS!
W-WHO'S PANICKING? I'M JUST TRYING TO KEEP UP WITH SCOOBY SO HE WON'T GET SCARED!
WHAM
LIKE, OOOPS!
DID YOU RUN INTO SOME HOLOGRAMS, TOO?
LIKE, BEFORE OR AFTER WE RAN INTO YOU?
ZOINKS! NOW EVEN THAT LAST BONE IS GONE! DID YOU TAKE IT, SCOOB?
RUH-UH! ROT RE!
THE MYSTERY DEEPENS!
WHICH CALLS FOR SOME DEEP THINKING--
VELMA, THAT DOESN'T LOOK VERY DIGNIFIED!
RELAX, DAPHNE! A CLUE-CHASING DETECTIVE HAS TO GET DIRTY ONCE IN A WHILE!
AHAH! JUST AS I SUSPECTED--
A WIRE! NOW TO FIND OUT WHERE IT LEADS TO!
LOOK AROUND FOR MORE CLUES, GUYS --I'M GOING TO FOLLOW THIS CLUE!

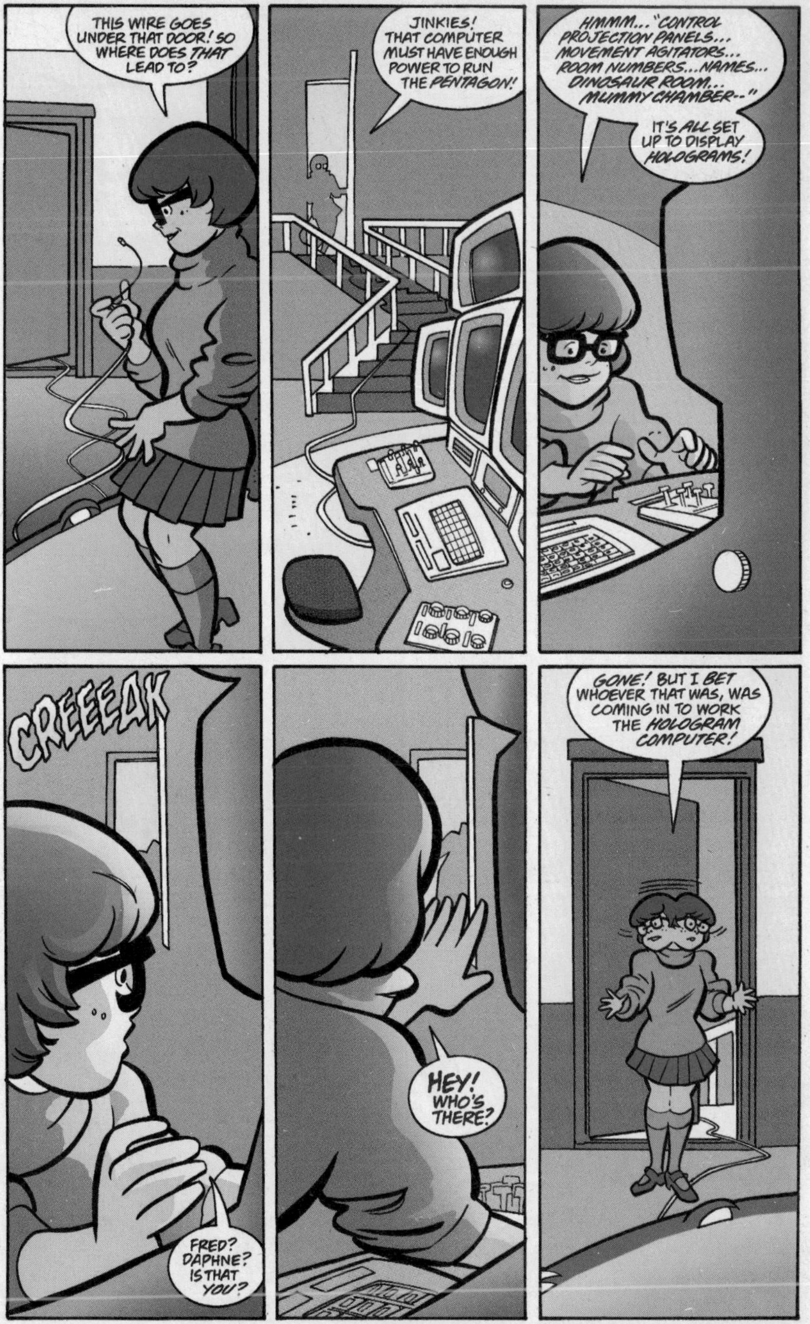
THIS WIRE GOES UNDER THAT DOOR! SO WHERE DOES THAT LEAD TO?
JINKIES! THAT COMPUTER MUST HAVE ENOUGH POWER TO RUN THE PENTAGON!
HMMM... "CONTROL PROJECTION PANELS... MOVEMENT AGITATORS... ROOM NUMBERS... NAMES... DINOSAUR ROOM... MUMMY CHAMBER--"
IT'S ALL SET UP TO DISPLAY HOLOGRAMS!
CREEEAK
FRED? DAPHNE? IS THAT YOU?
HEY! WHO'S THERE?
GONE! BUT I BET WHOEVER THAT WAS, WAS COMING IN TO WORK THE HOLOGRAM COMPUTER!

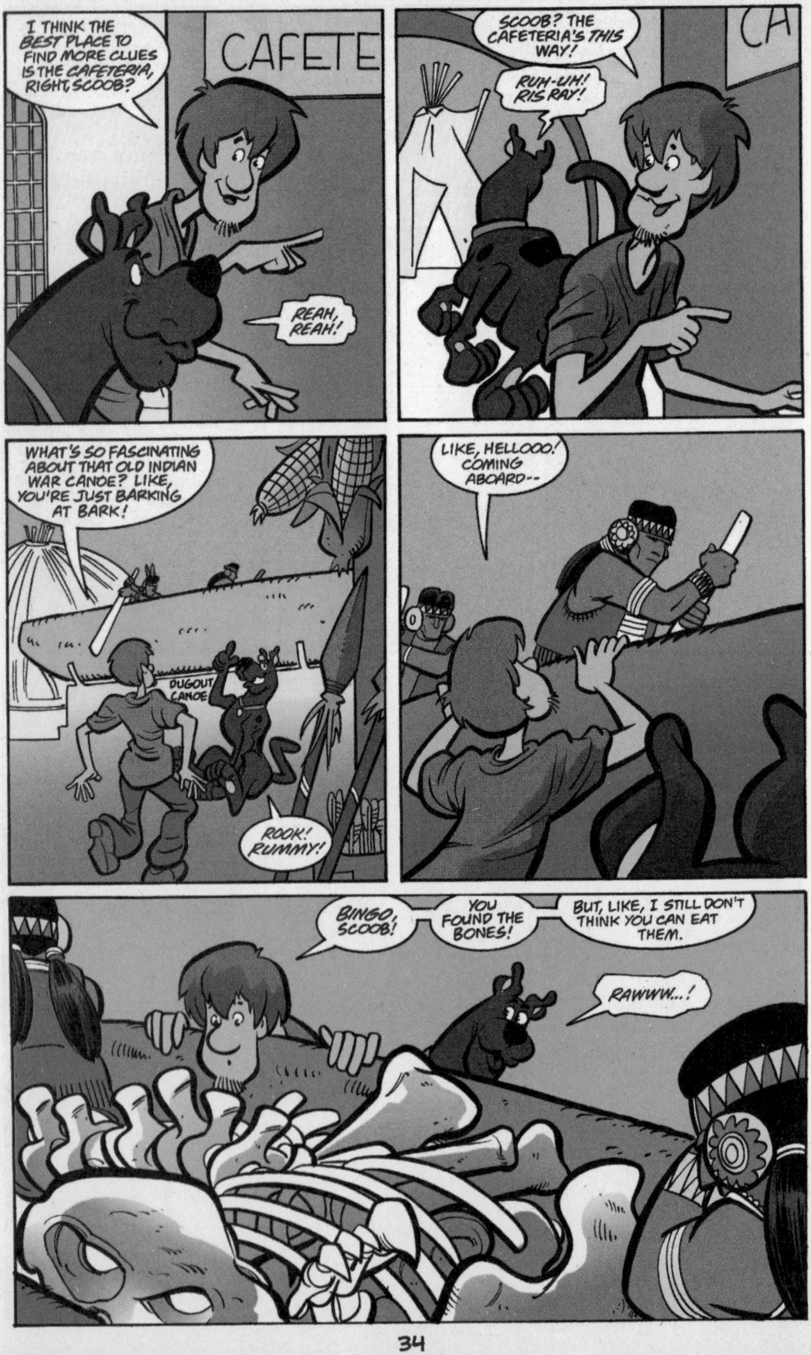
I THINK THE BEST PLACE TO FIND MORE CLUES IS THE CAFETERIA, RIGHT, SCOOB?
CAFETE
REAH, REAH!
SCOOB? THE CAFETERIA'S THIS WAY!
CA
RUH-UH! RIS RAY!
WHAT'S SO FASCINATING ABOUT THAT OLD INDIAN WAR CANOE? LIKE, YOU'RE JUST BARKING AT BARK!
DUGOUT CANOE
ROOK! RUMMY!
LIKE, HELLOOO! COMING ABOARD--
BINGO, SCOOB!
YOU FOUND THE BONES!
BUT, LIKE, I STILL DON'T THINK YOU CAN EAT THEM.
RAWWW...!

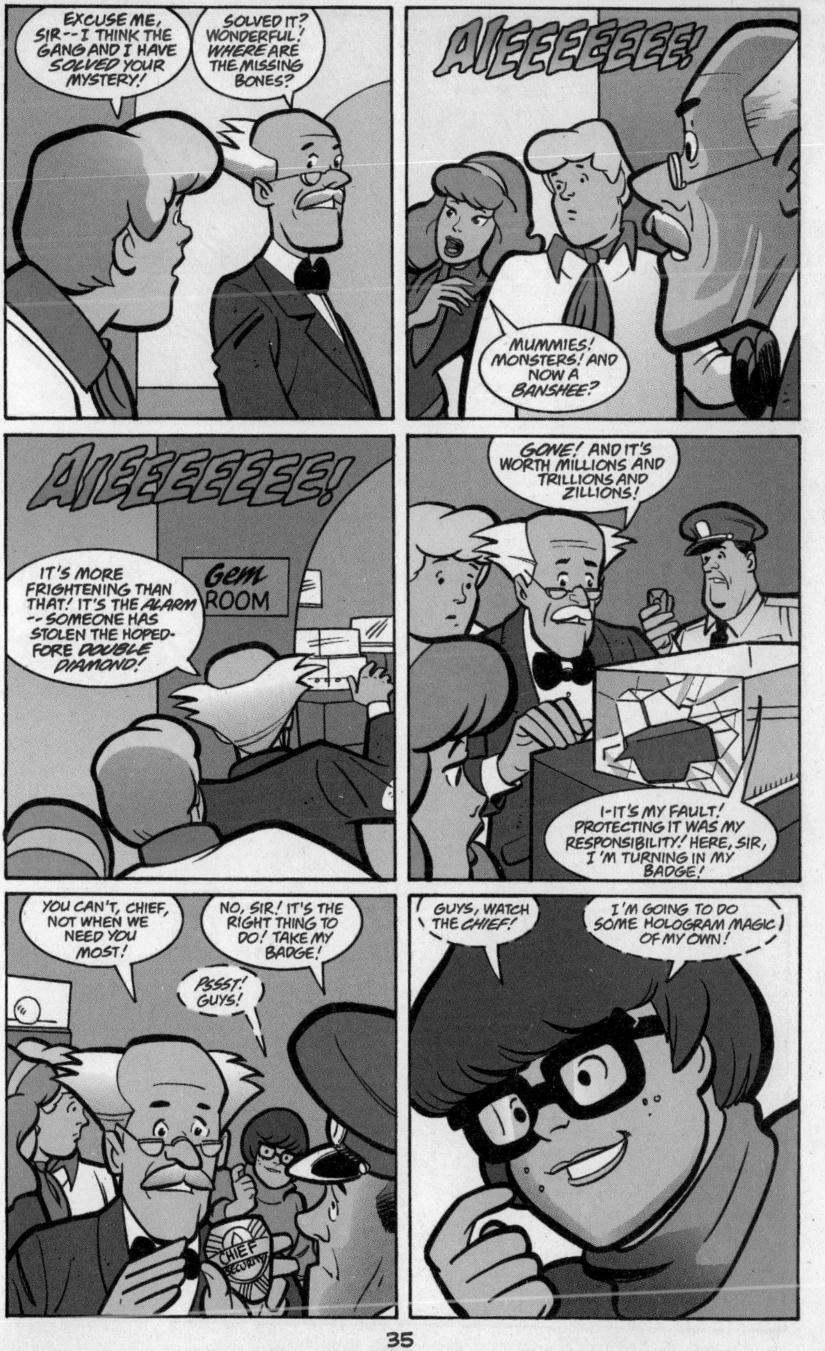
EXCUSE ME, SIR-- I THINK THE GANG AND I HAVE SOLVED YOUR MYSTERY!
SOLVED IT? WONDERFUL! WHERE ARE THE MISSING BONES?
AIEEEEEEEE!
MUMMIES! MONSTERS! AND NOW A BANSHEE?
AIEEEEEEEE!
IT'S MORE FRIGHTENING THAN THAT! IT'S THE ALARM -- SOMEONE HAS STOLEN THE HOPED-FORE DOUBLE DIAMOND!
Gem ROOM
GONE! AND IT'S WORTH MILLIONS AND TRILLIONS AND ZILLIONS!
I-IT'S MY FAULT! PROTECTING IT WAS MY RESPONSIBILITY! HERE, SIR, I'M TURNING IN MY BADGE!
YOU CAN'T, CHIEF, NOT WHEN WE NEED YOU MOST!
NO, SIR! IT'S THE RIGHT THING TO DO! TAKE MY BADGE!
PSSST! GUYS!
CHIEF SECURITY
GUYS, WATCH THE CHIEF!
I'M GOING TO DO SOME HOLOGRAM MAGIC OF MY OWN!

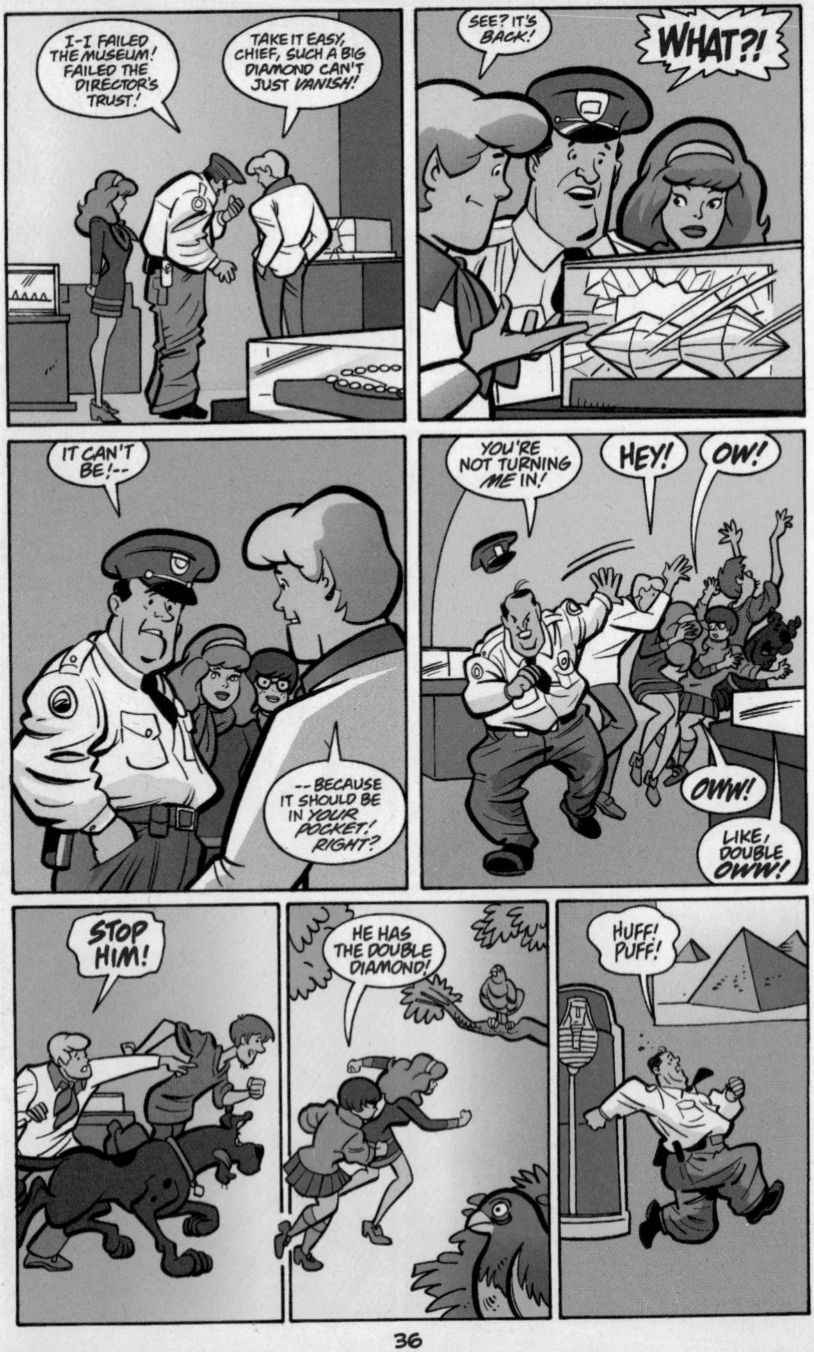
I-I FAILED THE MUSEUM! FAILED THE DIRECTOR'S TRUST!
TAKE IT EASY, CHIEF, SUCH A BIG DIAMOND CAN'T JUST VANISH!
SEE? IT'S BACK!
WHAT?!
IT CAN'T BE!--
--BECAUSE IT SHOULD BE IN YOUR POCKET! RIGHT?
YOU'RE NOT TURNING ME IN!
HEY!
OW!
OWW!
LIKE, DOUBLE OWW!
STOP HIM!
HE HAS THE DOUBLE DIAMOND!
HUFF! PUFF!

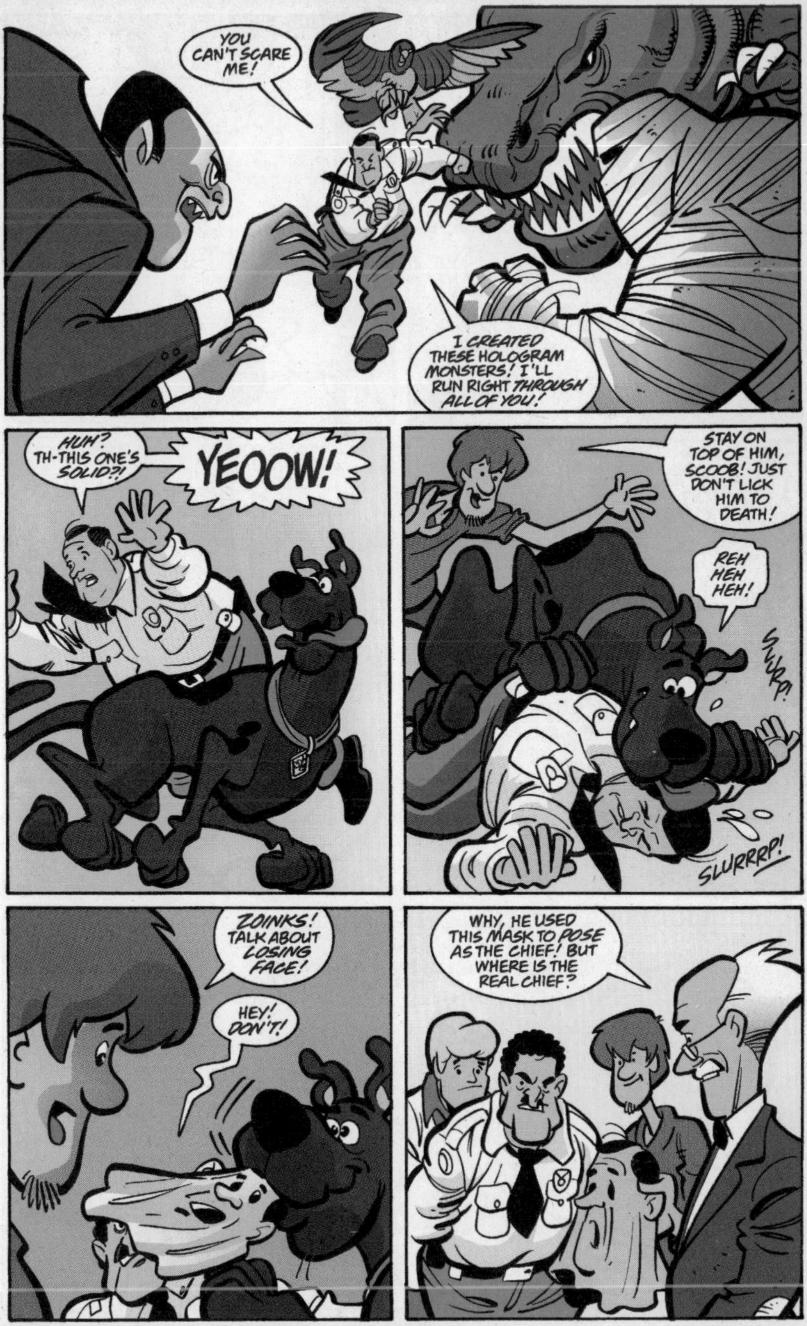
YOU CAN'T SCARE ME!
I CREATED THESE HOLOGRAM MONSTERS! I'LL RUN RIGHT THROUGH ALL OF YOU!
HUH? TH-THIS ONE'S SOLID?!
YEOOW!
STAY ON TOP OF HIM, SCOOB! JUST DON'T LICK HIM TO DEATH!
REH HEH HEH!
SLURP!
SLURRRP!
ZOINKS! TALK ABOUT LOSING FACE!
HEY! DON'T!
WHY, HE USED THIS MASK TO POSE AS THE CHIEF! BUT WHERE IS THE REAL CHIEF?

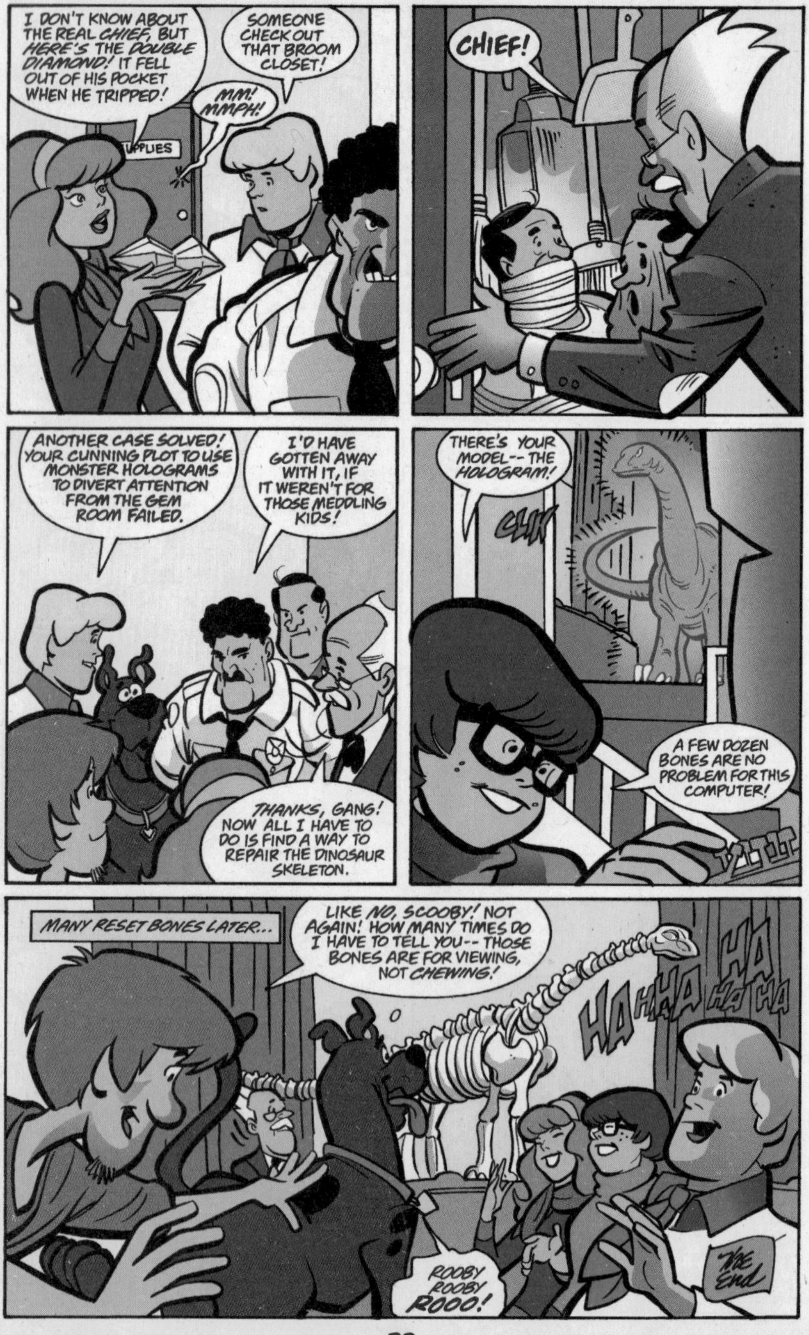
I DON'T KNOW ABOUT THE REAL CHIEF, BUT HERE'S THE DOUBLE DIAMOND! IT FELL OUT OF HIS POCKET WHEN HE TRIPPED!
SOMEONE CHECK OUT THAT BROOM CLOSET!
MM! MMPH!
SUPPLIES
CHIEF!
ANOTHER CASE SOLVED! YOUR CUNNING PLOT TO USE MONSTER HOLOGRAMS TO DIVERT ATTENTION FROM THE GEM ROOM FAILED.
I'D HAVE GOTTEN AWAY WITH IT, IF IT WEREN'T FOR THOSE MEDDLING KIDS!
THANKS, GANG! NOW ALL I HAVE TO DO IS FIND A WAY TO REPAIR THE DINOSAUR SKELETON.
THERE'S YOUR MODEL-- THE HOLOGRAM!
CLIK
A FEW DOZEN BONES ARE NO PROBLEM FOR THIS COMPUTER!
MANY RESET BONES LATER...
LIKE NO, SCOOBY! NOT AGAIN! HOW MANY TIMES DO I HAVE TO TELL YOU-- THOSE BONES ARE FOR VIEWING, NOT CHEWING!
HA HA HA HA HA HA HA
ROOBY ROOBY ROOO!
The End

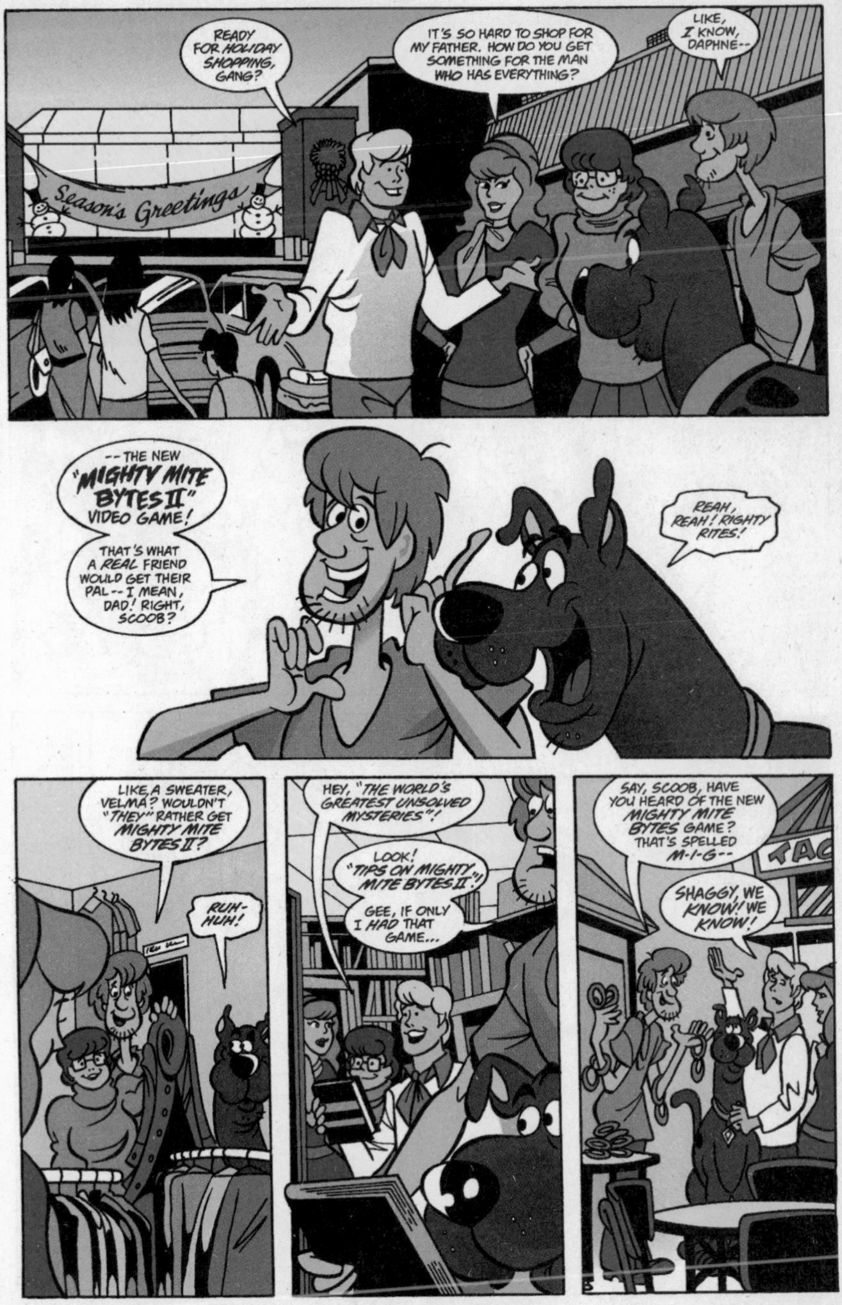
READY FOR HOLIDAY SHOPPING, GANG?
IT'S SO HARD TO SHOP FOR MY FATHER. HOW DO YOU GET SOMETHING FOR THE MAN WHO HAS EVERYTHING?
LIKE, I KNOW, DAPHNE--
Season's Greetings
--THE NEW "MIGHTY MITE BYTES II" VIDEO GAME!
THAT'S WHAT A REAL FRIEND WOULD GET THEIR PAL--I MEAN, DAD! RIGHT, SCOOB?
REAH, REAH! RIGHTY RITES!
LIKE, A SWEATER, VELMA? WOULDN'T "THEY" RATHER GET MIGHTY MITE BYTES II?
RUH-HUH!
HEY, "THE WORLD'S GREATEST UNSOLVED MYSTERIES"!
LOOK! "TIPS ON MIGHTY MITE BYTES II"!
GEE, IF ONLY I HAD THAT GAME...
SAY, SCOOB, HAVE YOU HEARD OF THE NEW MIGHTY MITE BYTES GAME? THAT'S SPELLED M-I-G--
SHAGGY, WE KNOW! WE KNOW!

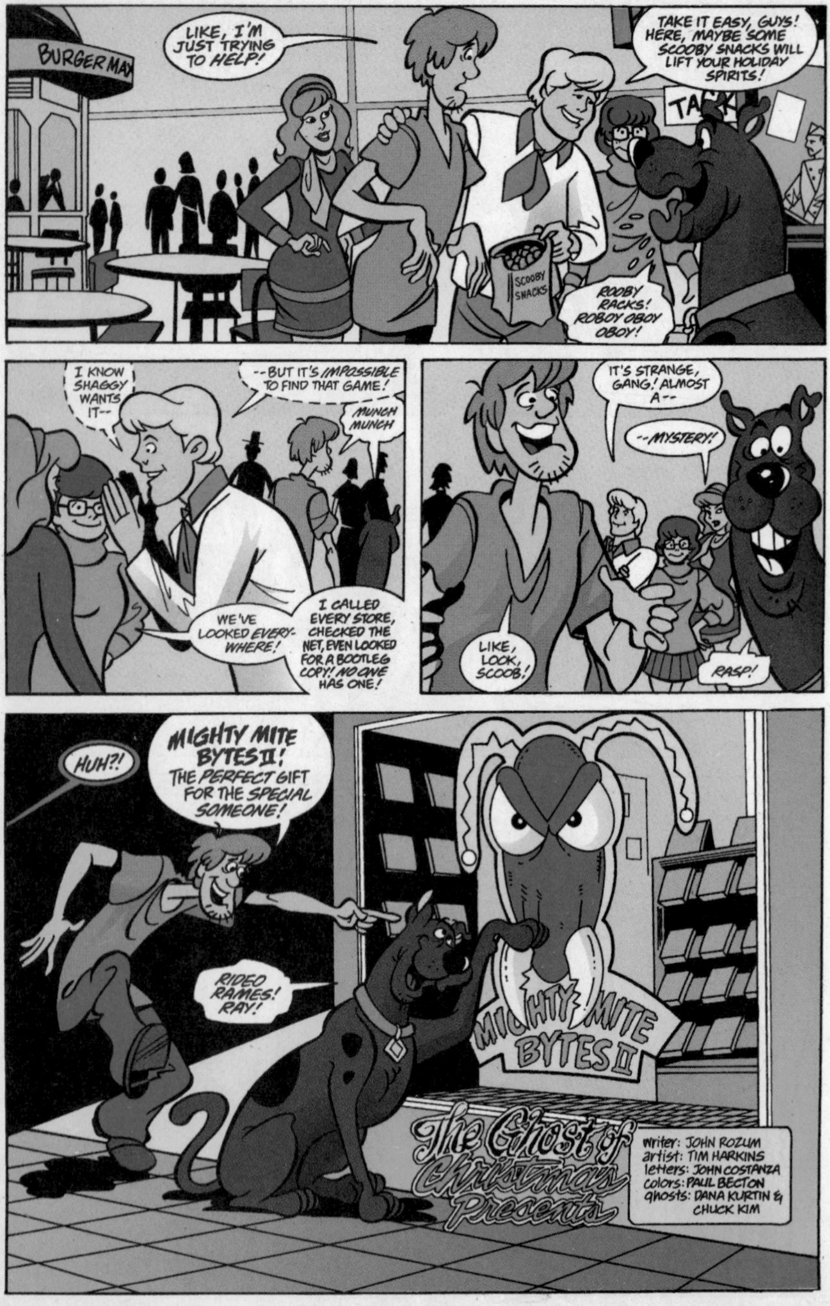
BURGER MAX
LIKE, I'M JUST TRYING TO HELP!
TAKE IT EASY, GUYS! HERE, MAYBE SOME SCOOBY SNACKS WILL LIFT YOUR HOLIDAY SPIRITS!
SCOOBY SNACKS
ROOBY RACKS! ROBOY OBOY OBOY!
I KNOW SHAGGY WANTS IT--
--BUT IT'S IMPOSSIBLE TO FIND THAT GAME!
MUNCH MUNCH
WE'VE LOOKED EVERYWHERE!
I CALLED EVERY STORE, CHECKED THE NET, EVEN LOOKED FOR A BOOTLEG COPY! NO ONE HAS ONE!
IT'S STRANGE, GANG! ALMOST A--
--MYSTERY!
LIKE, LOOK, SCOOB!
RASP!
HUH?!
MIGHTY MITE BYTES II! THE PERFECT GIFT FOR THE SPECIAL SOMEONE!
RIDEO RAMES! RAY!
MIGHTY MITE BYTES II
The Ghost of Christmas Presents
writer: JOHN ROZUM
artist: TIM HARKINS
letters: JOHN COSTANZA
colors: PAUL BECTON
ghosts: DANA KURTIN & CHUCK KIM

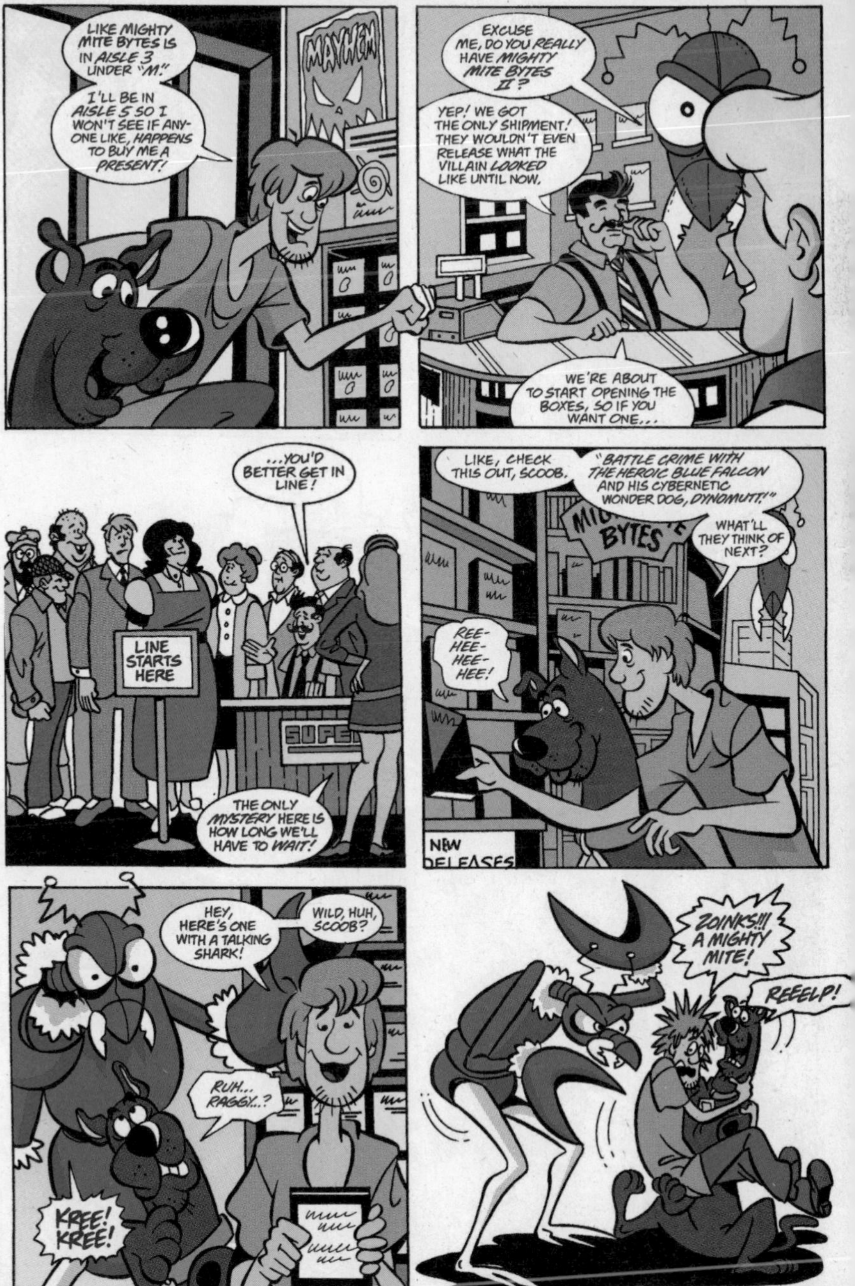

LIKE MIGHTY MITE BYTES IS IN AISLE 3 UNDER "M."
I'LL BE IN AISLE 5 SO I WON'T SEE IF ANYONE LIKE, HAPPENS TO BUY ME A PRESENT!
MAYHEM
EXCUSE ME, DO YOU REALLY HAVE MIGHTY MITE BYTES II ?
YEP! WE GOT THE ONLY SHIPMENT! THEY WOULDN'T EVEN RELEASE WHAT THE VILLAIN LOOKED LIKE UNTIL NOW.
WE'RE ABOUT TO START OPENING THE BOXES, SO IF YOU WANT ONE...
...YOU'D BETTER GET IN LINE!
LINE STARTS HERE
THE ONLY MYSTERY HERE IS HOW LONG WE'LL HAVE TO WAIT!
LIKE, CHECK THIS OUT, SCOOB.
"BATTLE CRIME WITH THE HEROIC BLUE FALCON AND HIS CYBERNETIC WONDER DOG, DYNOMUTT!"
WHAT'LL THEY THINK OF NEXT?
BYTES
REE-HEE-HEE-HEE!
NEW
HEY, HERE'S ONE WITH A TALKING SHARK!
WILD, HUH, SCOOB?
RUH... RAGGY...?
KREE! KREE!
ZOINKS!!! A MIGHTY MITE!
REEELP!

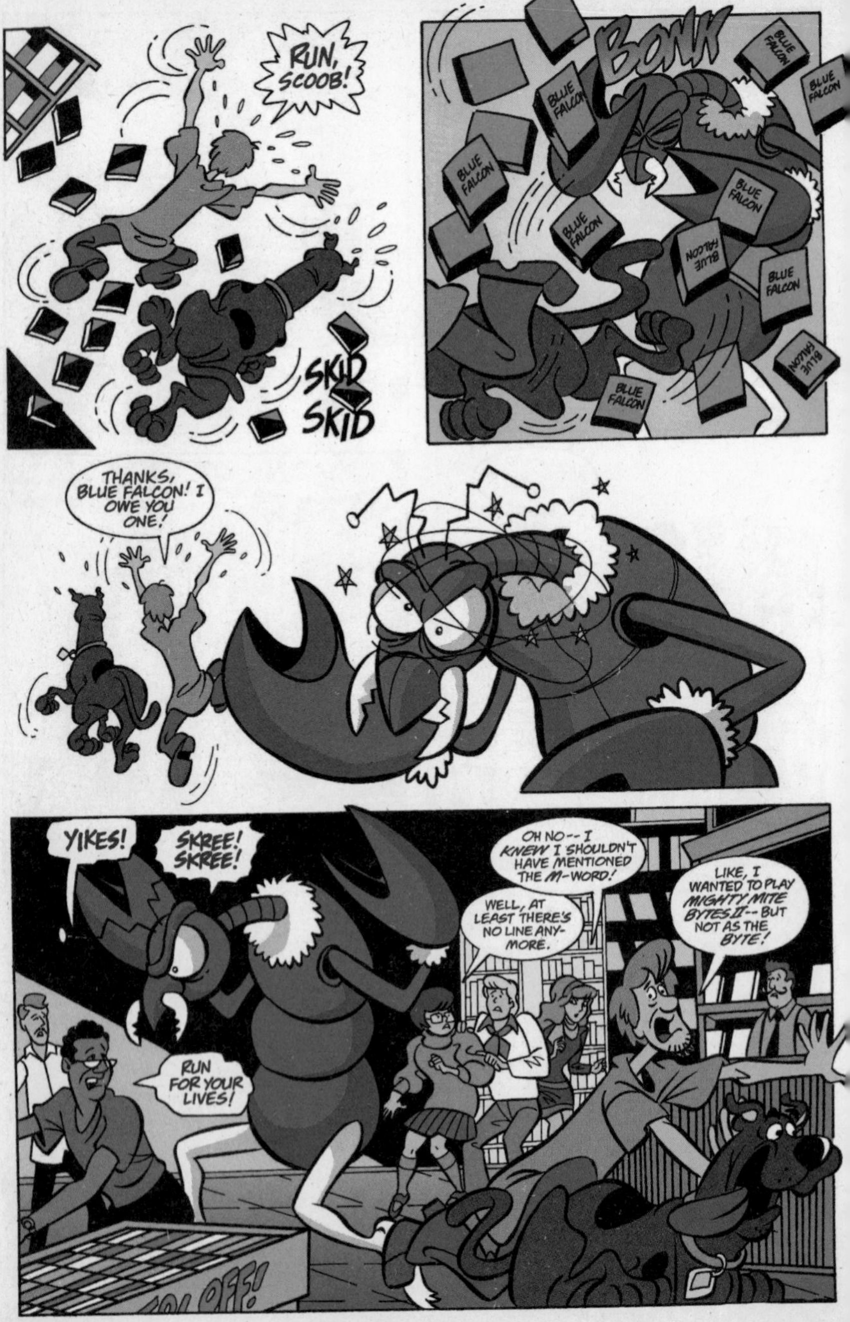
RUN, SCOOB!
SKID
SKID
BONK
BLUE FALCON
THANKS, BLUE FALCON! I OWE YOU ONE!
YIKES!
SKREE! SKREE!
OH NO-- I KNEW I SHOULDN'T HAVE MENTIONED THE M-WORD!
WELL, AT LEAST THERE'S NO LINE ANY-MORE.
LIKE, I WANTED TO PLAY MIGHTY MITE BYTES II-- BUT NOT AS THE BYTE!
RUN FOR YOUR LIVES!

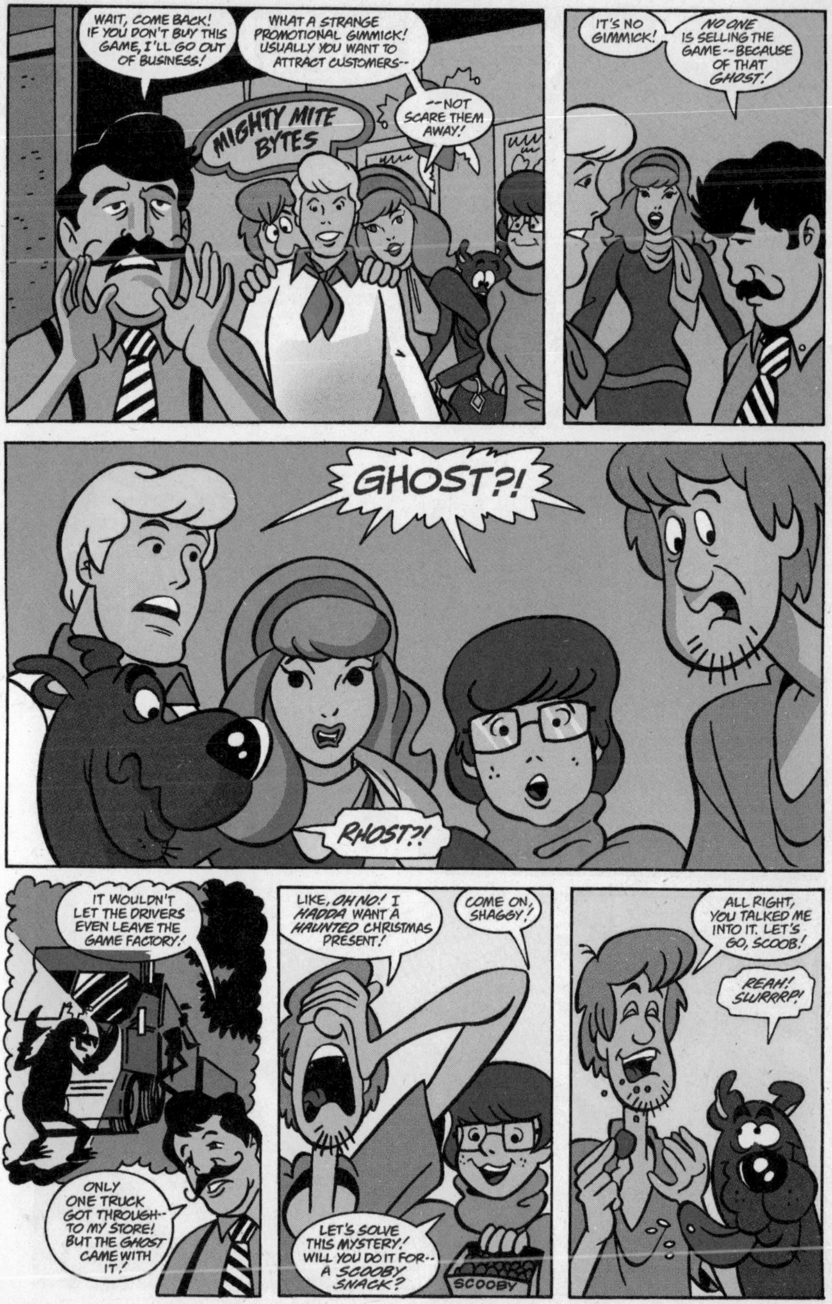
WAIT, COME BACK! IF YOU DON'T BUY THIS GAME, I'LL GO OUT OF BUSINESS!
WHAT A STRANGE PROMOTIONAL GIMMICK! USUALLY YOU WANT TO ATTRACT CUSTOMERS--
--NOT SCARE THEM AWAY!
MIGHTY MITE BYTES
IT'S NO GIMMICK!
NO ONE IS SELLING THE GAME--BECAUSE OF THAT GHOST!
GHOST?!
RHOST?!
IT WOULDN'T LET THE DRIVERS EVEN LEAVE THE GAME FACTORY!
ONLY ONE TRUCK GOT THROUGH--TO MY STORE! BUT THE GHOST CAME WITH IT!
LIKE, OH NO! I HADDA WANT A HAUNTED CHRISTMAS PRESENT!
COME ON, SHAGGY!
LET'S SOLVE THIS MYSTERY! WILL YOU DO IT FOR--A SCOOBY SNACK?
SCOOBY
ALL RIGHT, YOU TALKED ME INTO IT. LET'S GO, SCOOB!
REAH! SLURRRP!

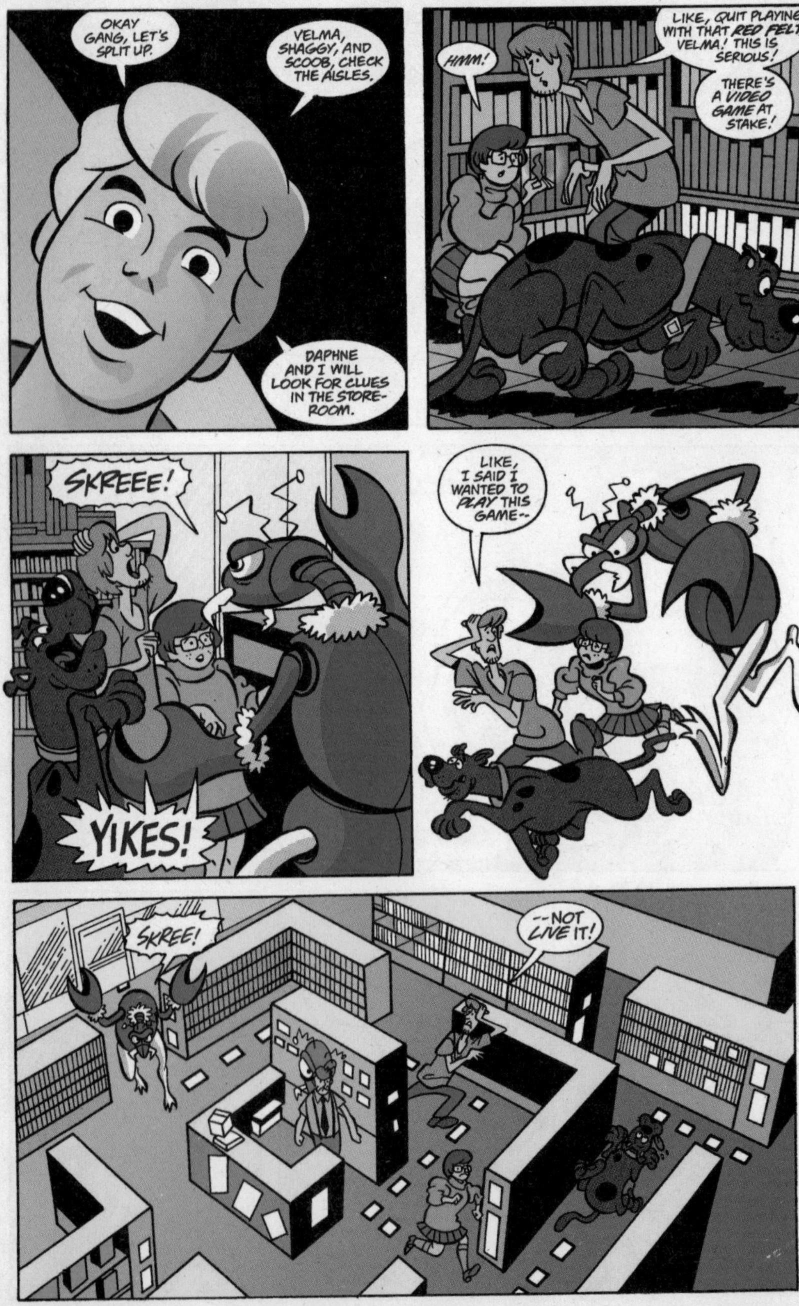
OKAY GANG, LET'S SPLIT UP.
VELMA, SHAGGY, AND SCOOB, CHECK THE AISLES.
DAPHNE AND I WILL LOOK FOR CLUES IN THE STORE-ROOM.
HMM!
LIKE, QUIT PLAYING WITH THAT RED FELT, VELMA! THIS IS SERIOUS!
THERE'S A VIDEO GAME AT STAKE!
SKREEE!
YIKES!
LIKE, I SAID I WANTED TO PLAY THIS GAME--
SKREE!
--NOT LIVE IT!

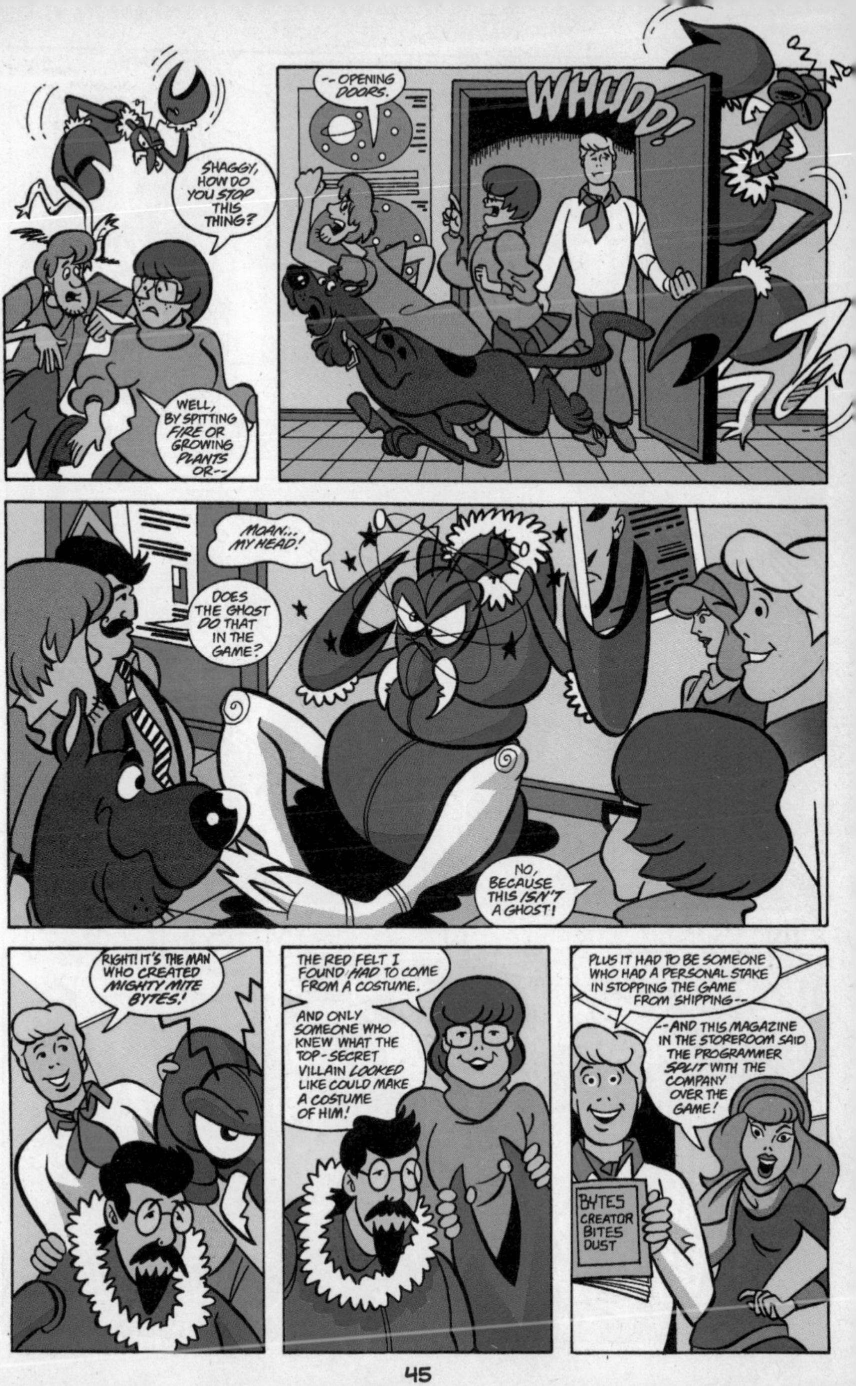
SHAGGY, HOW DO YOU *STOP* THIS THING?
WELL, BY SPITTING *FIRE* OR GROWING *PLANTS* OR--
--OPENING *DOORS*.
WHUDD!
MOAN... MY HEAD!
DOES THE GHOST *DO* THAT IN THE GAME?
NO, BECAUSE THIS *ISN'T* A GHOST!
RIGHT! IT'S THE MAN WHO CREATED *MIGHTY MITE BYTES!*
THE RED FELT I FOUND *HAD* TO COME FROM A COSTUME.
AND ONLY SOMEONE WHO KNEW WHAT THE TOP-SECRET VILLAIN *LOOKED* LIKE COULD MAKE A COSTUME OF HIM!
PLUS IT HAD TO BE SOMEONE WHO HAD A PERSONAL STAKE IN STOPPING THE GAME FROM SHIPPING--
--AND THIS MAGAZINE IN THE STOREROOM SAID THE PROGRAMMER *SPLIT* WITH THE COMPANY OVER THE GAME!
BYTES CREATOR BITES DUST

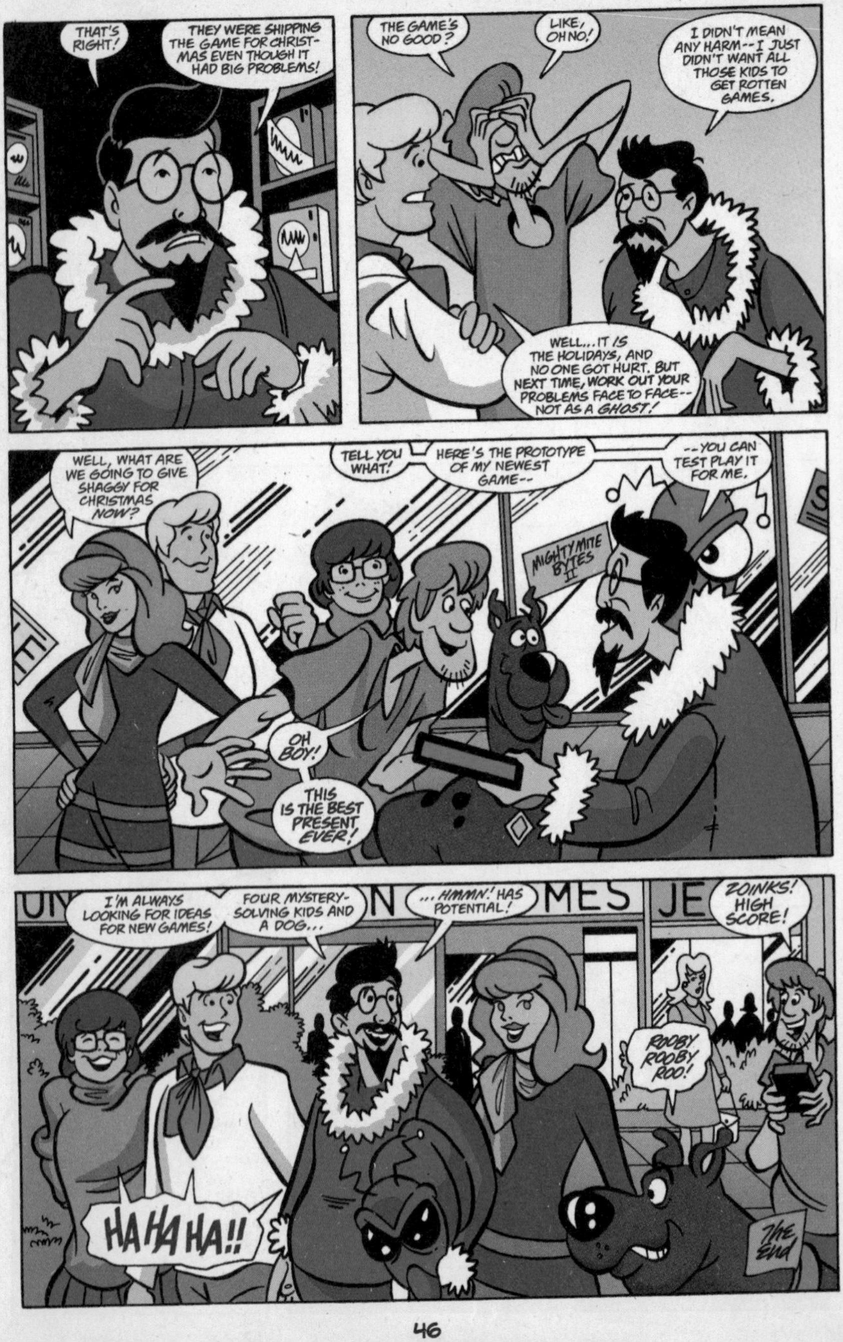
THAT'S RIGHT!
THEY WERE SHIPPING THE GAME FOR CHRISTMAS EVEN THOUGH IT HAD BIG PROBLEMS!
THE GAME'S NO GOOD?
LIKE, OH NO!
I DIDN'T MEAN ANY HARM-- I JUST DIDN'T WANT ALL THOSE KIDS TO GET ROTTEN GAMES.
WELL... IT IS THE HOLIDAYS, AND NO ONE GOT HURT. BUT NEXT TIME, WORK OUT YOUR PROBLEMS FACE TO FACE-- NOT AS A GHOST!
WELL, WHAT ARE WE GOING TO GIVE SHAGGY FOR CHRISTMAS NOW?
TELL YOU WHAT!
HERE'S THE PROTOTYPE OF MY NEWEST GAME--
--YOU CAN TEST PLAY IT FOR ME.
MIGHTY MITE BYTES II
OH BOY!
THIS IS THE BEST PRESENT EVER!
I'M ALWAYS LOOKING FOR IDEAS FOR NEW GAMES!
FOUR MYSTERY-SOLVING KIDS AND A DOG...
...HMMN! HAS POTENTIAL!
ZOINKS! HIGH SCORE!
ROOBY ROOBY ROO!
HA HA HA!!
The End

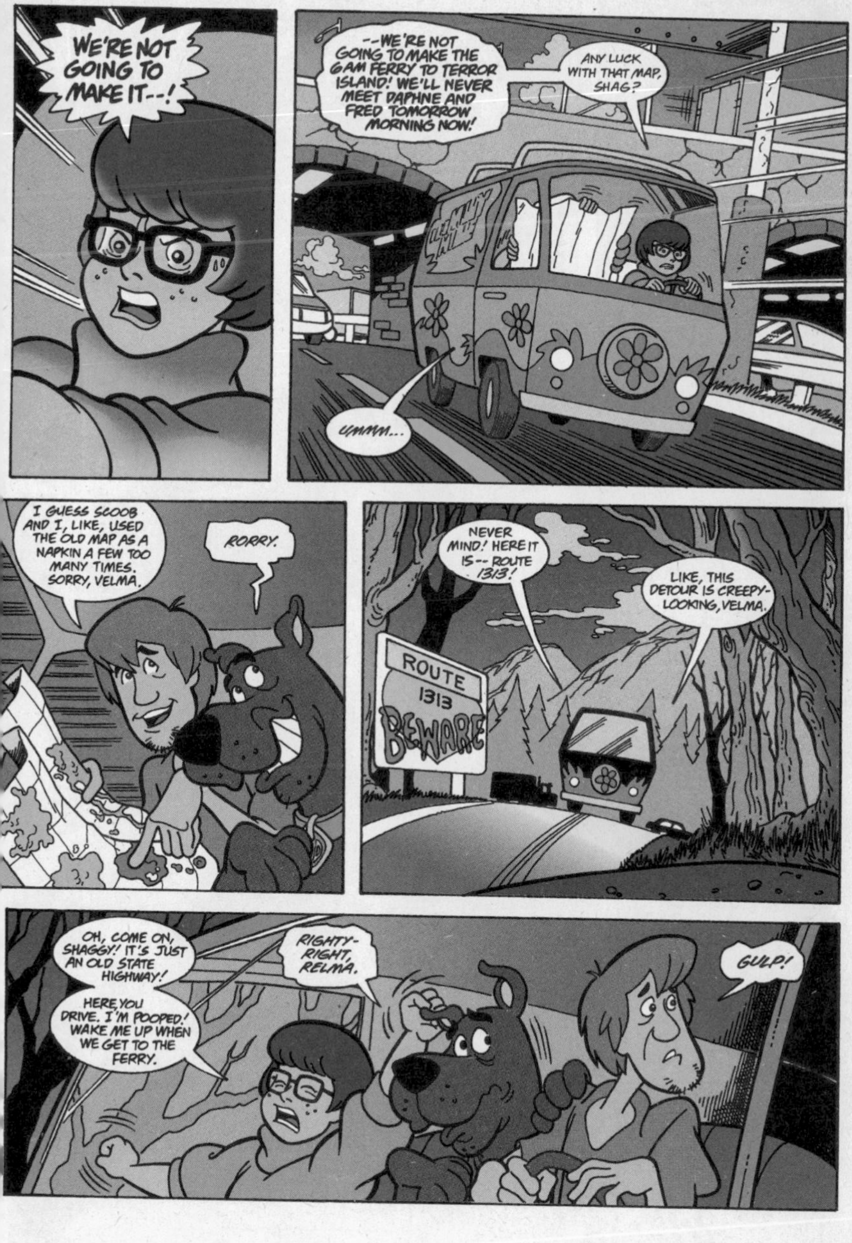
WE'RE NOT GOING TO MAKE IT--!
--WE'RE NOT GOING TO MAKE THE 6AM FERRY TO TERROR ISLAND! WE'LL NEVER MEET DAPHNE AND FRED TOMORROW MORNING NOW!
ANY LUCK WITH THAT MAP, SHAG?
UMMM...
I GUESS SCOOB AND I, LIKE, USED THE OLD MAP AS A NAPKIN A FEW TOO MANY TIMES. SORRY, VELMA.
RORRY.
NEVER MIND! HERE IT IS-- ROUTE 1313!
LIKE, THIS DETOUR IS CREEPY-LOOKING, VELMA.
ROUTE 1313
BEWARE
OH, COME ON, SHAGGY! IT'S JUST AN OLD STATE HIGHWAY!
HERE, YOU DRIVE. I'M POOPED! WAKE ME UP WHEN WE GET TO THE FERRY.
RIGHTY-RIGHT, RELMA.
GULP!

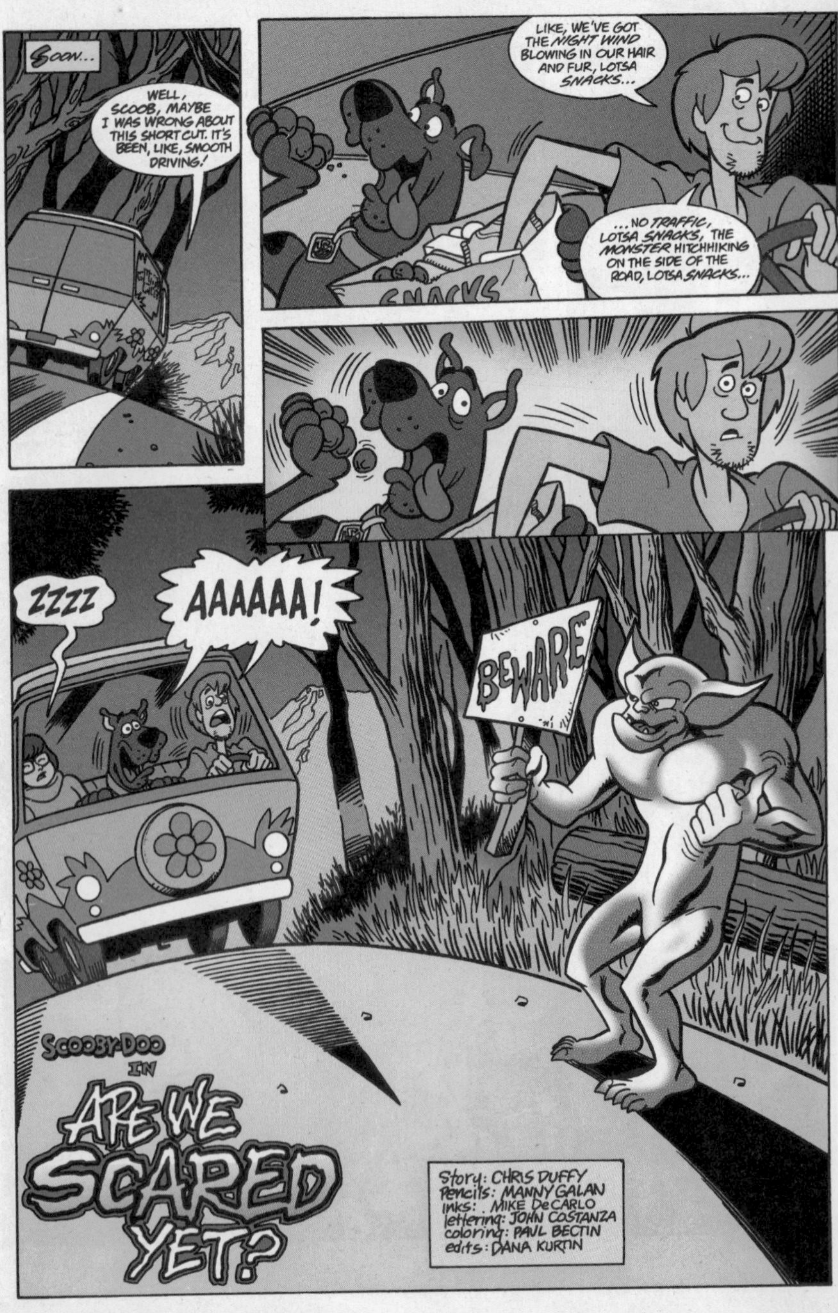
SOON...
WELL, SCOOB, MAYBE I WAS WRONG ABOUT THIS SHORT CUT. IT'S BEEN, LIKE, SMOOTH DRIVING!
LIKE, WE'VE GOT THE NIGHT WIND BLOWING IN OUR HAIR AND FUR, LOTSA SNACKS...
...NO TRAFFIC, LOTSA SNACKS, THE MONSTER HITCHHIKING ON THE SIDE OF THE ROAD, LOTSA SNACKS...
SNACKS
ZZZZ
AAAAAA!
BEWARE
SCOOBY-DOO IN
ARE WE SCARED YET?
Story: CHRIS DUFFY
Pencils: MANNY GALAN
Inks: MIKE DeCARLO
lettering: JOHN COSTANZA
coloring: PAUL BECTIN
edits: DANA KURTIN

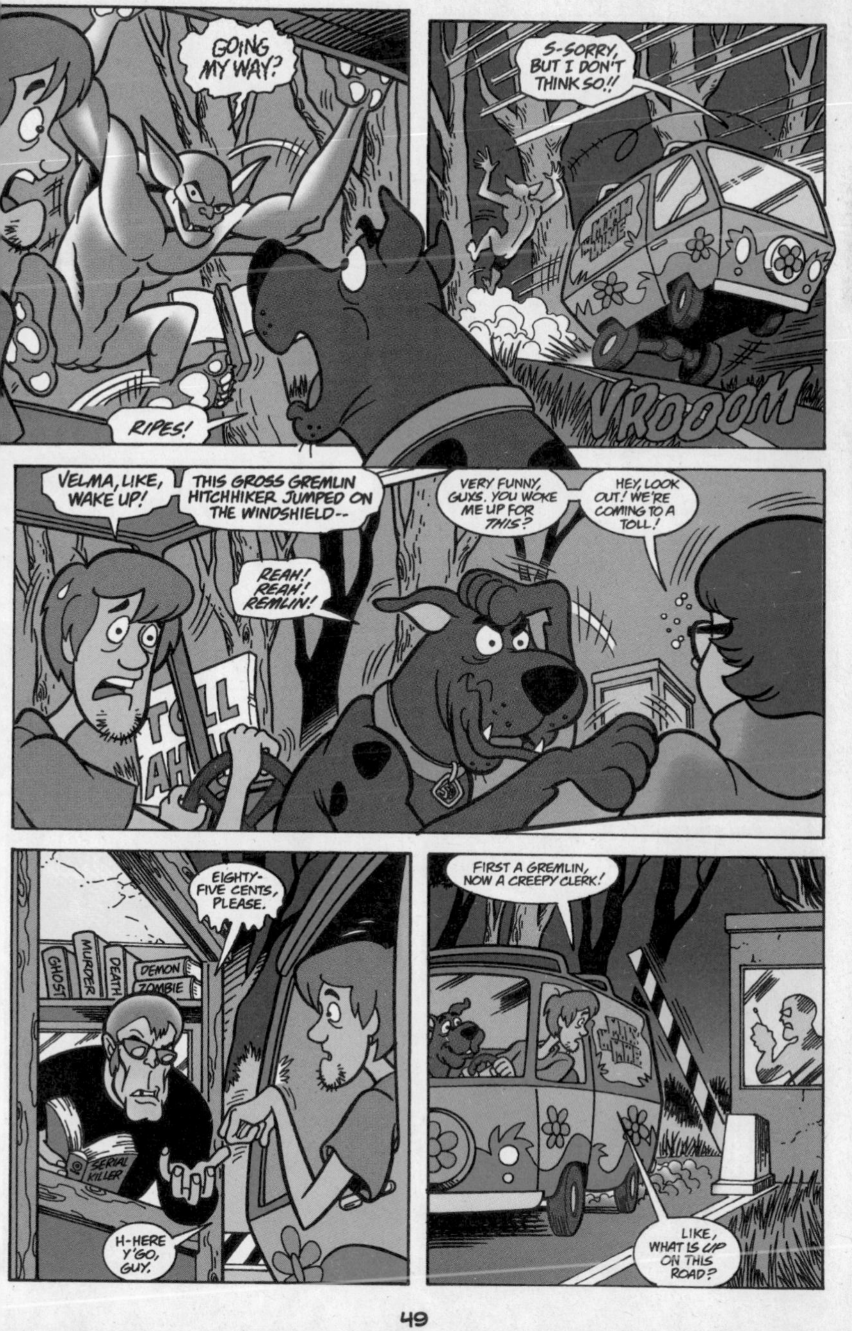
GOING MY WAY?
RIPES!
S-SORRY, BUT I DON'T THINK SO!!
VROOOM
VELMA, LIKE, WAKE UP!
THIS GROSS GREMLIN HITCHHIKER JUMPED ON THE WINDSHIELD--
REAH! REAH! REMLIN!
VERY FUNNY, GUYS. YOU WOKE ME UP FOR THIS?
HEY, LOOK OUT! WE'RE COMING TO A TOLL!
GHOST
MURDER
DEATH
DEMON
ZOMBIE
EIGHTY-FIVE CENTS, PLEASE.
SERIAL KILLER
H-HERE Y'GO, GUY.
FIRST A GREMLIN, NOW A CREEPY CLERK!
LIKE, WHAT IS UP ON THIS ROAD?

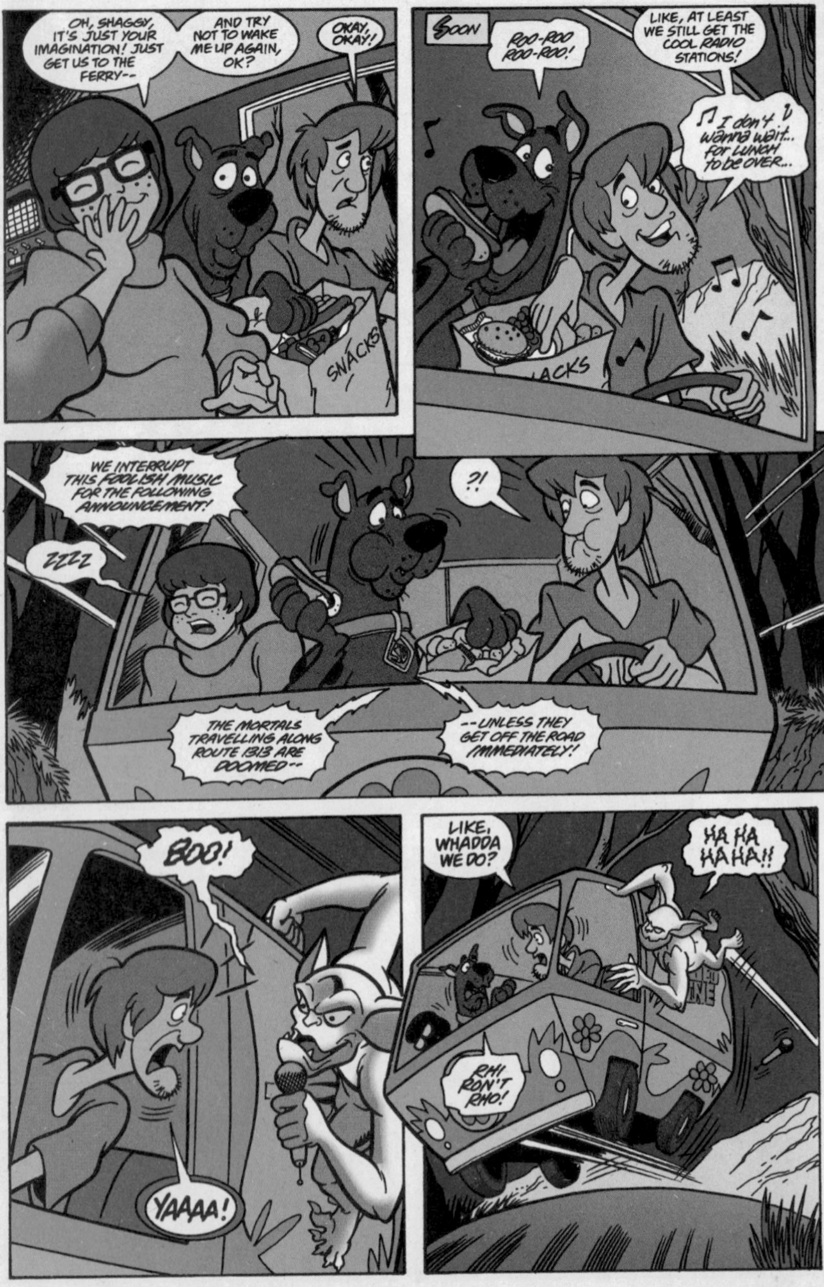
OH, SHAGGY, IT'S JUST YOUR IMAGINATION! JUST GET US TO THE FERRY--
AND TRY NOT TO WAKE ME UP AGAIN, OK?
OKAY, OKAY!
SNACKS
SOON
ROO-ROO ROO-ROO!
LIKE, AT LEAST WE STILL GET THE COOL RADIO STATIONS!
I don't wanna wait... for LUNCH to be OVER...
WE INTERRUPT THIS FOOLISH MUSIC FOR THE FOLLOWING ANNOUNCEMENT!
?!
ZZZZ
THE MORTALS TRAVELLING ALONG ROUTE 1313 ARE DOOMED--
--UNLESS THEY GET OFF THE ROAD IMMEDIATELY!
BOO!
YAAAA!
LIKE, WHADDA WE DO?
HA HA HA HA!!
RH! RON'T RHO!

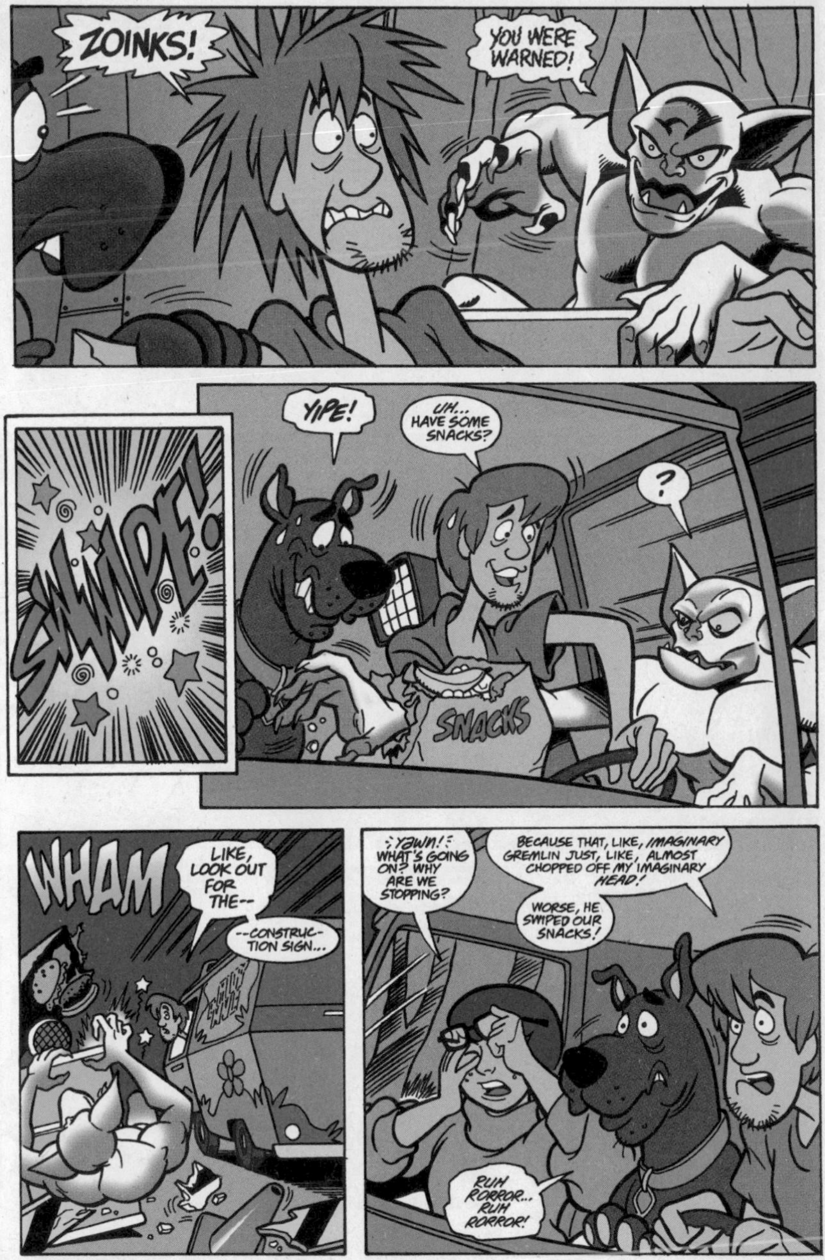
ZOINKS!
YOU WERE WARNED!
SWIPE!
YIPE!
UH... HAVE SOME SNACKS?
?
SNACKS
WHAM
LIKE, LOOK OUT FOR THE--
--CONSTRUCTION SIGN...
:YAWN!: WHAT'S GOING ON? WHY ARE WE STOPPING?
BECAUSE THAT, LIKE, IMAGINARY GREMLIN JUST, LIKE, ALMOST CHOPPED OFF MY IMAGINARY HEAD!
WORSE, HE SWIPED OUR SNACKS!
RUH RORROR... RUH RORROR!

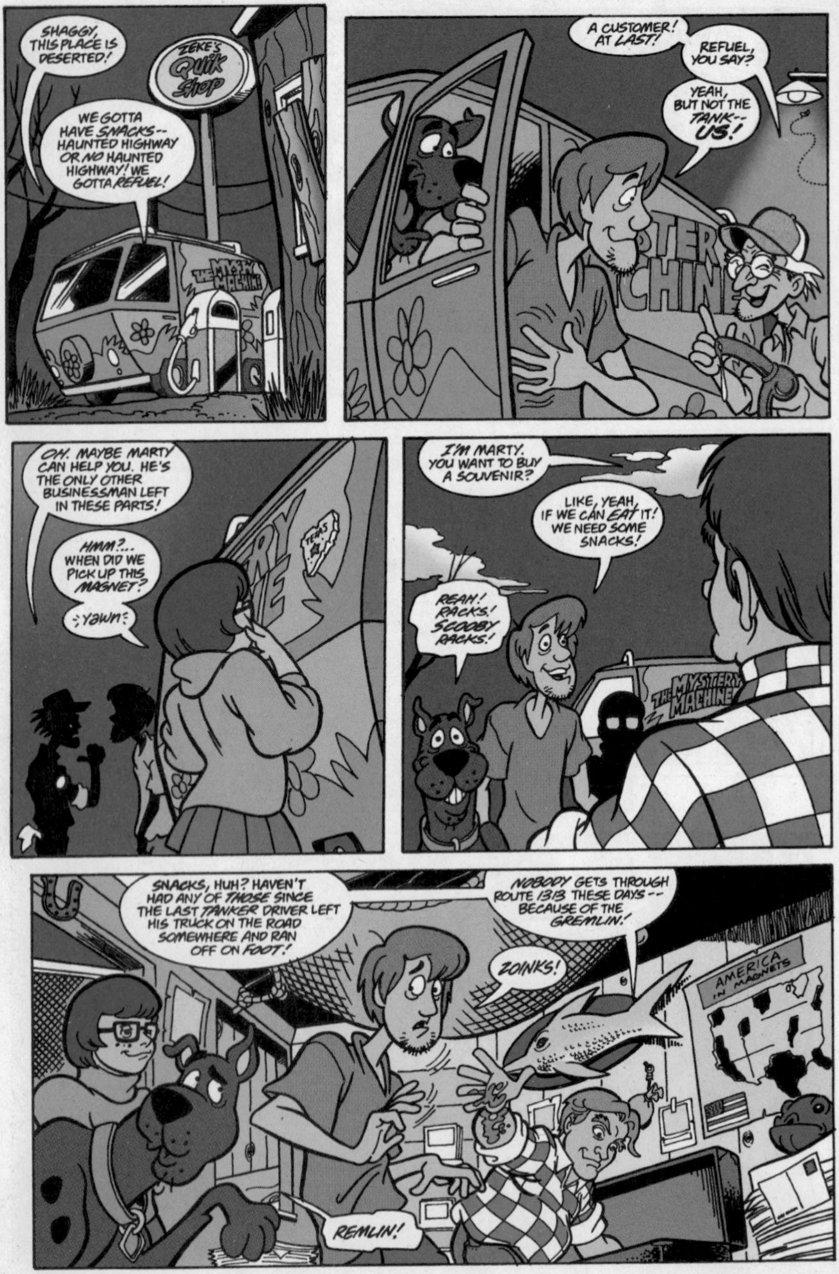
SHAGGY, THIS PLACE IS DESERTED!
ZEKE'S Quik Shop
WE GOTTA HAVE SNACKS-- HAUNTED HIGHWAY OR NO HAUNTED HIGHWAY! WE GOTTA REFUEL!
A CUSTOMER! AT LAST!
REFUEL, YOU SAY?
YEAH, BUT NOT THE TANK-- US!
OH. MAYBE MARTY CAN HELP YOU. HE'S THE ONLY OTHER BUSINESSMAN LEFT IN THESE PARTS!
HMM?... WHEN DID WE PICK UP THIS MAGNET?
yawn
I'M MARTY. YOU WANT TO BUY A SOUVENIR?
LIKE, YEAH, IF WE CAN EAT IT! WE NEED SOME SNACKS!
REAH! RACKS! SCOOBY RACKS!
THE MYSTERY MACHINE
SNACKS, HUH? HAVEN'T HAD ANY OF THOSE SINCE THE LAST TANKER DRIVER LEFT HIS TRUCK ON THE ROAD SOMEWHERE AND RAN OFF ON FOOT!
NOBODY GETS THROUGH ROUTE 1313 THESE DAYS-- BECAUSE OF THE GREMLIN!
ZOINKS!
AMERICA IN MAGNETS
REMLIN!

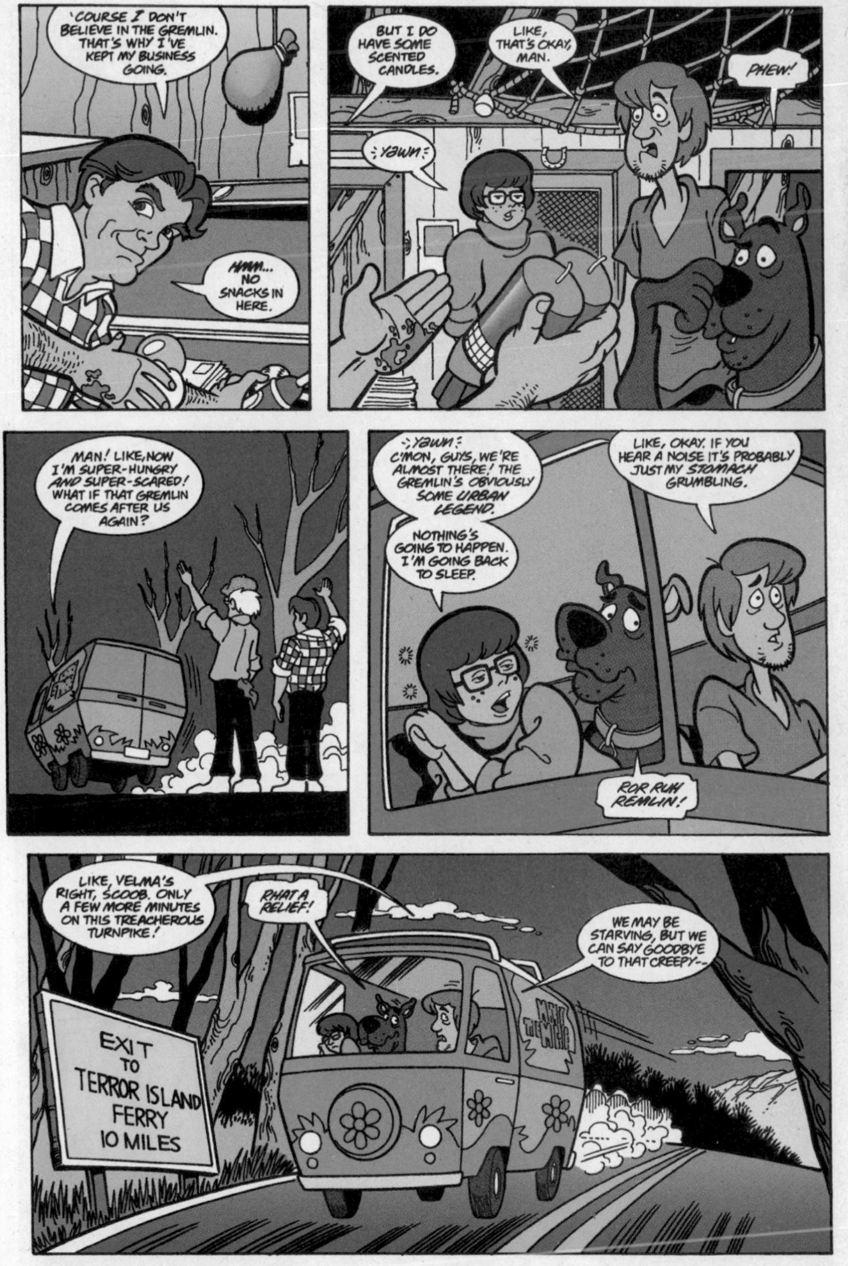
'COURSE I DON'T BELIEVE IN THE GREMLIN. THAT'S WHY I'VE KEPT MY BUSINESS GOING.
HMM... NO SNACKS IN HERE.
BUT I DO HAVE SOME SCENTED CANDLES.
LIKE, THAT'S OKAY, MAN.
PHEW!
YAWN
MAN! LIKE, NOW I'M SUPER-HUNGRY AND SUPER-SCARED! WHAT IF THAT GREMLIN COMES AFTER US AGAIN?
YAWN
C'MON, GUYS, WE'RE ALMOST THERE! THE GREMLIN'S OBVIOUSLY SOME URBAN LEGEND.
NOTHING'S GOING TO HAPPEN. I'M GOING BACK TO SLEEP.
LIKE, OKAY. IF YOU HEAR A NOISE IT'S PROBABLY JUST MY STOMACH GRUMBLING.
ROR RUH REMLIN!
LIKE, VELMA'S RIGHT, SCOOB. ONLY A FEW MORE MINUTES ON THIS TREACHEROUS TURNPIKE!
RHAT A RELIEF!
WE MAY BE STARVING, BUT WE CAN SAY GOODBYE TO THAT CREEPY--
EXIT TO TERROR ISLAND FERRY 10 MILES

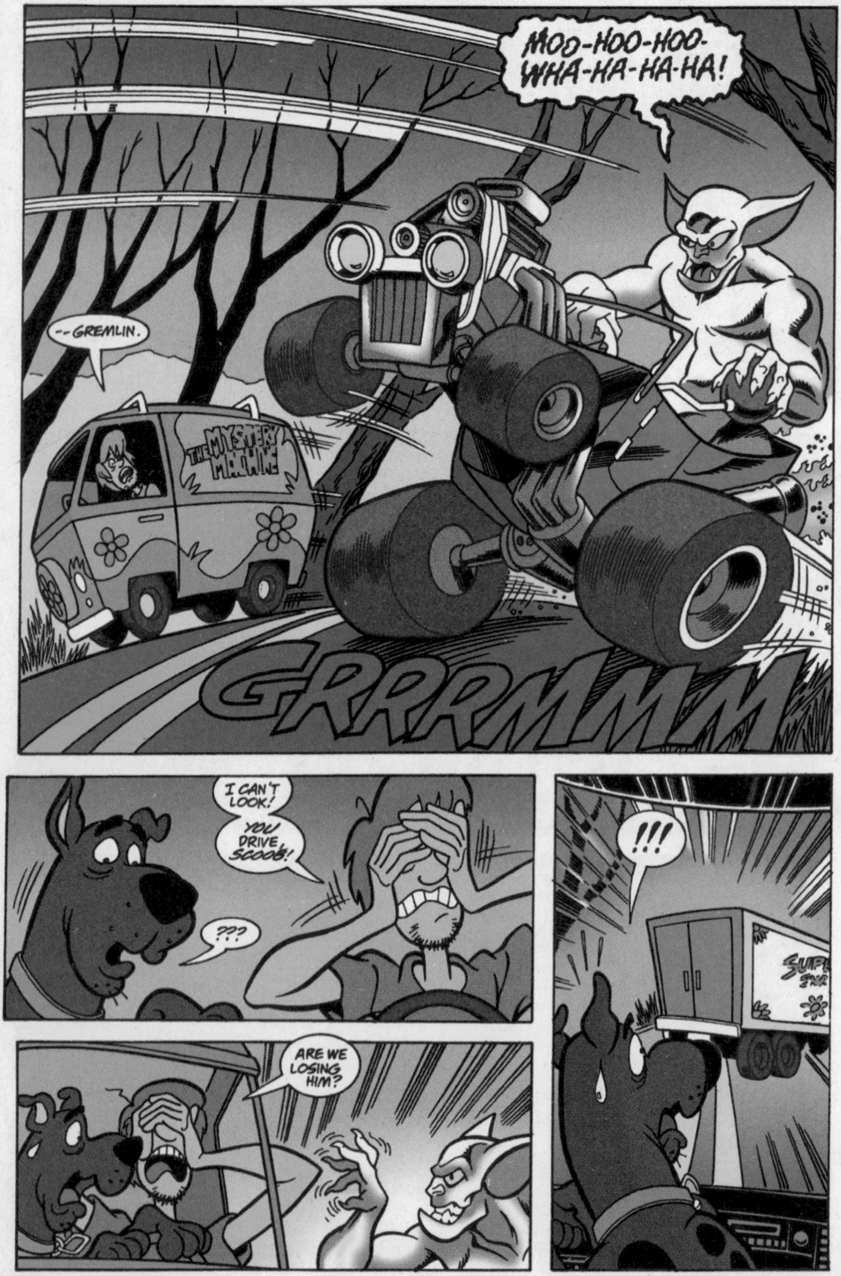
MOO-HOO-HOO-WHA-HA-HA-HA!
--GREMLIN.
THE MYSTERY MACHINE
GRRRMMMM
I CAN'T LOOK!
YOU DRIVE, SCOOB!
???
!!!
ARE WE LOSING HIM?

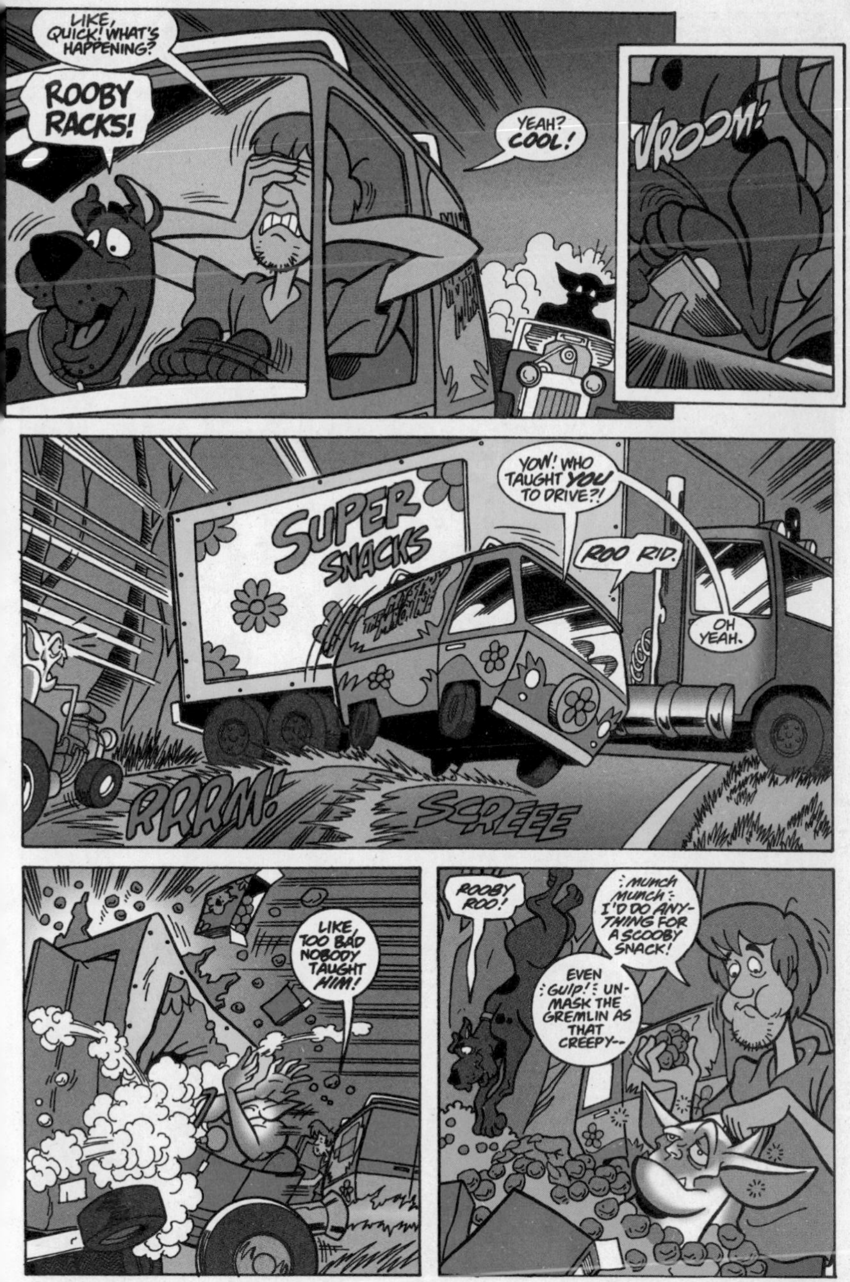
LIKE, QUICK! WHAT'S HAPPENING?
ROOBY RACKS!
YEAH? COOL!
VROOM!
YOW! WHO TAUGHT YOU TO DRIVE?!
ROO RID.
OH YEAH.
SUPER SNACKS
RRRM!
SCREEE
LIKE, TOO BAD NOBODY TAUGHT HIM!
ROOBY ROO!
munch munch I'D DO ANYTHING FOR A SCOOBY SNACK!
EVEN Gulp! UNMASK THE GREMLIN AS THAT CREEPY--

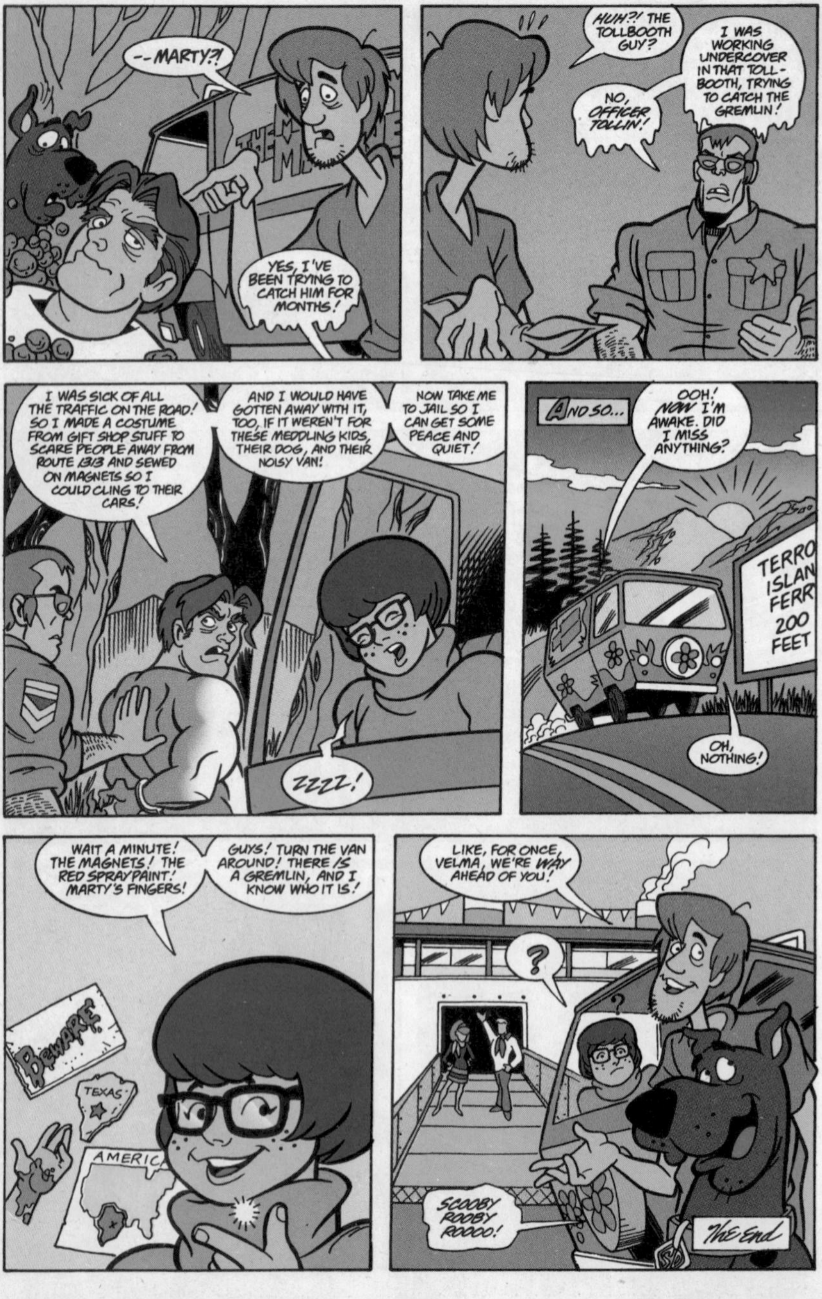

-- MARTY?!
YES, I'VE BEEN TRYING TO CATCH HIM FOR MONTHS!
HUH?! THE TOLLBOOTH GUY?
NO, OFFICER TOLLIN!
I WAS WORKING UNDERCOVER IN THAT TOLL-BOOTH, TRYING TO CATCH THE GREMLIN!
I WAS SICK OF ALL THE TRAFFIC ON THE ROAD! SO I MADE A COSTUME FROM GIFT SHOP STUFF TO SCARE PEOPLE AWAY FROM ROUTE 1313 AND SEWED ON MAGNETS SO I COULD CLING TO THEIR CARS!
AND I WOULD HAVE GOTTEN AWAY WITH IT, TOO, IF IT WEREN'T FOR THESE MEDDLING KIDS, THEIR DOG, AND THEIR NOISY VAN!
NOW TAKE ME TO JAIL SO I CAN GET SOME PEACE AND QUIET!
ZZZZ!
AND SO...
OOH! NOW I'M AWAKE. DID I MISS ANYTHING?
TERRO ISLAN FERR 200 FEET
OH, NOTHING!
WAIT A MINUTE! THE MAGNETS! THE RED SPRAY PAINT! MARTY'S FINGERS!
GUYS! TURN THE VAN AROUND! THERE IS A GREMLIN, AND I KNOW WHO IT IS!
BEWARE
TEXAS
AMERIC
LIKE, FOR ONCE, VELMA, WE'RE WAY AHEAD OF YOU!
?
SCOOBY ROOBY ROOOO!
The End

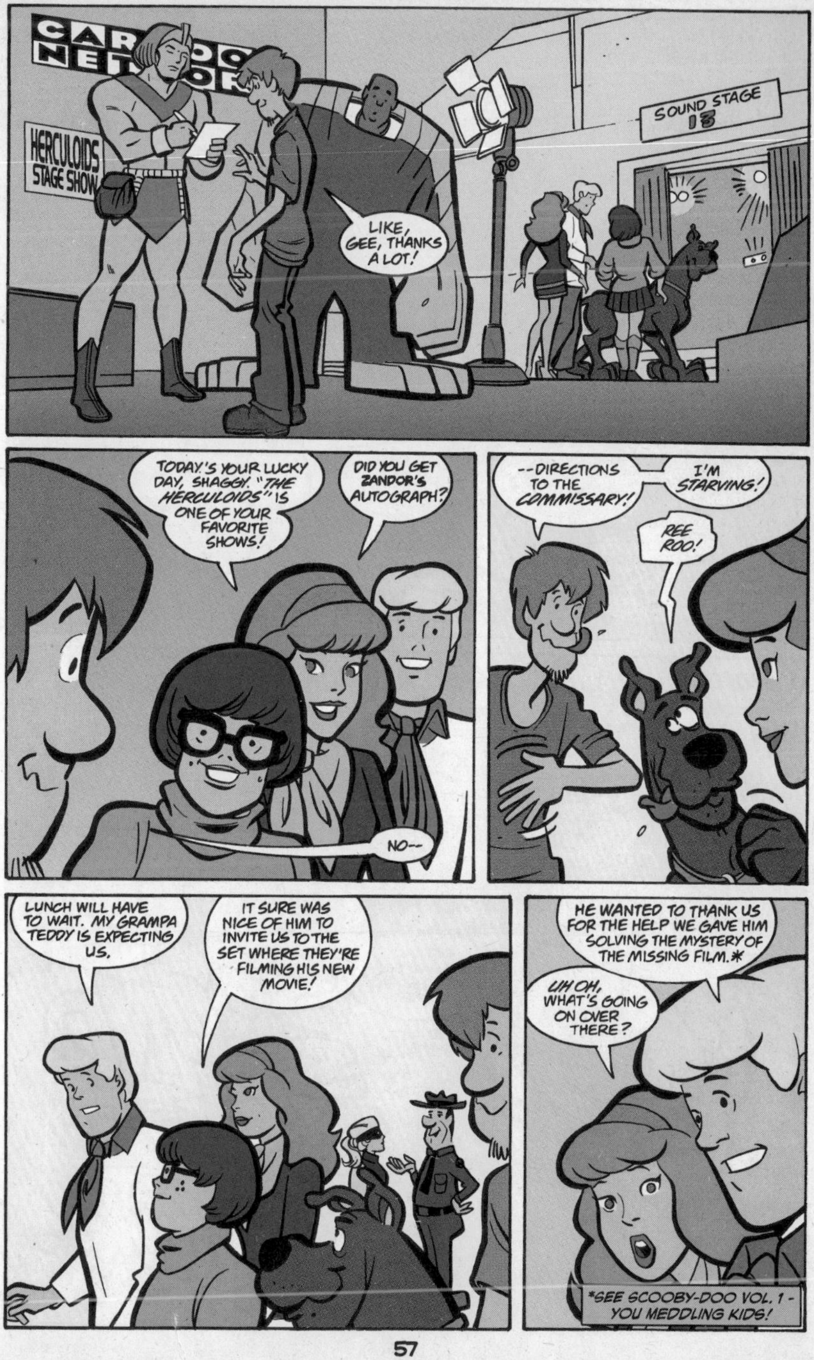
CARTOON NETWORK
HERCULOIDS STAGE SHOW
SOUND STAGE 18
LIKE, GEE, THANKS A LOT!
TODAY'S YOUR LUCKY DAY, SHAGGY. "THE HERCULOIDS" IS ONE OF YOUR FAVORITE SHOWS!
DID YOU GET ZANDOR'S AUTOGRAPH?
NO--
--DIRECTIONS TO THE COMMISSARY!
I'M STARVING!
REE ROO!
LUNCH WILL HAVE TO WAIT. MY GRAMPA TEDDY IS EXPECTING US.
IT SURE WAS NICE OF HIM TO INVITE US TO THE SET WHERE THEY'RE FILMING HIS NEW MOVIE!
HE WANTED TO THANK US FOR THE HELP WE GAVE HIM SOLVING THE MYSTERY OF THE MISSING FILM.*
UH OH, WHAT'S GOING ON OVER THERE?
*SEE SCOOBY-DOO VOL. 1 - YOU MEDDLING KIDS!

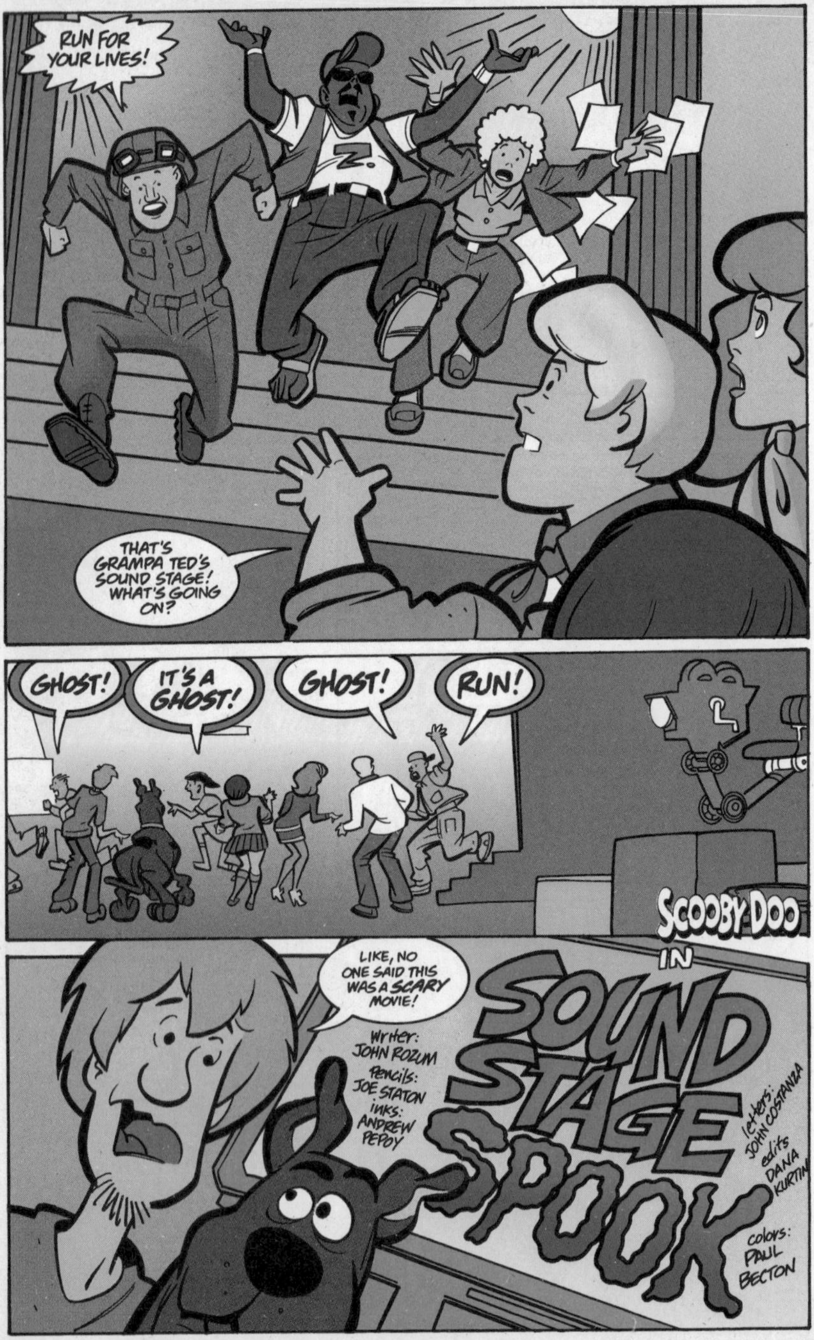
RUN FOR YOUR LIVES!
THAT'S GRAMPA TED'S SOUND STAGE! WHAT'S GOING ON?
GHOST!
IT'S A GHOST!
GHOST!
RUN!
SCOOBY-DOO IN
LIKE, NO ONE SAID THIS WAS A SCARY MOVIE!
SOUND STAGE SPOOK
Writer: JOHN ROZUM
Pencils: JOE STATON
inks: ANDREW PEPOY
letters: JOHN COSTANZA
edits DANA KURTIN
colors: PAUL BECTON

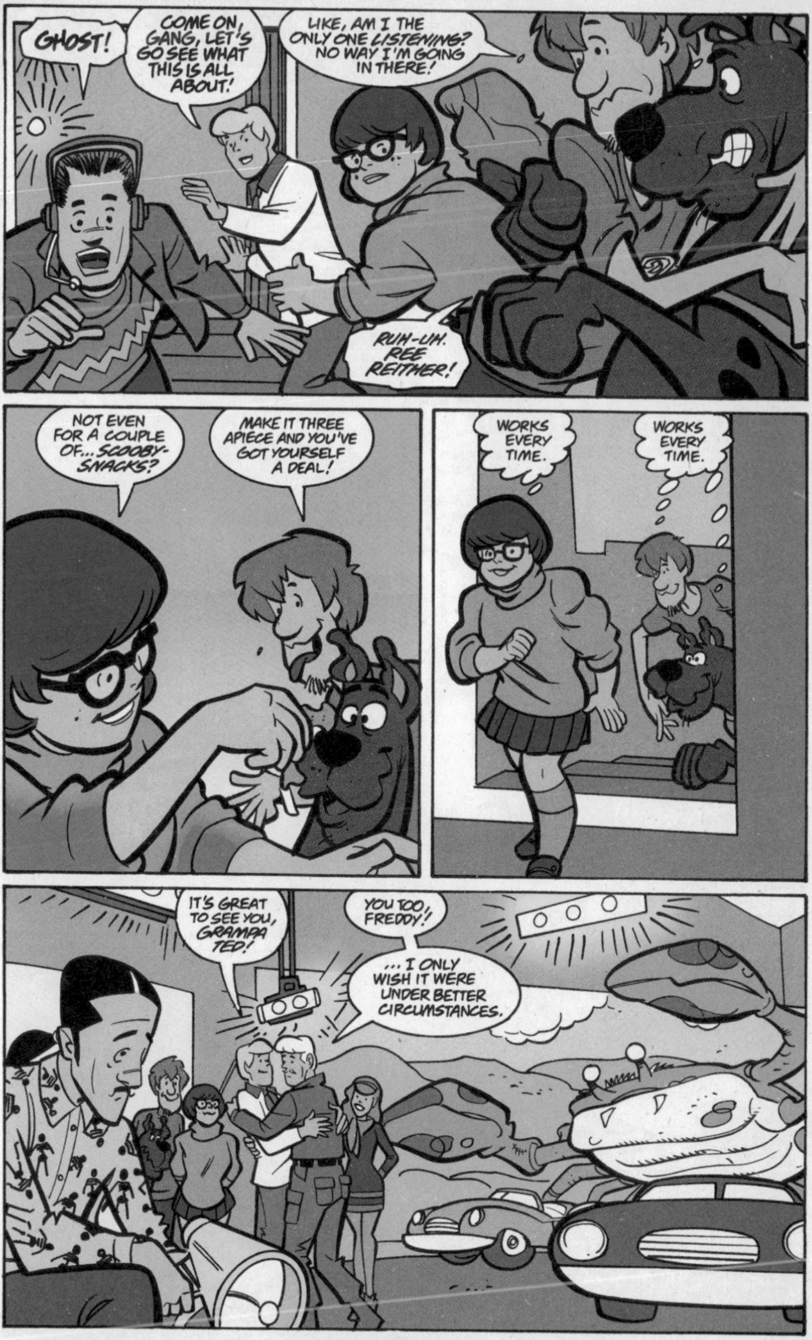
GHOST!
COME ON, GANG, LET'S GO SEE WHAT THIS IS ALL ABOUT!
LIKE, AM I THE ONLY ONE LISTENING? NO WAY I'M GOING IN THERE!
RUH-UH. REE REITHER!
NOT EVEN FOR A COUPLE OF... SCOOBY-SNACKS?
MAKE IT THREE APIECE AND YOU'VE GOT YOURSELF A DEAL!
WORKS EVERY TIME.
WORKS EVERY TIME.
IT'S GREAT TO SEE YOU, GRAMPA TED!
YOU TOO, FREDDY!
... I ONLY WISH IT WERE UNDER BETTER CIRCUMSTANCES.

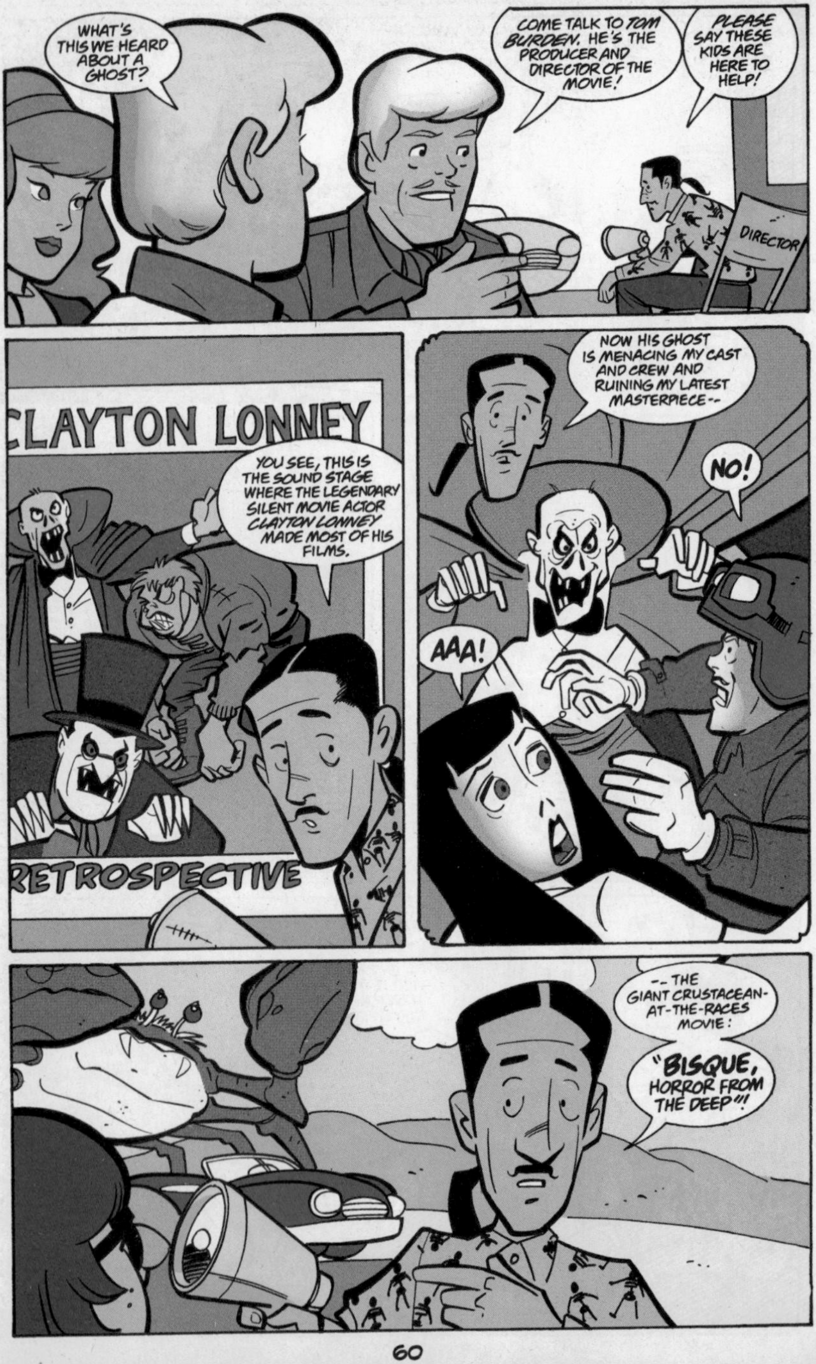
WHAT'S THIS WE HEARD ABOUT A GHOST?
COME TALK TO TOM BURDEN. HE'S THE PRODUCER AND DIRECTOR OF THE MOVIE!
PLEASE SAY THESE KIDS ARE HERE TO HELP!
DIRECTOR
CLAYTON LONNEY
RETROSPECTIVE
YOU SEE, THIS IS THE SOUND STAGE WHERE THE LEGENDARY SILENT MOVIE ACTOR CLAYTON LONNEY MADE MOST OF HIS FILMS.
NOW HIS GHOST IS MENACING MY CAST AND CREW AND RUINING MY LATEST MASTERPIECE--
NO!
AAA!
--THE GIANT CRUSTACEAN-AT-THE-RACES MOVIE:
"BISQUE, HORROR FROM THE DEEP"!!
-..

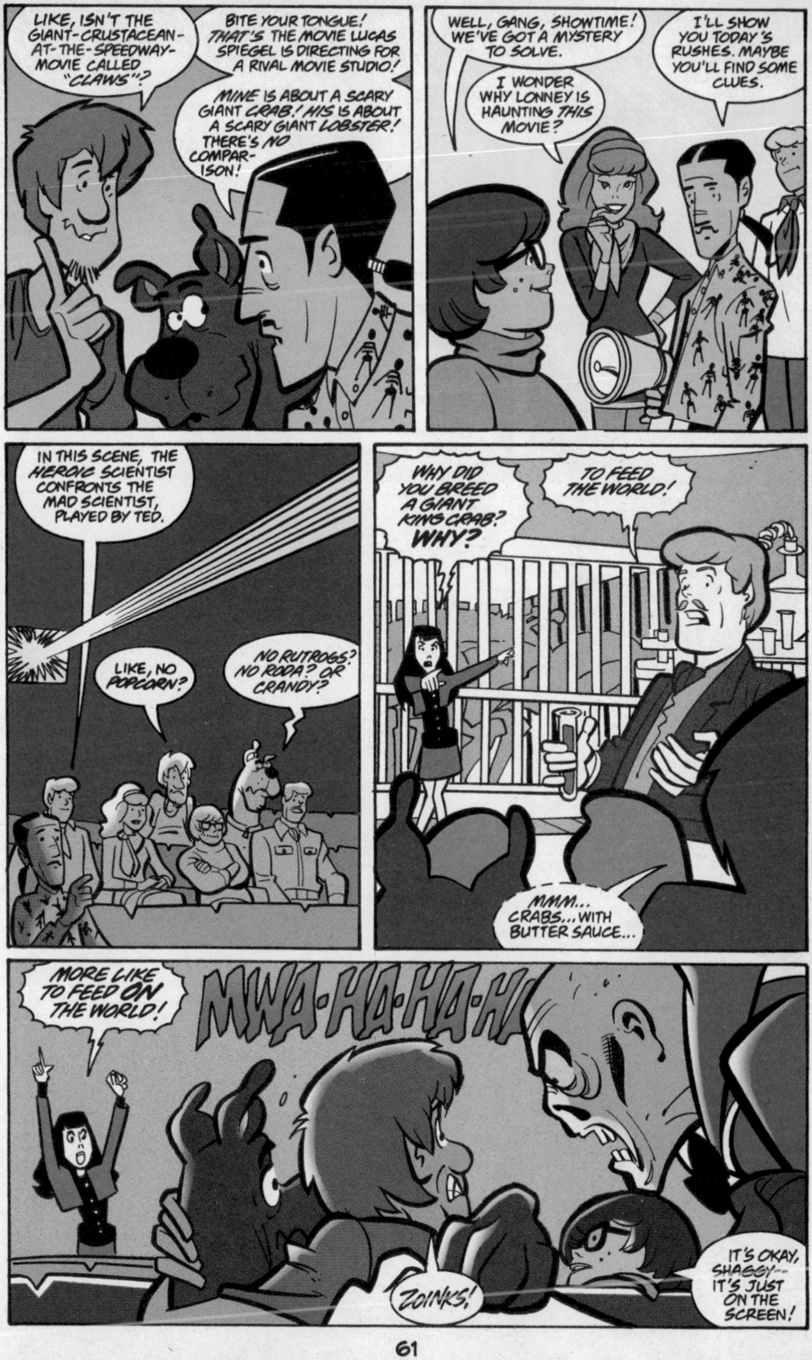
LIKE, ISN'T THE GIANT-CRUSTACEAN-AT-THE-SPEEDWAY-MOVIE CALLED "CLAWS"?
BITE YOUR TONGUE! THAT'S THE MOVIE LUCAS SPIEGEL IS DIRECTING FOR A RIVAL MOVIE STUDIO!
MINE IS ABOUT A SCARY GIANT CRAB! HIS IS ABOUT A SCARY GIANT LOBSTER! THERE'S NO COMPARISON!
WELL, GANG, SHOWTIME! WE'VE GOT A MYSTERY TO SOLVE.
I WONDER WHY LONNEY IS HAUNTING THIS MOVIE?
I'LL SHOW YOU TODAY'S RUSHES. MAYBE YOU'LL FIND SOME CLUES.
IN THIS SCENE, THE HEROIC SCIENTIST CONFRONTS THE MAD SCIENTIST, PLAYED BY TED.
LIKE, NO POPCORN?
NO RUTROGS? NO RODA? OR CRANDY?
WHY DID YOU BREED A GIANT KING CRAB? WHY?
TO FEED THE WORLD!
MMM... CRABS... WITH BUTTER SAUCE...
MORE LIKE TO FEED ON THE WORLD!
MWA-HA-HA-HA-H
ZOINKS!
IT'S OKAY, SHAGGY-- IT'S JUST ON THE SCREEN!

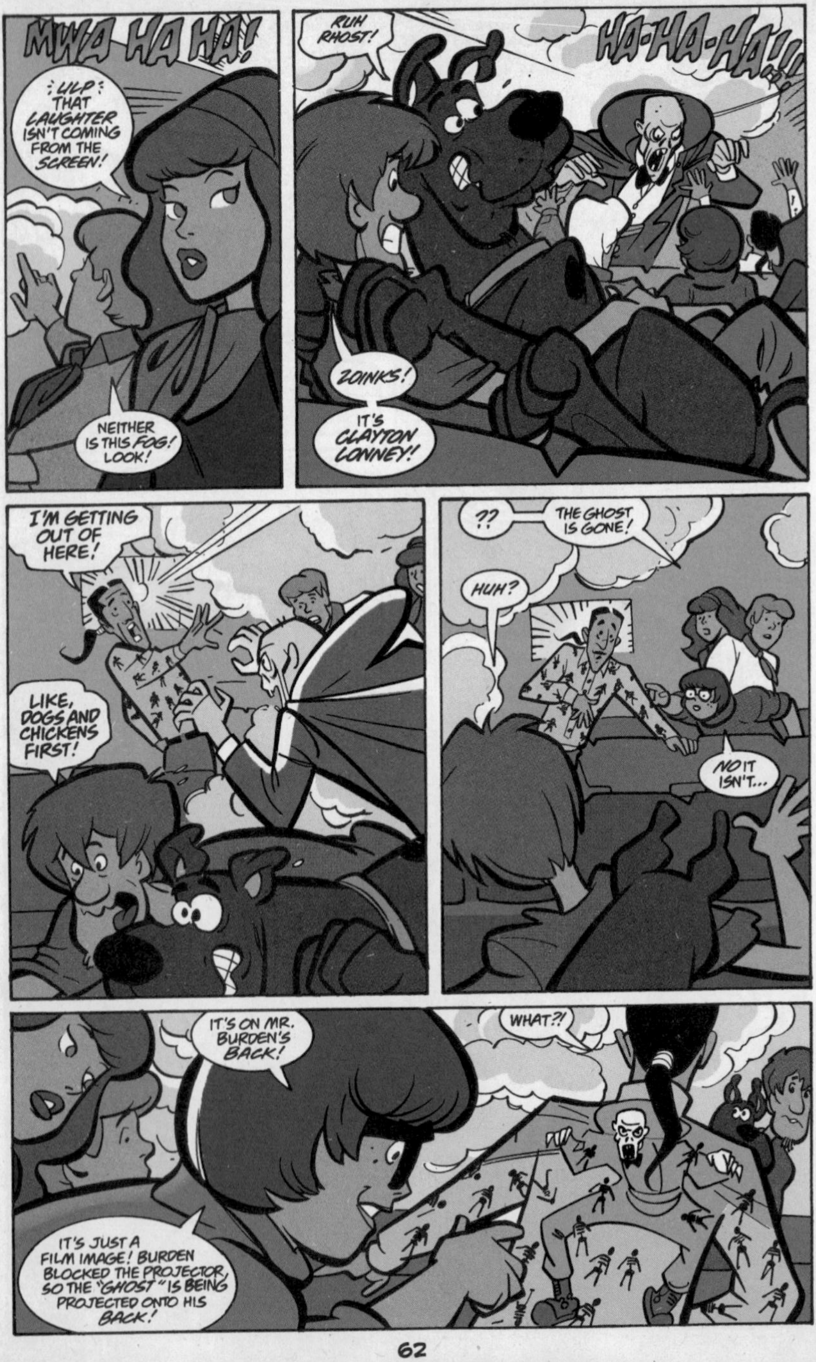
MWA HA HA!
ULP THAT LAUGHTER ISN'T COMING FROM THE SCREEN!
NEITHER IS THIS FOG! LOOK!
RUH RHOST!
HA-HA-HA!!!
ZOINKS!
IT'S CLAYTON LONNEY!
I'M GETTING OUT OF HERE!
LIKE, DOGS AND CHICKENS FIRST!
??
THE GHOST IS GONE!
HUH?
NO IT ISN'T...
IT'S ON MR. BURDEN'S BACK!
WHAT?!
IT'S JUST A FILM IMAGE! BURDEN BLOCKED THE PROJECTOR, SO THE "GHOST" IS BEING PROJECTED ONTO HIS BACK!

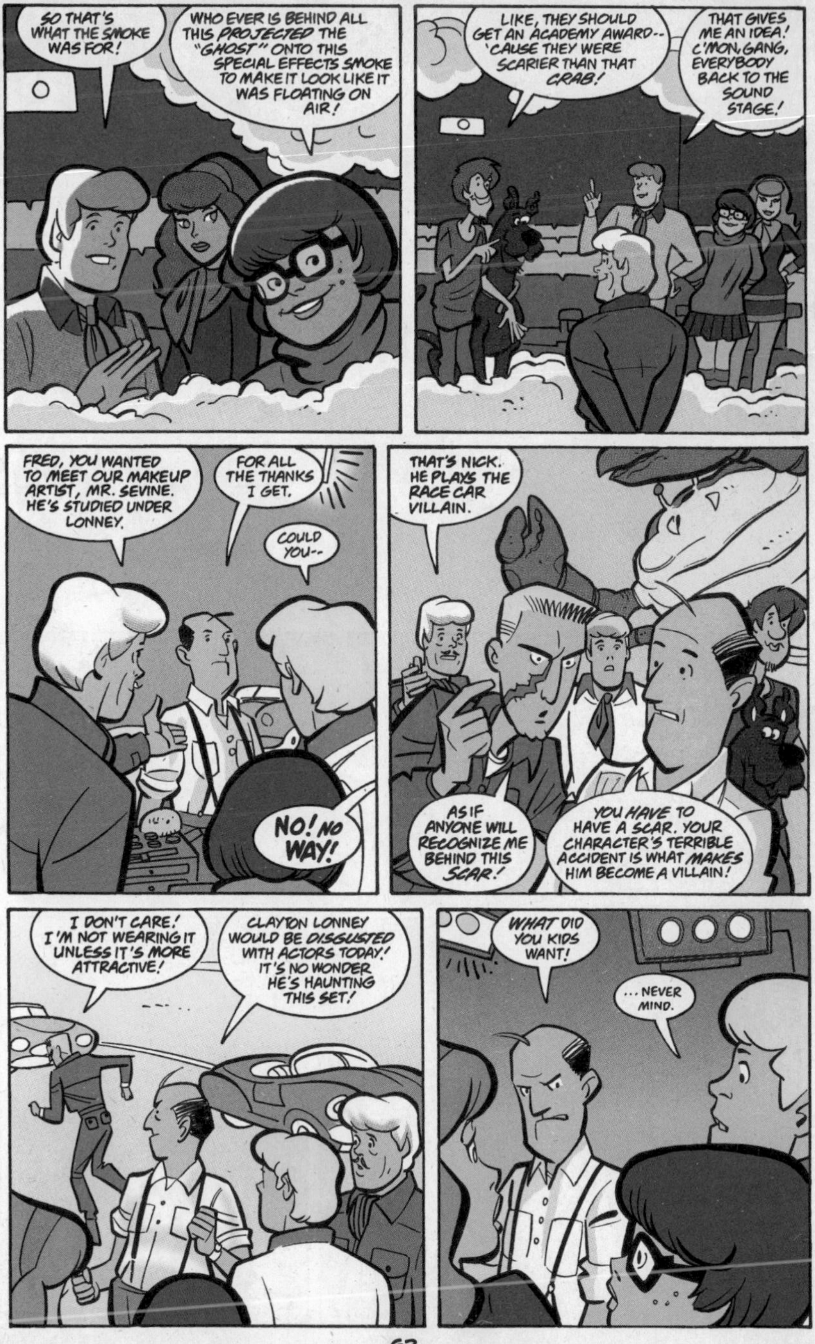
SO THAT'S WHAT THE SMOKE WAS FOR!
WHO EVER IS BEHIND ALL THIS PROJECTED THE "GHOST" ONTO THIS SPECIAL EFFECTS SMOKE TO MAKE IT LOOK LIKE IT WAS FLOATING ON AIR!
LIKE, THEY SHOULD GET AN ACADEMY AWARD-- 'CAUSE THEY WERE SCARIER THAN THAT CRAB!
THAT GIVES ME AN IDEA! C'MON, GANG, EVERYBODY BACK TO THE SOUND STAGE!
FRED, YOU WANTED TO MEET OUR MAKEUP ARTIST, MR. SEVINE. HE'S STUDIED UNDER LONNEY.
FOR ALL THE THANKS I GET.
COULD YOU--
NO! NO WAY!
THAT'S NICK. HE PLAYS THE RACE CAR VILLAIN.
AS IF ANYONE WILL RECOGNIZE ME BEHIND THIS SCAR!
YOU HAVE TO HAVE A SCAR. YOUR CHARACTER'S TERRIBLE ACCIDENT IS WHAT MAKES HIM BECOME A VILLAIN!
I DON'T CARE! I'M NOT WEARING IT UNLESS IT'S MORE ATTRACTIVE!
CLAYTON LONNEY WOULD BE DISGUSTED WITH ACTORS TODAY! IT'S NO WONDER HE'S HAUNTING THIS SET!
WHAT DID YOU KIDS WANT!
...NEVER MIND.

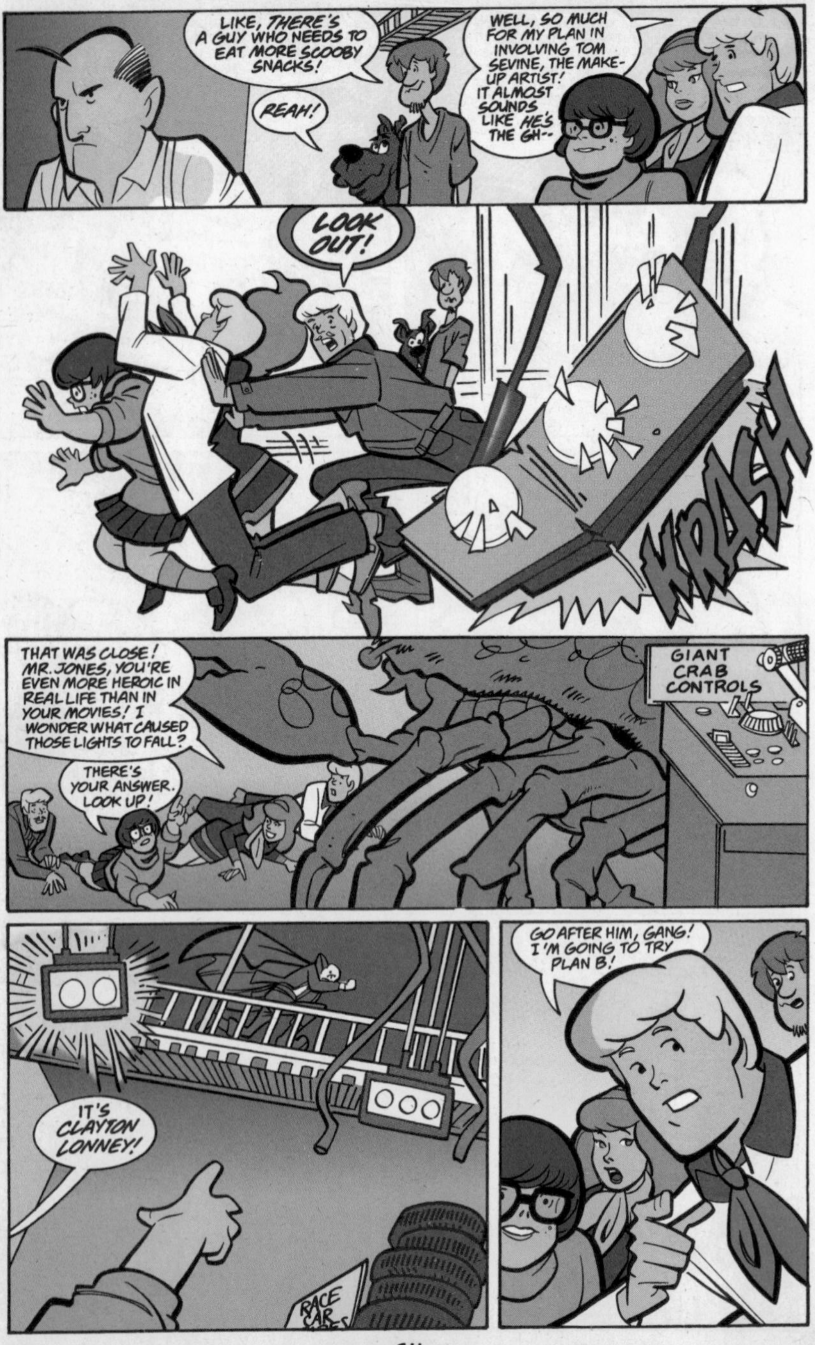
LIKE, THERE'S A GUY WHO NEEDS TO EAT MORE SCOOBY SNACKS!
REAH!
WELL, SO MUCH FOR MY PLAN IN INVOLVING TOM SEVINE, THE MAKE-UP ARTIST! IT ALMOST SOUNDS LIKE HE'S THE GH--
LOOK OUT!
KRASH
THAT WAS CLOSE! MR. JONES, YOU'RE EVEN MORE HEROIC IN REAL LIFE THAN IN YOUR MOVIES! I WONDER WHAT CAUSED THOSE LIGHTS TO FALL?
GIANT CRAB CONTROLS
THERE'S YOUR ANSWER. LOOK UP!
IT'S CLAYTON LONNEY!
RACE CAR
GO AFTER HIM, GANG! I'M GOING TO TRY PLAN B!

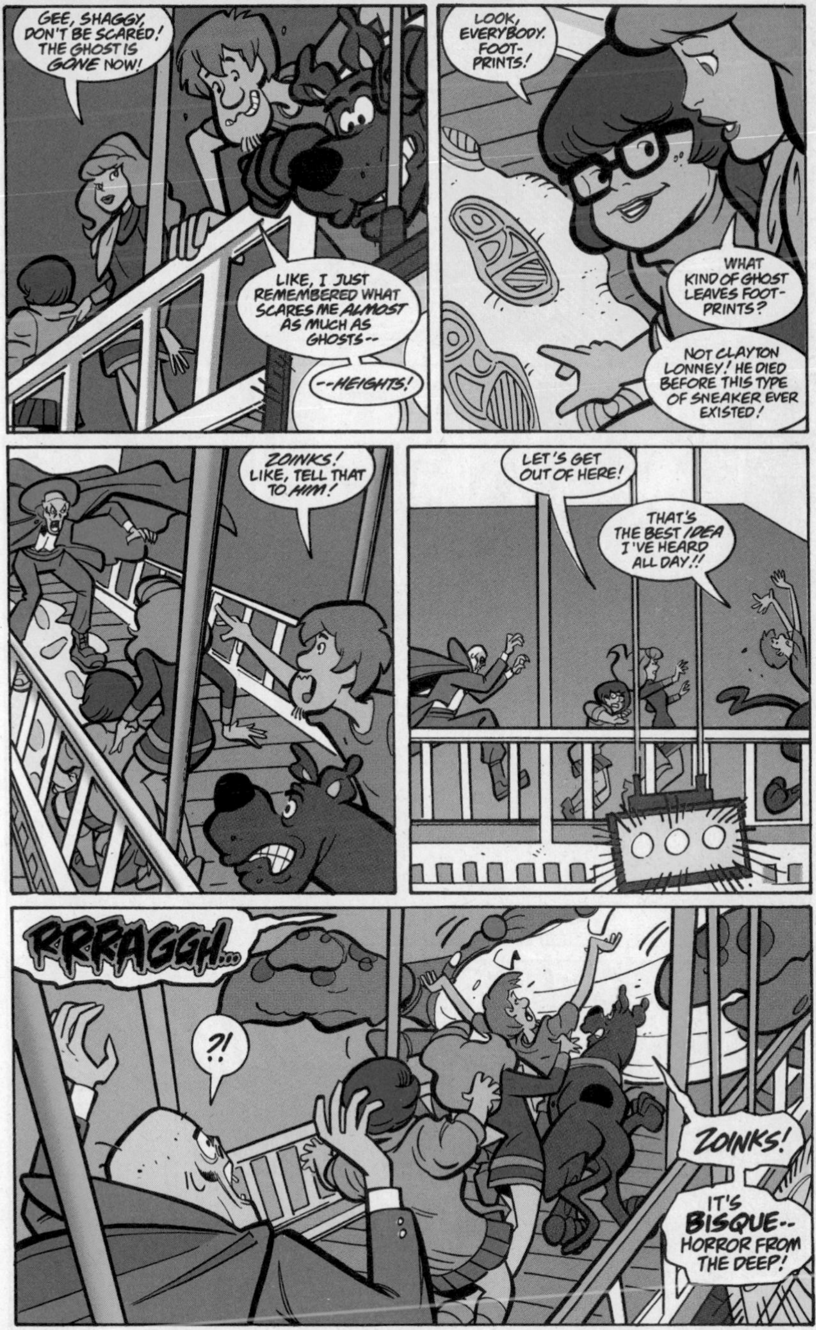
GEE, SHAGGY, DON'T BE SCARED! THE GHOST IS GONE NOW!
LIKE, I JUST REMEMBERED WHAT SCARES ME ALMOST AS MUCH AS GHOSTS--
--HEIGHTS!
LOOK, EVERYBODY. FOOT-PRINTS!
WHAT KIND OF GHOST LEAVES FOOT-PRINTS?
NOT CLAYTON LONNEY! HE DIED BEFORE THIS TYPE OF SNEAKER EVER EXISTED!
ZOINKS! LIKE, TELL THAT TO HIM!
LET'S GET OUT OF HERE!
THAT'S THE BEST IDEA I'VE HEARD ALL DAY!!
RRRAGGH...
?!
ZOINKS!
IT'S BISQUE-- HORROR FROM THE DEEP!

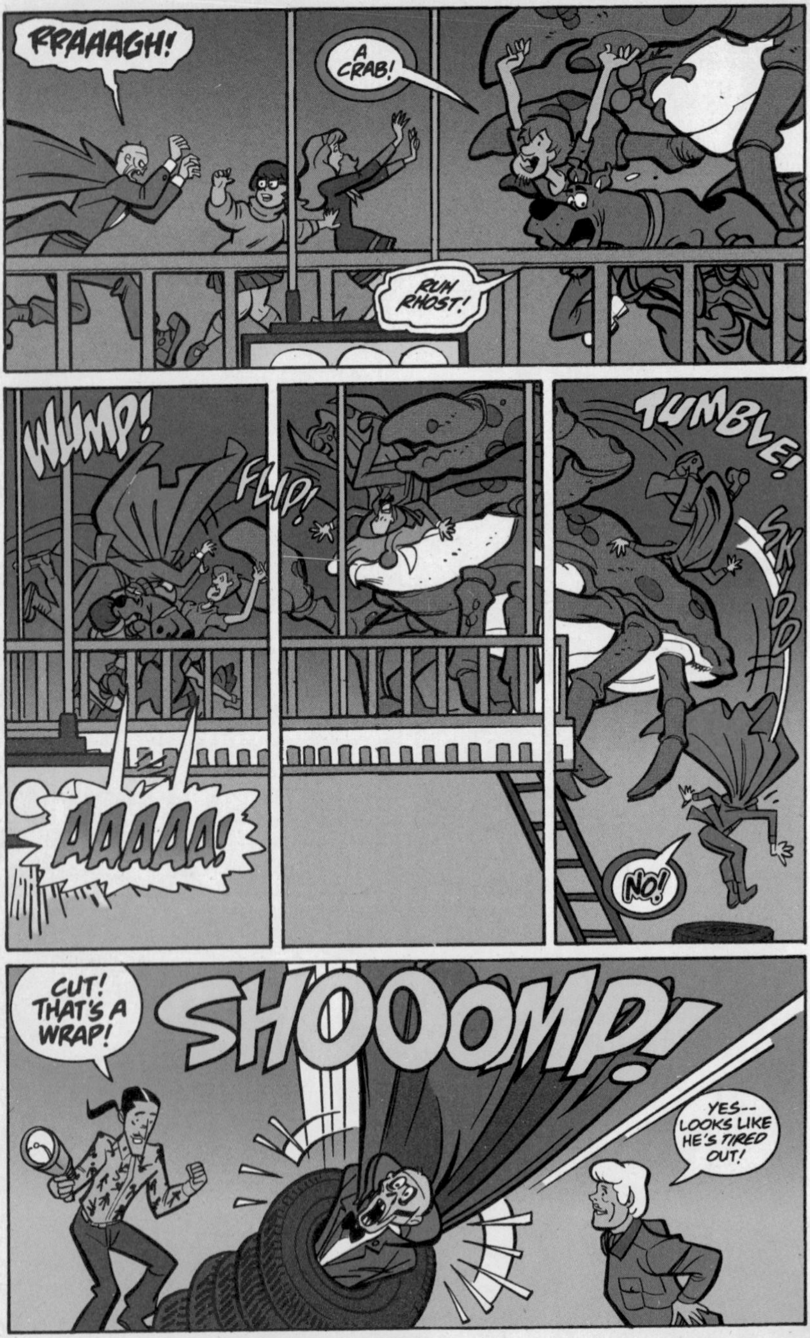
FRAAAGH!
A CRAB!
RUN RHOST!
WUMP!
FLIP!
TUMBLE!
SKIDOO
AAAAA!
NO!
CUT! THAT'S A WRAP!
SHOOOMP!
YES-- LOOKS LIKE HE'S TIRED OUT!

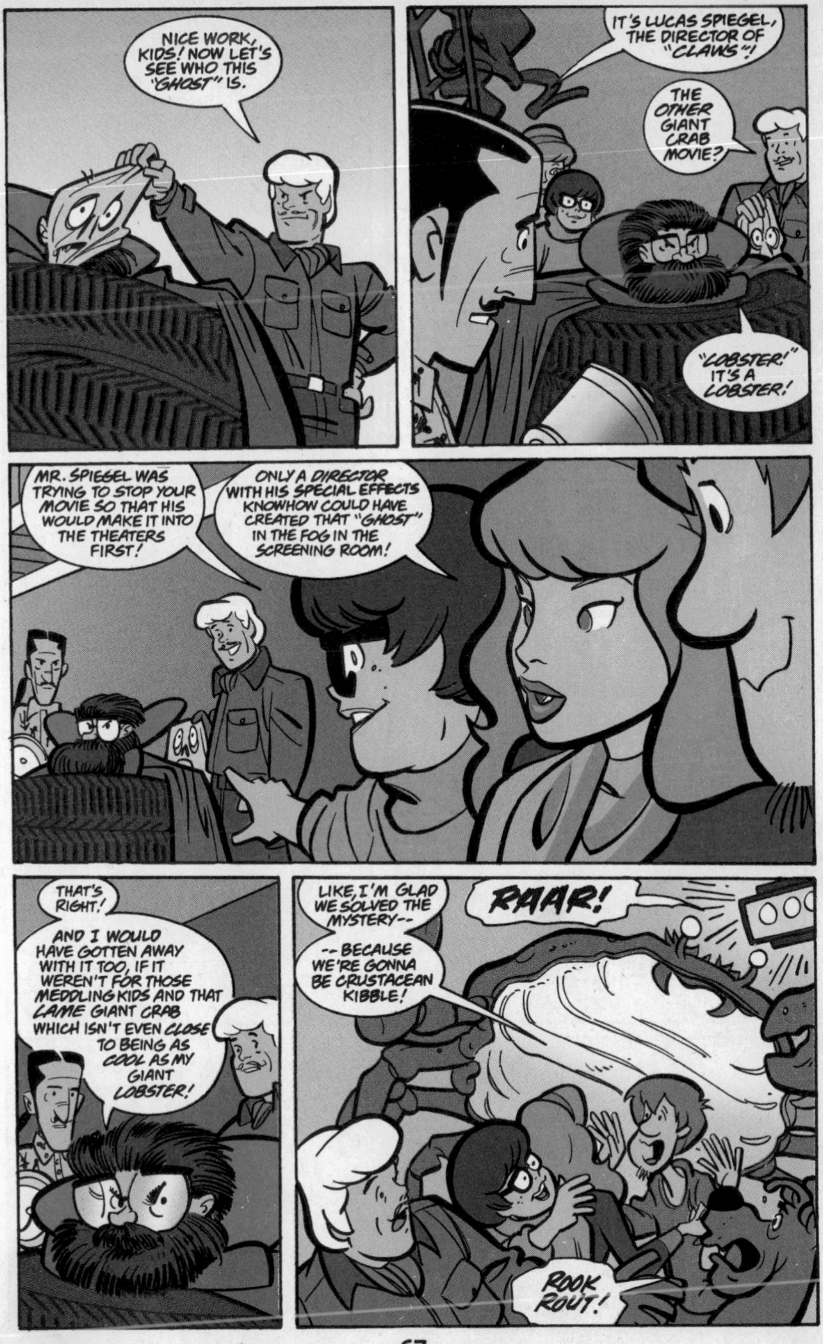

NICE WORK, KIDS! NOW LET'S SEE WHO THIS "GHOST" IS.
IT'S LUCAS SPIEGEL, THE DIRECTOR OF "CLAWS"!
THE OTHER GIANT CRAB MOVIE?
"LOBSTER!" IT'S A LOBSTER!
MR. SPIEGEL WAS TRYING TO STOP YOUR MOVIE SO THAT HIS WOULD MAKE IT INTO THE THEATERS FIRST!
ONLY A DIRECTOR WITH HIS SPECIAL EFFECTS KNOWHOW COULD HAVE CREATED THAT "GHOST" IN THE FOG IN THE SCREENING ROOM!
THAT'S RIGHT!
AND I WOULD HAVE GOTTEN AWAY WITH IT TOO, IF IT WEREN'T FOR THOSE MEDDLING KIDS AND THAT LAME GIANT CRAB WHICH ISN'T EVEN CLOSE TO BEING AS COOL AS MY GIANT LOBSTER!
LIKE, I'M GLAD WE SOLVED THE MYSTERY--
RAAR!
-- BECAUSE WE'RE GONNA BE CRUSTACEAN KIBBLE!
ROOK ROUT!

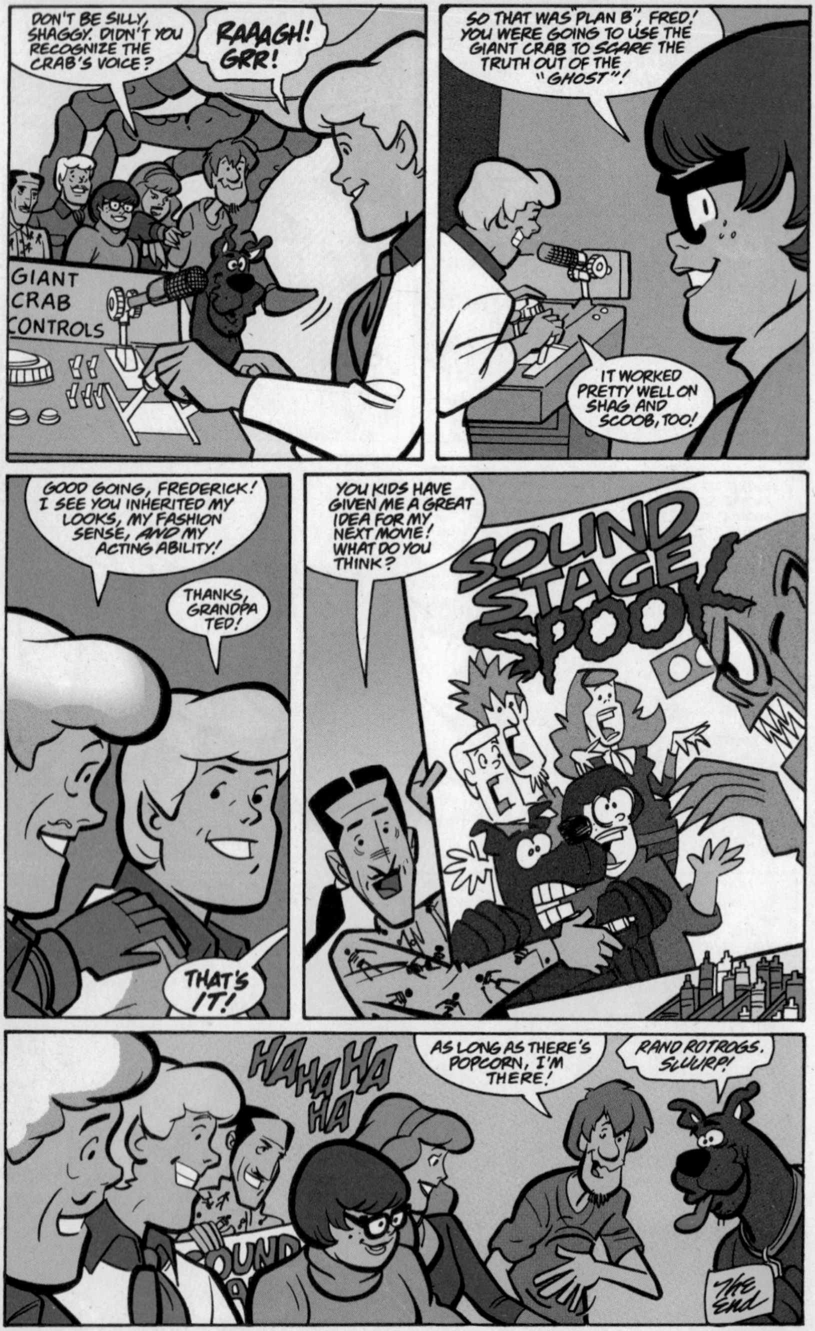
DON'T BE SILLY, SHAGGY. DIDN'T YOU RECOGNIZE THE CRAB'S VOICE?
RAAAGH! GRR!
GIANT CRAB CONTROLS
SO THAT WAS "PLAN B", FRED! YOU WERE GOING TO USE THE GIANT CRAB TO SCARE THE TRUTH OUT OF THE "GHOST"!
IT WORKED PRETTY WELL ON SHAG AND SCOOB, TOO!
GOOD GOING, FREDERICK! I SEE YOU INHERITED MY LOOKS, MY FASHION SENSE, AND MY ACTING ABILITY!
THANKS, GRANDPA TED!
THAT'S IT!
YOU KIDS HAVE GIVEN ME A GREAT IDEA FOR MY NEXT MOVIE! WHAT DO YOU THINK?
SOUND STAGE SPOOK
HA HA HA HA HA
AS LONG AS THERE'S POPCORN, I'M THERE!
RAND ROTROGS. SLUURP!
THE END

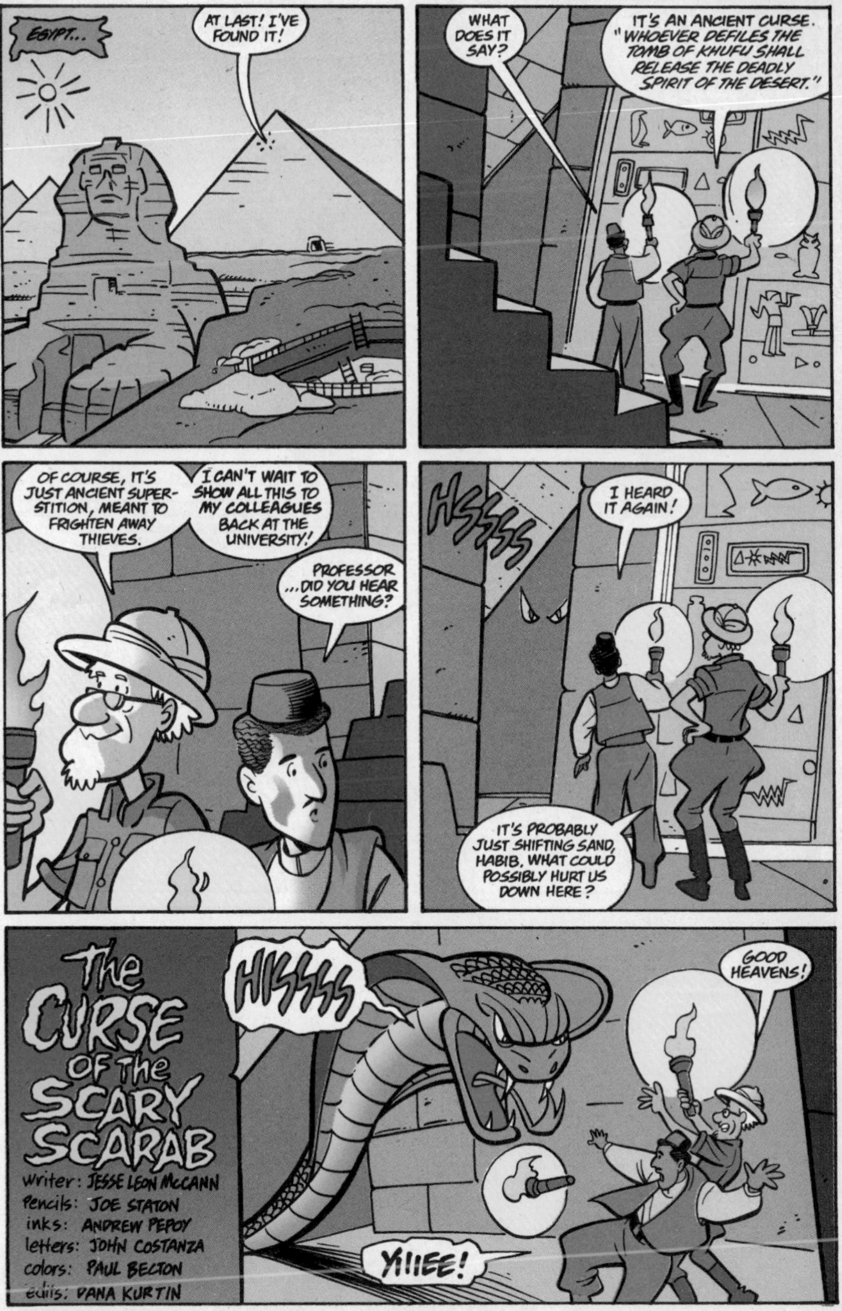
EGYPT...
AT LAST! I'VE FOUND IT!
WHAT DOES IT SAY?
IT'S AN ANCIENT CURSE. "WHOEVER DEFILES THE TOMB OF KHUFU SHALL RELEASE THE DEADLY SPIRIT OF THE DESERT."
OF COURSE, IT'S JUST ANCIENT SUPER-STITION, MEANT TO FRIGHTEN AWAY THIEVES.
I CAN'T WAIT TO SHOW ALL THIS TO MY COLLEAGUES BACK AT THE UNIVERSITY!
PROFESSOR ...DID YOU HEAR SOMETHING?
HSSSS
I HEARD IT AGAIN!
IT'S PROBABLY JUST SHIFTING SAND, HABIB. WHAT COULD POSSIBLY HURT US DOWN HERE?
The CURSE of the SCARY SCARAB
writer: JESSE LEON McCANN
Pencils: JOE STATON
inks: ANDREW PEPOY
letters: JOHN COSTANZA
colors: PAUL BECTON
edits: DANA KURTIN
HISSSS
GOOD HEAVENS!
YIIIEE!

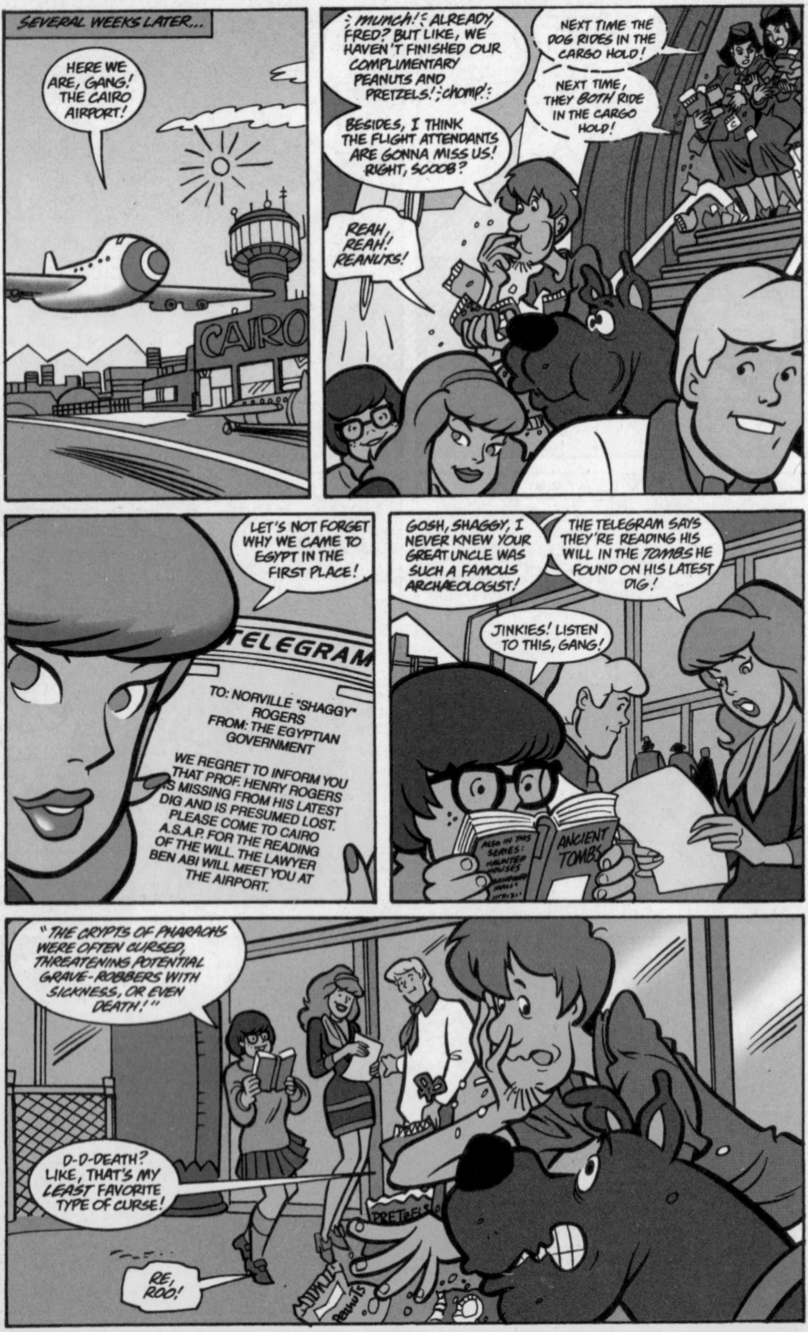
SEVERAL WEEKS LATER...
HERE WE ARE, GANG! THE CAIRO AIRPORT!
CAIRO
:munch!: ALREADY, FRED? BUT LIKE, WE HAVEN'T FINISHED OUR COMPLIMENTARY PEANUTS AND PRETZELS! :chomp!:
BESIDES, I THINK THE FLIGHT ATTENDANTS ARE GONNA MISS US! RIGHT, SCOOB?
REAH, REAH! REANUTS!
NEXT TIME THE DOG RIDES IN THE CARGO HOLD!
NEXT TIME, THEY BOTH RIDE IN THE CARGO HOLD!
LET'S NOT FORGET WHY WE CAME TO EGYPT IN THE FIRST PLACE!
TELEGRAM
TO: NORVILLE "SHAGGY" ROGERS
FROM: THE EGYPTIAN GOVERNMENT
WE REGRET TO INFORM YOU THAT PROF. HENRY ROGERS IS MISSING FROM HIS LATEST DIG AND IS PRESUMED LOST. PLEASE COME TO CAIRO A.S.A.P. FOR THE READING OF THE WILL. THE LAWYER BEN ABI WILL MEET YOU AT THE AIRPORT.
GOSH, SHAGGY, I NEVER KNEW YOUR GREAT UNCLE WAS SUCH A FAMOUS ARCHAEOLOGIST!
THE TELEGRAM SAYS THEY'RE READING HIS WILL IN THE TOMBS HE FOUND ON HIS LATEST DIG!
JINKIES! LISTEN TO THIS, GANG!
ANCIENT TOMBS
"THE CRYPTS OF PHARAOHS WERE OFTEN CURSED, THREATENING POTENTIAL GRAVE-ROBBERS WITH SICKNESS, OR EVEN DEATH!"
D-D-DEATH? LIKE, THAT'S MY LEAST FAVORITE TYPE OF CURSE!
RE, ROO!
PRETZELS
PEANUTS

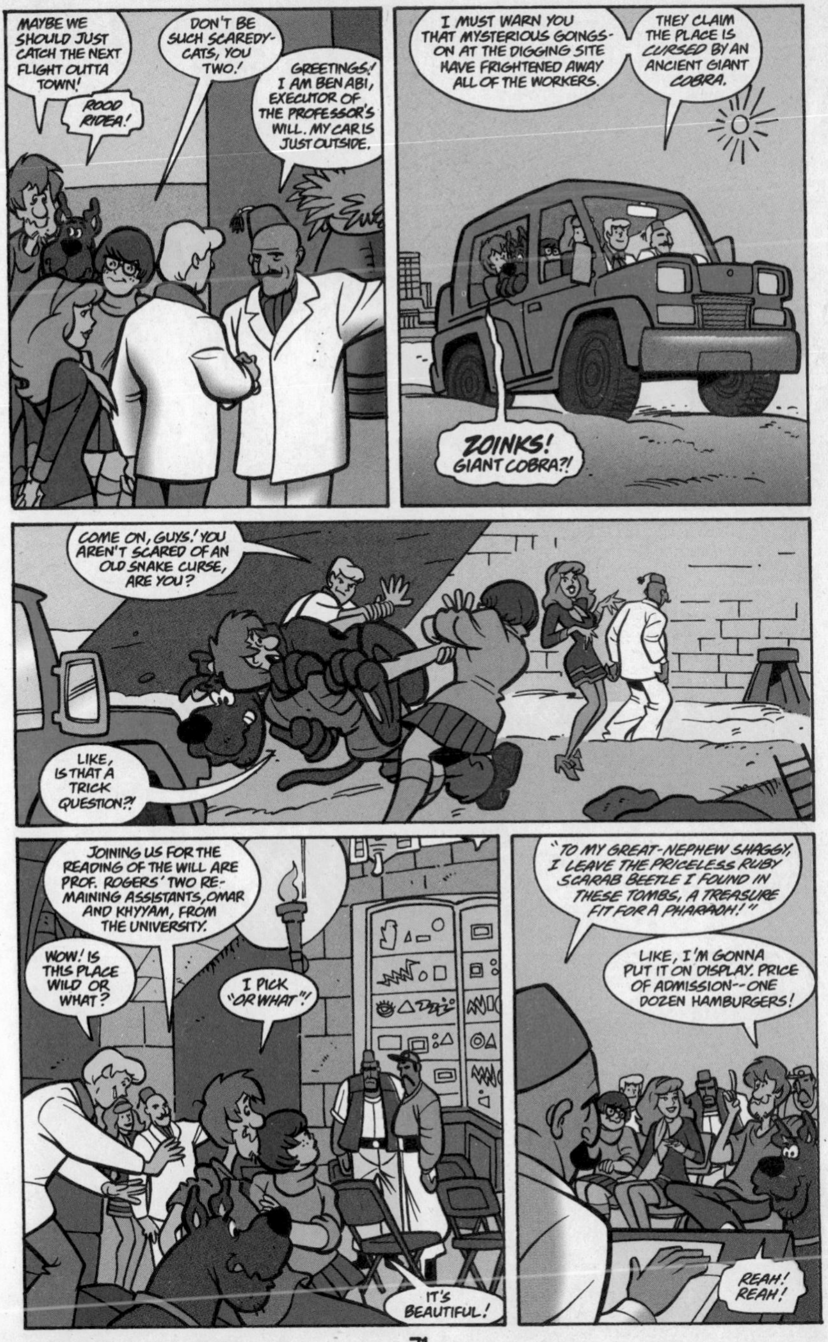
MAYBE WE SHOULD JUST CATCH THE NEXT FLIGHT OUTTA TOWN!
ROOD RIDEA!
DON'T BE SUCH SCAREDY-CATS, YOU TWO!
GREETINGS! I AM BEN ABI, EXECUTOR OF THE PROFESSOR'S WILL. MY CAR IS JUST OUTSIDE.
I MUST WARN YOU THAT MYSTERIOUS GOINGS-ON AT THE DIGGING SITE HAVE FRIGHTENED AWAY ALL OF THE WORKERS.
THEY CLAIM THE PLACE IS CURSED BY AN ANCIENT GIANT COBRA.
ZOINKS! GIANT COBRA?!
COME ON, GUYS! YOU AREN'T SCARED OF AN OLD SNAKE CURSE, ARE YOU?
LIKE, IS THAT A TRICK QUESTION?!
JOINING US FOR THE READING OF THE WILL ARE PROF. ROGERS' TWO REMAINING ASSISTANTS, OMAR AND KHYYAM, FROM THE UNIVERSITY.
WOW! IS THIS PLACE WILD OR WHAT?
I PICK "OR WHAT"!
IT'S BEAUTIFUL!
"TO MY GREAT-NEPHEW SHAGGY, I LEAVE THE PRICELESS RUBY SCARAB BEETLE I FOUND IN THESE TOMBS, A TREASURE FIT FOR A PHARAOH!"
LIKE, I'M GONNA PUT IT ON DISPLAY. PRICE OF ADMISSION--ONE DOZEN HAMBURGERS!
REAH! REAH!

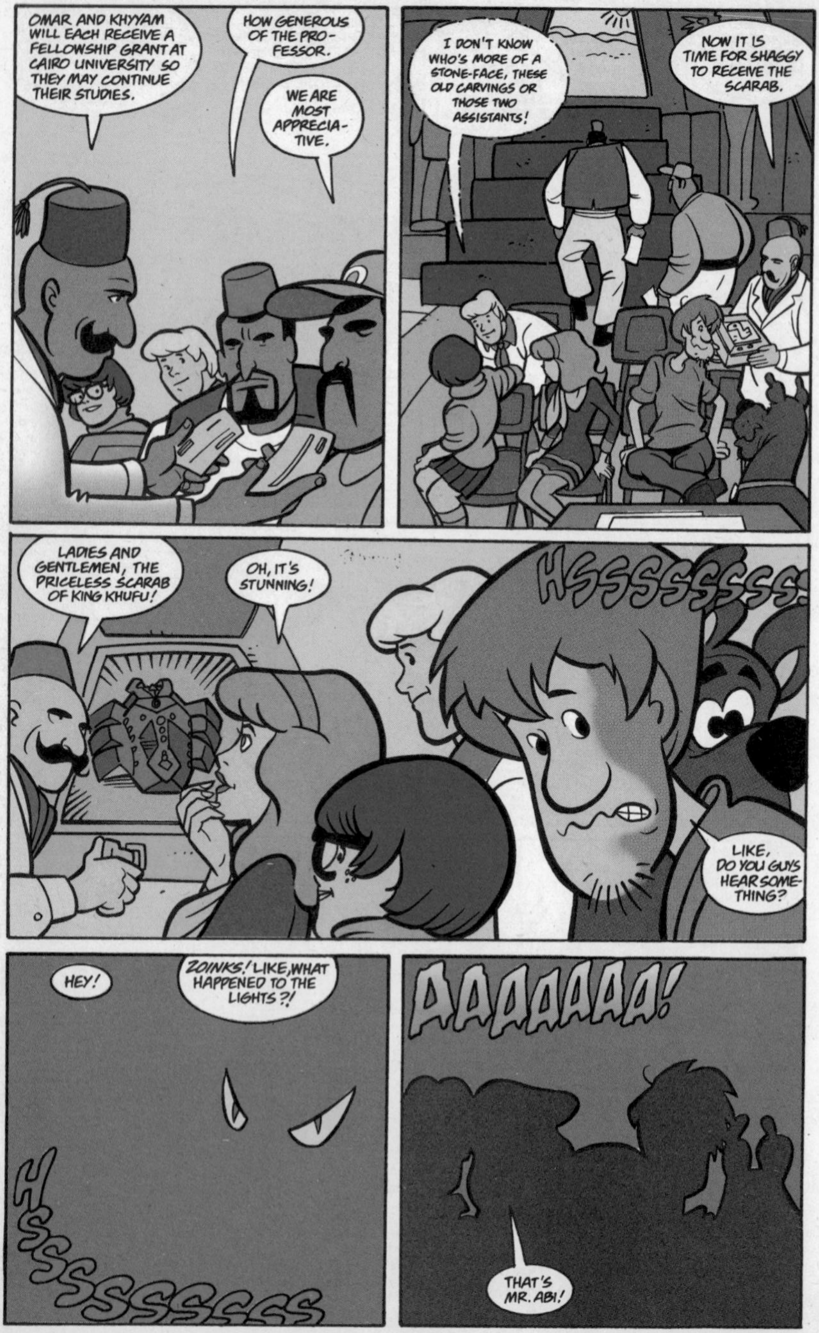
OMAR AND KHYYAM WILL EACH RECEIVE A FELLOWSHIP GRANT AT CAIRO UNIVERSITY SO THEY MAY CONTINUE THEIR STUDIES.
HOW GENEROUS OF THE PRO-FESSOR.
WE ARE MOST APPRECIA-TIVE.
I DON'T KNOW WHO'S MORE OF A STONE-FACE, THESE OLD CARVINGS OR THOSE TWO ASSISTANTS!
NOW IT IS TIME FOR SHAGGY TO RECEIVE THE SCARAB.
LADIES AND GENTLEMEN, THE PRICELESS SCARAB OF KING KHUFU!
OH, IT'S STUNNING!
HSSSSSSSSS!
LIKE, DO YOU GUYS HEAR SOME-THING?
HEY!
ZOINKS! LIKE, WHAT HAPPENED TO THE LIGHTS?!
HSSSSSSSSSS
AAAAAAA!
THAT'S MR. ABI!

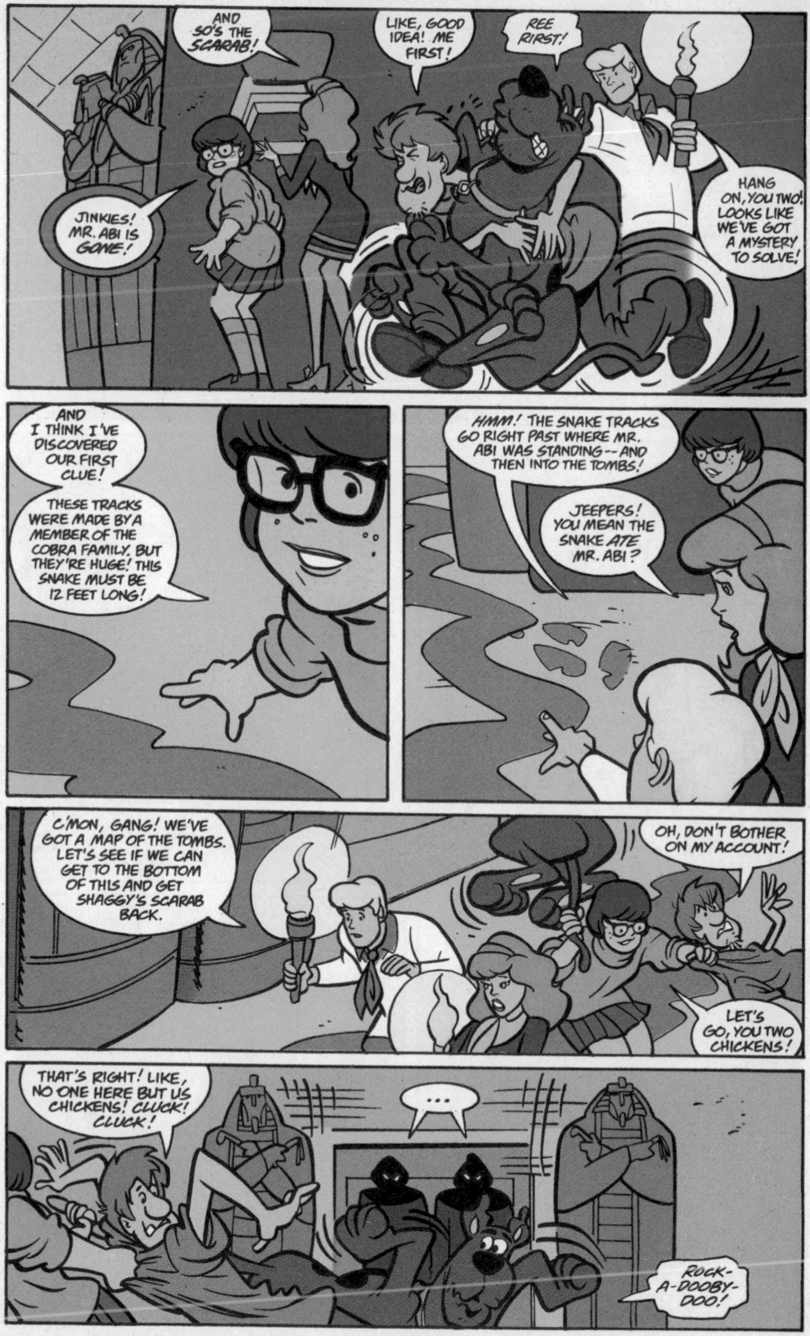
AND SO'S THE SCARAB!
LIKE, GOOD IDEA! ME FIRST!
REE RIRST!
JINKIES! MR. ABI IS GONE!
HANG ON, YOU TWO! LOOKS LIKE WE'VE GOT A MYSTERY TO SOLVE!
AND I THINK I'VE DISCOVERED OUR FIRST CLUE!
THESE TRACKS WERE MADE BY A MEMBER OF THE COBRA FAMILY. BUT THEY'RE HUGE! THIS SNAKE MUST BE 12 FEET LONG!
HMM! THE SNAKE TRACKS GO RIGHT PAST WHERE MR. ABI WAS STANDING--AND THEN INTO THE TOMBS!
JEEPERS! YOU MEAN THE SNAKE ATE MR. ABI?
C'MON, GANG! WE'VE GOT A MAP OF THE TOMBS. LET'S SEE IF WE CAN GET TO THE BOTTOM OF THIS AND GET SHAGGY'S SCARAB BACK.
OH, DON'T BOTHER ON MY ACCOUNT!
LET'S GO, YOU TWO CHICKENS!
THAT'S RIGHT! LIKE, NO ONE HERE BUT US CHICKENS! CLUCK! CLUCK!
...
ROCK-A-DOOBY-DOO!

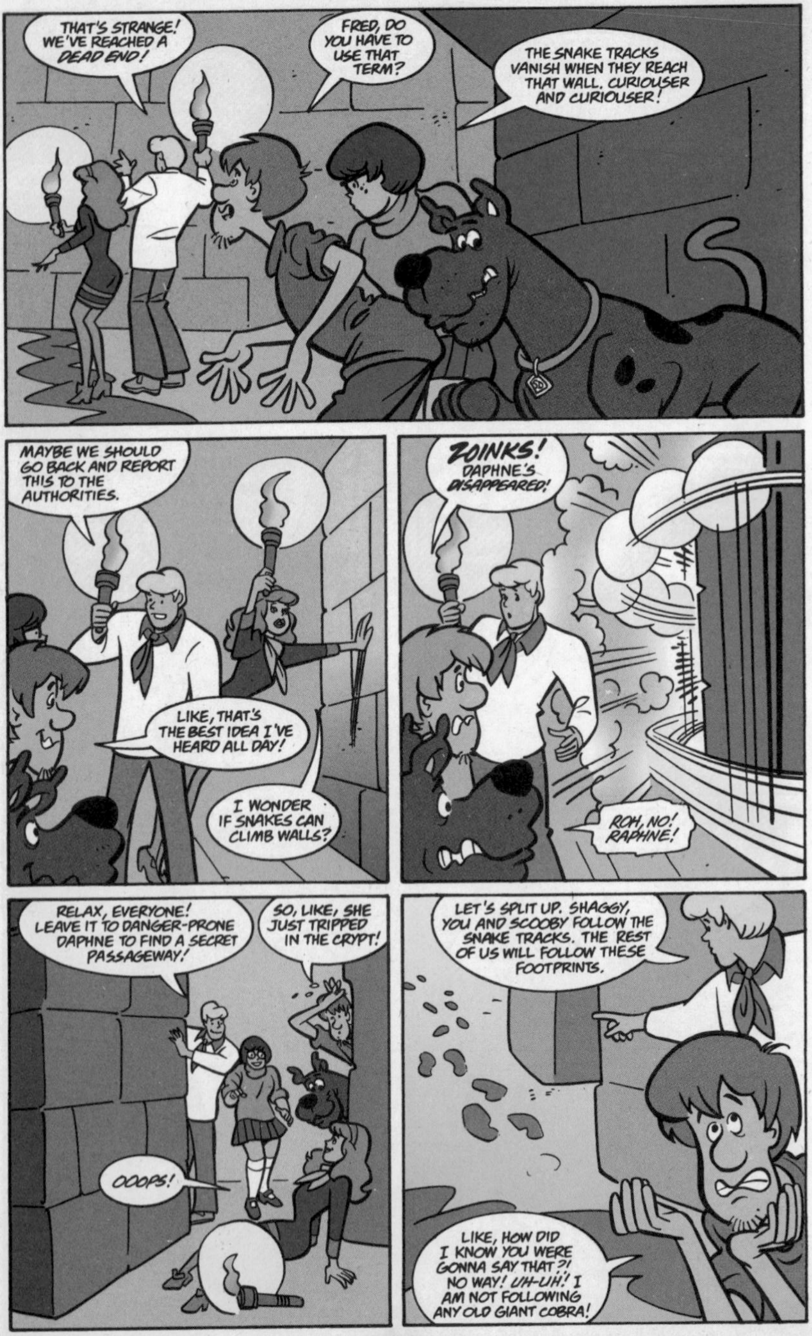
THAT'S STRANGE! WE'VE REACHED A DEAD END!
FRED, DO YOU HAVE TO USE THAT TERM?
THE SNAKE TRACKS VANISH WHEN THEY REACH THAT WALL. CURIOUSER AND CURIOUSER!
MAYBE WE SHOULD GO BACK AND REPORT THIS TO THE AUTHORITIES.
LIKE, THAT'S THE BEST IDEA I'VE HEARD ALL DAY!
I WONDER IF SNAKES CAN CLIMB WALLS?
ZOINKS! DAPHNE'S DISAPPEARED!
ROH, NO! RAPHNE!
RELAX, EVERYONE! LEAVE IT TO DANGER-PRONE DAPHNE TO FIND A SECRET PASSAGEWAY!
SO, LIKE, SHE JUST TRIPPED IN THE CRYPT!
OOOPS!
LET'S SPLIT UP. SHAGGY, YOU AND SCOOBY FOLLOW THE SNAKE TRACKS. THE REST OF US WILL FOLLOW THESE FOOTPRINTS.
LIKE, HOW DID I KNOW YOU WERE GONNA SAY THAT?! NO WAY! UH-UH! I AM NOT FOLLOWING ANY OLD GIANT COBRA!

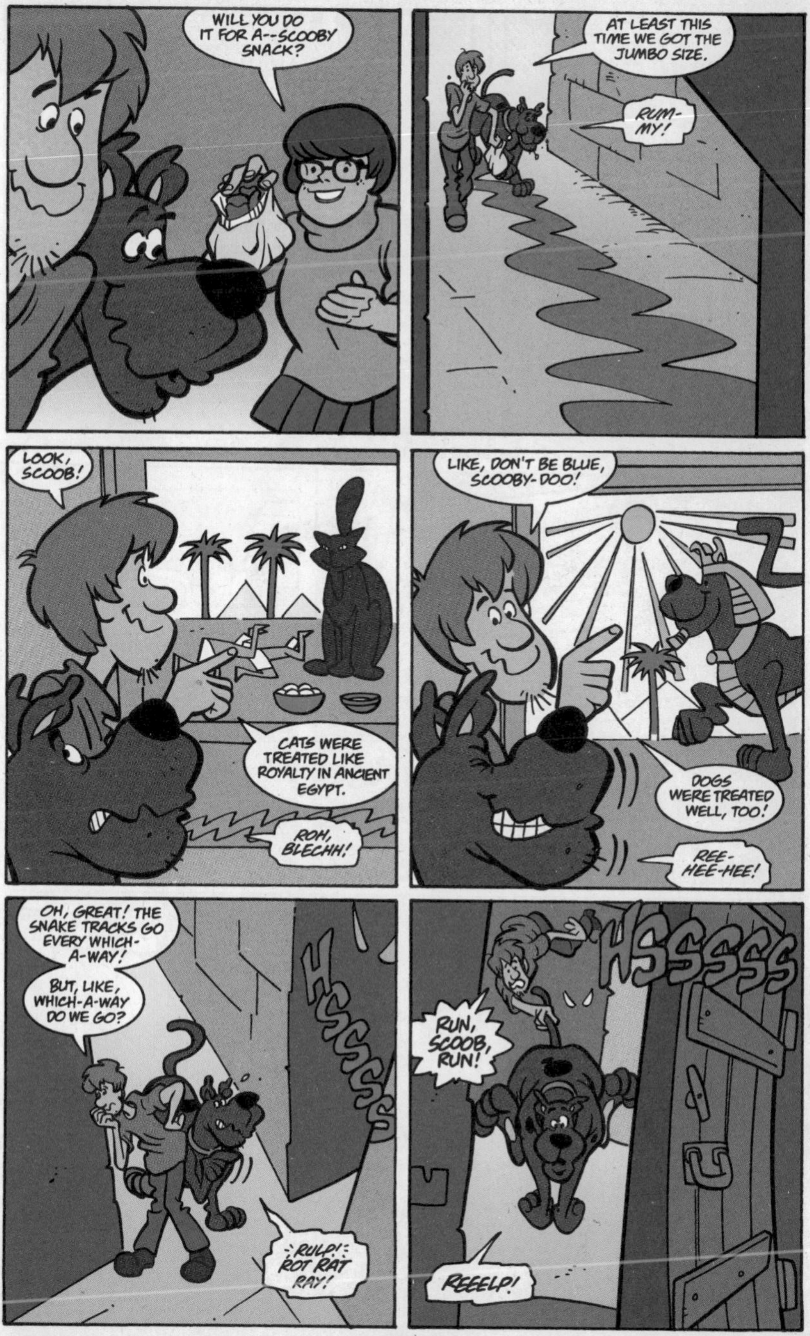
WILL YOU DO IT FOR A--SCOOBY SNACK?
AT LEAST THIS TIME WE GOT THE JUMBO SIZE.
RUM-MY!
LOOK, SCOOB!
CATS WERE TREATED LIKE ROYALTY IN ANCIENT EGYPT.
ROH, BLECHH!
LIKE, DON'T BE BLUE, SCOOBY-DOO!
DOGS WERE TREATED WELL, TOO!
REE-HEE-HEE!
OH, GREAT! THE SNAKE TRACKS GO EVERY WHICH-A-WAY!
BUT, LIKE, WHICH-A-WAY DO WE GO?
HSSSSS
RULP! ROT RAT RAY!
HSSSSS
RUN, SCOOB, RUN!
REEELP!

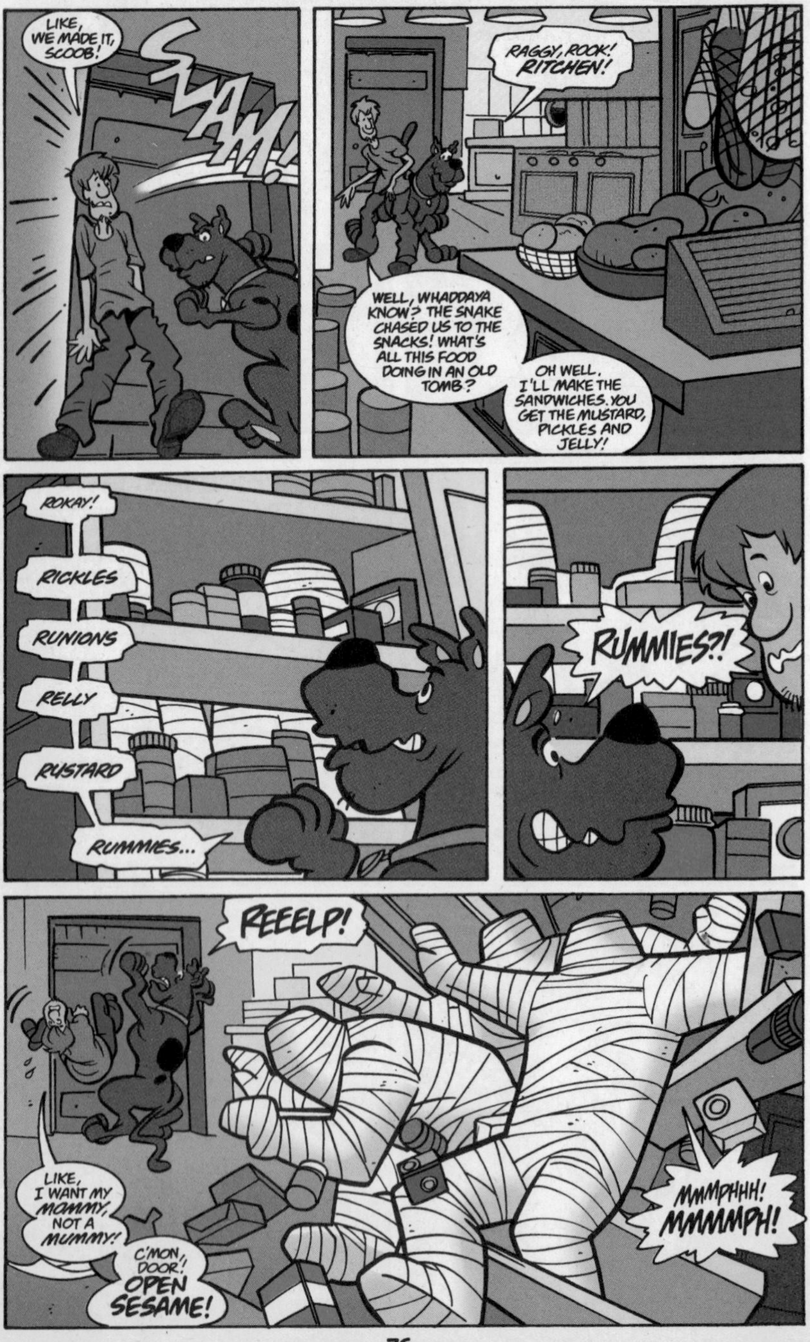
LIKE, WE MADE IT, SCOOB!
SLAM!
RAGGY, ROOK! RITCHEN!
WELL, WHADDAYA KNOW? THE SNAKE CHASED US TO THE SNACKS! WHAT'S ALL THIS FOOD DOING IN AN OLD TOMB?
OH WELL. I'LL MAKE THE SANDWICHES. YOU GET THE MUSTARD, PICKLES AND JELLY!
ROKAY!
RICKLES
RUNIONS
RELLY
RUSTARD
RUMMIES...
RUMMIES?!
REEELP!
LIKE, I WANT MY MOMMY, NOT A MUMMY!
C'MON, DOOR! OPEN SESAME!
MMMPHHH! MMMMPH!

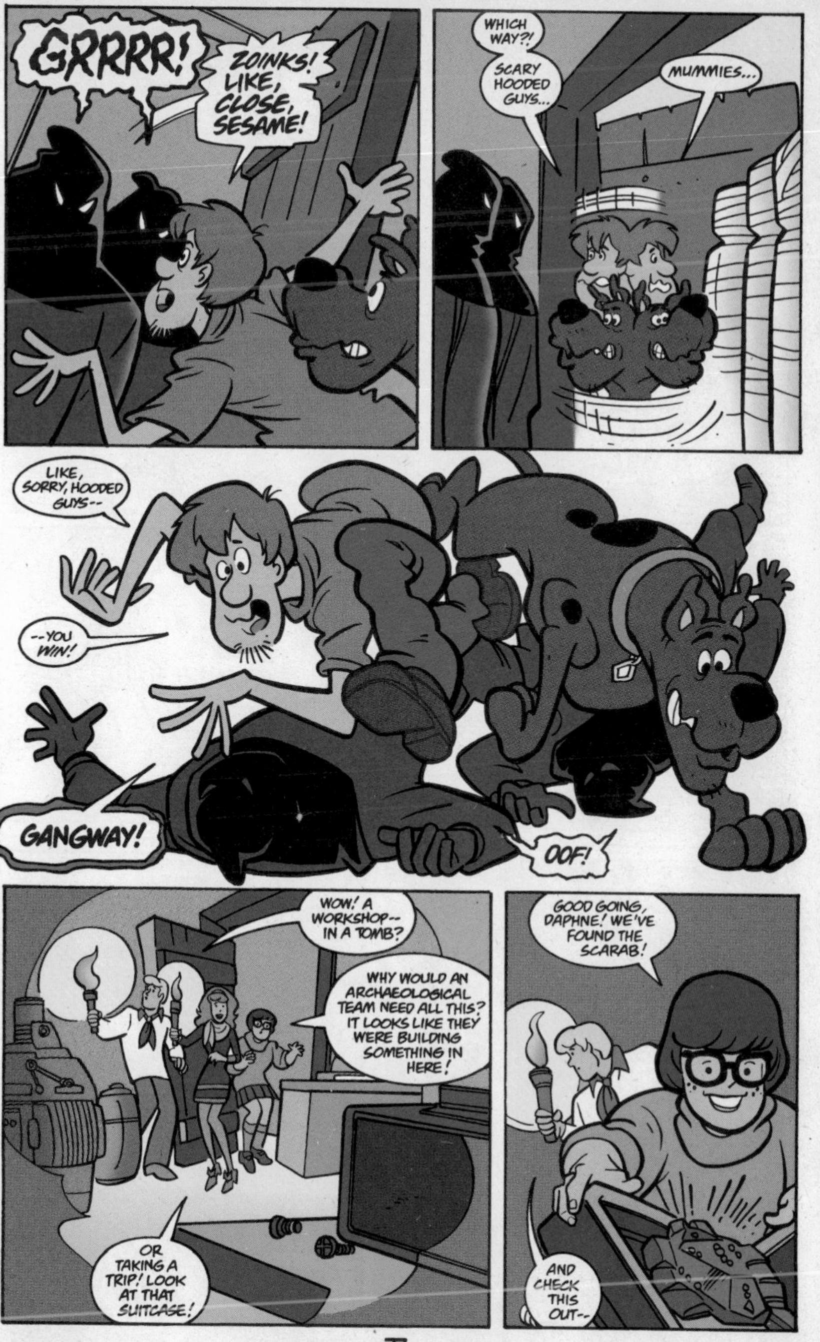
GRRRR!
ZOINKS! LIKE, CLOSE, SESAME!
WHICH WAY?!
SCARY HOODED GUYS...
MUMMIES...
LIKE, SORRY, HOODED GUYS--
--YOU WIN!
GANGWAY!
OOF!
WOW! A WORKSHOP-- IN A TOMB?
WHY WOULD AN ARCHAEOLOGICAL TEAM NEED ALL THIS? IT LOOKS LIKE THEY WERE BUILDING SOMETHING IN HERE!
OR TAKING A TRIP! LOOK AT THAT SUITCASE!
GOOD GOING, DAPHNE! WE'VE FOUND THE SCARAB!
AND CHECK THIS OUT--

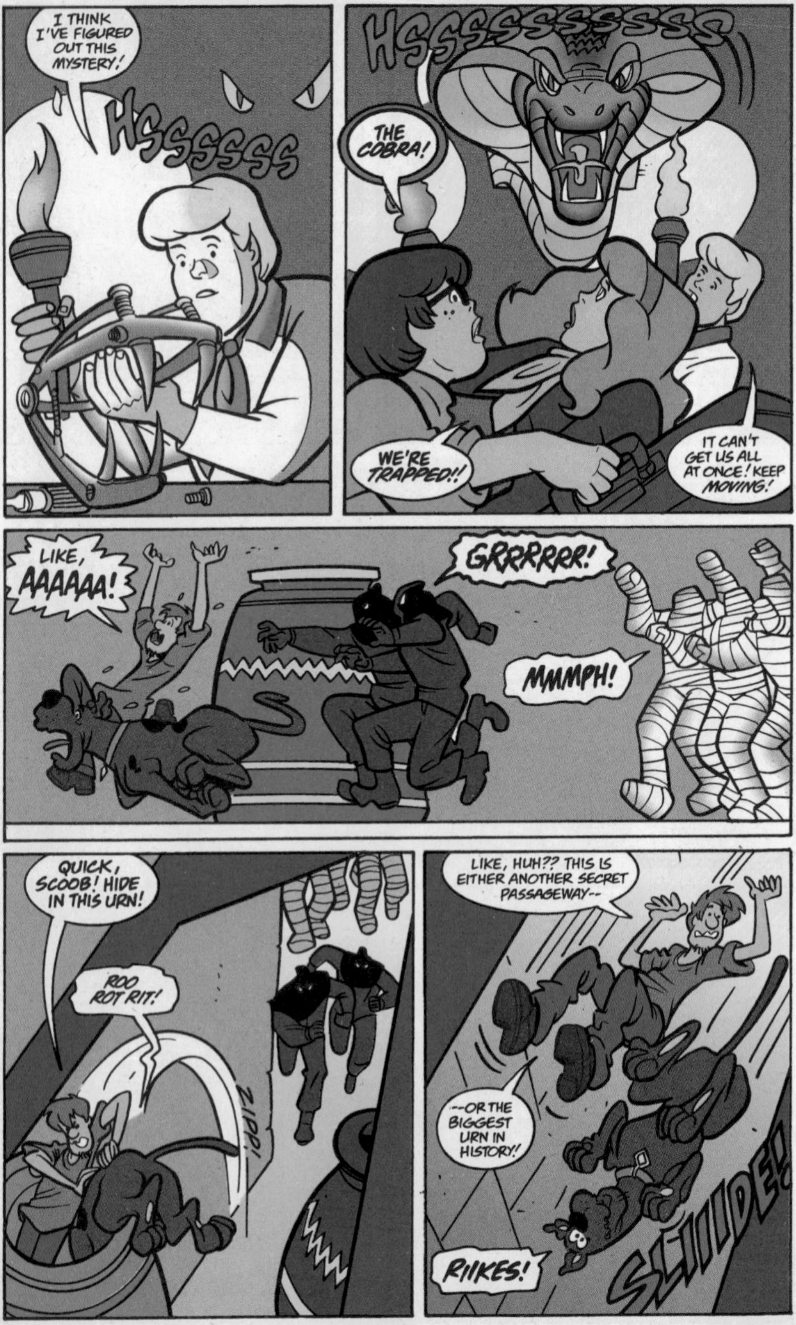
I THINK I'VE FIGURED OUT THIS MYSTERY!
HSSSSSSS
HSSSSSSSSSSS
THE COBRA!
WE'RE TRAPPED!!
IT CAN'T GET US ALL AT ONCE! KEEP MOVING!
LIKE, AAAAAA!
GRRRRRR!
MMMPH!
QUICK, SCOOB! HIDE IN THIS URN!
ROO ROT RIT!
ZIPP!
LIKE, HUH?? THIS IS EITHER ANOTHER SECRET PASSAGEWAY--
--OR THE BIGGEST URN IN HISTORY!
RIIKES!
SLIIIDE!

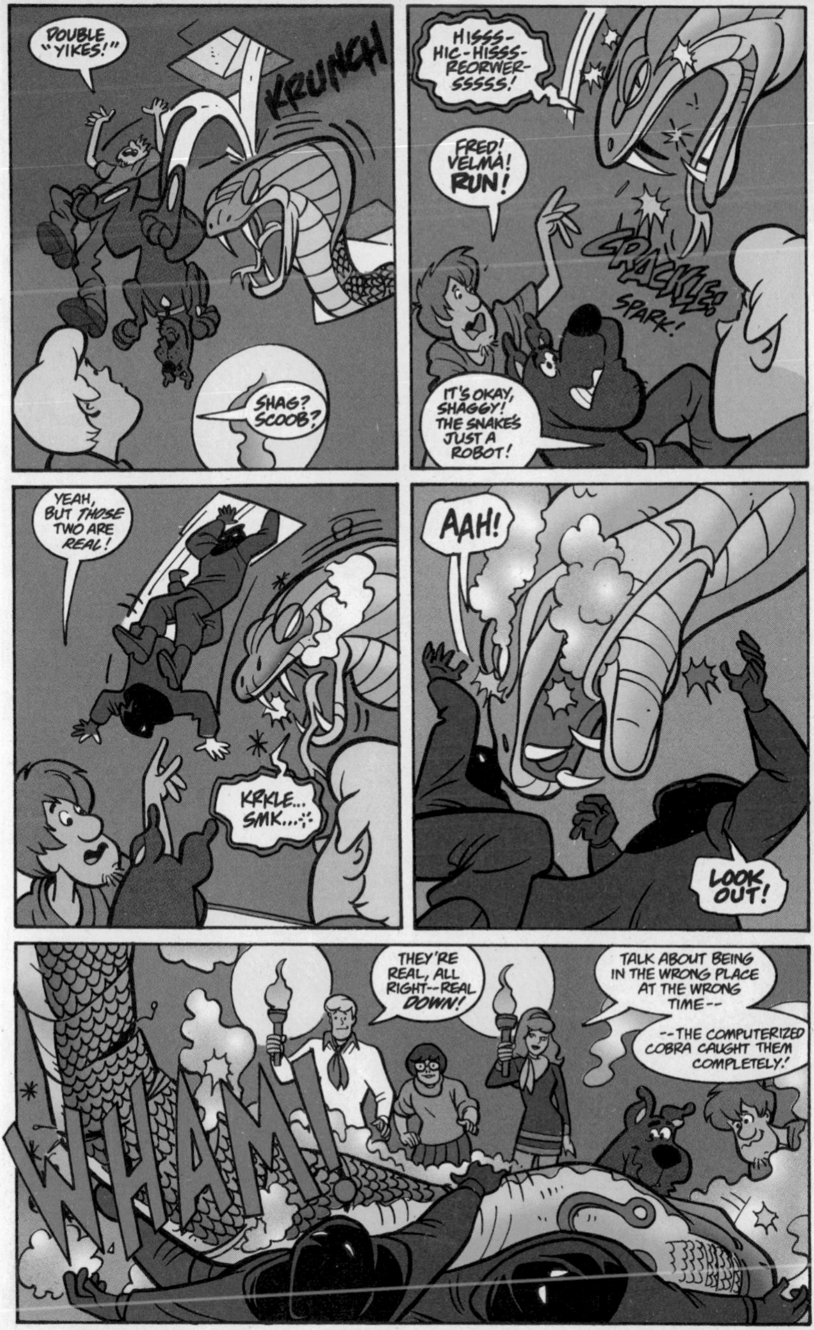
DOUBLE "YIKES!"
KRUNCH
SHAG? SCOOB?
HISSS-HIC-HISSS-REORWER-SSSSS!
FRED! VELMA! RUN!
CRACKLE!
SPARK!
IT'S OKAY, SHAGGY! THE SNAKE'S JUST A ROBOT!
YEAH, BUT THOSE TWO ARE REAL!
KRKLE... SMK...
AAH!
LOOK OUT!
THEY'RE REAL, ALL RIGHT--REAL DOWN!
TALK ABOUT BEING IN THE WRONG PLACE AT THE WRONG TIME--
--THE COMPUTERIZED COBRA CAUGHT THEM COMPLETELY!
WHAM!

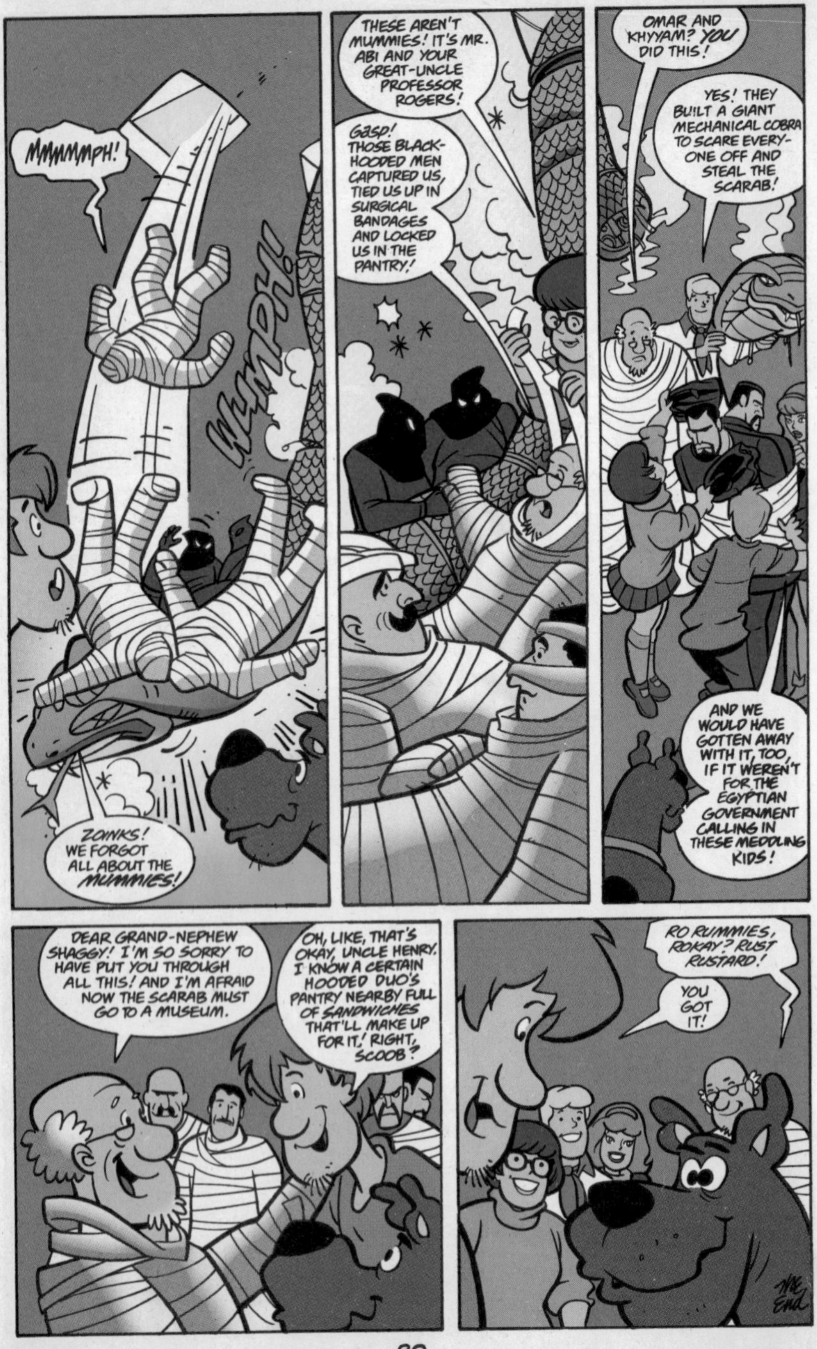
MMMMMPH!
WUMPH!
ZOINKS! WE FORGOT ALL ABOUT THE MUMMIES!
THESE AREN'T MUMMIES! IT'S MR. ABI AND YOUR GREAT-UNCLE PROFESSOR ROGERS!
Gasp! THOSE BLACK-HOODED MEN CAPTURED US, TIED US UP IN SURGICAL BANDAGES AND LOCKED US IN THE PANTRY!
OMAR AND KHYYAM? YOU DID THIS!
YES! THEY BUILT A GIANT MECHANICAL COBRA TO SCARE EVERY-ONE OFF AND STEAL THE SCARAB!
AND WE WOULD HAVE GOTTEN AWAY WITH IT, TOO, IF IT WEREN'T FOR THE EGYPTIAN GOVERNMENT CALLING IN THESE MEDDLING KIDS!
DEAR GRAND-NEPHEW SHAGGY! I'M SO SORRY TO HAVE PUT YOU THROUGH ALL THIS! AND I'M AFRAID NOW THE SCARAB MUST GO TO A MUSEUM.
OH, LIKE, THAT'S OKAY, UNCLE HENRY. I KNOW A CERTAIN HOODED DUO'S PANTRY NEARBY FULL OF SANDWICHES THAT'LL MAKE UP FOR IT! RIGHT, SCOOB?
RO RUMMIES, ROKAY? RUST RUSTARD!
YOU GOT IT!
THE END

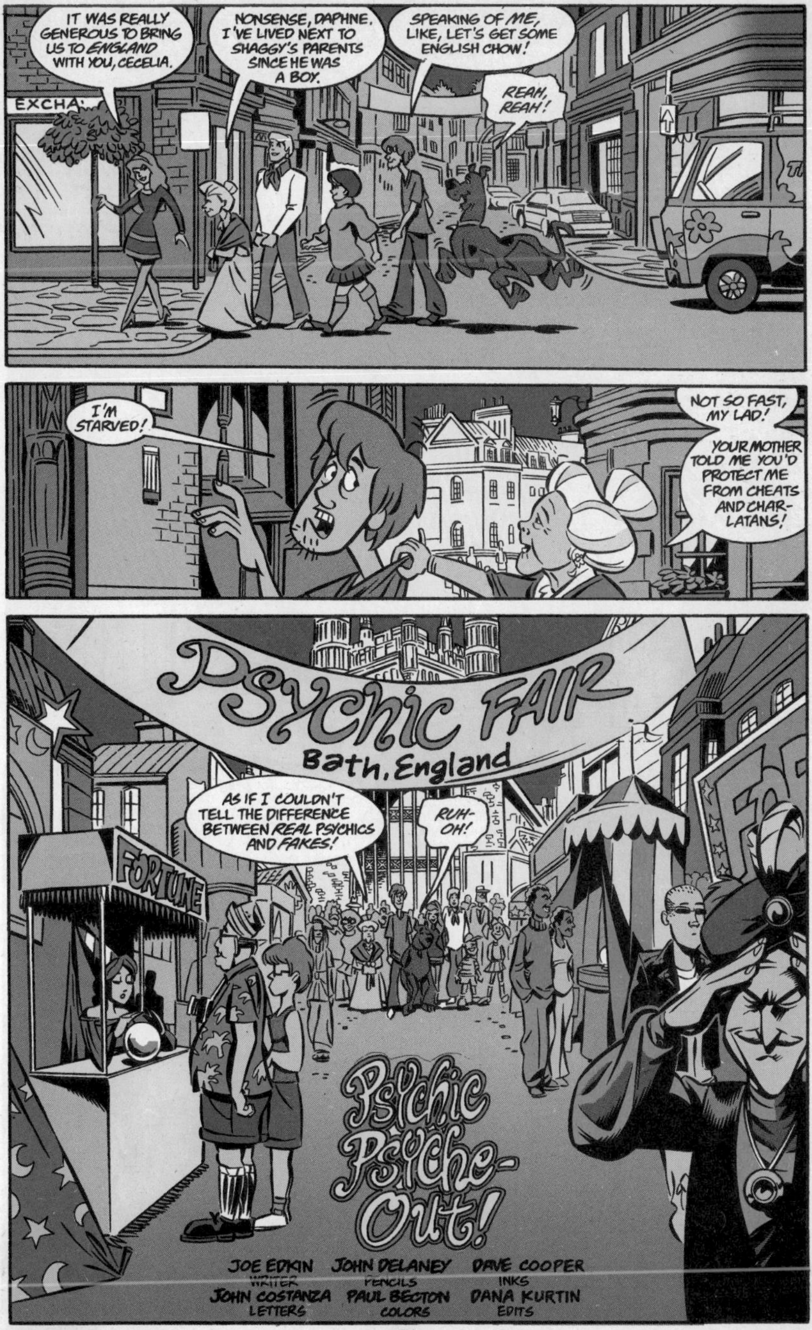
EXCHA
IT WAS REALLY GENEROUS TO BRING US TO ENGLAND WITH YOU, CECELIA.
NONSENSE, DAPHNE. I'VE LIVED NEXT TO SHAGGY'S PARENTS SINCE HE WAS A BOY.
SPEAKING OF ME, LIKE, LET'S GET SOME ENGLISH CHOW!
REAH, REAH!
I'M STARVED!
NOT SO FAST, MY LAD!
YOUR MOTHER TOLD ME YOU'D PROTECT ME FROM CHEATS AND CHAR-LATANS!
PSYCHIC FAIR
Bath, England
AS IF I COULDN'T TELL THE DIFFERENCE BETWEEN REAL PSYCHICS AND FAKES!
RUH-OH!
FORTUNE
Psychic Psyche-Out!
JOE EDKIN WRITER
JOHN DELANEY PENCILS
DAVE COOPER INKS
JOHN COSTANZA LETTERS
PAUL BECTON COLORS
DANA KURTIN EDITS

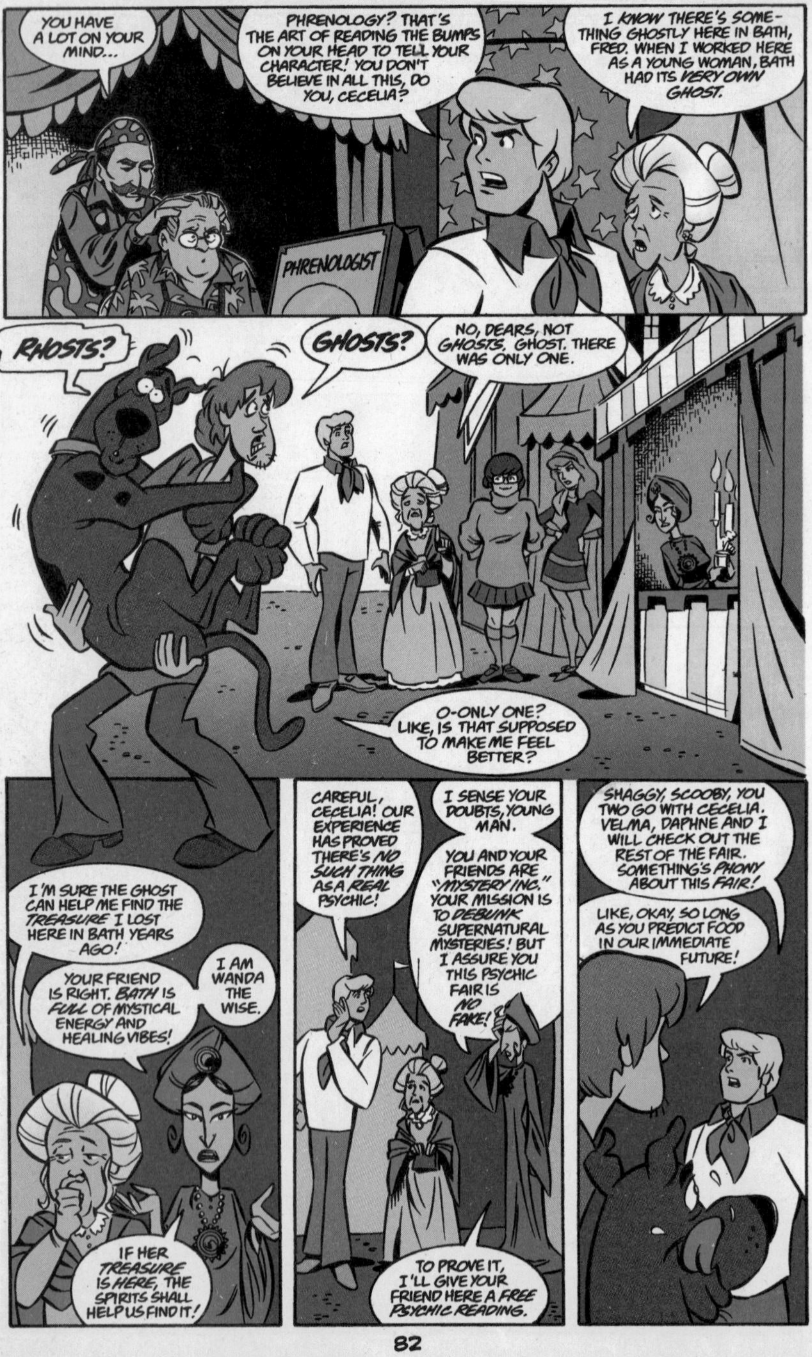
YOU HAVE A LOT ON YOUR MIND...
PHRENOLOGY? THAT'S THE ART OF READING THE BUMPS ON YOUR HEAD TO TELL YOUR CHARACTER! YOU DON'T BELIEVE IN ALL THIS, DO YOU, CECELIA?
PHRENOLOGIST
I KNOW THERE'S SOMETHING GHOSTLY HERE IN BATH, FRED. WHEN I WORKED HERE AS A YOUNG WOMAN, BATH HAD ITS VERY OWN GHOST.
RHOSTS?
GHOSTS?
NO, DEARS, NOT GHOSTS, GHOST. THERE WAS ONLY ONE.
O-ONLY ONE? LIKE, IS THAT SUPPOSED TO MAKE ME FEEL BETTER?
I'M SURE THE GHOST CAN HELP ME FIND THE TREASURE I LOST HERE IN BATH YEARS AGO!
YOUR FRIEND IS RIGHT. BATH IS FULL OF MYSTICAL ENERGY AND HEALING VIBES!
I AM WANDA THE WISE.
IF HER TREASURE IS HERE, THE SPIRITS SHALL HELP US FIND IT!
CAREFUL, CECELIA! OUR EXPERIENCE HAS PROVED THERE'S NO SUCH THING AS A REAL PSYCHIC!
I SENSE YOUR DOUBTS, YOUNG MAN.
YOU AND YOUR FRIENDS ARE "MYSTERY INC." YOUR MISSION IS TO DEBUNK SUPERNATURAL MYSTERIES! BUT I ASSURE YOU THIS PSYCHIC FAIR IS NO FAKE!
TO PROVE IT, I'LL GIVE YOUR FRIEND HERE A FREE PSYCHIC READING.
SHAGGY, SCOOBY, YOU TWO GO WITH CECELIA. VELMA, DAPHNE AND I WILL CHECK OUT THE REST OF THE FAIR. SOMETHING'S PHONY ABOUT THIS FAIR!
LIKE, OKAY, SO LONG AS YOU PREDICT FOOD IN OUR IMMEDIATE FUTURE!

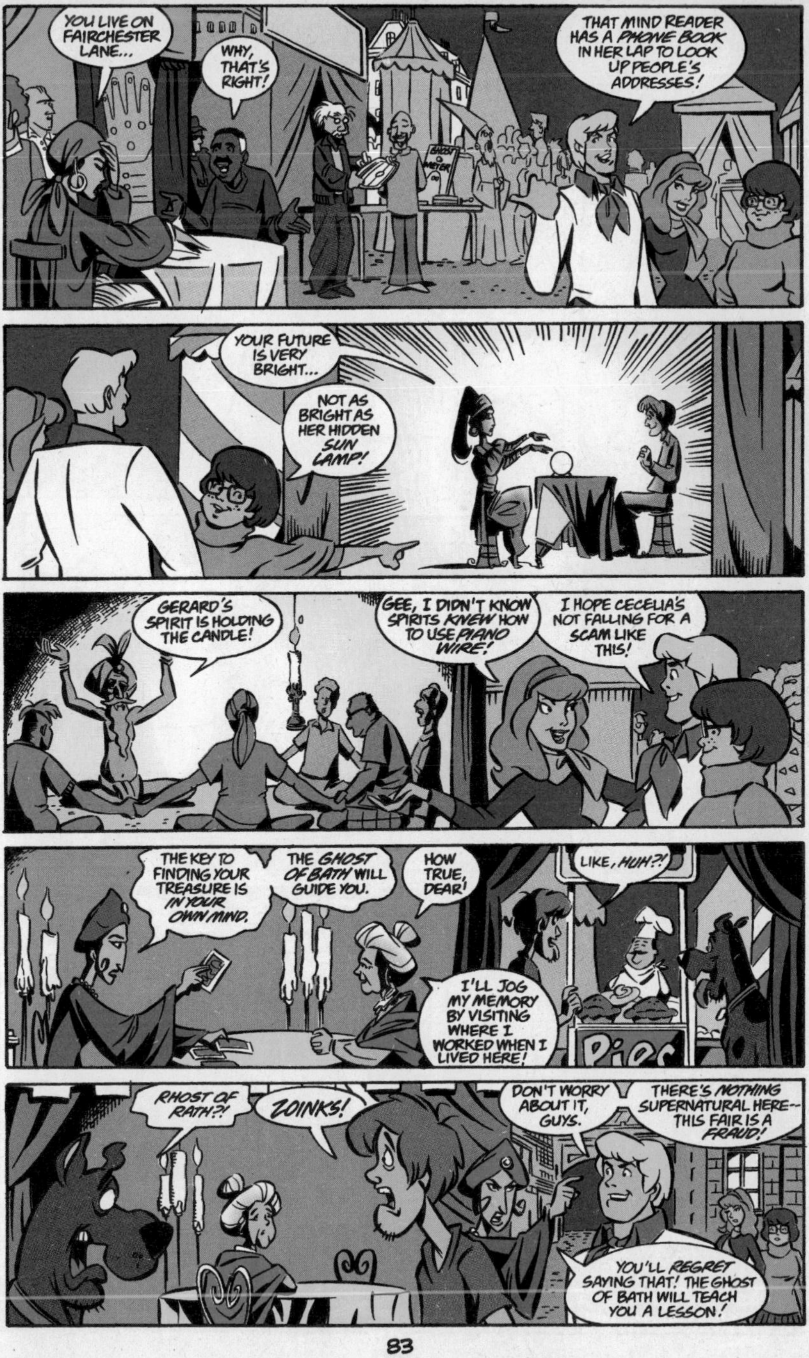
YOU LIVE ON FAIRCHESTER LANE...
WHY, THAT'S RIGHT!
THAT MIND READER HAS A PHONE BOOK IN HER LAP TO LOOK UP PEOPLE'S ADDRESSES!
GHOST METER
YOUR FUTURE IS VERY BRIGHT...
NOT AS BRIGHT AS HER HIDDEN SUN LAMP!
GERARD'S SPIRIT IS HOLDING THE CANDLE!
GEE, I DIDN'T KNOW SPIRITS KNEW HOW TO USE PIANO WIRE!
I HOPE CECELIA'S NOT FALLING FOR A SCAM LIKE THIS!
THE KEY TO FINDING YOUR TREASURE IS IN YOUR OWN MIND.
THE GHOST OF BATH WILL GUIDE YOU.
HOW TRUE, DEAR!
LIKE, HUH?!
I'LL JOG MY MEMORY BY VISITING WHERE I WORKED WHEN I LIVED HERE!
PIES
RHOST OF RATH?!
ZOINKS!
DON'T WORRY ABOUT IT, GUYS.
THERE'S NOTHING SUPERNATURAL HERE-- THIS FAIR IS A FRAUD!
YOU'LL REGRET SAYING THAT! THE GHOST OF BATH WILL TEACH YOU A LESSON!

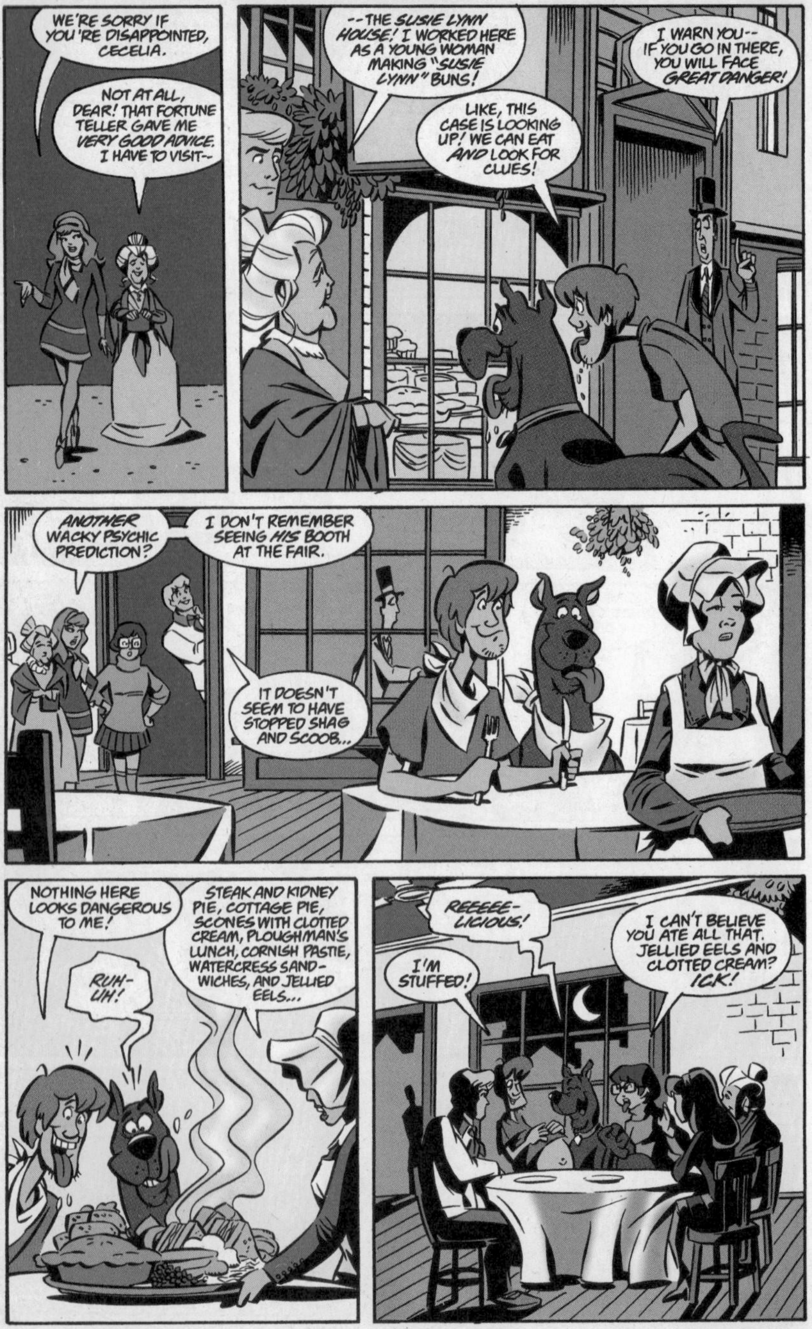
WE'RE SORRY IF YOU'RE DISAPPOINTED, CECELIA.
NOT AT ALL, DEAR! THAT FORTUNE TELLER GAVE ME VERY GOOD ADVICE. I HAVE TO VISIT--
--THE SUSIE LYNN HOUSE! I WORKED HERE AS A YOUNG WOMAN MAKING "SUSIE LYNN" BUNS!
LIKE, THIS CASE IS LOOKING UP! WE CAN EAT AND LOOK FOR CLUES!
I WARN YOU-- IF YOU GO IN THERE, YOU WILL FACE GREAT DANGER!
ANOTHER WACKY PSYCHIC PREDICTION?
I DON'T REMEMBER SEEING HIS BOOTH AT THE FAIR.
IT DOESN'T SEEM TO HAVE STOPPED SHAG AND SCOOB...
NOTHING HERE LOOKS DANGEROUS TO ME!
RUH-UH!
STEAK AND KIDNEY PIE, COTTAGE PIE, SCONES WITH CLOTTED CREAM, PLOUGHMAN'S LUNCH, CORNISH PASTIE, WATERCRESS SANDWICHES, AND JELLIED EELS...
REEEEE-LICIOUS!
I'M STUFFED!
I CAN'T BELIEVE YOU ATE ALL THAT. JELLIED EELS AND CLOTTED CREAM? ICK!

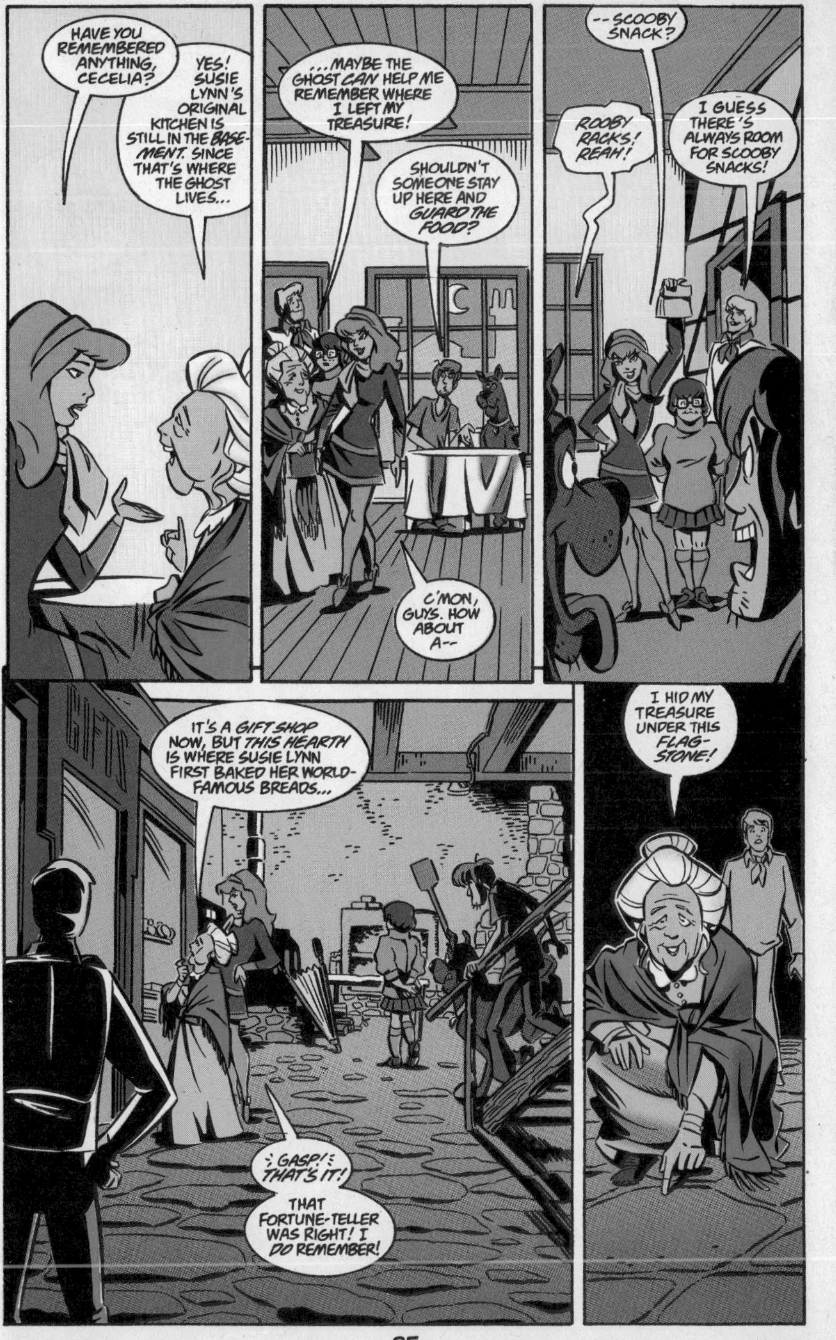
HAVE YOU REMEMBERED ANYTHING, CECELIA?
YES! SUSIE LYNN'S ORIGINAL KITCHEN IS STILL IN THE BASEMENT. SINCE THAT'S WHERE THE GHOST LIVES...
...MAYBE THE GHOST CAN HELP ME REMEMBER WHERE I LEFT MY TREASURE!
SHOULDN'T SOMEONE STAY UP HERE AND GUARD THE FOOD?
C'MON, GUYS. HOW ABOUT A--
--SCOOBY SNACK?
ROOBY RACKS! REAH!
I GUESS THERE'S ALWAYS ROOM FOR SCOOBY SNACKS!
GIFTS
IT'S A GIFT SHOP NOW, BUT THIS HEARTH IS WHERE SUSIE LYNN FIRST BAKED HER WORLD-FAMOUS BREADS...
GASP! THAT'S IT!
THAT FORTUNE-TELLER WAS RIGHT! I DO REMEMBER!
I HID MY TREASURE UNDER THIS FLAG-STONE!

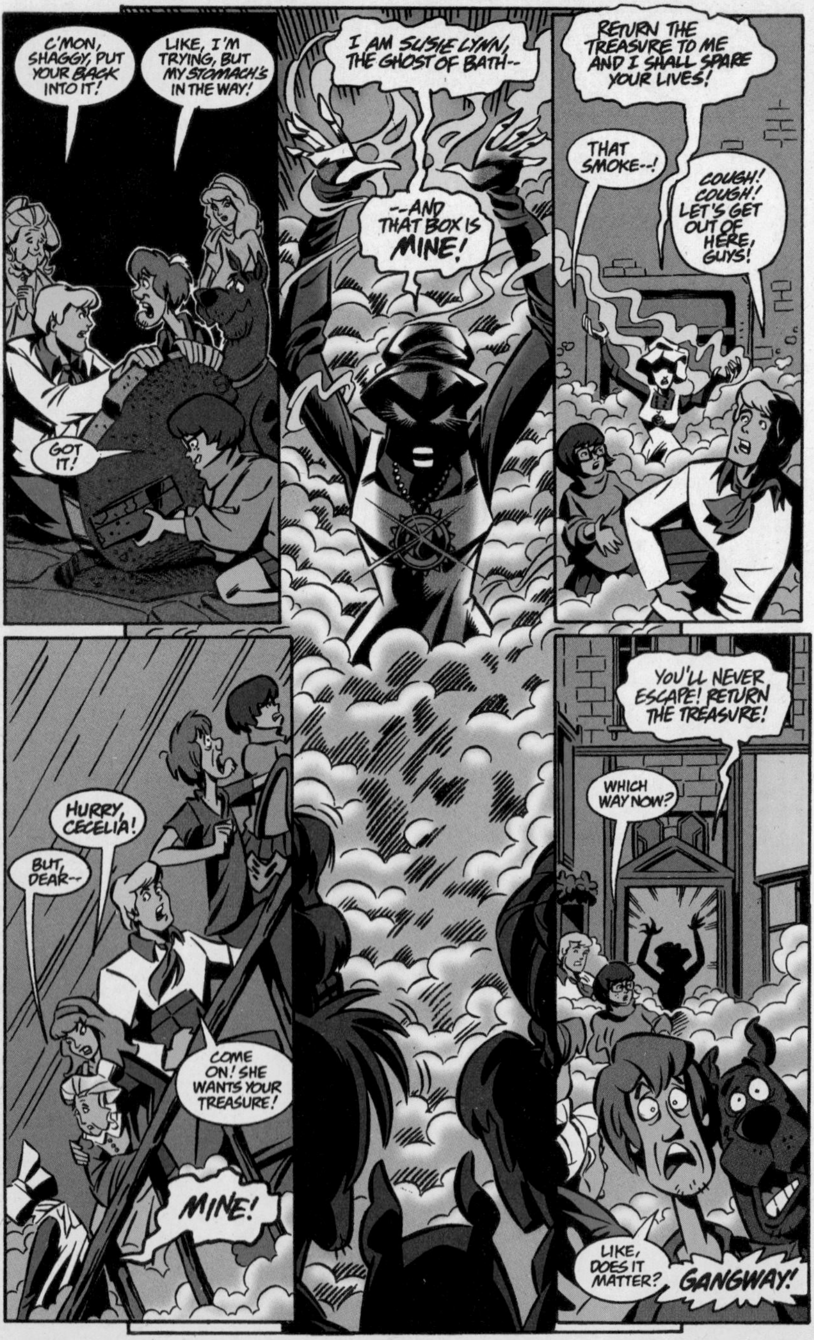
C'MON, SHAGGY, PUT YOUR BACK INTO IT!
LIKE, I'M TRYING, BUT MY STOMACH'S IN THE WAY!
GOT IT!
I AM SUSIE LYNN, THE GHOST OF BATH--
--AND THAT BOX IS MINE!
RETURN THE TREASURE TO ME AND I SHALL SPARE YOUR LIVES!
THAT SMOKE--!
COUGH! COUGH! LET'S GET OUT OF HERE, GUYS!
HURRY, CECELIA!
BUT, DEAR--
COME ON! SHE WANTS YOUR TREASURE!
MINE!
YOU'LL NEVER ESCAPE! RETURN THE TREASURE!
WHICH WAY NOW?
LIKE, DOES IT MATTER?
GANGWAY!

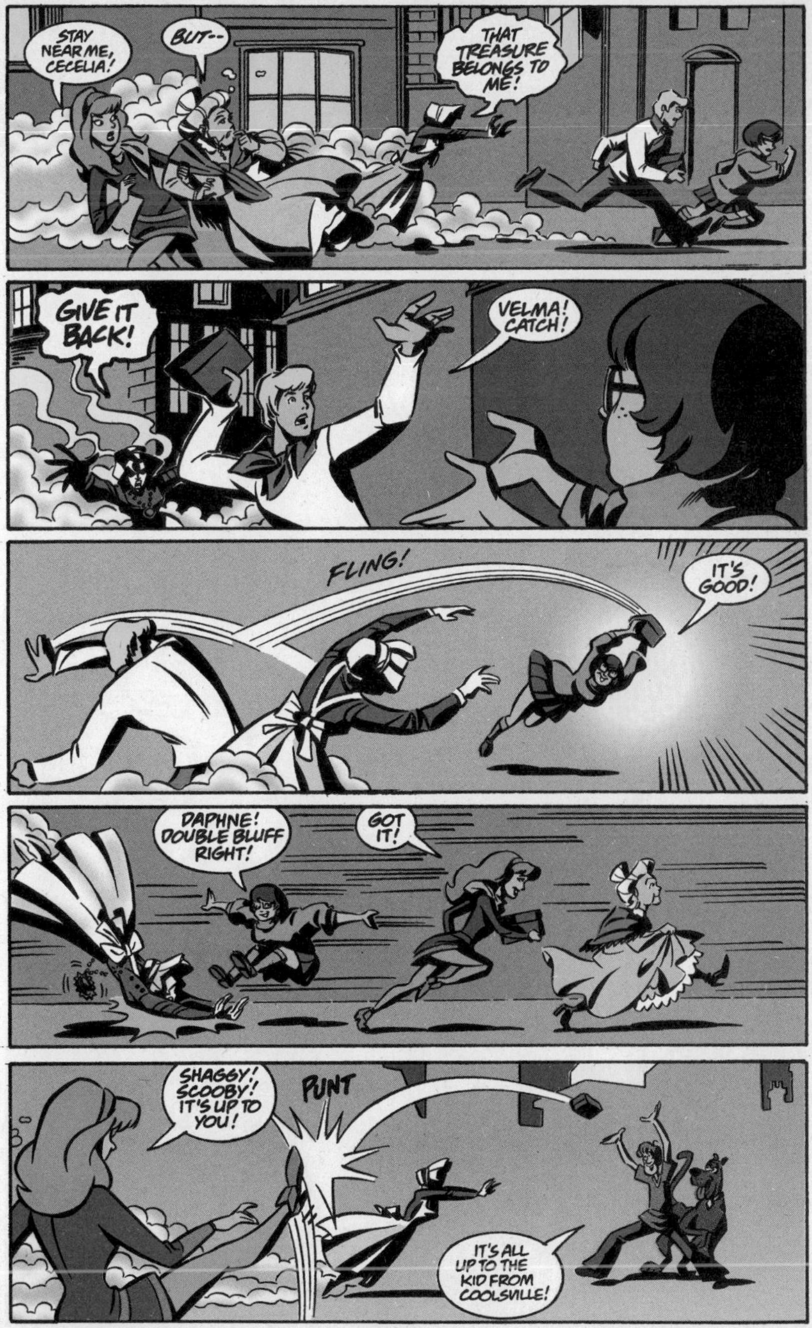
STAY NEAR ME, CECELIA!
BUT--
THAT TREASURE BELONGS TO ME!
GIVE IT BACK!
VELMA! CATCH!
FLING!
IT'S GOOD!
DAPHNE! DOUBLE BLUFF RIGHT!
GOT IT!
SHAGGY! SCOOBY! IT'S UP TO YOU!
PUNT
IT'S ALL UP TO THE KID FROM COOLSVILLE!

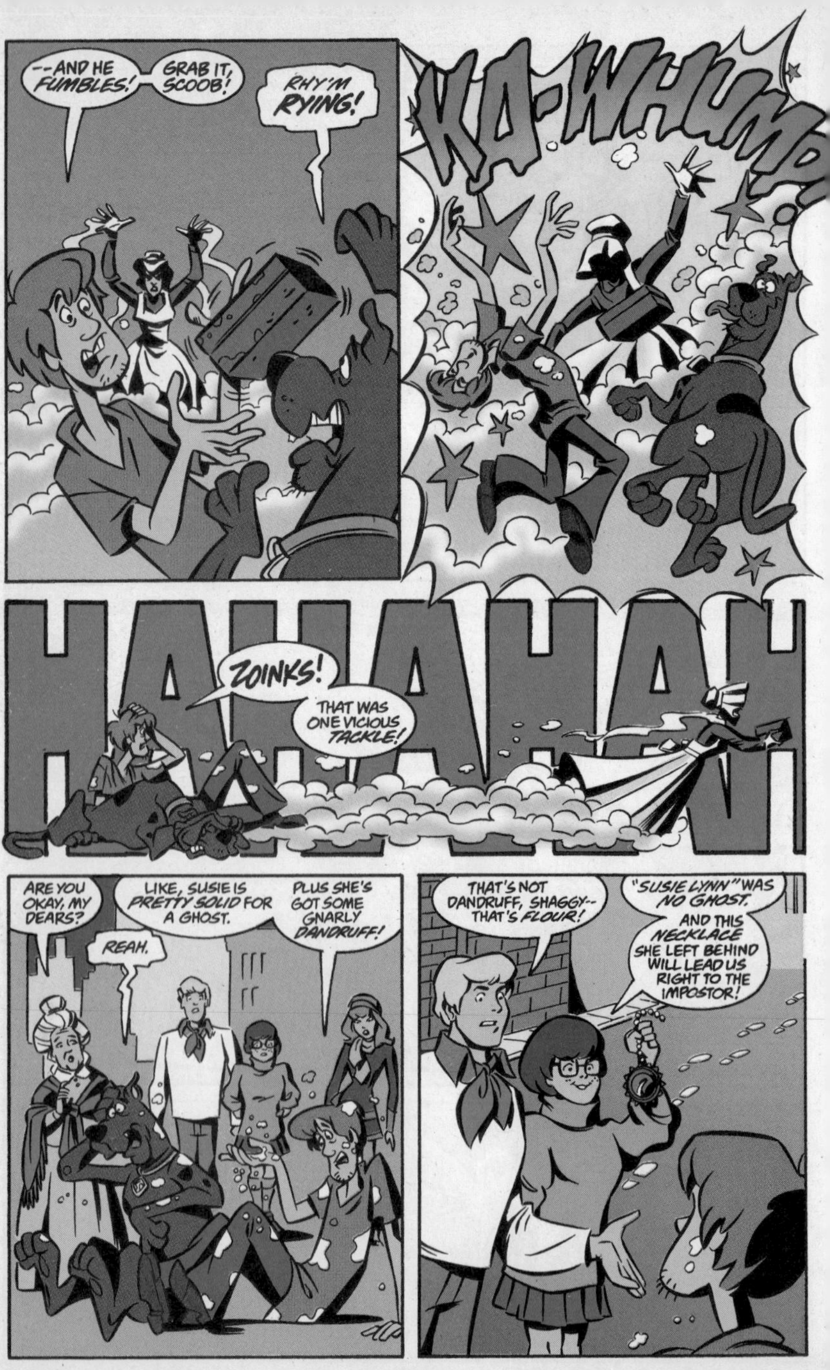
--AND HE FUMBLES!
GRAB IT, SCOOB!
RHY'M RYING!
KA-WHUMP!
HAHAH
ZOINKS!
THAT WAS ONE VICIOUS TACKLE!
ARE YOU OKAY, MY DEARS?
REAH.
LIKE, SUSIE IS PRETTY SOLID FOR A GHOST.
PLUS SHE'S GOT SOME GNARLY DANDRUFF!
THAT'S NOT DANDRUFF, SHAGGY-- THAT'S FLOUR!
"SUSIE LYNN" WAS NO GHOST.
AND THIS NECKLACE SHE LEFT BEHIND WILL LEAD US RIGHT TO THE IMPOSTOR!

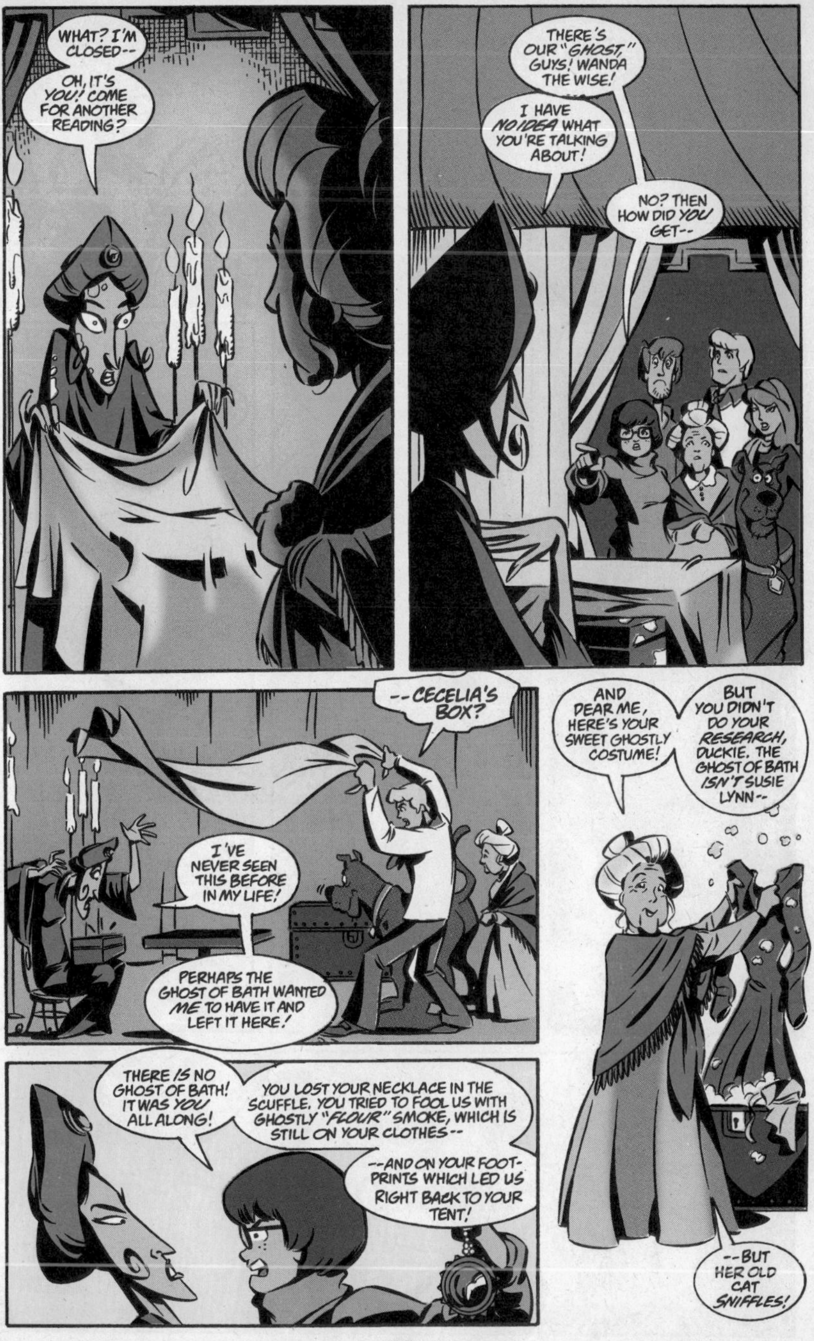
WHAT? I'M CLOSED--
OH, IT'S YOU! COME FOR ANOTHER READING?
THERE'S OUR "GHOST," GUYS! WANDA THE WISE!
I HAVE NO IDEA WHAT YOU'RE TALKING ABOUT!
NO? THEN HOW DID YOU GET--
--CECELIA'S BOX?
I'VE NEVER SEEN THIS BEFORE IN MY LIFE!
PERHAPS THE GHOST OF BATH WANTED ME TO HAVE IT AND LEFT IT HERE!
AND DEAR ME, HERE'S YOUR SWEET GHOSTLY COSTUME!
BUT YOU DIDN'T DO YOUR RESEARCH, DUCKIE. THE GHOST OF BATH ISN'T SUSIE LYNN--
--BUT HER OLD CAT SNIFFLES!
THERE IS NO GHOST OF BATH! IT WAS YOU ALL ALONG!
YOU LOST YOUR NECKLACE IN THE SCUFFLE. YOU TRIED TO FOOL US WITH GHOSTLY "FLOUR" SMOKE, WHICH IS STILL ON YOUR CLOTHES--
--AND ON YOUR FOOT-PRINTS WHICH LED US RIGHT BACK TO YOUR TENT!

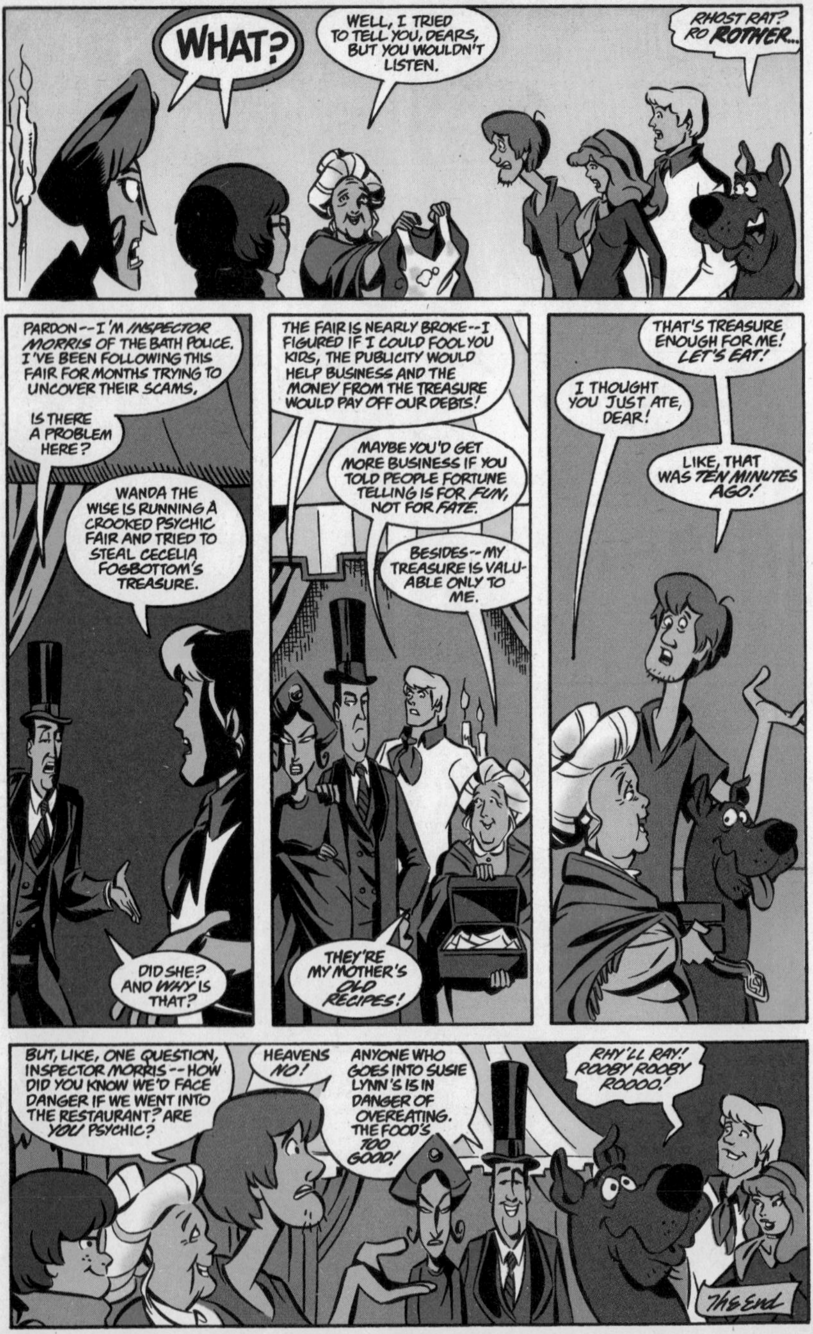
WHAT?
WELL, I TRIED TO TELL YOU, DEARS, BUT YOU WOULDN'T LISTEN.
RHOST RAT? RO ROTHER...
PARDON--I'M INSPECTOR MORRIS OF THE BATH POLICE. I'VE BEEN FOLLOWING THIS FAIR FOR MONTHS TRYING TO UNCOVER THEIR SCAMS.
IS THERE A PROBLEM HERE?
WANDA THE WISE IS RUNNING A CROOKED PSYCHIC FAIR AND TRIED TO STEAL CECELIA FOGBOTTOM'S TREASURE.
DID SHE? AND WHY IS THAT?
THE FAIR IS NEARLY BROKE--I FIGURED IF I COULD FOOL YOU KIDS, THE PUBLICITY WOULD HELP BUSINESS AND THE MONEY FROM THE TREASURE WOULD PAY OFF OUR DEBTS!
MAYBE YOU'D GET MORE BUSINESS IF YOU TOLD PEOPLE FORTUNE TELLING IS FOR FUN, NOT FOR FATE.
BESIDES--MY TREASURE IS VALU-ABLE ONLY TO ME.
THEY'RE MY MOTHER'S OLD RECIPES!
THAT'S TREASURE ENOUGH FOR ME! LET'S EAT!
I THOUGHT YOU JUST ATE, DEAR!
LIKE, THAT WAS TEN MINUTES AGO!
BUT, LIKE, ONE QUESTION, INSPECTOR MORRIS--HOW DID YOU KNOW WE'D FACE DANGER IF WE WENT INTO THE RESTAURANT? ARE YOU PSYCHIC?
HEAVENS NO!
ANYONE WHO GOES INTO SUSIE LYNN'S IS IN DANGER OF OVEREATING. THE FOOD'S TOO GOOD!
RHY'LL RAY! ROOBY ROOBY ROOOO!
The End

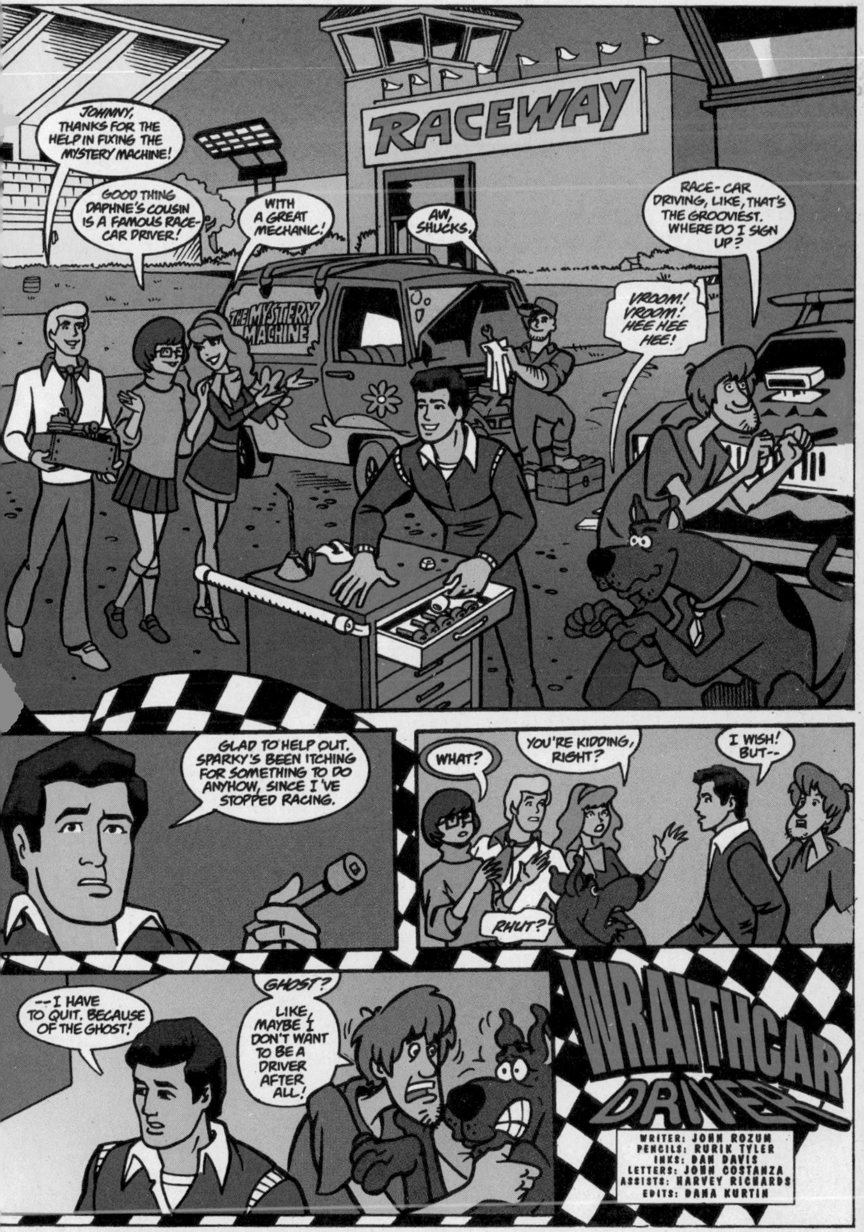
RACEWAY
JOHNNY, THANKS FOR THE HELP IN FIXING THE MYSTERY MACHINE!
GOOD THING DAPHNE'S COUSIN IS A FAMOUS RACE-CAR DRIVER!
WITH A GREAT MECHANIC!
AW, SHUCKS.
RACE-CAR DRIVING, LIKE, THAT'S THE GROOVIEST. WHERE DO I SIGN UP?
THE MYSTERY MACHINE
VROOM! VROOM! HEE HEE HEE!
GLAD TO HELP OUT. SPARKY'S BEEN ITCHING FOR SOMETHING TO DO ANYHOW, SINCE I'VE STOPPED RACING.
WHAT?
YOU'RE KIDDING, RIGHT?
I WISH! BUT--
RHUT?
--I HAVE TO QUIT. BECAUSE OF THE GHOST!
GHOST?
LIKE, MAYBE I DON'T WANT TO BE A DRIVER AFTER ALL!
WRAITHCAR DRIVER
WRITER: JOHN ROZUM
PENCILS: RURIK TYLER
INKS: DAN DAVIS
LETTERS: JOHN COSTANZA
ASSISTS: HARVEY RICHARDS
EDITS: DANA KURTIN

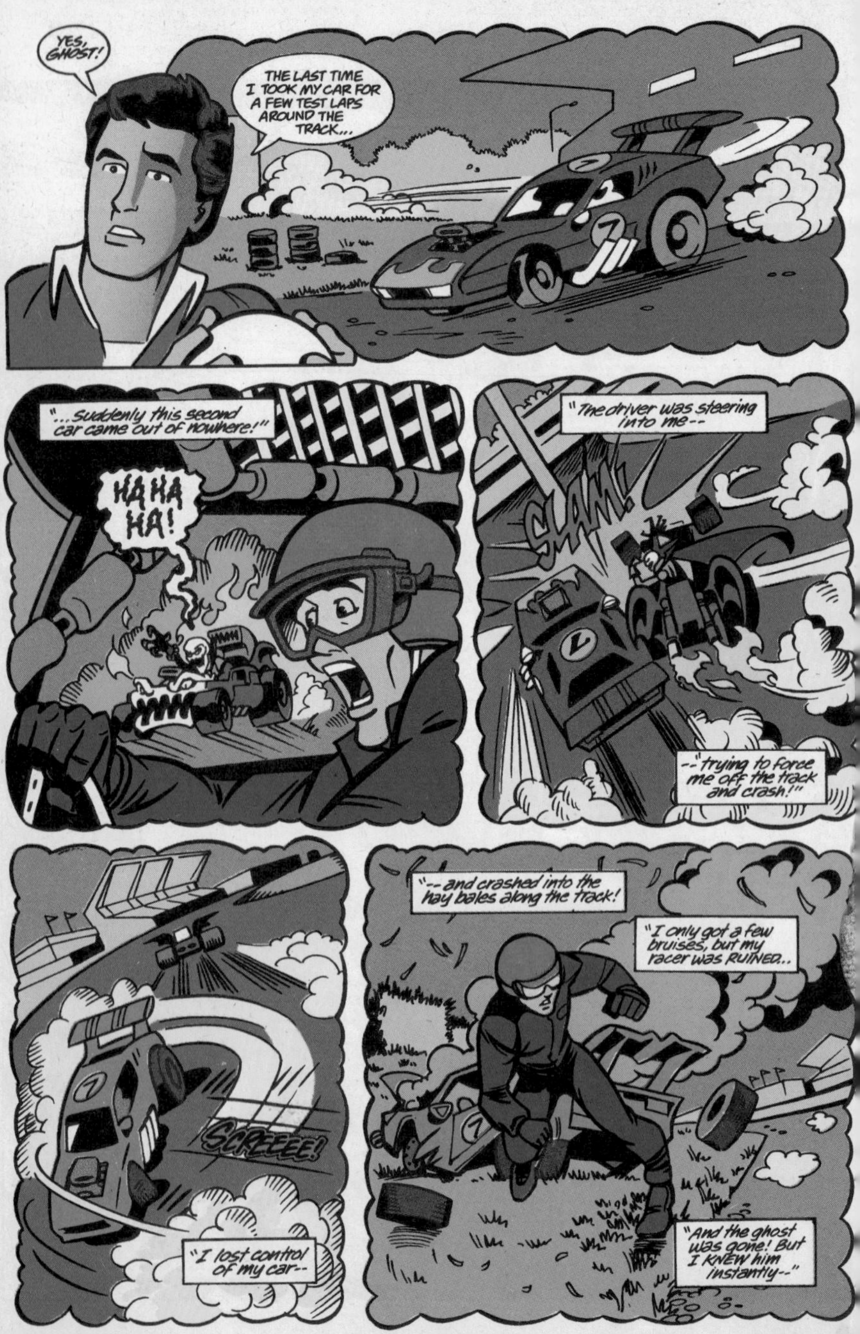
YES, GHOST!
THE LAST TIME I TOOK MY CAR FOR A FEW TEST LAPS AROUND THE TRACK...
"...Suddenly this second car came out of nowhere!"
HA HA HA!
"The driver was steering into me--
SLAM!
--"trying to force me off the track and crash!"
SCREEEEE!
"I lost control of my car--
"-- and crashed into the hay bales along the track!
"I only got a few bruises, but my racer was RUINED...
"And the ghost was gone! But I KNEW him instantly--"

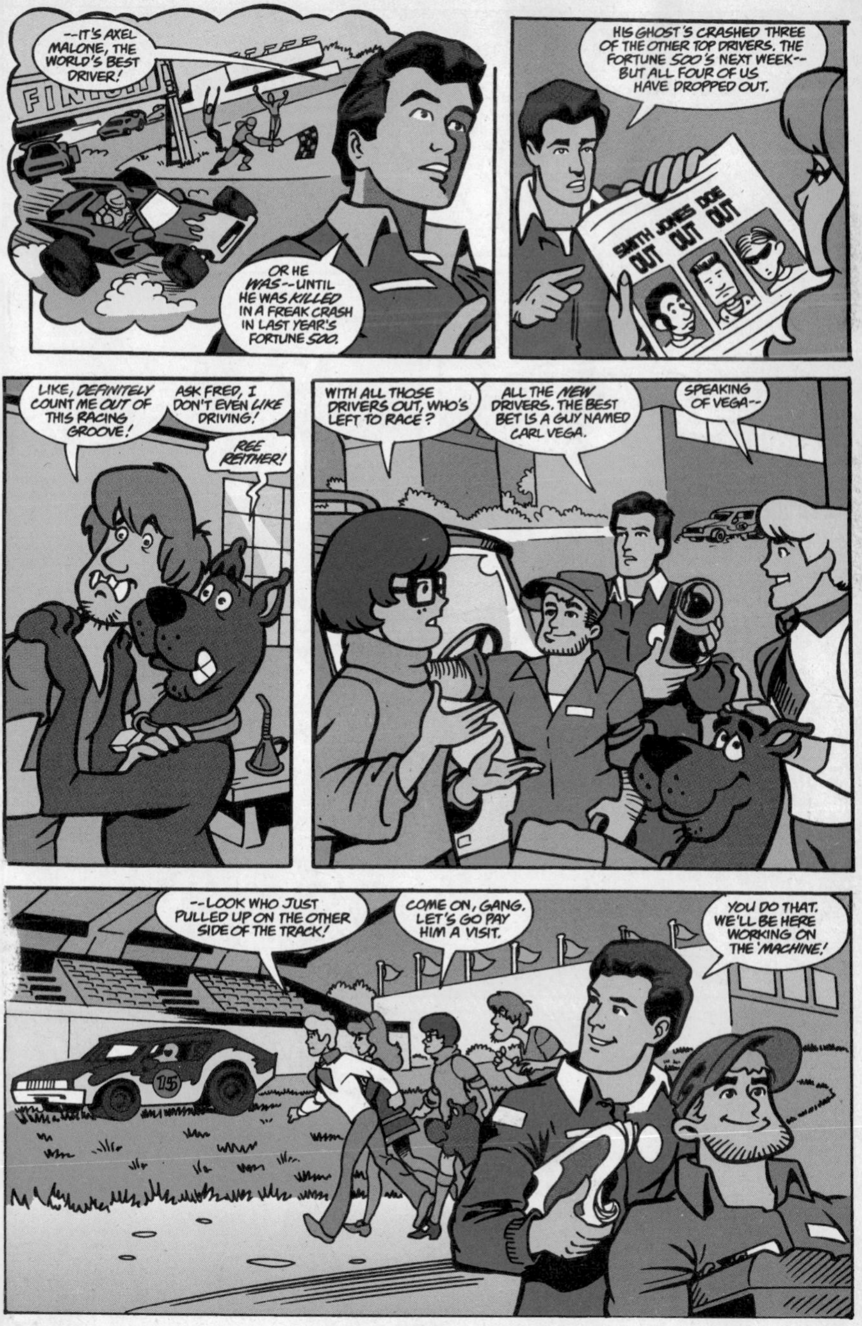
--IT'S AXEL MALONE, THE WORLD'S BEST DRIVER!
FINISH
OR HE WAS--UNTIL HE WAS KILLED IN A FREAK CRASH IN LAST YEAR'S FORTUNE 500.
HIS GHOST'S CRASHED THREE OF THE OTHER TOP DRIVERS. THE FORTUNE 500'S NEXT WEEK--BUT ALL FOUR OF US HAVE DROPPED OUT.
SMITH JONES DOE
OUT OUT OUT
LIKE, DEFINITELY COUNT ME OUT OF THIS RACING GROOVE!
ASK FRED, I DON'T EVEN LIKE DRIVING!
REE REITHER!
WITH ALL THOSE DRIVERS OUT, WHO'S LEFT TO RACE?
ALL THE NEW DRIVERS. THE BEST BET IS A GUY NAMED CARL VEGA.
SPEAKING OF VEGA--
--LOOK WHO JUST PULLED UP ON THE OTHER SIDE OF THE TRACK!
COME ON, GANG. LET'S GO PAY HIM A VISIT.
YOU DO THAT. WE'LL BE HERE WORKING ON THE 'MACHINE!
15

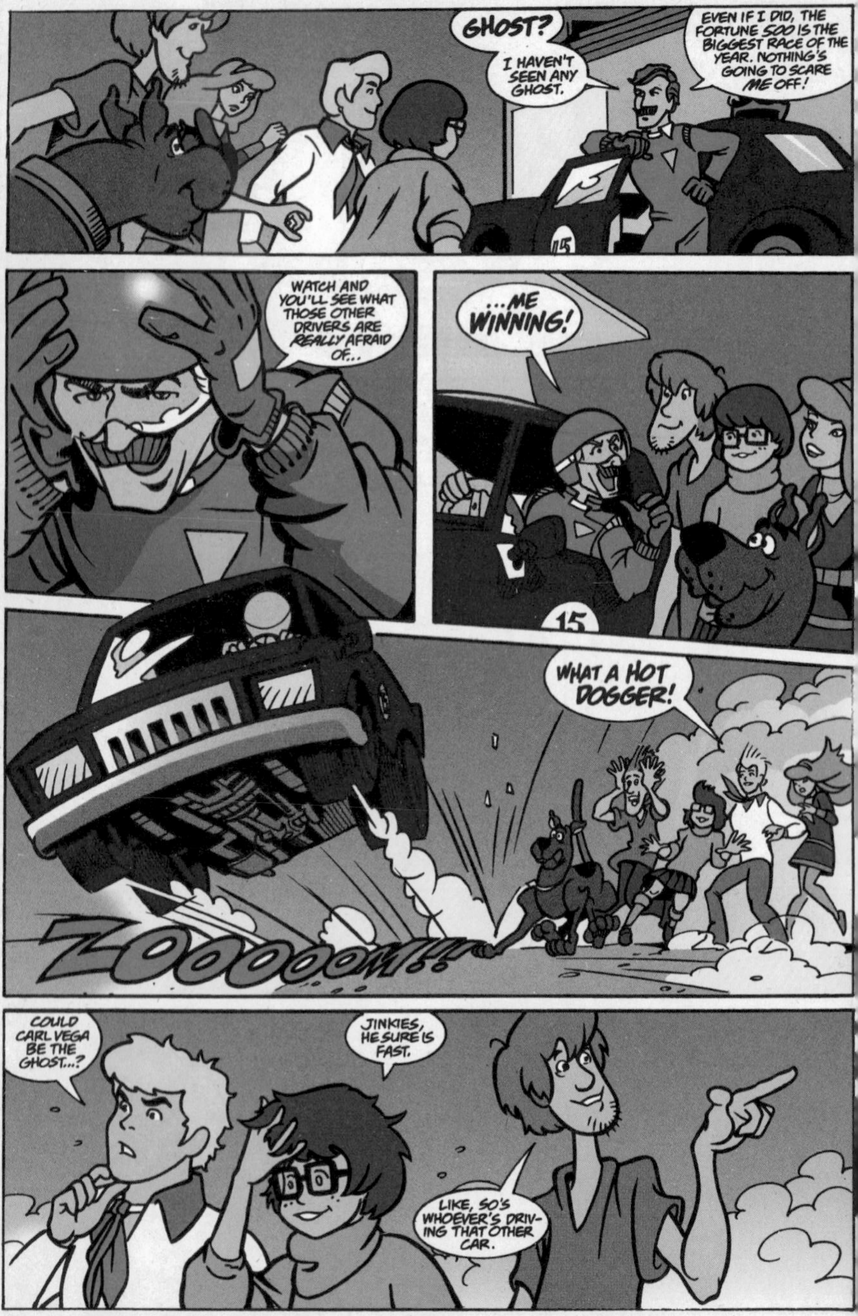
GHOST?
I HAVEN'T SEEN ANY GHOST.
EVEN IF I DID, THE FORTUNE 500 IS THE BIGGEST RACE OF THE YEAR. NOTHING'S GOING TO SCARE ME OFF!
WATCH AND YOU'LL SEE WHAT THOSE OTHER DRIVERS ARE REALLY AFRAID OF...
...ME WINNING!
15
WHAT A HOT DOGGER!
ZOOOOOOM!!!
COULD CARL VEGA BE THE GHOST...?
JINKIES, HE SURE IS FAST.
LIKE, SO'S WHOEVER'S DRIV-ING THAT OTHER CAR.

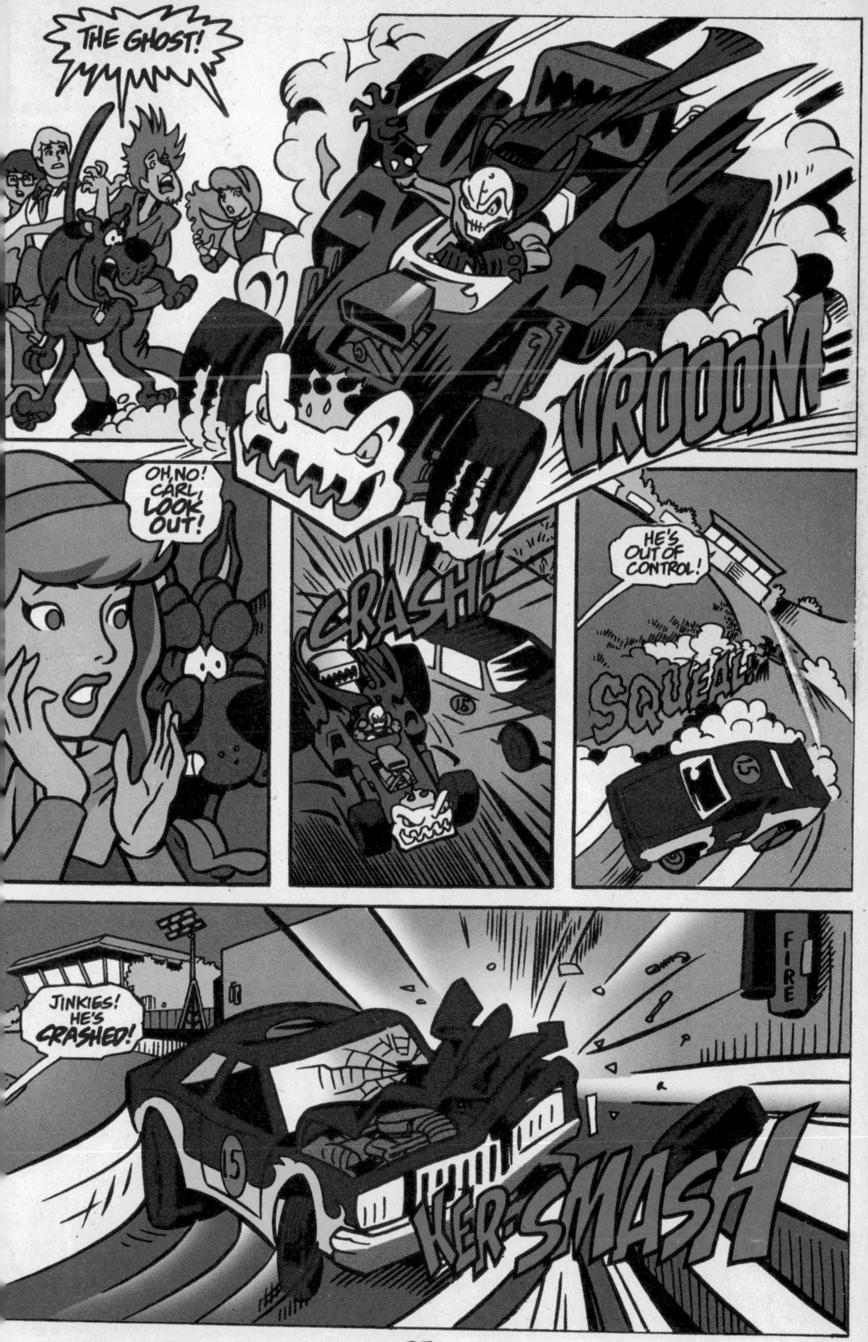
THE GHOST!
VROOOM
OH, NO! CARL, LOOK OUT!
CRASH!
HE'S OUT OF CONTROL!
SQUEAL!
FIRE
JINKIES! HE'S CRASHED!
KER-SMASH

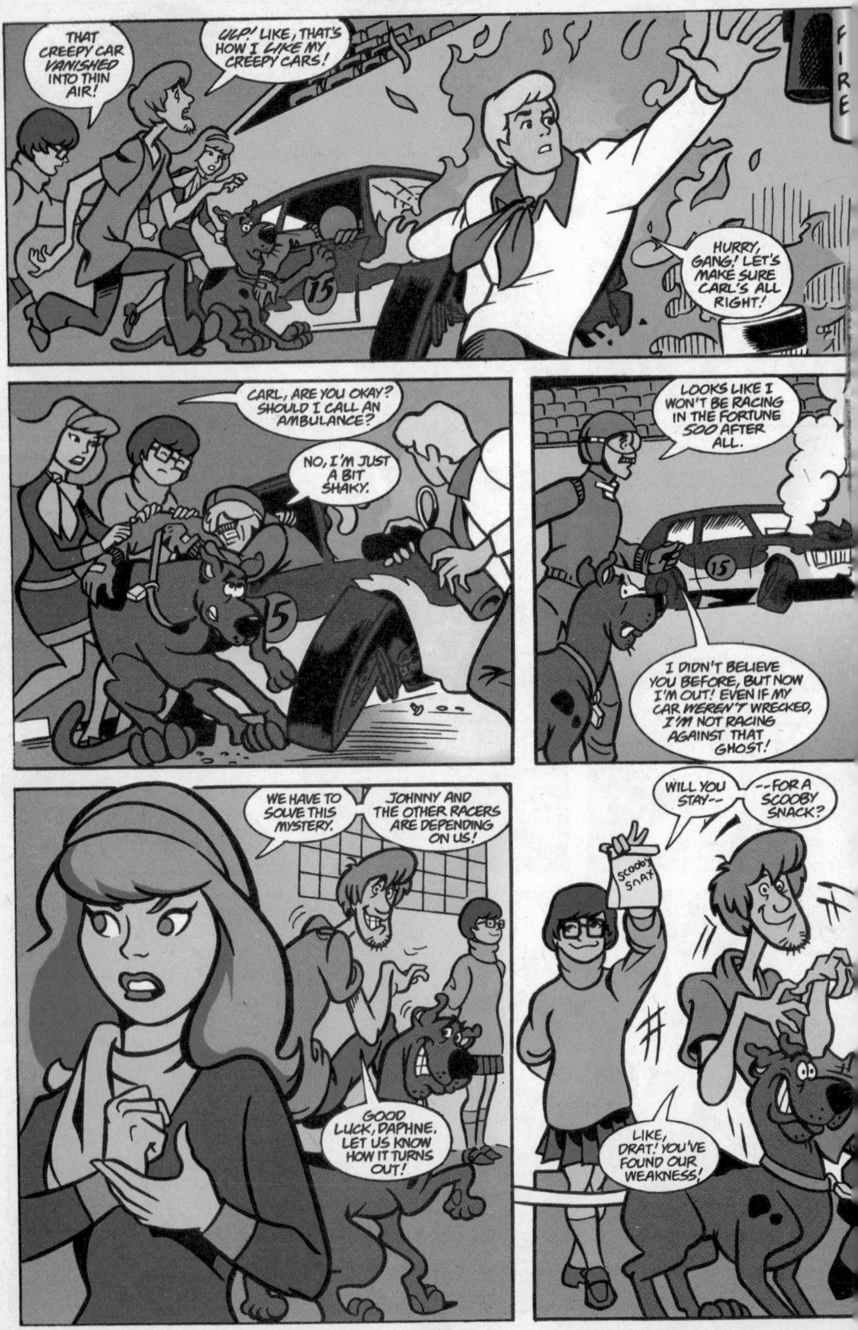
THAT CREEPY CAR VANISHED INTO THIN AIR!
ULP! LIKE, THAT'S HOW I LIKE MY CREEPY CARS!
FIRE
HURRY, GANG! LET'S MAKE SURE CARL'S ALL RIGHT!
CARL, ARE YOU OKAY? SHOULD I CALL AN AMBULANCE?
NO, I'M JUST A BIT SHAKY.
LOOKS LIKE I WON'T BE RACING IN THE FORTUNE 500 AFTER ALL.
I DIDN'T BELIEVE YOU BEFORE, BUT NOW I'M OUT! EVEN IF MY CAR WEREN'T WRECKED, I'M NOT RACING AGAINST THAT GHOST!
WE HAVE TO SOLVE THIS MYSTERY.
JOHNNY AND THE OTHER RACERS ARE DEPENDING ON US!
GOOD LUCK, DAPHNE. LET US KNOW HOW IT TURNS OUT!
WILL YOU STAY--
--FOR A SCOOBY SNACK?
Scooby Snax
LIKE, DRAT! YOU'VE FOUND OUR WEAKNESS!

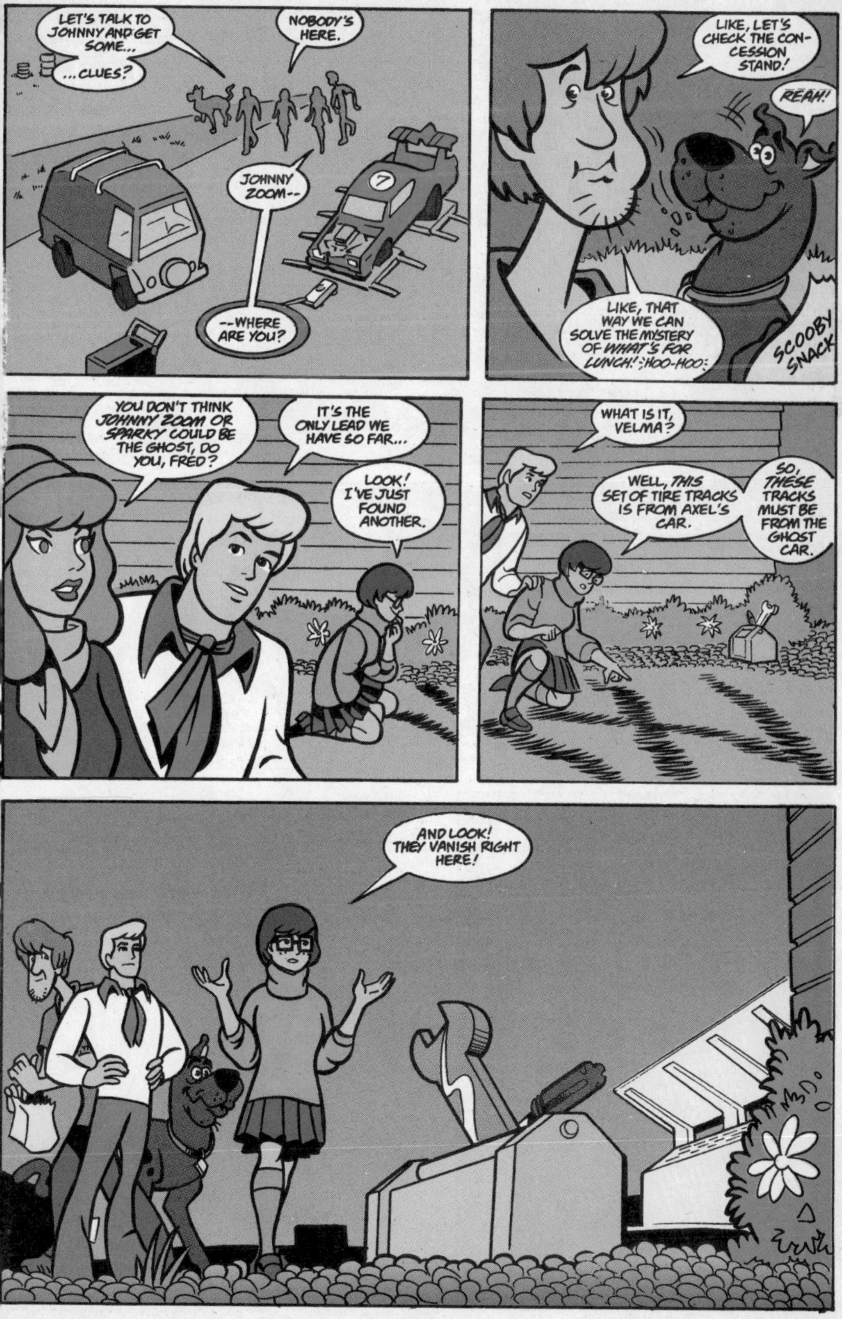
LET'S TALK TO JOHNNY AND GET SOME...
NOBODY'S HERE.
...CLUES?
JOHNNY ZOOM--
--WHERE ARE YOU?
LIKE, LET'S CHECK THE CON-CESSION STAND!
REAH!
LIKE, THAT WAY WE CAN SOLVE THE MYSTERY OF WHAT'S FOR LUNCH! HOO-HOO
SCOOBY SNACK
YOU DON'T THINK JOHNNY ZOOM OR SPARKY COULD BE THE GHOST, DO YOU, FRED?
IT'S THE ONLY LEAD WE HAVE SO FAR...
LOOK! I'VE JUST FOUND ANOTHER.
WHAT IS IT, VELMA?
WELL, THIS SET OF TIRE TRACKS IS FROM AXEL'S CAR.
SO, THESE TRACKS MUST BE FROM THE GHOST CAR.
AND LOOK! THEY VANISH RIGHT HERE!

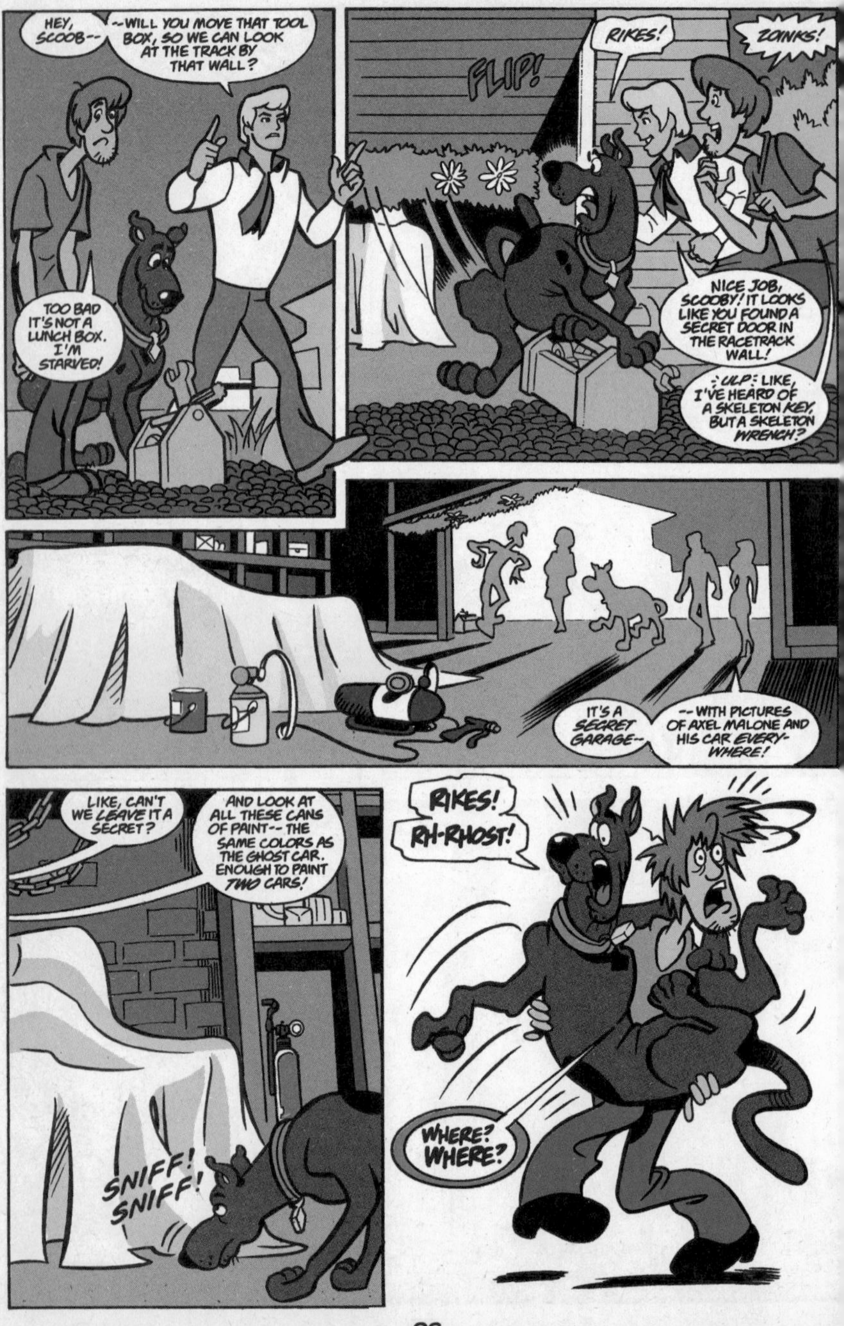
HEY, SCOOB--
--WILL YOU MOVE THAT TOOL BOX, SO WE CAN LOOK AT THE TRACK BY THAT WALL?
TOO BAD IT'S NOT A LUNCH BOX. I'M STARVED!
FLIP!
RIKES!
ZOINKS!
NICE JOB, SCOOBY! IT LOOKS LIKE YOU FOUND A SECRET DOOR IN THE RACETRACK WALL!
:ULP: LIKE, I'VE HEARD OF A SKELETON KEY, BUT A SKELETON WRENCH?
IT'S A SECRET GARAGE--
--WITH PICTURES OF AXEL MALONE AND HIS CAR EVERYWHERE!
LIKE, CAN'T WE LEAVE IT A SECRET?
AND LOOK AT ALL THESE CANS OF PAINT-- THE SAME COLORS AS THE GHOST CAR. ENOUGH TO PAINT TWO CARS!
SNIFF! SNIFF!
RIKES! RH-RHOST!
WHERE? WHERE?

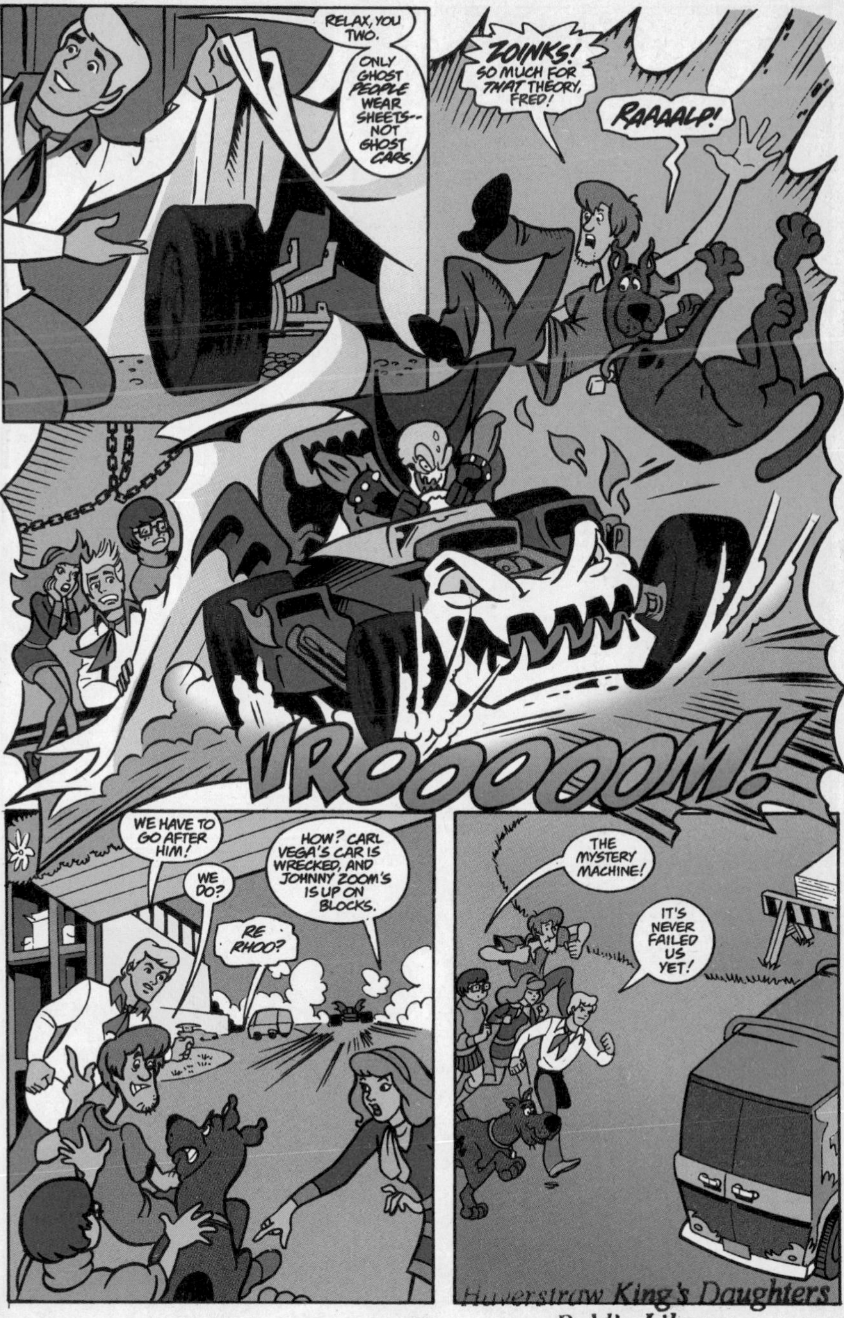
RELAX, YOU TWO.
ONLY GHOST PEOPLE WEAR SHEETS-- NOT GHOST CARS.
ZOINKS! SO MUCH FOR THAT THEORY, FRED!
RAAAALP!
VROOOOOOM!
WE HAVE TO GO AFTER HIM!
WE DO?
HOW? CARL VEGA'S CAR IS WRECKED, AND JOHNNY ZOOM'S IS UP ON BLOCKS.
RE RHOO?
THE MYSTERY MACHINE!
IT'S NEVER FAILED US YET!

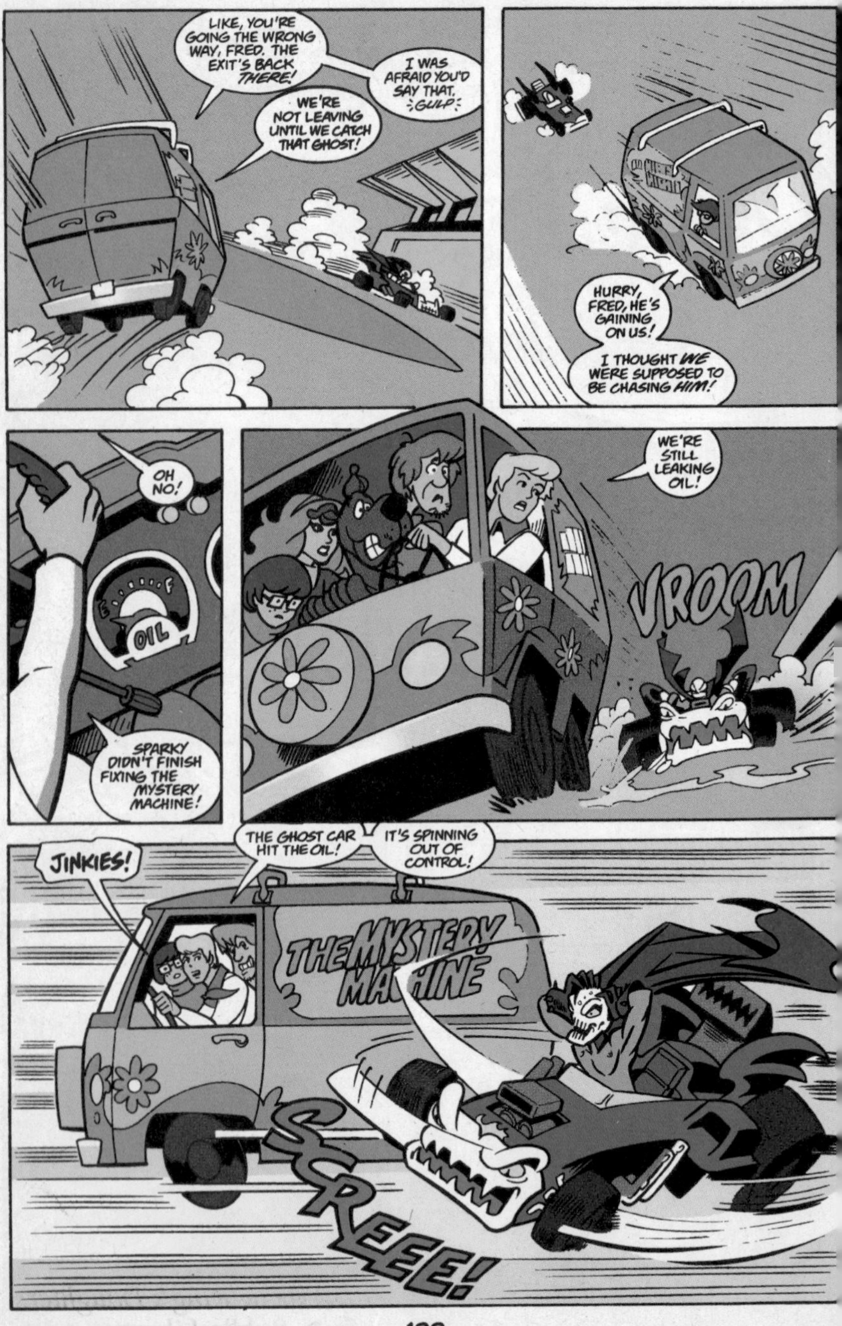

LIKE, YOU'RE GOING THE WRONG WAY, FRED. THE EXIT'S BACK THERE!
WE'RE NOT LEAVING UNTIL WE CATCH THAT GHOST!
I WAS AFRAID YOU'D SAY THAT. GULP
HURRY, FRED, HE'S GAINING ON US!
I THOUGHT WE WERE SUPPOSED TO BE CHASING HIM!
OH NO!
E F
OIL
SPARKY DIDN'T FINISH FIXING THE MYSTERY MACHINE!
WE'RE STILL LEAKING OIL!
VROOM
JINKIES!
THE GHOST CAR HIT THE OIL!
IT'S SPINNING OUT OF CONTROL!
THE MYSTERY MACHINE
SCREEE!

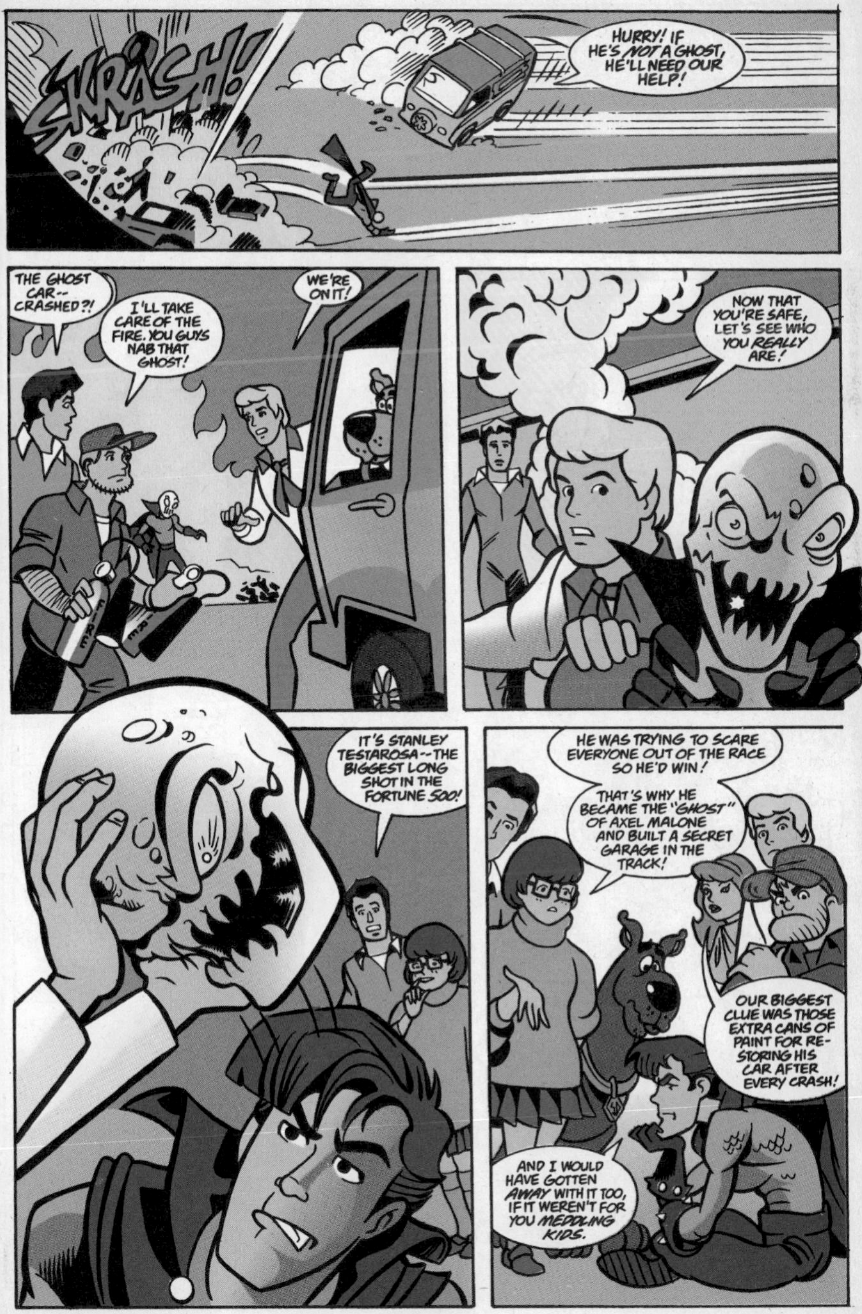
SKRASH!
HURRY! IF HE'S NOT A GHOST, HE'LL NEED OUR HELP!
THE GHOST CAR-- CRASHED?!
I'LL TAKE CARE OF THE FIRE. YOU GUYS NAB THAT GHOST!
WE'RE ON IT!
NOW THAT YOU'RE SAFE, LET'S SEE WHO YOU REALLY ARE!
IT'S STANLEY TESTAROSA--THE BIGGEST LONG SHOT IN THE FORTUNE 500!
HE WAS TRYING TO SCARE EVERYONE OUT OF THE RACE SO HE'D WIN!
THAT'S WHY HE BECAME THE "GHOST" OF AXEL MALONE AND BUILT A SECRET GARAGE IN THE TRACK!
OUR BIGGEST CLUE WAS THOSE EXTRA CANS OF PAINT FOR RE-STORING HIS CAR AFTER EVERY CRASH!
AND I WOULD HAVE GOTTEN AWAY WITH IT TOO, IF IT WEREN'T FOR YOU MEDDLING KIDS.

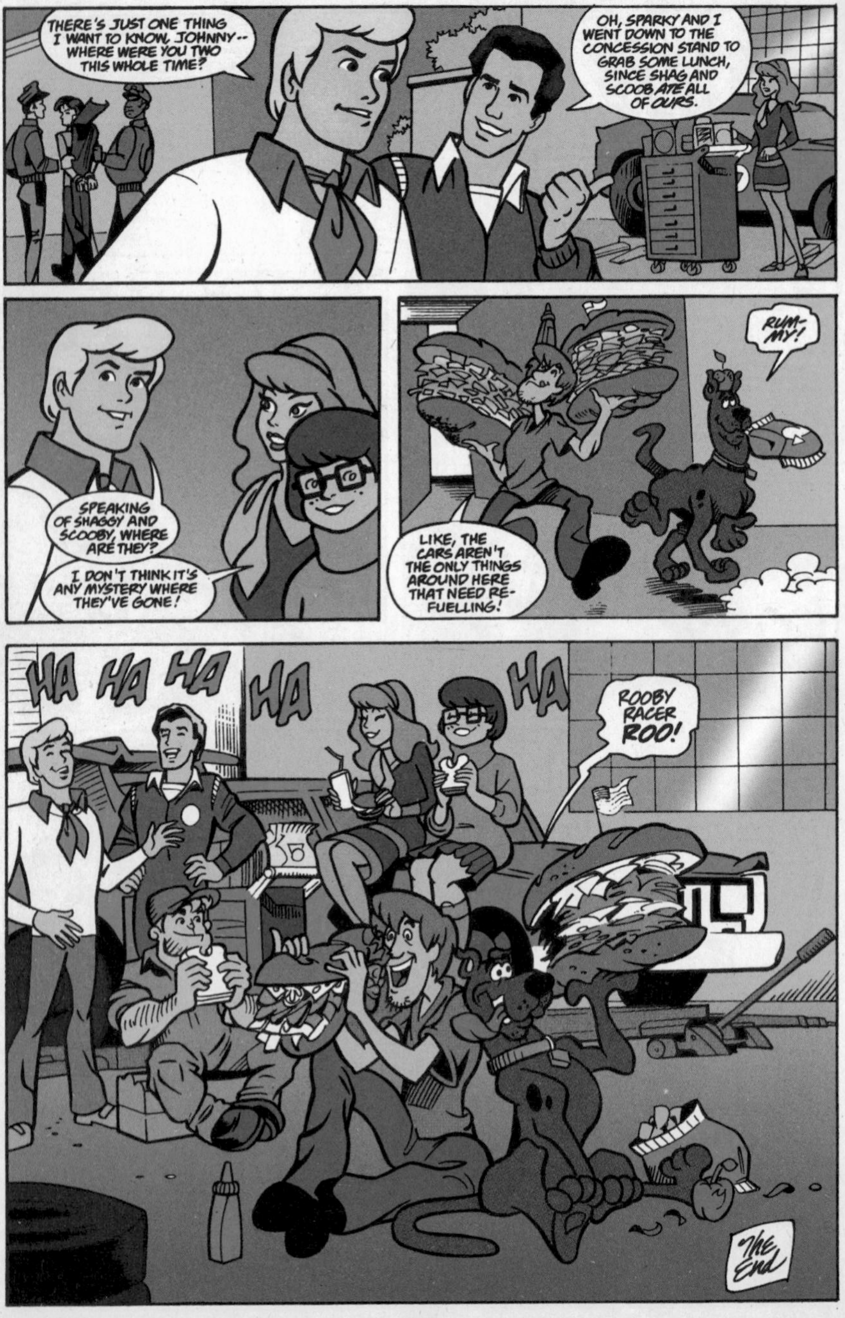
THERE'S JUST ONE THING I WANT TO KNOW, JOHNNY-- WHERE WERE YOU TWO THIS WHOLE TIME?
OH, SPARKY AND I WENT DOWN TO THE CONCESSION STAND TO GRAB SOME LUNCH, SINCE SHAG AND SCOOB ATE ALL OF OURS.
SPEAKING OF SHAGGY AND SCOOBY, WHERE ARE THEY?
I DON'T THINK IT'S ANY MYSTERY WHERE THEY'VE GONE!
RUM-MY!
LIKE, THE CARS AREN'T THE ONLY THINGS AROUND HERE THAT NEED RE-FUELLING!
HA HA HA HA HA
ROOBY RACER ROO!
The End

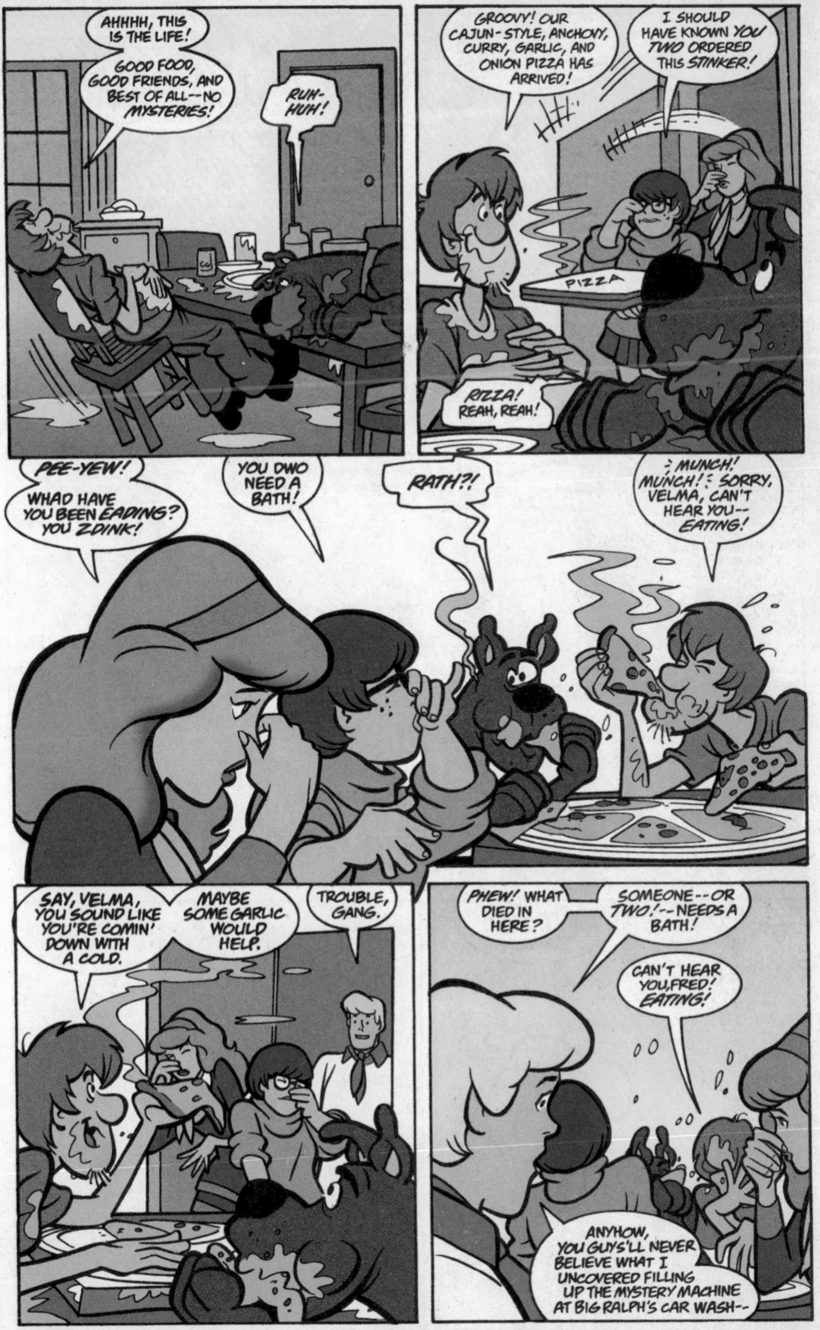
AHHHH, THIS IS THE LIFE!
GOOD FOOD, GOOD FRIENDS, AND BEST OF ALL--NO MYSTERIES!
RUH-HUH!
GROOVY! OUR CAJUN-STYLE, ANCHOVY, CURRY, GARLIC, AND ONION PIZZA HAS ARRIVED!
I SHOULD HAVE KNOWN YOU TWO ORDERED THIS STINKER!
PIZZA
RIZZA! REAH, REAH!
PEE-YEW!
WHAD HAVE YOU BEEN EADING? YOU ZDINK!
YOU DWO NEED A BATH!
RATH?!
MUNCH! MUNCH! SORRY, VELMA, CAN'T HEAR YOU--EATING!
SAY, VELMA, YOU SOUND LIKE YOU'RE COMIN' DOWN WITH A COLD.
MAYBE SOME GARLIC WOULD HELP.
TROUBLE, GANG.
PHEW! WHAT DIED IN HERE?
SOMEONE--OR TWO!--NEEDS A BATH!
CAN'T HEAR YOU, FRED! EATING!
ANYHOW, YOU GUYS'LL NEVER BELIEVE WHAT I UNCOVERED FILLING UP THE MYSTERY MACHINE AT BIG RALPH'S CAR WASH--

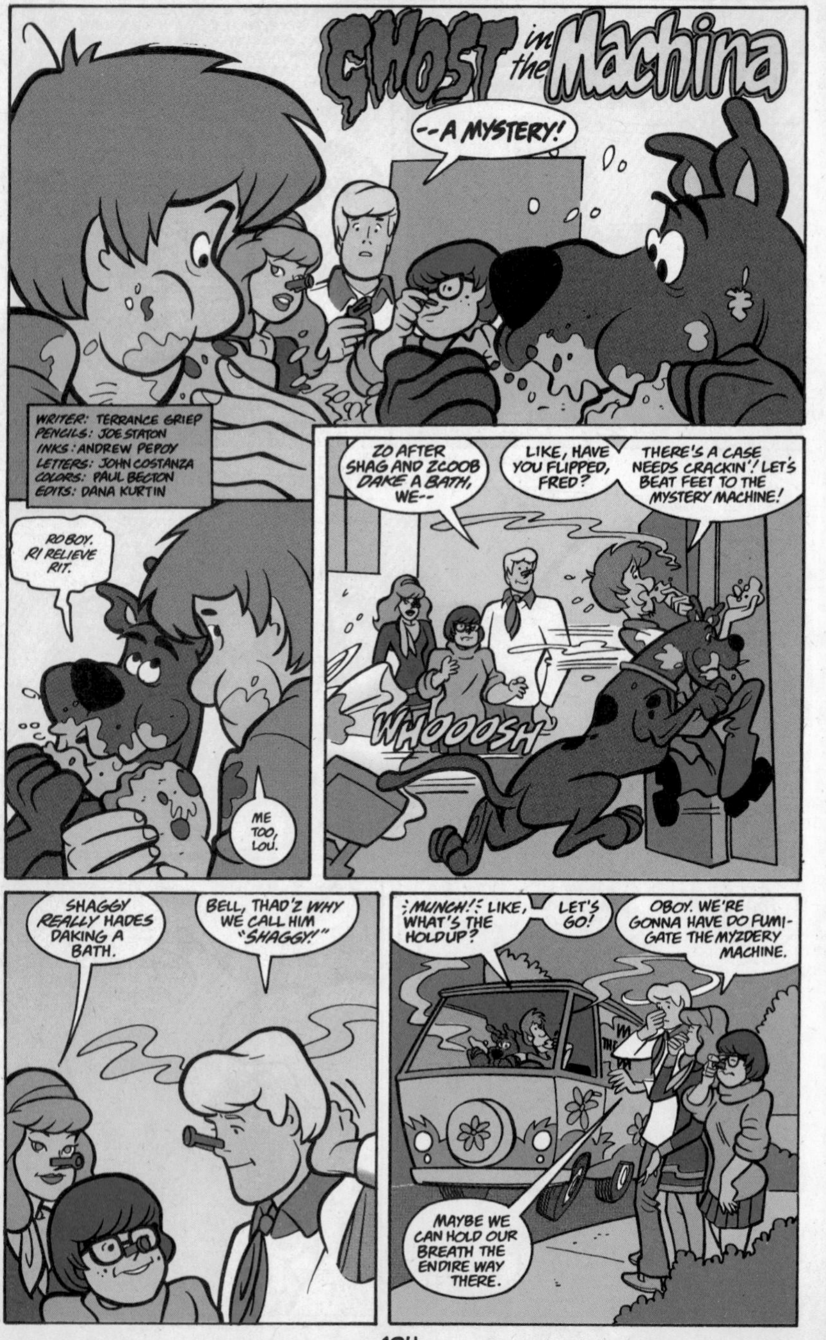
GHOST in the Machina
--A MYSTERY!
WRITER: TERRANCE GRIEP
PENCILS: JOE STATON
INKS: ANDREW PEPOY
LETTERS: JOHN COSTANZA
COLORS: PAUL BECTON
EDITS: DANA KURTIN
RO BOY. RI RELIEVE RIT.
ME TOO, LOU.
ZO AFTER SHAG AND ZCOOB DAKE A BATH, WE--
LIKE, HAVE YOU FLIPPED, FRED?
THERE'S A CASE NEEDS CRACKIN'! LET'S BEAT FEET TO THE MYSTERY MACHINE!
WHOOOSH
SHAGGY REALLY HADES DAKING A BATH.
BELL, THAD'Z WHY WE CALL HIM "SHAGGY!"
;MUNCH!; LIKE, WHAT'S THE HOLDUP?
LET'S GO!
OBOY. WE'RE GONNA HAVE DO FUMI-GATE THE MYZDERY MACHINE.
MAYBE WE CAN HOLD OUR BREATH THE ENDIRE WAY THERE.

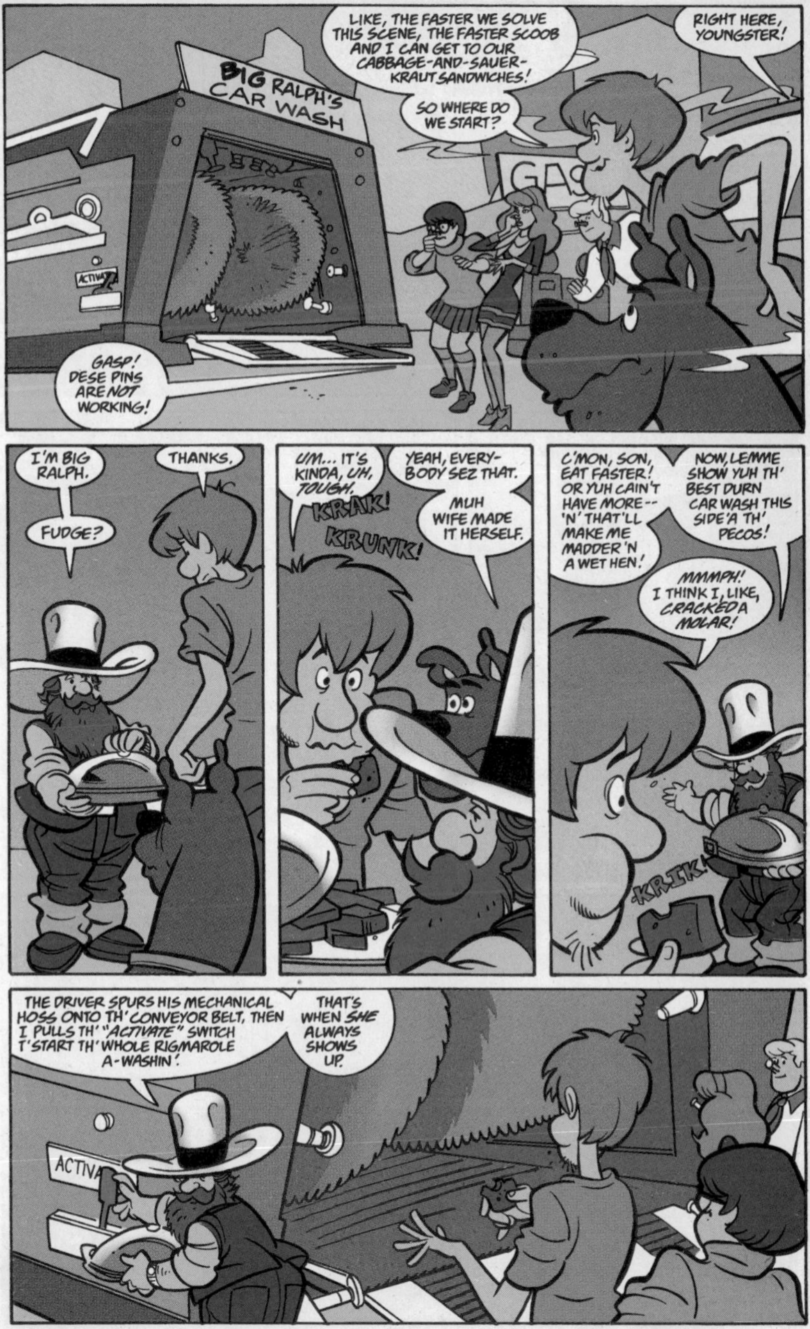
BIG RALPH'S CAR WASH
LIKE, THE FASTER WE SOLVE THIS SCENE, THE FASTER SCOOB AND I CAN GET TO OUR CABBAGE-AND-SAUER-KRAUT SANDWICHES!
SO WHERE DO WE START?
RIGHT HERE, YOUNGSTER!
GASP! DESE PINS ARE *NOT* WORKING!
I'M BIG RALPH.
FUDGE?
THANKS.
UM... IT'S KINDA, *UH*, *TOUGH*.
KRAK!
KRUNK!
YEAH, EVERY-BODY SEZ THAT.
MUH WIFE MADE IT HERSELF.
C'MON, SON, EAT FASTER! OR YUH CAIN'T HAVE MORE-- 'N' THAT'LL MAKE ME MADDER 'N A WET HEN!
NOW, LEMME SHOW YUH TH' BEST DURN CAR WASH THIS SIDE'A TH' PECOS!
MMMPH! I THINK I, LIKE, *CRACKED A MOLAR!*
KRIK!
THE DRIVER SPURS HIS MECHANICAL HOSS ONTO TH' CONVEYOR BELT, THEN I PULLS TH' "*ACTIVATE*" SWITCH T'START TH' WHOLE RIGMAROLE A-WASHIN'.
THAT'S WHEN *SHE* ALWAYS SHOWS UP.
ACTIVA

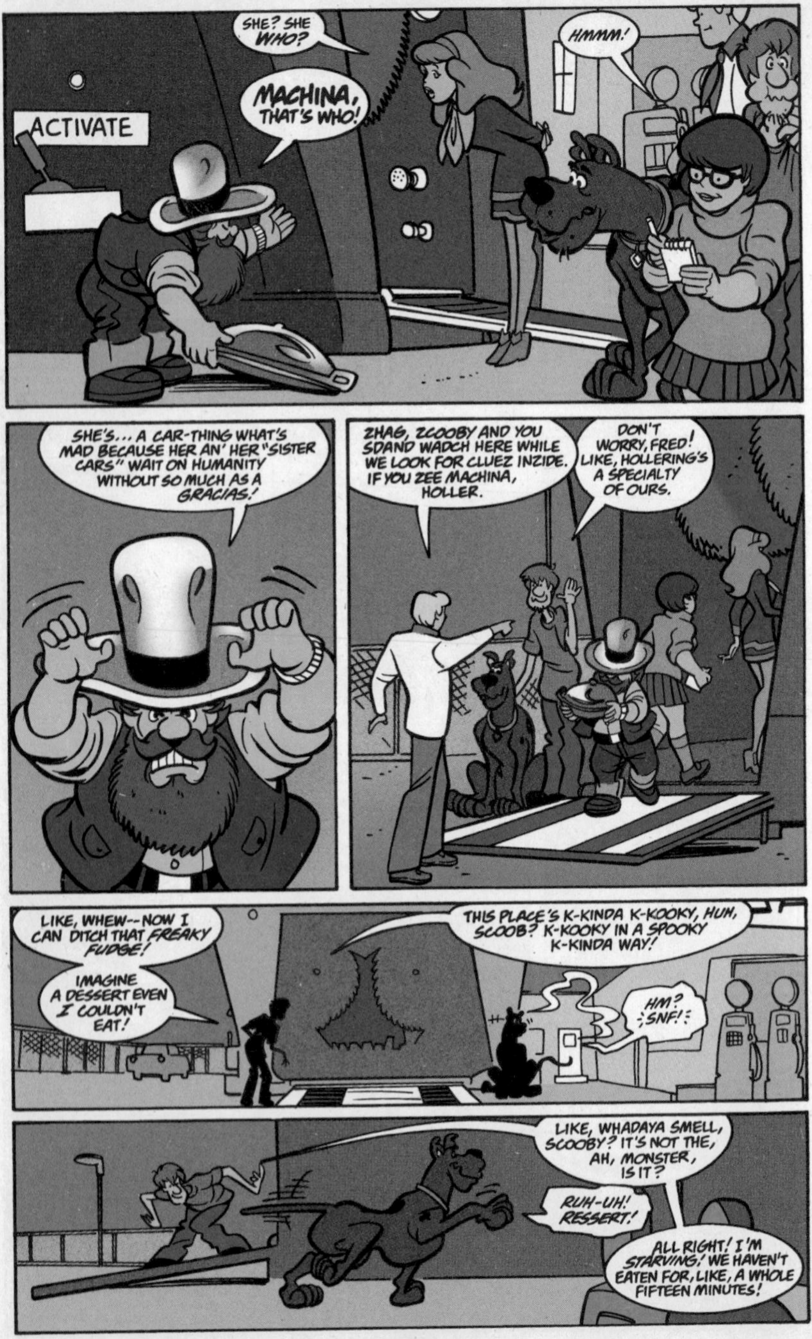
SHE? SHE WHO?
MACHINA, THAT'S WHO!
HMMM!
ACTIVATE
SHE'S... A CAR-THING WHAT'S MAD BECAUSE HER AN' HER "SISTER CARS" WAIT ON HUMANITY WITHOUT SO MUCH AS A GRACIAS!
ZHAG, ZCOOBY AND YOU SDAND WADCH HERE WHILE WE LOOK FOR CLUEZ INZIDE. IF YOU ZEE MACHINA, HOLLER.
DON'T WORRY, FRED! LIKE, HOLLERING'S A SPECIALTY OF OURS.
LIKE, WHEW--NOW I CAN DITCH THAT FREAKY FUDGE!
IMAGINE A DESSERT EVEN I COULDN'T EAT!
THIS PLACE'S K-KINDA K-KOOKY, HUH, SCOOB? K-KOOKY IN A SPOOKY K-KINDA WAY!
HM? SNF!
LIKE, WHADAYA SMELL, SCOOBY? IT'S NOT THE, AH, MONSTER, IS IT?
RUH-UH! RESSERT!
ALL RIGHT! I'M STARVING! WE HAVEN'T EATEN FOR, LIKE, A WHOLE FIFTEEN MINUTES!

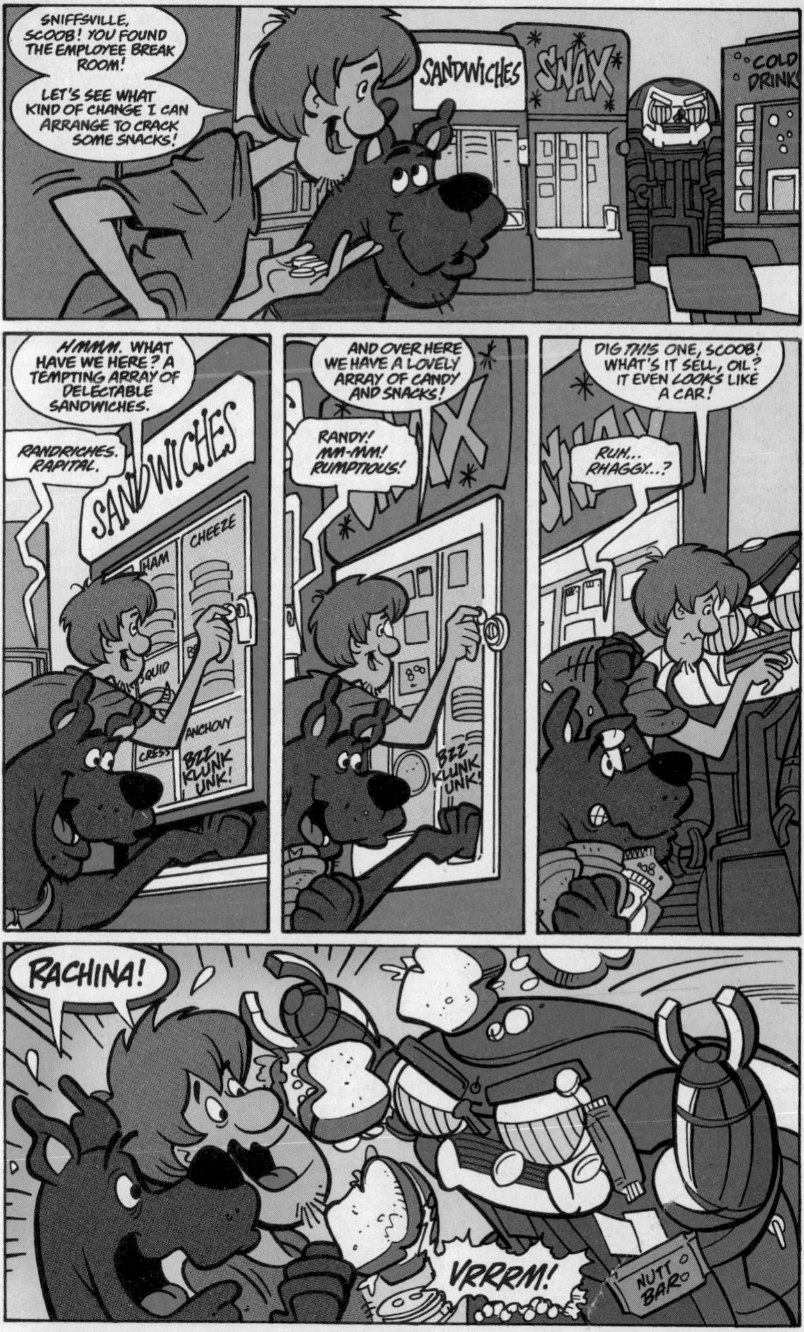
SNIFFSVILLE, SCOOB! YOU FOUND THE EMPLOYEE BREAK ROOM!
LET'S SEE WHAT KIND OF CHANGE I CAN ARRANGE TO CRACK SOME SNACKS!
SANDWICHES
SNAX
COLD DRINKS
HMMM. WHAT HAVE WE HERE? A TEMPTING ARRAY OF DELECTABLE SANDWICHES.
RANDRICHES. RAPITAL.
SANDWICHES
HAM
CHEEZE
SQUID
ANCHOVY
CRESS
BZZ KLUNK UNK!
AND OVER HERE WE HAVE A LOVELY ARRAY OF CANDY AND SNACKS!
RANDY! MM-MM! RUMPTIOUS!
BZZ KLUNK UNK!
DIG THIS ONE, SCOOB! WHAT'S IT SELL, OIL? IT EVEN LOOKS LIKE A CAR!
RUH... RHAGGY...?
RACHINA!
VRRRM!
NUTT BAR

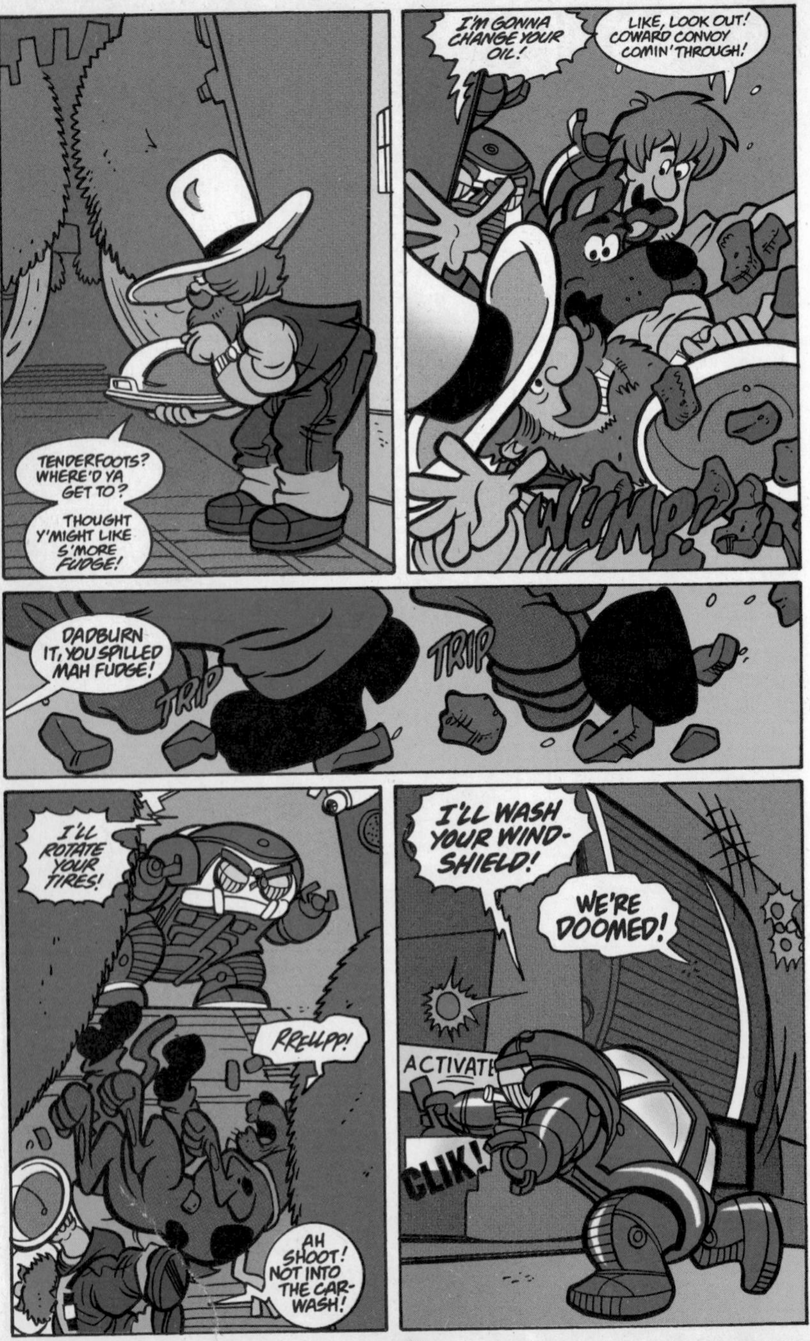

TENDERFOOTS? WHERE'D YA GET TO?
THOUGHT Y'MIGHT LIKE S'MORE FUDGE!
I'M GONNA CHANGE YOUR OIL!
LIKE, LOOK OUT! COWARD CONVOY COMIN' THROUGH!
WUMP!
DADBURN IT, YOU SPILLED MAH FUDGE!
TRIP
TRIP
I'LL ROTATE YOUR TIRES!
RRELLPP!
AH SHOOT! NOT INTO THE CAR-WASH!
I'LL WASH YOUR WIND-SHIELD!
WE'RE DOOMED!
ACTIVATE
CLIK!

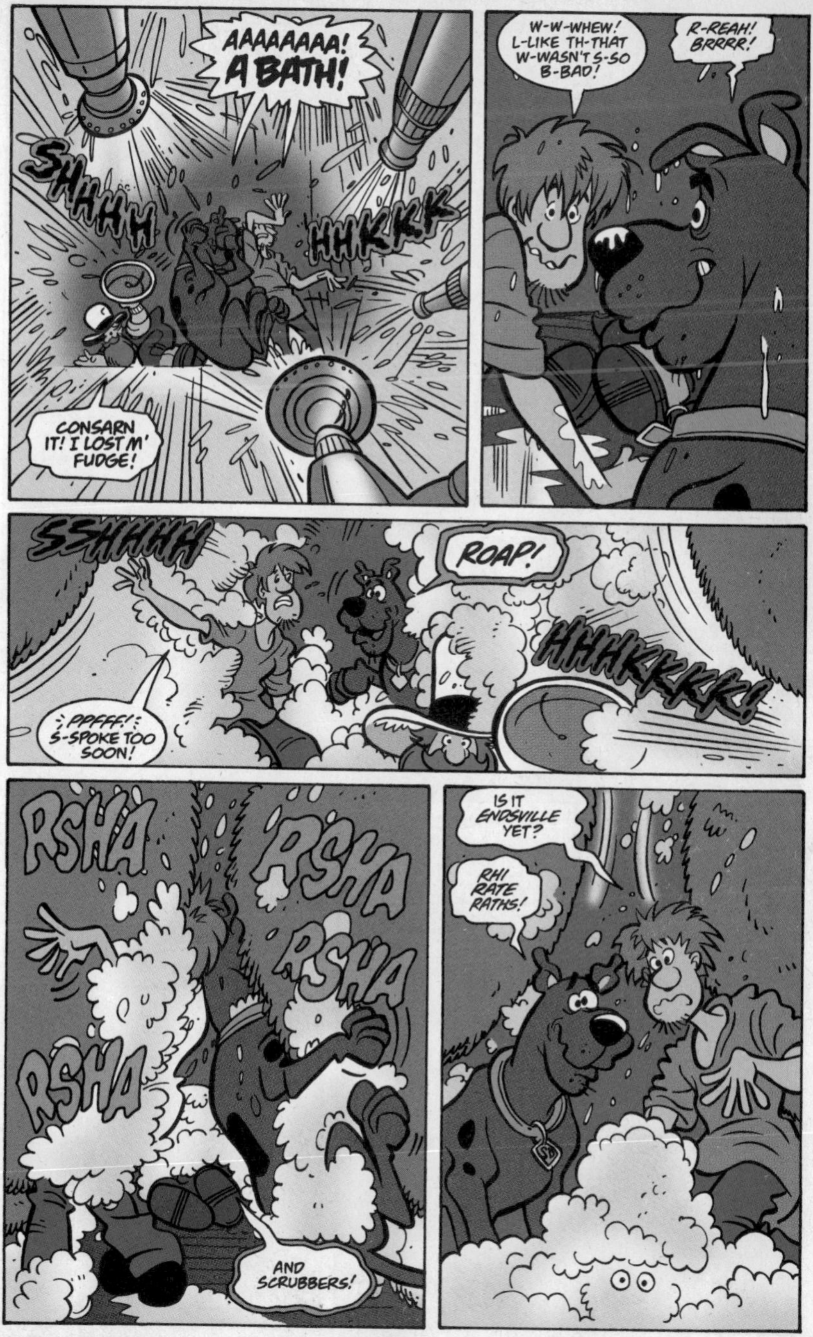
AAAAAAAA! A BATH!
SHHHHH
HHKKK
CONSARN IT! I LOST M' FUDGE!
W-W-WHEW! L-LIKE TH-THAT W-WASN'T S-SO B-BAD!
R-REAH! BRRRR!
SSHHHH
ROAP!
HHHKKKK!
PPFFF! S-SPOKE TOO SOON!
RSHA
RSHA
RSHA
RSHA
AND SCRUBBERS!
IS IT ENDSVILLE YET?
RHI RATE RATHS!

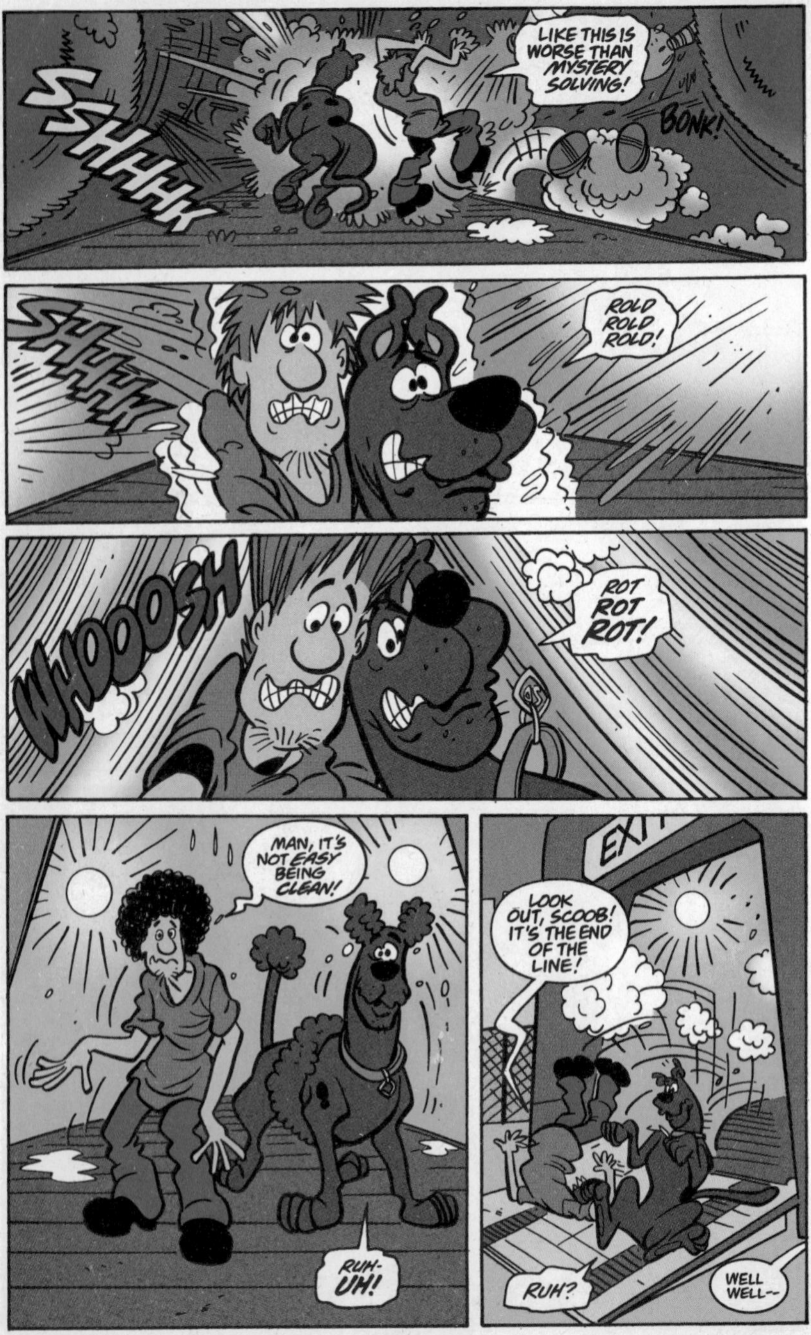
SSHHHKK
LIKE THIS IS WORSE THAN MYSTERY SOLVING!
BONK!
SHHHK
ROLD ROLD ROLD!
WHOOOSH
ROT ROT ROT!
MAN, IT'S NOT EASY BEING CLEAN!
RUH-UH!
EXI
LOOK OUT, SCOOB! IT'S THE END OF THE LINE!
RUH?
WELL WELL--

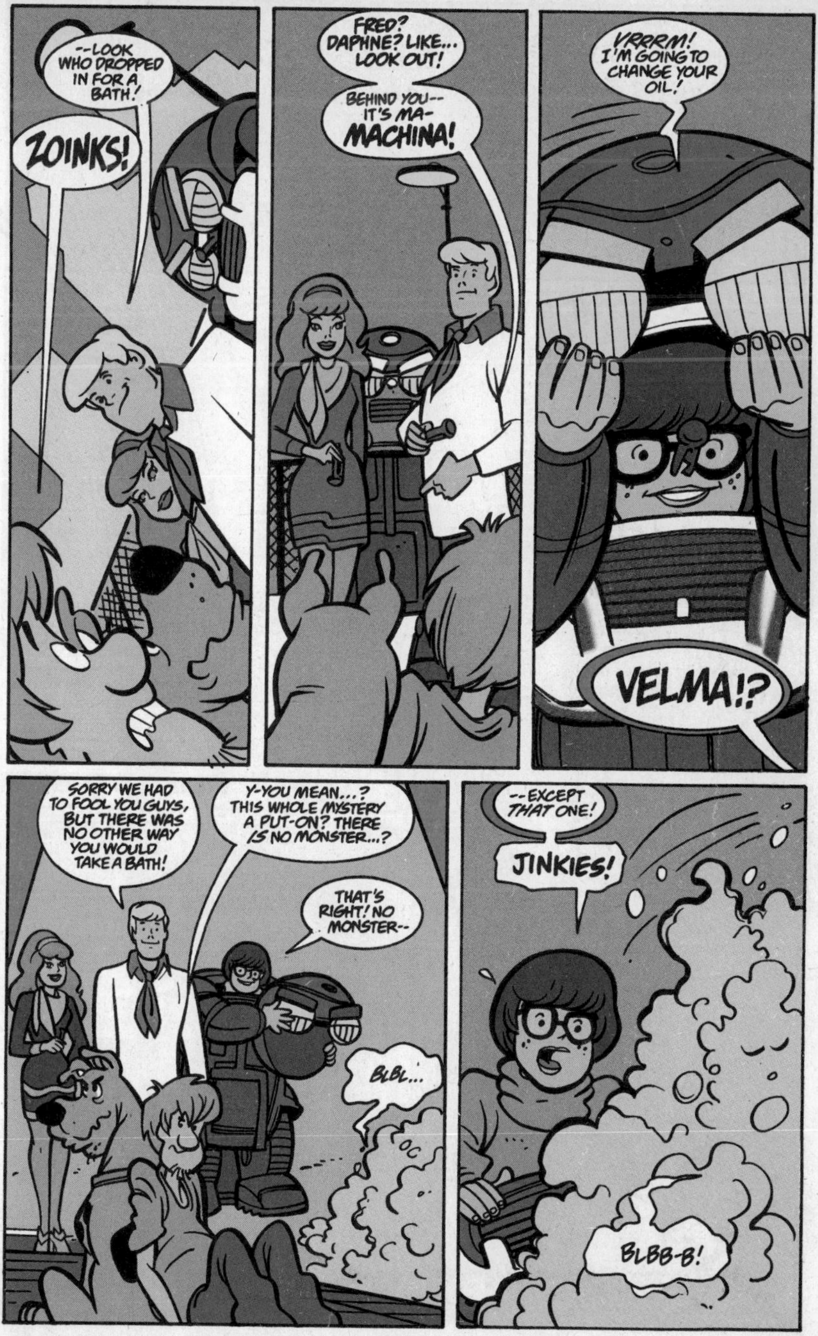
--LOOK WHO DROPPED IN FOR A BATH!
ZOINKS!
FRED? DAPHNE? LIKE... LOOK OUT!
BEHIND YOU-- IT'S MA-MACHINA!
VRRRM! I'M GOING TO CHANGE YOUR OIL!
VELMA!?
SORRY WE HAD TO FOOL YOU GUYS, BUT THERE WAS NO OTHER WAY YOU WOULD TAKE A BATH!
Y-YOU MEAN...? THIS WHOLE MYSTERY A PUT-ON? THERE IS NO MONSTER...?
THAT'S RIGHT! NO MONSTER--
BLBL...
--EXCEPT THAT ONE!
JINKIES!
BLBB-B!

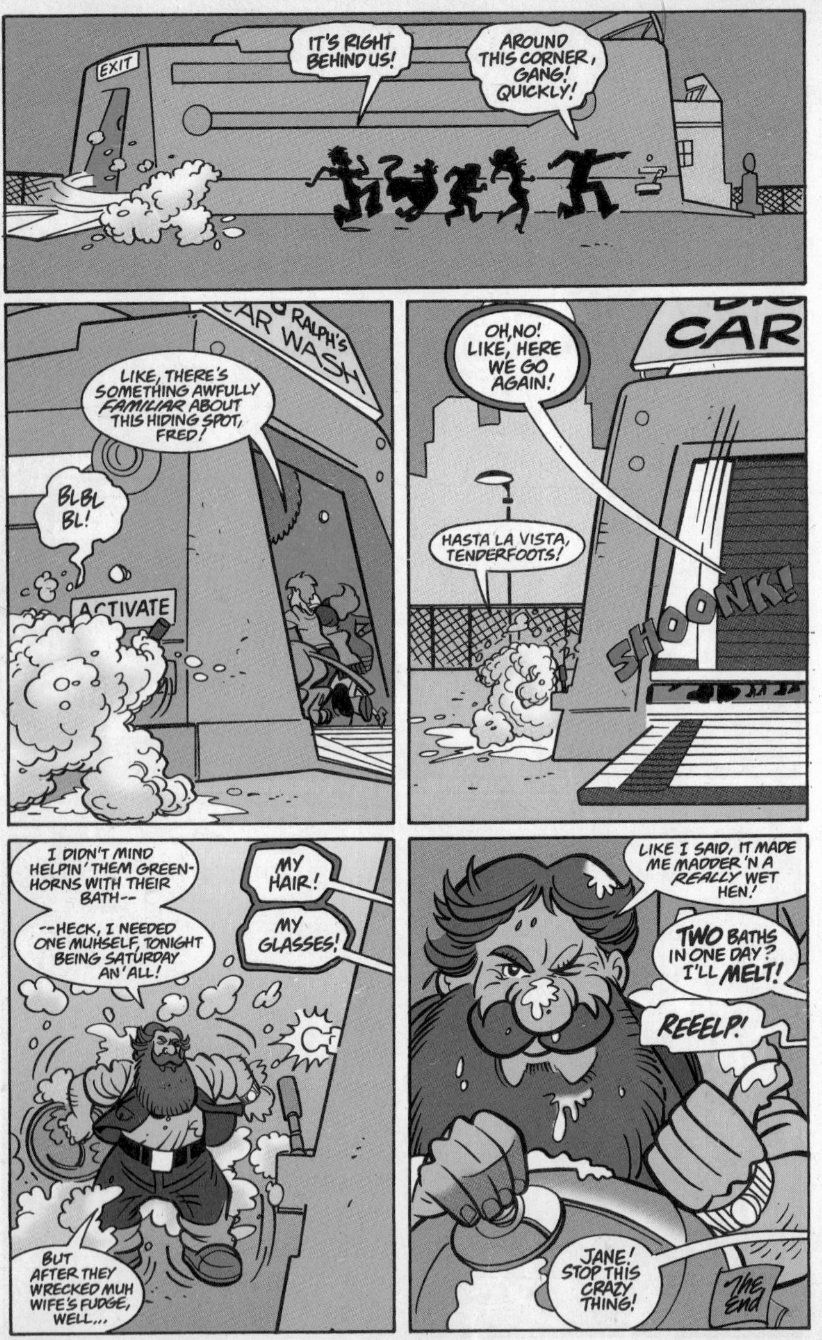
EXIT
IT'S RIGHT BEHIND US!
AROUND THIS CORNER, GANG! QUICKLY!
RALPH'S CAR WASH
LIKE, THERE'S SOMETHING AWFULLY FAMILIAR ABOUT THIS HIDING SPOT, FRED!
BLBL BL!
ACTIVATE
OH, NO! LIKE, HERE WE GO AGAIN!
CAR
HASTA LA VISTA, TENDERFOOTS!
SHOONK!
I DIDN'T MIND HELPIN' THEM GREENHORNS WITH THEIR BATH--
--HECK, I NEEDED ONE MUHSELF, TONIGHT BEING SATURDAY AN' ALL!
MY HAIR!
MY GLASSES!
BUT AFTER THEY WRECKED MUH WIFE'S FUDGE, WELL...
LIKE I SAID, IT MADE ME MADDER 'N A REALLY WET HEN!
TWO BATHS IN ONE DAY? I'LL MELT!
REEELP!
JANE! STOP THIS CRAZY THING!
The End